D1645995

THE REAPER

MYA RICHTER

Dedicated to anyone who has ever felt silenced.
You are heard.

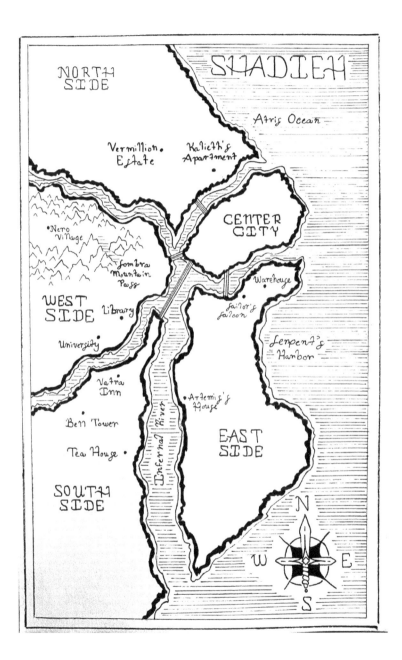

Prologue

Record #1

Where I come from, the fate of a person relies solely on their shadow.

The darkness that festers at our backs taints us. The darker our shadows, the more corrupted we become. The night hungers to claim our souls. It wishes to be all-consuming. For it is in the darkness where the burning lights of our souls are tested. A heavy enough shadow will douse the flame, and we will be plunged into eternal nothingness.

But the darkness is the final test. The first is life. Our shadows form with our first sin. They grow darker and heavier with each wrongdoing. The worst of us have night itself clinging to our backs. The weight of such shadows is said to break even the strongest of warriors. There is no one more dangerous than a person with a heavy shadow.

Some say that when we wrinkle with age, it is our shadows that drive us mad. They whisper in our ears, promising eternal peace and dreams. When we finally succumb to it– to the beckoning of Death himself– it is our shadow that decides our fate. After Death claims us, our soul will attempt to ascend to the Land Above the Stars. If our shadow is too heavy, it will instead drag our soul down into the Realm of the Damned, the Shadow Realm. Starlight does not reach that place. Nothing does. It's a void filled with irredeemable spirits. Those who journey there can never be reborn.

The very concept of shadows and fate being braided together began long ago. There was said to be two young kings locked in a brutal war. Their names had long been forgotten, but their story lived on for eons. One of them hid behind his walls and sent his loyal soldiers off to do his bidding. Somehow, by sending other men to their deaths and keeping his own hands clean, he managed to meet his timely death with no shadow at his back. He's said to be the first man to die pure and ascend. He's called the King of Stars, or the King above, because it's believed that he now rules over the Land Above the Stars.

The other king's story did not have such a happy ending. Because he fought honorably with his men, and spilled blood with his own sword, his shadow grew to be darker than most. Some say that seeing his own shadow drove him into madness. Others say that he continued on with his killing spree because he *wanted* to darken his shadow. He wanted to test the limits and see what may happen if he embraced the darkness instead of running from it.

All the stories differ from that point on. But my family believed that after a certain point, his shadow became so dark and so heavy, that it became its own entity. He was able to control the shadow and force it to do his bidding. When he mastered that skill, he could control any shadow he came across. Soon he commanded his own army of mindless beings that could not be killed. He wielded Death's power. Some even believe that he brought the Long Night to the mortal realm, consuming the mainland with a dark mist that hid the sun away for years.

When the second king died, his shadow army descended with him into the Shadow Realm. The people of my town believe that he continues to rule over the shadows there, and he punishes any soul that descends for attempting to follow in his footsteps. He has many names. Most people, however, call him the Accuser. He is the King of Shadows– the King below.

The tale of two kings became exaggerated and twisted over time. But the main themes of the story stayed true. Children hear the same speech over and over again. *Do not lie. Do not cheat. Do not steal. The Accuser watches. He will come for you if your shadow grows too heavy.*

The twisted history of the kings somehow lived on, and in doing so, kept the two kingdoms from ever living in peace. The Eternal War plagued our lands long before I was born. I can only assume it will continue to rage on long after my demise.

The Southern Kingdom, once the Accuser's kingdom, is the place I call home. Its vast borders stretch across the mainland for hundreds of miles, and even go beyond the East shores into the rough seas. To journey across the entire nation would mean travelling through dense forests, glacial mountains, and expansive farmlands.

The Northern Kingdom, once the King of Star's domain, shares our Northern border. Travelling between the two kingdoms has been prohibited for centuries. I've only heard stories, passed down from generation to generation, from a time long before the war, about what lies in the north. There are only the tall tales from a time when the kingdoms lived in harmony, to tell us what might be up there. If truth can be found in the old tales, then the Northern Kingdom is also home to forests and mountains, but beyond that lies the tundra. There, the spirits of the two kings sometimes battle in the afterlife, and otherworldly streaks of light dance in the night sky.

With war raging in both realms, the kingdoms fell victim to degrading stereotypes. The Northerners see the Southerners as scheming, murderous low lives. The Southerners, on the other hand, view the Northerners as cowardly snobs incapable of solving their own conflicts, just like the High Lord that came before them. Young children of one nation learn to despise the citizens of the other long before they report for their first round of training.

Serving in the King's army is required of every citizen in the Southern Kingdom. At the age of sixteen, children are subjected to testing. The tests determine whether the child descends from a mystical bloodline. If they test positive, they have a magical gift that cannot be overlooked. They are unable to appeal the Southern King's call to service; the required five years in the army. After receiving positive results, they are immediately sent to an academy to further explore their power. If and when they master that power, they are sent to the front lines. Because of this, mystical bloodlines are quite rare to come across. Many of them died off after decades of being the first defense against the Northern Kingdom's merciless attacks. The Mystic Academy has fewer students each year.

There are four mystic ranks in the king's army. The first, and most common, is *heilaris,* healers. They can cure wounds of war and plagues of the mind alike. The second is *elemefnis,* benders of nature. The second rank is an umbrella term, really. Mystics with a range of powers comprise it. *Shifklov,* the third rank, are shapeshifters. They are nearly extinct now. The final rank, *Decivok,* manipulators of the mind, were the most powerful, but the last of them were killed off centuries ago. Children are assigned their ranks upon the positive results of their tests.

For most children, their tests return negative, and they are sent to a training camp a few miles inland from the front lines. The training soldiers are the last line of defense in absolute emergencies. They are trained in all aspects of war, including combat, strategy, tracking, and wilderness survival. All trainees practice these skills to perfection for over three years. Then, they graduate as soldiers and serve their five years.

While most able-bodied men and women serve the nation, the cities and villages within the Southern Kingdom's borders have become fair game to other ambitious men seeking power. The powerful families in each city rose and took control. They still follow their king's commands, but they do what they please with the citizens that live beneath them, and the money they earn is spent on anything and everything but the needs of the city.

In the city of Shadieh, medicine and food are scarce. The majority of all supplies goes toward our soldiers, so, falling ill is a death sentence, and lower-class children are lucky to find a scrap of soggy bread on the ground to eat for supper. Many have tried to change the ways of the city since the war started, but all have failed. The rich don't want things to change. The Vermillion family, who run the city, refuse to do anything. They have it easy. They don't find themselves fighting to survive on the streets, either dying from starvation or illness. They reap the benefits of this war with no regard for the suffering around them.

Outside of the city, in the farmlands, several families live in peace. They keep small portions of what they grow to feed themselves and surrender the rest to the King's army for a small profit. Their lives are relatively uneventful, but they happily accept that over anything else.

There was one specific family, however, that appeared like the rest. Happy, kind, and average. But no one knew that a monster hid in their midst. No one knew that the future of Shadieh, and the entire world for that matter, lied in this man's hands. He fled the safety of the farmlands with vengeance plaguing his mind.

They say the Reaper is a descendant of the Accuser himself. Others believe he is the Accuser reincarnated. He came into the city like a whisper in the wind; quiet but swift.

Like a shadow in the dead of night, he remains unseen. Over thirteen kills were attributed to him within two days. Just like that, he earned his name.

He sparked fear in everyone's hearts. Not just because of his bloodlust but because he shows his face to no one. Those who claimed to have seen him say he is a living shadow, a silhouette with an assassin's mask covering his mouth and nose, and a hood covering his brow.

What's worse, he never speaks a single word.

The housewives believe that if a person hears his voice, it is because Death will find them sooner than their lips could tell his story.

Fear and curiosity drove the entire city into madness. At first, no one knew what he was after. Townsfolk boarded up their houses and hid their children in the cellars. Rumors about the faceless man spread like wildfire. Prophets predicted that the Accuser returned, and the High Lord would not be far behind. Seers, magical beings blessed with visions of the future, foretold that the Long Night was coming once more, and it would swallow the Reaper and his infamous shadow. They said it would drag him down into the depths of the Realm of the Damned and condemn his soul to eternal torment.

They are right about change. It is coming for us all; in ways we can't begin to imagine. They are wrong about the Reaper. Night is coming, and judgement day with it. But night doesn't swallow the shadows. It fuels them. It makes them harder to find. Harder to kill. Invisible.

Night is coming because the Reaper is bringing it with him.

CHAPTER

1

Kalieth

I assumed the Reaper would be nothing more than a faceless rumor. Another exaggerated fairytale that is whispered among the commoners.

I was wrong.

The night that my sister burned, everyone in the city of Shadieh rejoiced. I didn't know why they cheered and danced in the streets. I had no idea that it was one of my father's warehouses that went up in flames, and the citizens celebrated the fact that the King of Shadows was finally giving our family what we deserved. I watched the fire from a distance as it bathed the entire North Side of the city in an orange glow. I pitied the poor bastard whose estate collapsed in on itself.

It wasn't until the next night, when I returned to the Vermillion estate, that my father broke the news to my brothers and me. Three more of our properties burned across the city, and our beloved sister was nothing more than ash in the wind. My little sister, only thirteen years of age, was lost to us.

Devastation was too weak a word for what I felt.

The thought of Octavia suffocating in the smoke– the thought of her skin burning–

Grief was a weight sitting on my chest. It pressed down on my heart and lungs until I couldn't breathe. I forced air into my throat through great gasps, clutching at my chest as if the emotion was some sort of leach I could claw off and toss away. Everything else faded as my mind fogged. All I could see was my beautiful sister. All I could hear was her laugh. The world began to spin. Round and round it went until all I saw were streaks of light. I couldn't make out a word being said by my family. I tried to listen, but my stomach was flipping, threatening to spill my dinner onto the floor. I used the last of my strength to run out into the night, screaming my frustration to the stars. The sound echoed into the sky, and then died off into nothing more than a whisper to the mountaintops.

There was nothing I could do. She was gone. I was supposed to protect her, and I failed.

Weeks passed. The days dragged on. My anger only festered. Our mail overflowed with cards from all manner of folk. I didn't care enough to open them. Inside would be another one-liner expressing sympathy in the blandest way possible. I threw them away. I wanted to burn them, to shred them. How dare they? They steal someone else's words, sign their name on the card, and expect a thank you? Did they think it would help to assuage the endless pit of sorrow that found its place in me?

But my anger had not yet reached a breaking point. No, it wasn't until later, when my father told us about the Reaper, the man responsible for my sister's death, that I saw red. The criminal came to the city a short time ago, hellbent, for whatever reason, on destroying everything associated with the Vermillion name. We were the wealthiest, most powerful family in the city.

My father, Xaphan Vermillion, became the leader of the Southern Trading Circle long before I was born. He did so well that the king named him Master of Trade and Coin. All the tradesmen and merchants within the Southern Kingdom answered to him, and he only answered to the king himself. That was until the Reaper crawled from the shadows to mess with our affairs.

Within months of his arrival, we lost nearly everything. Our associates stopped all communication with us. Our revenue dropped to nearly nothing. Our empire– my inheritance– was gone after mere weeks.

He never hit us directly, not until Octavia. He went after our assets first. Crippled us. Destroyed our boats and carriages. Burned our warehouses to the ground. Shortly after, our business partners and colleagues started to disappear. It was no coincidence, and he made sure we knew it. In the ashes of our warehouses– at the scene of every murder– he left a piece of obsidian stone for us to find. A soldier's threat. In the army, they're given a small stone for each kill. It's believed that the

11

stone wards off evil spirits, the spirits of the fallen. Soldiers sew them into their uniform to keep the dead from haunting them. By leaving the stone instead of wearing it, the Reaper insulted my family and his victims. The gesture told us that he was not afraid of whatever vengeance the spirits might have. It implied that he did not fear us. It implied that he felt no shame in what he'd done, or toward the scenes he left behind.

Desperation drove our household into chaos. My elder brothers scrambled to heighten security around the estate. The eldest, Azazel, even tried to hunt down the Reaper himself, but it seemed that he was no good at hunting a wraith. My younger brothers doubled the hours of their combat training and attempted to help my father with the mountains of paperwork on his desk. We were all preparing for the worst.

My father started to show signs of paranoia. He would speak to us, but his eyes would never leave the shadows. He was constantly scanning, searching. He wanted the Reaper dead more than anything else. He refused to let his name go down in history as the Vermillion who lost everything. So, he hired hitmen and mercenaries. He sent them after the Reaper, offering them a hefty sum in return for his head. Not a single man returned. Well, not in one piece. Sometimes the Reaper would send us their heads.

After months of failure, my father turned to the best bounty hunter he knew.

"I didn't want to ask this of you," he'd said to me on that moonless night. "I understand if you refuse. But if you choose to fight, for this family,

12

for your legacy, know that you will be honored for decades. Your name will not be forgotten. No words would be able to describe my pride."

My father was not a loving man. My six brothers and I fought for his attention as children. Even now, at twenty-two years of age, I felt nothing but joy at the fact that he came to me first, excitement at the fact that I might earn his pride, and determination to destroy the man who killed my baby sister. The Reaper would pay for all he'd done. Those were the only words that drove me forward, past the grief. I vowed to kill him that night with my father as a witness. I'd watch him burn, just as he did to my sister.

My hunt began in the South Side of the city. I ruled out the other sides quickly. The North Side, my home, housed all the wealthy families. Large estates, infamous restaurants, and elegant theaters did not make good refuge for criminals. The West Side seemed unlikely. The only people who venture there are university students, scholars, and scribes. Center City was nothing but markets and shops. Unless the Reaper stood beside a cart to sell his dismembered victims, I wouldn't find him there. That left the East and South Sides– the unfavorable parts of Shadieh. The East Side had a reputation for rambunctious night life, both legal and not. Because the East Side bordered the vast Atris Ocean, it often hosted bands of vikings, pirates, merchants, and sailors, all of which are known to gamble in the underground fighting rings, drink their sorrows away, and find a bed in a brothel. While I knew the Reaper could hold his own in a place like that, there was far too much activity there for the assassin to stay without being seen. That left the South.

The South Side was a living beast. The grooves between the cobblestones were like its network of veins, bleeding out into the Infernal River. The rounded roofs of the houses packed together were scales, curling in on themselves as if they were cowering from the streets. The stench of rotten flesh, either from the rats in the streets or the body of another fallen gangster, was the very air drawn in through the beast's gaping mouth. The main strip lured newcomers in with bright lights and lively music. Before long, the beast's teeth sinks into them, injecting them with the venom of laced drinks and addictive drugs until they're nothing more than another body on the street for the beast to swallow. Another victim of the South Side.

I refused to become one of those victims. My search needed to be swift, and the capture of the Reaper had to be clean. After nearly a week of fruitless searching, I found a tavern which was the scene of many of the Reaper's brawls. The Sinner's Tavern lived up to its horrid reputation. The building sat on the corner of a filthy street. Beggars lined both sides of the outer walls, pleading anyone passing-by to lend them a bronze mark. I felt bad for them. Not because of their situation but because they were stupid enough to stand beside a poor man's tavern and expect recompense. One of them got too close for my liking, so I let him have a glance at the blades strapped to my belt and he backed off quick enough.

I didn't want to be here any longer than necessary. Nothing about this part of the city was warm or welcoming. It was a cold, dreary place that seemed to give you a push in the opposite direction. I could already feel bumps rising along my neck, as if the King above was sending me a warning. I picked up the pace as I walked toward the tavern's entrance. The wooden doors were half-rotten, and unless the owner made the decision to splatter red paint everywhere, I'd say it was overdue for a makeover.

The dim light inside gave everyone's skin a warm glow. It made the corners impossibly dark, and I had to squint to try to read the labels on the liquor bottles behind the counter. It made the barmaid's blonde hair, tied back tight, glisten. Her green eyes scanned over the customers at her counter over and over again. She didn't even look down as she poured an ale for the man in front of her. She was searching for something. Someone.

I took an empty stool by the bar. An older man sat a few seats down at the very end, and a soldier sat one seat over. I gestured to the barmaid and waited for her to make her way to me. I noticed she had a faint limp; a remnant of an old injury that either didn't heal right, or never had the chance to heal completely.

"Awful dark in here," I said as she approached.

"Folks 'round these parts are sinners. They come here to forget. Less light, less chance they see their shadows and remember," she responded, leaning heavily against the counter. I noted her East Verin accent, a land far from our city of Shadieh. She poured me a drink and slid it over carelessly. The liquid churned in the glass, nearly spilling over.

"I'm looking for the Reaper. Know where I can find him?" I asked. Even the sound of his name on my lips made my blood boil.

At the sound of the name, the soldier stood abruptly. He tossed a bronze mark onto the counter and shrugged on his cloak.

The barmaid's gaze snapped to meet mine. Shock crossed over her face, then fear, and then suspicion. She stood up straight, searching my expression through narrowed eyes. I purposefully left my face void of all emotion as I weathered her gaze. "It's awful foolish of you to speak that name in my bar," she muttered.

"Why's that?"

"Lot of rumors associated with that name. I don't need those rumors makin' themselves a home here. You say that name in my bar, it'll be empty for weeks. Men like you tend to go missin' when they speak of him."

"Tell me where to find him and I'll be on my way."

"What makes you think I know?"

I smiled and looked down to the drink in my hand. "He's been here quite a few times, so the records say," I gestured to her right leg. "I'm willing to bet that wound was a warning from the man I'm looking for. A warning to keep quiet?"

She crossed her arms over her chest and glanced at the old man beside me. When she was sure he wasn't listening, she leaned forward until she was close enough to whisper, "You want to find the Reaper? You've got to look where all the monsters hide when they walk in the daylight. The shadows."

I almost laughed in her face. But when she pulled away, I saw the look in her eye. I felt the sudden tension that crackled in the air. She was completely serious. I pulled a gold mark out of my pocket for the drink. The thin slip of paper could probably pay her rent in a horrid place like the South Side. "Here. No change. Get yourself out of this place."

Her eyes narrowed slightly, and the corners of her lips twitched up in the smallest hint of a smile, but that was her only reaction. "Good luck," she said as I handed her the money. "I've heard the Reaper works for the Accuser himself."

I stood from my chair, pulling my cloak over my shoulders. "Really? I thought the rumor was that the Reaper *is* the Accuser."

The old man at the end of the bar set down his drink suddenly. A chuckle sounded from the back of his throat, echoing off the walls in a dark, haunting way. "You've got that all wrong. The Accuser saw the Reaper, and he ran as fast as he could." He nodded to me. "If the King below flees from the Reaper, we should all do the same."

The man didn't wait for any sort of response. He set down three bronze marks before getting up and walking out. The barmaid was right. With the Reaper's name hanging in the air, the bar was clearing out. He truly did strike fear into the hearts of these people.

I turned to find that the soldier was still there, standing just behind me. He raised his chin. He looked me up and down, calculating. He huffed a laugh and shook his head. "You don't find the Reaper, kid. He finds you. Judging from that gold mark you just set down, I'll assume you're a Vermillion. A word of advice? Run. He probably already knows you're here."

Their warnings paved the way for fear to brush down my back in a cold caress. A shudder worked through me. I clutched my cloak tighter around my arms as I strode out into the street again. Suddenly, I had the odd feeling that I was being watched. I looked around, but I was alone on the dark road. I huffed a laugh at my own ridiculous fear. I wouldn't let strangers' words steer me off course. For my sister, my honor, and my legacy, I had to continue my search.

He finds you. The soldier's words were meant to scare me off, but instead they gave me an idea. I didn't need to search for the Reaper. He was after my family. All I had to do was make my presence in the South Side known. Then he would come, and I would be ready for him.

I sent a raven to my father. My letter told him to station the best of his guards at our safehouse in the South Side and give them orders to kill the Reaper on sight. I will lead him there. I'll watch him burn, then bring his charred skull to my father. We'll display it proudly for all to see, as a reminder of what happens to those who defy us.

I watched the raven fly off into the night, toward the Vermillion estate in the North Side. I knew, as it at last faded from my view, that a battle was coming. One I intended to win.

And so, it begins.

CHAPTER 2

Kalieth

Two days and three nights passed since I sent that raven. I visited every tavern, inn, and brothel in the South Side. I was sure to give them my true name and declare my search for the Reaper. I voiced threats and challenged the Reaper in public.

Nothing.

There was no response to my public displays. There were no whispered hints of any whereabouts. There were no new sightings of him. It was like he retreated into the shadows, waiting to strike.

I refused to return to my father without the Reaper's head. So, I made myself seen each night.

I walked up and down the cobblestone streets for hours. I looked under bridges and in alleyways, in every place he was reported to be seen in the past. Every night, I found nothing. Not even a footprint or drop of blood. He was a wraith– a ghost.

For the fourth night in a row, frustration, hunger, and exhaustion started to affect my tendency to be thorough. My boots dragged on the ground as I walked. My limbs felt unbearably heavy, and the small pain in my back was quickly turning into a muscle spasm. It annoyed me to turn around and call it a night, but I did so with the intention of returning to my hunt in the early hours of the morning.

The abrupt pivot on my heels caught the man behind me off guard. We crashed into each other, hard enough to send me stumbling backward. He caught my arm and helped to steady me again.

I only caught a brief glance of the face beneath the hood of his black cloak. I saw a flash of golden eyes, brown skin, a scar that ran through his left eye, and another along his jaw. A few stray strands of hair fell over his brow, showing shoulder-length waves that, for the most part, were tied back within the dark depths of the hood. He gave me a curt nod before going on about his night, leaving me to stand alone. I turned to get another look at him, but he'd already disappeared.

As I scanned the street, searching for him, I noticed that the city was quiet– too quiet. I could hear the wind whistling in the distance. There was even a hint of the water roaring in the Infernal River a few blocks away. It seemed like every person on this side of the city locked themselves in their homes. The streets were utterly empty. There was no music or chatter from the taverns. Silence ruled the South Side.

The hairs on the back of my neck stood up, but I paid it no mind. I decided to head back to my own filthy room in the run-down inn a few blocks over. It wasn't the sort of place I was used to staying, like the Gold Palace or Royal Tavern, but it had a bed and a fireplace. That's all that mattered.

As I walked, I noticed that something felt off. I felt... lighter.

I pulled the fabric of my cloak away to find that my belt was gone, and my blades with it. The cloaked man robbed me. A homeless man passing by, covered in dirt and limping, laughed at me.

"The night is coming," the man said between cackles. "He watches, he disarms, and then he comes."

I froze. The night turned cold. "What did you say?"

The man stopped, looking back at me through wide, horrifying eyes. "The Reaper, of course."

"You know where I can find him?"

The man broke down into another fit of laughter. Cackling was a better word for what he did. The shrill sounds echoed down the empty streets. He clutched his stomach, leaning down close to the ground as his entire body convulsed with his laughter. I quickly realized that he was not in his right mind. I turned to leave, but it was his next words that stopped me in my tracks. "A Vermillion should know that the darkest shadows are the ones at your back."

I didn't need to look over my shoulder to know someone else was there. I could sense it. I could tell from the tension in the air. I felt it in the way that the evening's chill breeze sent a shiver down my spine. Bumps rose along my arms. The sensation set in so fast and sharp that it was almost painful. The laughter of the homeless man died off rather abruptly, and then silence ensued once more.

I turned slowly. The man was gone. In his place stood a cloaked figure. I would've thought it was the thief who just stole from me, but this silhouette was short and petite in comparison. It wasn't the Reaper either. This was a woman who wore no mask.

She pulled her hood back, and I recognized her as the barmaid from my first night in the South Side. Her limp magically disappeared, and she stood with utter confidence. She smirked and winked at me. "Hey pretty boy." Her accent changed as well. She sounded local now.

"No limp?"

She shrugged. "I had to sell the part." While she spoke, two more hooded figures approached me on either side. I reached for my blades, forgetting that they'd been stolen. I was surrounded and vulnerable. The barmaid waved a hand in their direction. "Allow me to introduce my friends, Ace and Quinn."

Ace took his hood down, revealing his scarred face. He was the thief I bumped into moments ago. He flashed his teeth in a crooked grin, dangling my belt in the air. "Looking for this?" he sneered.

Quinn did not pull his hood down or show his face, but as Ace moved closer, so did he. I raised my fists as they inched forward.

The barmaid rolled her eyes at the sight. "You're unarmed and outnumbered. Just stand down." But I refused, so she sighed and, with a wave of a hand, said, "Take him."

Ace and Quinn struck faster than lightning. They grabbed my arms and forced them behind my back. I thrashed around, putting all my weight into the swing of my legs, to try and loosen their grip. It only succeeded in earning me a punch to the nose. I heard a sickening crack. My vision blurred for a few horrible moments. Searing pain erupted across my face. Something warm and thick trickled from my nostrils as they dragged me away with my feet bent behind me. My shoes creased, and my breeches were soon soiled by the filthy city streets.

Ace kept my blades out of reach, but that didn't stop me from trying to get to them. I was rewarded with a kick to my abdomen, knocking the air out of my lungs. It became blatantly obvious that fighting them was no use. I went limp in their hold as the barmaid led us into an alleyway.

"Where are you taking me?" I snapped at her. She didn't so much as glance my way. I was vaguely aware of her scoffing at my question, a disrespect that I would make her regret later. Either way, I didn't really need her answer. I knew where they were taking me. Rather, I knew *who* they were taking me to. The day of reckoning had come. Tonight, I would look upon the Reaper's face.

The sound of a door being kicked in broke me away from my thoughts. I was thrown into an abandoned pub. My clothes were coated in dust and cobwebs from the floorboards. Even my footprints could be seen through the thick layer of filth on the wooden floors. The place was crawling with rodents and insects. I could practically hear the chittering of rodents in the walls. The floorboards creaked beneath our weight. I was surprised they didn't give way.

The barmaid unlocked the door at the back of the main room and gestured for me to take the lead. I glared at her as I walked by, through a cloud of stirred up dust, and got a wink in return.

The doorway led into a narrow staircase. Cracked, half-rotten boards made up the stairs. A few steps were missing from the set entirely. By the looks of them, even a feather-light touch would have them collapsing.

I glanced back at my captors, wordlessly asking if they were serious. The barmaid crossed her arms over her chest, nodding toward the stairs. Ace leaned against the wall to her left. He narrowed his eyes, watching expectantly. Quinn waited in the doorway; silent. His face was hidden in the shadows of his hood, so I couldn't see whatever expression he wore.

I tested my weight on the first board. When I was sure it would hold, I did the same to the next. Slowly, I climbed upward. The group followed in my footsteps. I purposefully kicked up as much dust as I could, hoping I'd be able to hit one of them right in the eyes. I had no luck.

Another wooden door sat at the top of the stairs. The barmaid pushed past me and opened it, walking out onto the rooftop with nothing but the moon to light her path. Ace and Quinn took up my arms, pushed me out onto the roof, then kicked in my knees.

Suddenly I was kneeling before two new figures. One faced me while the other looked down at the street below. The street I'd just been standing on. They'd been watching from above the whole time.

The man who faced me wore the same cloak as the others, but he did not hide his face. He held his head high, looking down at me through silver eyes, a color I'd never seen before. I could barely see his black hair through the night, and his dark skin made his movements impossible to track through the shadows.

The second man did not turn to face me, but I knew who he was, nevertheless. The Reaper. The man I'd been looking for.

After all the time I'd spent searching, he'd been watching. Waiting. When he saw an opportunity, he sent his allies to jump me in an alleyway. I don't know why I was surprised. It only made sense that the man who let a thirteen-year-old girl burn alive would be a coward who sends his henchmen to do his dirty work for him.

"This is the one I told you about. What did I say about the barmaid job? Didn't I tell you it was a good idea?" the woman asked excitedly.

Ace rolled his eyes and tossed her a bronze mark. "Fine," he grunted. She caught the mark with a triumphant huff.

Quinn finally took his hood down. He had short black hair, round, brown eyes, and skin which was tanned in a birth-given way. He looked like a kid– a scrawny teenager. "You bet money on the practicality of her barmaid job?" he asked.

"By the Kings above and below, Quinn. Must you speak like a virgin professor constantly?" the woman said as she rolled her eyes.

"My apologies, Bryce. I'll be sure to act illiterate just as soon as you learn to stop acting like an overpaid woman of the night," Quinn snapped back.

The smirk on Bryce's face dropped. Her jaw clenched, and she spoke through her teeth. "What did you call me?" She reached toward her hip to unsheathe her dagger, but before her fingertips reached her belt, a throwing knife flew past my head, barely missing the tip of my nose, and hit Bryce's wrist. I sucked in a breath, waiting for blood to spill. The throwing knife clattered to the ground. The blade appeared pristine. Not a single drop of blood tainted it.

The Reaper now faced us, his arm still outstretched. He threw the knife with such trust in his own hand that he knew the hilt side of the blade would miss me and hit Bryce's wrist. He meant to catch her attention, not hurt her. The skill needed for something like that... I was awe-stricken.

The Reaper's cloaked henchmen went silent and backed away from me. They sank into the dark corners of the rooftop, watching from the shadows. I turned my attention to the Reaper. His shadow lived up to its reputation. It was so large and so dark, that it surrounded him completely and clung to his back as if it were the night itself. Just as the rumors stated, the hood of his cloak sat low enough to cover his entire brow. He wore an assassin's mask that shielded his neck up to the bridge of his nose. The only part of him left uncovered were his silver eyes, and the dark skin around them. He was shorter than I thought he'd be. Even kneeling, my head passed his abdomen. I couldn't tell whether he'd be a challenge in combat. His cloak was too bulky to show off any of the muscle he might have.

By the silver eye color alone, I assumed that the Reaper and the man beside him were brothers. Even though they were both cloaked, I could tell the difference. The Reaper's eyes seemed to glow through the darkness. They were orbs of liquid silver, with white flames of pure rage crackling deep within.

His brother's eyes were different. They glowed in the same way, but there was no fire within them. His eyes reminded me of a silver river. Always moving, rippling, changing, but in a peaceful manner, not with the hungry need to devour like the flames in the Reaper's irises.

My gaze settled on the Reaper. "Is this how you best all of your opponents?" I asked bitterly. "Rob them of their weapons, jump them in an alley, and have your henchmen hold them down while you finish them off with one clean strike?"

He tilted his head, saying nothing.

I took his silence as an opportunity to continue. "I should have known. The infamous

Reaper, nothing more than a coward in a costume, gaining his fame with dishonest fights."

The Reaper's cloak flowed behind him in the breeze as he walked toward me, coming so close that I had to fight the urge to reach for his knife on the ground. He stopped in front of me, his feet nearly touching my knees. He looked down at me for a long moment. I refused to shy away from his menacing gaze. Instead, I stared back, matching his intensity. I stared straight into the silver eyes of the man who killed my sister. I wanted him to see all the hatred and rage I felt for him.

If he saw it, he showed no sign of caring. After a moment, he beckoned with a gloved hand for one of his men to come forward. It was Ace that stepped out of the shadows.

He walked toward us, never taking his eyes off me, and placed my belt and blades in the Reaper's hand. The Reaper took them, examining them while Ace slunk back into the darkness. The Reaper withdrew my broadsword. He stared at it for a long moment, and if I didn't know any better, I would've thought that he was admiring the blade as it glinted in the moonlight.

I clenched my fists at my sides, assuming the Reaper planned to steal my sword, the sword my father gave me. I had others, but the thought of a lowlife like him touching the blade of a Vermillion irked me, let alone a blade carrying our family crest on the hilt.

But he only examined it for a moment before twirling it in his hand, offering it to me by the hilt.

It caught me off guard. I was slow to react as I reached up and took the sword from him. I wondered if he smiled beneath his mask as he watched me, judging from the slight squint of his eyes. As soon as I had a hold on the broadsword, he stepped back, pulling both sides of his cloak back to reveal his own belt. He had five throwing knives on each side, as well as one long dagger. The weapon that took me by surprise was the sai, one on each side of his belt. I knew only a handful of men trained to use that weapon with skill.

I struggled to see his blades in the dark. My heart dropped when I realized why. Each one was made from obsidian stone. The amount of stone he would have needed to earn to forge all those blades– the number of kills he must've had... I shuddered at the thought.

"You asked for a fair fight. The Reaper has graciously accepted your challenge," his brother said. "Pick his weapon."

I stood, shaking the dust off my breeches. I surveyed his belt again as I tightened my grip on the hilt of my sword. His throwing knives were too small to keep track of on a dark rooftop. His sai would provide him with good defense against my sword. But using his dagger would require him to get into close range. I'd be ready for that.

"The dagger," I said.

Someone behind me snickered. The Reaper said nothing. He reached down and withdrew the dagger from its sheath. He removed his belt and tossed it to his brother, who caught it without hesitation.

I raised my sword, widened my stance, and bent my knees. It'd been a long time since I had to fight anyone. But the Reaper should be the one trembling with fear. I was trained by the best swordsmen in the kingdom, and I'm a bounty hunter fueled by rage. He didn't stand a chance.

The Reaper circled me. He wanted me to make the first move. That was a mistake. Any teacher will tell you to seize the offensive instead of waiting for a counterattack. I waited until he was at my backside before quickly turning on my heel and attempting to strike him first. With deception being the key to winning any swordfight, I took my sword one way and my eyes the other.

He moved faster than I could blink. One second, he was in the path of my blade, and the next he was several strides away.

I was fully prepared for my blade to hit something solid, so when it didn't, it threw me off balance. I stumbled, caught myself, and whirled around, expecting to see the Reaper raising his dagger at my back.

He stood on the other side of the rooftop, waiting for me to steady myself. Humiliated and angered, I took up my fighting stance once more. I charged him this time, hoping to intimidate him. I swung out with the sword, aiming a strike for his chest. He anticipated my move and dropped to his knees. He slid gracefully under my blade and was back on his feet in one fluid motion.

I didn't wait for him to ready himself as he did for me. I raised the broadsword over my head and brought it down as hard as I could. The Reaper ducked and side-stepped. Once my sword was pointed downward, as were my arms, he kicked me squarely in the chest.

I fell back with a grunt, pressing a hand to the ache. His henchmen laughed and snickered from all different corners of the rooftop. I ignored them all. I cracked my neck and tossed the sword between my hands.

The Reaper's walk reeked of confidence. He stalked, like a predator did its prey. He twirled the dagger in his hands, pivoted on his feet, and raised the blade above his head, his eyes focused on my shoulder.

I raised my sword to counter his attack, but as soon as I did, he lowered the dagger and put all his weight into kicking my exposed midsection, knocking the breath out of me and sending me stumbling backward. I'd fallen for his deception, and it was about to cost me. He had me backed up against the roof's edge.

Panicking from his proximity, I swung out again, one-handed. He dodged my half-hearted swing with ease. He aimed to strike my chest again, but I saw it coming and raised my sword. Exactly what he wanted me to do. He went downward for my legs, kicking them out from under me. I fell to the ground. My sword clattered out of my hand.

I realized in that moment that I would not be able to beat the Reaper in combat. His movements were too quick. His motions were so fluid that he seemed to be a living shadow. He dodged my blows and threw his own jabs as if we were engaged in some sort of dance, and I'd forgotten all the moves. He was toying with me. He could've killed me three strikes ago. For whatever reason, he was keeping me alive.

My plan required sudden readjustments. I hadn't realized that the Reaper worked with a team. I didn't anticipate a close circle of friends, and I knew I wouldn't be able to bribe one of them to help me. Honor among thieves was a bond thicker than blood.

If I couldn't beat him in combat, and I couldn't convince one of his companions to do it for me, I needed to come up with something else.

There was only one way to take down an operation like this. From within. I had to get them to trust me. Then, and only then, could I tear them apart, and take the Reaper's head to my father. The only way I could get them to my father's warehouse would be if they followed willingly.

So, I reached into the hidden pocket within my jacket. I pulled out my pistol and cocked it before the Reaper had a chance to move away.

Time froze. No one moved. No one spoke. No one appeared to breath. The tension in the air thickened to the point of making it hard to swallow.

"Cocky bastard," Bryce snarled from behind me. "Called the Reaper a coward, meanwhile he brought a gun to a sword fight."

"You could kill him, but we'd kill you before you could run," Ace added from somewhere to my right.

"Trust a Vermillion to have an outlawed weapon while the war rages on," Quinn said.

I drowned out their voices. My focus was solely on the Reaper, and his on me. I saw no fear in his eyes. Only curiosity. He wanted to know if I'd do it.

I wanted to.

I wanted nothing more than to see that silver light leave his eyes. But I couldn't. It would be too quick. Too easy. I needed to see him suffer after all he did to my family. I switched the safety back on and rose to my feet, stretching out my hand to offer the gun to the Reaper. "I want to help you."

He made no move to come forward and take the gun from me. Instead, his thief swiped it.

"Help us with what, exactly?" the Reaper's brother asked.

"My name is—"

"We know who you are," he interrupted. "Answer the question."

I ignored my rapid heartbeat. I drew a long breath through my nose and raised my chin. I said the first thing I could think of to gain their trust. "I want to help you kill my father."

CHAPTER

3

Bryce

The Reaper found me before he found the others. It was a few seasons back. I was doing honest work as a barmaid at the Sinner's Tavern. I earned next to nothing, but I was able to leave my past behind me, and that was enough. No one asked questions in the South Side. I liked it that way.

Each day I followed the same routine. I woke before dawn, which alone made me want to vomit and crawl back into the warmth of my bed. When the initial nausea passed, I left the remote, windowless basement I called home. It was infested with rats, the paint faded off years ago, and an odd smell emanated from a mysterious stain on the floor. I absolutely hated it, but it was all I could afford. The mean old veteran I rented from let me stay for two silver marks a month so long as I didn't report him for foul living conditions.

In the early hours of the morning, before the sun rose over the horizon, I walked through the main strip of Center City. I looked through the windows of all the shops meant to ward off the poor and draw in the rich, I imagined myself walking through the doors one day, wearing a double strand of pearls and a dress made with high-end fabric. I would buy the black display dress I always admired from the street, with a lace back and real gold flakes decorating the skirt. The shopkeeper would package it for me with a smile on his face, and he'd hand me the bag without questioning me about my class.

Every now and then, a dress, a pair of earrings, or shoes would disappear from a local shop. The shopkeepers would cause a scene, yelling for the king's guard to come and find the missing product. A single officer would come, file a report, take it to the library to be documented, and go about his day without thinking about it again. It killed me to take the items I loved only to sell them off to the highest bidder, but I had to pay rent on the apartment I hated.

After daydreaming, stealing, and selling, I'd go to work at the tavern. Each night consisted of tongue-biting and fist clenching from the comments of drunken men. I wanted nothing more than to quit and find a job on the North Side of Shadieh, but I would never be accepted there. They'd take one look at my split ends and chewed fingernails and they would know I didn't belong. I couldn't have them asking questions or doing background checks. That would bring everything good I'd worked for to an end. So, I worked from sun-high to moon-high in the poor man's tavern. I kept my hands to myself, even when others didn't, because I knew that if I let myself fight, I'd win. I couldn't risk drawing that kind of attention to myself.

When the moon reached its peak, my shift was finally over. I'd return to my sad little basement. I'd let my hair down, wincing at how tight I kept it. I'd sit down, groaning at the tight muscles in my back finally relaxing after a long day.

I hated the nights the most. I hated crawling into bed. I hated the basement, my job, and my life. I hated that I had to lay my head on the pillow and envision a better life to have good dreams, and ward off the nightmares of my past. I hated the moments before sleep where all I had were my own thoughts. Eventually, I'd drift off, only to wake up in a pool of sweat with horrid screams echoing from my memories.

My days went exactly like that, over and over, for many seasons. With each day that passed, it seemed as though I became numbed toward my surroundings. Life dragged on with no regard for my state. I got closer to wondering what life would be like if I passed on early into the Shadow Realm.

Everything changed when the Reaper found me.

That night started like any other. I was restocking the liquor bottles, expecting a larger crowd since the Southern army suffered a tremendous loss after the Northern soldiers overtook Serpent's Harbour. Friends and families of everyone lost would be funneling into the taverns, drinking to forget their grief.

I knew someone approached the bar counter, but I didn't turn at first. I wanted to finish the task at hand before serving anyone.

"Bryce Reitenour?" a deep voice drawled from behind me.

A shiver ran up my spine. No one had called me that name in a long time. I didn't want to turn for fear of who I'd see standing behind me. An enemy? A soldier here to take me away? One of my old teachers returning to identify me?

"No. Never heard the name." I replied without turning. I had to concentrate on keeping my voice steady.

Something dropped onto the counter. I turned just enough to see a file marked 'CONFIDENTIAL.' Beneath the bolded word was my name, who I used to be.

"One of the best fighters in the army, a mystic. She was considered an *elemefnis,* but she was one of the only fire summoners ever recorded. Trained in the mystic academy and sent straight to the front lines afterward. Many Northerners perished in her flames," the man read aloud.

My mouth went dry. "Sounds like some woman."

The man didn't miss a beat. "Her entire unit died. She went with them. It's said that their shadows consumed their souls and dragged them downward."

My heart dropped to the floor. "Shame."

"It is. Because if she were alive, she'd have a hell of a proposition headed her way," he said, closing the file.

I faced him fully then. That was when I saw him for the first time. My eyes skimmed over his textured black hair, cut close to his scalp, and went straight to the captivating silver eyes that would soon haunt my dreams. My gaze fell to his chiseled jaw and the knot in his throat that bobbed when he spoke. I was rendered speechless for all of five seconds, and he smirked at me, as if he knew exactly where my thoughts wandered.

I snapped out of my trance at the sight of his arrogance. "I imagine she would be interested."

His smirk widened. He leaned down on the counter, interlocking his fingers. "They called you 'the Harbinger.' What exactly were you the harbinger of?"

Alright then, no more pretending. I set down the rag and bottle in my hands. "Death."

"We could use someone with *your*... skillset."

I approached the counter and leaned down with him, drawing his attention as my hands searched the underside of the counter. "Which skillset?" I asked seductively. "Business or pleasure?"

I caught him off guard. His eyes widened slightly, and his lips parted. His shock lasted half a second, but that was all I needed. My fingers found the hidden dagger. I drew it out, grabbed him by the collar of his tight jacket, and pressed the blade to his chest, just above his heart.

"Who are you? How did you find me?" My lip curled in slight disgust as I thought of who might be behind this.

The cold kiss of metal pressed against my throat. The man in my grasp winked at me. He'd been the distraction all along as his companion snuck up behind me. I withdrew my dagger and held my hands up. The man behind me took my blade and backed me away.

"The name's Ryder," the first man said, fixing the lapels of his jacket. "The one behind you is the Reaper."

My breath caught. I'd heard the rumors, but I didn't think they were true. I wanted to look back and see if he truly wore the mask people spoke of, but he still had his blade pressed to my neck.

"You have a choice," Ryder continued. "You can keep living the miserable life that you are, stealing and hiding, or you can join us, and be the Reaper's Firemaster."

"You've been watching me?" I asked, infuriated.

Ryder huffed a laugh. "I wouldn't say watching. Call it scoping out the candidate."

I rolled my eyes. "Well, the dagger pressed to my throat doesn't make me feel like I have much of a choice."

To my surprise, the blade was promptly removed, and the Reaper backed away. I glanced over to see the menacing man of shadows that the drunks whispered about after dark. With the hood, gloves, and assassin's mask, there was nothing about him that could be seen. It had an uneasy feeling running up my spine.

"If you refuse us, we'll burn this file, and you'll never hear from us again. But if you agree to come with us, you'll be helping us fix this city," Ryder explained, pouring himself a drink as he spoke.

I agreed to join them. I wanted the Vermillions dead. Plus, Ryder spoke with divine persuasion, telling me that we'd make a difference and end the suffering in the city. The Reaper said nothing. He simply watched and listened.

That's how I ended up on the rooftop with the new team, watching the Reaper make a joke of the Vermillion son in combat.

"We know who you are," Ryder spat him.

As if we didn't have to just look to his sleeve. There, in gold embroidery, was the Vermillion family crest. A rearing horse, for speed and power, with a bird flying overhead, to symbolize travel, both a nod to the family's role in the trading system. My body went cold at the sight of that awful crest. Bile rose up my throat at the memories it brought back.

"I want to help you kill my father."

Ace and I exchanged a knowing glance. His lips pressed into a thin line, stretching the scar along his jaw. We agreed, then. A Vermillion was not to be trusted.

"That's why I've been trying to find you. I know you want to take him down. This way, we both get what we want. You kill my father and I gain my inheritance," Vermillion continued. He looked up at the Reaper with wide eyes, like a lost puppy.

The Reaper never uttered a word to anyone, but we all knew he was far too smart to fall for that cheap excuse. The Reaper circled the rich boy, twirling his dagger in his hand. Ryder, Quinn, Ace, and I all stepped closer to surround him, so he had nowhere to run.

"Prove it," Ryder said. He acted as a translator for the Reaper's gestures. Ryder always knew what his brother wanted to say.

"There's another property– a vault that he keeps his emergency funds in. I can take you to it. We break in and empty it. It's the only one you've left untouched. Without this last vault, my family will be completely out of options," he explained. When no one said anything, he continued, "I swear it! My father might even be so desperate as to come to you himself."

That caught the Reaper's attention. He stopped pacing. He stood straight, staring off into the horizon. I'd come to learn that staring off meant he was considering the matter at hand.

It only took a few seconds for the Reaper to turn back to the Vermillion boy and offer a gloved hand to help him up.

I couldn't believe it. By the looks of the wide eyes and dropped jaws of my companions, they couldn't either. Even Ryder seemed surprised by his brother's gesture, but he didn't show it as much as we did.

The Vermillion boy looked skeptical at first, but he slowly took the Reaper's hand and allowed him to tug him to his feet. He dusted the dirt off his breeches and anxiously looked around at the rest of us, as if waiting for us to jump him again. I wished we could. But I imagined that if I tried to harm him after the Reaper expressed interest in keeping him around, well, the Reaper might just withhold my cut of the next vault we hit.

"He comes with us?" Ace asked, his voice breathy from disbelief.

The Reaper gave us one curt nod for confirmation. We all looked at him as though he grew a second head. How were we meant to trust the enemy? Let alone bring him back to our living space. He seemed like the type of cowardly prick that would slice our throats while we slept.

The Reaper motioned for us to leave. He took his belt back from Ryder and strapped it on, sheathing his dagger once again. He led the way off the rooftop, followed by Ace, who shoved the Vermillion boy along. Ryder, Quinn, and I hung back to keep an eye on him, far enough to be out of earshot but close enough to see him in the dim moonlight.

"What's his name?" I asked. Quinn and I fell into step next to each other. Quinn was the youngest of us, just nineteen years old, but I took a liking to him. I took him under my wing. He was no fighter, but where he lacked physical strength, he made up for it with a sharp mind. He spent years studying to become a scribe.

"Kalieth," Quinn replied. "Vermillion's fifth son. A bounty hunter. He lives away from home for the most part, so not much is known about him."

As Quinn and I walked, I purposefully turned my back to Ryder. I still saw the pained look in his eye at my open gesture of resentment. I hated that the sight of it hurt me. I hated that he still had an effect on me at all. I hated it so much that I completely shut out all thoughts of him and gave my attention over to Quinn. It was harder than I thought to forget about his presence as he fell into line a few yards behind us.

"Why are we bringing him back with us? He can't be trusted." We spoke in hushed whispers.

Quinn raised one shoulder in an awkward half-shrug. "Maybe the Reaper secretly has a death wish."

Ryder chimed in from behind us. "I trust my brother. Everything he does is calculated. There's a reason that he's doing this."

Quinn tried to stop walking for Ryder to catch up, but I looped my arm through his and hurried us forward. I didn't bother looking back, despite wishing that Ryder could see the angry, partially disgusted look on my face.

"Calculated or not, it's unwise to let an enemy into our home," I snapped back, keeping my eyes forward.

We rounded a corner to catch up with the others, only to see that they were stopped. The Reaper was tying a piece of fabric over Kalieth's eyes. He at least had the decency to ensure that the enemy didn't see our home. When he finished, he left Vermillion in the care of Ace and Ryder, who found it amusing to let go and watch him walk blindly into poles. Childish bastards.

"What are we meant to do with him now? Treat him like our newest member?" I whispered harshly.

Quinn sighed. "Bryce, honestly, I don't know."

"How did that taste coming out of your mouth?"

"Like poison," he muttered under his breath, cringing as if there truly was a foul taste in his mouth.

I said nothing more as we continued down the old cobblestone road, walking in the shadows. We weaved our way through alleyways and courtyards until we finally reached the old bell tower. Centuries ago, it acted as the dragon bell. The guards rang it when a dragon was spotted in the skies as a warning for all the families to take cover. Since the dragons went extinct, the tower stands as nothing but a forgotten past. Both the tower and adjoining cathedral were sealed off ages ago. The Reaper made us a home there. He stayed in the top room. From there, he watched over the entire city like a hawk in its nest. The rest of us stayed on the lower levels. We wanted to be ready for a quick escape should it be needed. Kalieth Vermillion being under the same roof as the rest of us may result in one of those quick escapes, one way or another.

We slipped through the rotting boards nailed across the threshold. Through dim torchlight, we walked down the stone entrance hall and into the main room. Quinn and Ace stayed with Kalieth. They chained him to the wall so that he couldn't wander and relieved him of his blindfold. The Vermillion son squinted to adjust his eyes to the light. He took one look at the chains binding him and glared at us. Ace laughed. "Get comfortable, Vermillion."

The Reaper didn't wait to for Kalieth's response. He immediately made for the stairs, ascending toward his nest. Ryder was right on his heels. Our eyes connected when he glanced back, but instinct told me to look away.

"I don't get you two," Ace said as he sank into a chair.

My brows pulled together. "What do you mean?"

"He means that one moment you're all over each other, then the next, there couldn't be enough space in the world to put between you," Quinn responded.

They didn't understand the sudden rift between Ryder and me, which was something I didn't want to think about. The fight we had. The words we exchanged. The horrible things he said and the awful things I countered him with.

"He loves you, Bryce," Ace added. "You know that don't you?"

"No, I wouldn't know that. It's not like he tells me anything. I'd honestly be surprised if the word 'communication' was in his vocabulary," I scoffed.

"He never told me either. He didn't have to. It's obvious. I've never seen a guy so absolutely whipped, Bryce. Which is how I know it had to be you that called it quits. So, why'd you do it?" Ace asked, plopping down into one of the reading chairs.

"Why do you care so much?" I countered. Ace never seemed to care about anything. His expression showed a constant state of boredom aside from the occasional smirk.

"I don't. But this is a small place, and I get bored."

Quinn rolled his eyes. "Nice."

I laughed. "While I'm glad that my love life is amusing to you, I will not be your entertainment tonight." I gestured to Kalieth and said, "Play with your new pet instead."

Kalieth pressed himself against the wall. Ace's eyes flashed with wicked excitement at the sight of Vermillion's fear. He sat forward in his chair, leaning on his knees. I'd seen that look before. It was the viking-raised warrior's promise of pain.

"Just don't keep me up with screams," I called over my shoulder. I climbed the stairs to my room on the second level. When the cathedral was in use, it served as the preacher's quarters. It was small, tucked away in the corner. After dusting and furnishing, I like to think I made it quite cozy.

Ryder was the first thing I saw when I opened the door. He was sprawled out on the bed, his tight jacket unbuttoned at the top. The loud creak of the door snapped him out of his thoughts, and he jolted upright to greet me.

A sigh escaped my lips as I shook my head. My hand lingered on the handle, holding the door open for him to leave. "I'm too tired for this, Ryder. I don't want to talk to you."

He ran a hand over his clenched jaw, shaking his head. "I've lost count of the number of times I've apologized to you, Bryce. Please, tell me what else I can do."

I pushed the door open wider. "You can go."

He took a step forward. "It's over. I get that. You've made it perfectly clear." His voice was deeper than usual, and his eyes suddenly found the floor to be very interesting. "But I deserve a reason. Was it something I did? Is there someone else?"

I wanted so desperately to laugh when I realized just how clueless he really was to the reality that there could be no one else for me. But I also fought tears, because after all this time, he thought so little of me.

"No, Ryder, there's no one else," I whispered. I couldn't bring myself to say it any louder. It felt like a silly confession, one that he shouldn't have needed to hear.

"Then, why?" his voice broke over the words.

I couldn't tell him the real reason. I was barely able to admit it to myself. My mind scrambled to find an excuse.

"There is no future for us," I said with a shrug. "What happens after this? What will you do once the blood of the Vermillion family is finally on your hands? After your shadow has grown too large for your soul to have a shot at ascending? Do you really think that you'll want to go away with me? Can you see yourself settling down and having a family far away from here?"

He said nothing. His lips parted in surprise, but he didn't try to argue. I let the silence prove my point before continuing.

"Exactly. And do you want to know the best part? You never even told me why this means so much to you. I have no idea why you're going after the Vermillions because you don't talk to me."

He looked straight into my eyes, allowing me to lose myself in his beautiful silver irises. He shook his head slowly. "You have no idea how much I want to leave with you. I would follow you to the ends of the world, but I must stay here. I have to be one of the last people Xaphan Vermillion sees before he loses everything. After that, I can move on and commit my heart and soul to you." His jaw stiffened. "He killed my father."

The words were a bucket of ice water dumped over my head, tensing every muscle in my body. I wanted to console him, but the shock froze my tongue.

"What we're doing here... it's about more than revenge. Vermillion killed my father because he was trying to end the war. My father was persuading the Northern Kingdom's generals to lay down their arms when Xaphan killed him, silenced him. They don't want this war to end. We're going to figure out why. They're hiding something."

"That's why the Reaper started all this?"

He nodded. "He was very close to our father. He won't stop until he gets his revenge."

"So, there is a real man under that mask," I murmured to myself.

Ryder took another step toward me. "I'm not giving up on us, Bryce. I'll wait for you... as long as you need."

"And if Vermillion kills us first?"

"Then I'll find you in the next life," he vowed, placing his hand over his heart. He leaned over and placed a kiss on my cheek. His lips lingered against my skin for a second longer than I think he intended. When he did pull away, he walked out the door without another word.

I put myself to bed, unable to stop the flow of thoughts. I tossed and turned for hours, going over the conversation repeatedly. Xaphan Vermillion killed Ryder's father. The pieces slowly came together. Realization dawned, and I sat up with a shuddering gasp.

I assumed that the brothers chose Ace, Quinn, and I because of our skillsets. I had the magic, Ace had the strength, and Quinn had the intelligence. But it was much more than that. The brothers came to me because they needed me for something much more important than my mystic abilities. They came to us because we each have a personal stake in this. One of them knew my past. They knew that I would bring not just power to the table, but a hunger for vengeance as well.

I left the comfort and warmth of my wolf furs and fled the room entirely. I trudged up the winding staircase. It felt like eternity stretched on before I finally reached the bell room.

The ceiling towered far above my head and from it hung the bell. It was old and rusted, with a crack running halfway to the top, but it was still beautiful in a vintage way. Vines and moss covered the gold surface. The vines spread from the bell's center, across the ceiling, and wrapped their way down the stone beams. With the bell room being completely open, foliage grew unchecked. Stone pillars held up the ceiling, but there were no walls or windows, only open archways with a view of the city. I was exposed to the elements. Tonight, a the cold wind blew in from the Atris Ocean beyond the East Side of the city. I shivered and hugged my nightgown closer to my chest.

I squinted through the darkness, searching each shadow for movement. I didn't expect to find him in the light, sitting on the very edge of one of the archways, looking down at the city below. One of his legs hung over the edge, as if he had no fear of falling. His cloak flowed behind him in the wind, but his hood remained fixed over his brow.

I approached slowly, catching the glint of his mask in the light. The Reaper turned his head slightly, not enough to face me, but enough to let me know that he was aware of my presence.

"You knew, didn't you?" I asked. I had to raise my voice over the howling wind. "You never came to me all that time ago for my skillset. You came to me because you knew what the Vermillions did to me."

He stood up and faced me fully, not that it mattered. His silver eyes betrayed nothing.

"Does Ryder know?"

He shook his head.

A shuddering breath left me. I could hardly find my voice to ask my final question. "Do you know where they buried her?"

He stepped forward. His hands disappeared beneath his cloak, and out of instinct I stepped away. But after a moment he pulled out a folded-up piece of paper and held it out for me to take.

I hesitantly unfolded it. At first, I wasn't sure what I was looking at. I held it up to the light and felt my heart falter in my chest. My face was drawn onto the paper, but a few features were sharper, older. A scar slashed through her left brow. It was my sister. How he could've possibly known what she looked like, I had no idea.

I tried to speak, but the lump in my throat made it difficult. I had to shut my mouth and try again, ignoring the tears forming in my eyes. "She's dead," I whispered, shaking my head like a wet dog.

The Reaper shook his head, slow and smooth. He placed a small object in my hand. I looked down to see a gold ring with an amber gemstone. The gem glowed as if a fire burned within. I recognized it instantly, because it was an exact match to the one that I wore on my own finger.

I knew I would get no answer, but still I asked, "How did you get this?"

He raised an arm and pointed off into the distance. I followed his gesture towards the Vermillion estate that loomed over the city. Then, he gently placed two fingers beneath his eye.

Spies.

A lone tear escaped my eye. "She's been there this whole time?"

A curt nod in response.

Something like a sob ripped from my throat. I'd spent the past few years drowning in grief and sorrow. I convinced myself that there was no hope for my sister. A part of me, deep down, buried beneath shame and guilt, wished that she was dead.

Because if the Reaper was right...

If Alina still lived... If she was still trapped in that horrid place, living through every torture imaginable...

Emotions raced through my veins faster than I could process them. Flames rose from under my skin like a tidal wave, ready to destroy. I hadn't used my power in years. I forgot what it was like to feel it pushing beneath my fingertips, begging to be released. I forgot what it was like to have to fight that power, to suppress it. It had been too long. Control was a thin thread that slipped between my fingers.

Fire exploded from my hands, shooting two parallel beams of flame straight up into the ceiling. I fell to my knees, pulling my arms back into my chest to try to stop the raging inferno. The chaos of my power was simply a mirror of what was happening within my mind.

It was the first time since my days in the army that I let my power loose. Almost three years passed. As a result, I'd been weak and fatigued. Using my power now had my old strength returning. For all the wrong reasons, it felt amazing.

Reigning in my emotions took several long moments. My eyes met the Reaper's, and I was sure that mine were now glowing with small strands of red flame within. I stood up, regaining more of my power by the second.

I was too afraid before, but for Alina I'd face those demons. The Reaper knew it. He knew all along. He needed this revelation to happen. His burning of warehouses and sinking of ships was just the beginning.

But now we were closing in on the final act, and what better finale than having me bathe the Vermillions in flames?

Once, I was known as the Harbinger. Now, they will know me– they will *bow* to me– as the Reaper's Firemaster.

CHAPTER
4

Quinn

I absolutely hate everything about this life. It's not what I imagined for myself. The others might be perfectly content, but I always wanted more than this, more than running and hiding, more than living in abandoned towers. I wanted to be able to walk into the library and read a book. I wanted to go to a pub without having to look over my shoulder. Most of all, I wanted to publish my writings without fear of who might come after me for my words.

Funny enough, I was the one to seek the Reaper out in the first place. I needed his protection when Vermillion sent his assassins after me. But sometimes I wondered if letting them kill me would be better than staying with three idiots in their twenties and one aspiring Accuser with no end in sight. I didn't expect to become part of his twisted operation. I never wanted to break any laws or hurt anyone. The only bright side to the whole thing was that I could write about the Reaper's conquests from an inside perspective. I'd be the first scribe to contribute such a detailed record. That was if I ever escaped the mess that I got myself into.

I was forced to leave the university, my studies, and my friends. All I wanted was to earn my history degree and become a scribe. To write history as I watched it happen. But I got close to something. I don't even know what it was. I stuck my nose somewhere it wasn't supposed to be, and Vermillion wanted to put an end to me before I could dig any further.

The Reaper searched tirelessly through my work, looking for something on the Vermillions. I tried to tell him I had nothing, but he didn't listen. To no one's surprise, he remained empty-handed.

He brought me every book I looked through in the past. Every research paper and record. He demanded I look through it all again. I started months ago, and barely made it through half of the material.

Some nights, when it all seemed like too much, I would sneak out of the horrid bell tower, just to get some time to myself. It was the only time I felt some sort of freedom.

I couldn't stay out for longer than a bell chime or two, because I knew that Vermillion still had his goons looking for me. But getting a few seconds of fresh air to clear my head was worth the risk. I was a writer, after all. Mental breaks, fresh air, and clear heads are quite possibly the most important things for a scribe.

The night that we brought Kalieth Vermillion to the tower, I desperately needed one of those breaks. My head throbbed from trying to understand the Reaper's logic. Eventually, I gave up, and when everyone went to sleep, I snuck out of my room. There was only one moment of hesitation when I walked past Ace's door. I stopped, wanting to knock. I wondered if he would go with me, or if he would slam the door in my face and tell me to go to bed. I stood in the silence of the hall, contemplating, before shaking my head at my own foolishness and leaving the tower.

It honestly puzzled me how the group could all brag about their superior skills, and yet I could sneak by them so easily. I could leave for the entire night, and no one would notice my absence. I didn't know whether to be offended or relieved.

The outside world seemed like a foreign thing now. After being with the Reaper and his henchmen for so long, I felt like I was looking at the real world through a window.

The knowledge I had weighed me down. Knowing the difference between the fiction and reality in the rumors surrounding the Reaper was extremely frustrating. Upon hearing housewives or drunken veterans whispering about him, I wished I could shout, "that's not true!" or "I saw that myself!" But I couldn't, because then they'd ask how I knew so much, and I wouldn't be able to respond.

So, I simply watched the strangers on the streets. Living vicariously through them was my only outlet. Sometimes I'd make up backstories for the people I saw, just to pass the time. It was comforting, somehow, to feel like I was a part of these strangers' lives, even for a few seconds

The truth poured from me in my nightly writings, my records. I continued to write them in hopes that one day I'd submit them. I hoped that my name would be etched into the wall of the library, where each scribe that came before me was commemorated. I wanted to be referenced in books and articles. Scholars would know my name. But until then I'd have to live like a criminal.

I wondered if my parents had received news of my absence from the university yet. Anxiety gripped me at the thought of my mother lying awake at night, with a tear-stained face, wondering where I'd run off to. I grew scared at the thought of my father yelling at her, maybe even hitting her, if he was having a bad day, for agreeing to let me go to the city. He never wanted me to go to school. He wanted me to stay home and be a stableboy. I was meant to take over the farm one day. But that wasn't me. He never knew me, anyway.

Thoughts of my parents faded in my mind when I reached the steps of the university's library.

I hadn't even realized I walked so far. Somehow, I managed to walk into the West Side of the city. My feet acted on their own accord. My heart brought me here. It was the one place I always wanted to be, where I felt safe. It was home.

The polished stone road shined beneath my feet, despite the moss and ferns that grew across the steps and the vines that climbed the walls on all sides. From afar, the library looked like a beautiful mixture of nature and man. A fusion of the past and the present.

It was a large building with many marble steps and columns. I wanted to walk up the stairs and into the front room. I wanted to stare up in awe at the vast bookshelves that went from the floor to the ceiling. I wanted to look upon the ancient tree trunks that the library was built around, and the lush growth that surrounded them, covering the wall in plant life. I wished I could see the glowing orbs of light, faelights, that floated through the air like dust particles, casting an eerie blueish light over all the books.

I would give anything to set my eyes on all of it again, but I knew that if I tried the doors, they'd be locked. Even if they weren't, I knew that Vermillion had to have someone stationed nearby to monitor who walked in and out of those large, drearwood doors.

So, I admired the building's architecture for a few more seconds, and then I kept walking. I crossed the western bridge and found myself in Center City.

The streets of Center City were beautiful compared to the South Side. Instead of thugs and homeless folks, scholars and tradesmen roamed the avenues. People from all around came to mingle. Every shop and restaurant worth visiting were located along the main strip of road. Few people actually lived in Center City, but those that did were incredibly lucky. One day, I wanted to own one of the beautiful apartments above the storefronts, made from brick and cobblestone, with iron terraces overlooking the streets. I could watch travelers and make up stories about them for hours. Unfortunately, time was a luxury I did not have.

I made my way toward the southern bridge.

Historic bridges connected Center City to the North, South, West, and East Sides. Each bridge was decorated accordingly. The bridge to the South Side was carved from obsidian stone because it was believed to ward off shadowed spirits, and in turn, ward off the criminals from crossing.

I read about the origin of the bridges a few years back, from the records of the infamous scribe, Gavinus Lennox. He wrote that the war raged nearby, close enough for stray bullets to leave marks in the cobblestone buildings that can still be seen to this day.

The Northern Kingdom's forces were pushing our Southern troops back toward the city, gaining ground. But just when the Southern forces were going to surrender, a horrible sound came from the sea on the horizon. The ground shook and broke apart. Water rushed through the new cracks in the earth and flooded the city, breaking it apart into five sections.

Lennox wrote that the river was a sea serpent's creation. He wrote in his records that the sea serpent rose from the waves, bothered by the noise of war, and opened his powerful jaws. He rained enough sea water on the city and the valley beyond to create the Infernal River. I found it interesting that Gavinus's record was the only one to mention the serpent.

Either way, I brushed my fingertips over the cool obsidian stone of the bridge. I couldn't help but admire the way the moonlight glinted off it. How could something meant to ward off the ugliest of souls be so basely beautiful?

While my fingers traced over the grooves and dips of the stone railing, my eyes fell to the dark abyss below. The Infernal River roared beneath me. I became instantly mesmerized by how the water's surface reflected the darkness of the night sky above. Even the moonlight couldn't seem to penetrate the water's surface, which swirled below me like a pool of liquid shadows. The way it churned made it seem like the waves were arms stretching out to try to pull me over. The very thought of it sent me staggering away.

Somewhere in the back of my mind, I knew that I needed to return to the bell tower. I never strayed this far before or stayed out for longer than an hour. But tonight, with Kalieth Vermillion chained to a wall, Bryce and Ryder engaged in a strange lover's quarrel, Ace's very presence, and the Reaper's overbearing gaze, the thought of returning to the tower was especially unbearable.

I turned back with every intention of heading toward the tower, but at the sound of a band playing in the distance, I stopped. It had been so long since I last heard music. The tune carried on the wind. The sweet melody practically beckoned to me. I could hear the shrill yet hauntingly divine sound of the violin, accompanied by the guitar and a singer or two.

I hesitated for all of one moment before changing direction to walk toward the commotion.

I came across a lively tavern. The customers spilled out into the street, clapping, dancing, laughing, and stomping their feet to the music as the band played.

I watched from across the way as two men clanked their ale pints together, tossing the glasses back. They managed to get more ale on their clothes than they did in their mouths. A woman on the other side of the courtyard tripped over her dress and fell into the man beside her. They laughed it off and began to dance together.

All of it was so natural, so... warming. I wanted to drink an ale with the group of men. I wanted to dance with the boys to my left. I wished that I could strike up a conversation with the man holding my favorite book under his arm.

I don't know how long I stood there, watching through my imaginary window. It felt like an eternity. I knew that I could've stayed there forever, though. Watching the way people moved with one another, interacted with each other, it fascinated me.

"Do you plan to join them?" a voice asked from beside me, making me jump. I hadn't heard anyone approach.

I looked over to see a boy near my age, if not a year or two older. I couldn't help but think that he was strikingly handsome, yet somewhat familiar. His hair was a dark brown, but standing in the shadows at night, I nearly mistook it for black. The flames of a nearby torch reflected in his blue eyes, which made them appear hazel. His skin was pale, as if he hadn't seen sunlight in months. I couldn't see his shadow in the dim light, but something told me that it was a shade darker than average– just a shade.

Anxiety made my tongue feel heavy. I had to clear my throat before I dared speak any words aloud. "No," I said, turning back to the scene before me. "I don't dance."

"Sounds like a boring way to pass time, watching others with envy."

"I'm not envious."

"No?"

"No."

He sighed, leaning against the brick wall of the building behind us.

We stood in silence for a few long moments. Tension crackled in the air like electricity. I resisted the urge to wipe my sweaty hands off on my nice breeches.

I flinched when he started to laugh. It was out of the blue. There was no way I could've expected it. But the laugh was genuine and loud. He clutched his stomach and doubled over, struggling to breathe.

"What?" I said, chuckling awkwardly with him. "What is it?"

"Sorry," he waved a hand through the air. "I was just imagining how that woman would come over here and slap you silly if she catches you watching her like that. By the Kings, you look like you're about to stomp out there and criticize her waltz."

I rolled my eyes. "Maybe I am."

"I'd pay good money to see it."

"How much?"

He narrowed his eyes while looking me up and down. His lips twitched up in the slightest of smirks. "Ten bronze marks."

I scoffed. "It would take more than that."

"How about you grab an ale with me, and we can discuss it?"

I couldn't help the choked laugh that escaped my lips. "That was your best?" I asked with a raised brow.

"Are you always so critical?"

"Yes."

He smiled. It was a beautiful thing. I couldn't remember the last time I made someone else smile. I never realized how much I took that small thing for granted. His eyes darted to the ground before meeting mine again. "That ale?"

I gave him a suspicious look. "I don't even know your name."

"Alastor," he said, offering me his hand. "Alastor Vermillion."

My entire body went taut when the words left his lips. I was left staring down at his hand in silence. The lump in my throat made it hard to swallow. "Vermillion?"

His brows bunched together. "Is that a problem?"

I thought about the Reaper. His eyes, made of silver flames, haunted my mind as I stared, unseeing, at Alastor's hand. I knew the Reaper would kill me if he ever found out about this, but I couldn't remember why I cared. I couldn't recall a reason I shouldn't be able to have one drink.

I shook his hand. "No. Not a problem at all."

CHAPTER 5

Kalieth

The first week of being the Reaper's prisoner, I was terrified. The second week, I still sat awake at night completely on edge. Once the third week passed, I realized I had nothing to fear, because they had absolutely no idea what to do with me.

I couldn't believe that this was the team that killed my sister. My hatred for them did not wane in my time chained to a wall, but I did get to observe their routines and listen to their conversations. As much as I hated to admit it, I couldn't envision Bryce, Quinn, Ace, or Ryder to be the sort of people to murder an innocent child. I became convinced over the course of the three weeks that the henchmen didn't have to die when I brought them to their knees. They could serve time in the prisons or be sent to the front lines, but I didn't want their blood on my hands. I only wanted the Reaper's. No matter how much time I spent here, that wouldn't change. He will burn.

Nearly a season passed since I first started my search. The leaves started to turn. The chilly autumn breeze that once drifted through the building quickly turned to a frigid winter wind. I found myself shivering against the freezing stone walls.

The Reaper found me blowing hot air over my numbed hands. I straightened against the wall, pretending not to be absolutely gripped by the cold. I would not show this man weakness. I wouldn't give him the satisfaction of knowing I could hardly feel any part of my body.

It was odd to see the Reaper standing in the doorway alone. Normally Ryder stood right by his side. He appeared wearing his signature clothes, a black cloak covering his whole body with the assassin's mask covering his face. He came just before dawn, the coldest point of the morning. He stood in the doorway for a long moment, watching me shiver. I was barely able to spot him in the dark.

He walked forward and fiddled with my chains. I grunted when the iron cuffs shifted places on my wrists, rubbing against the chaffed, sensitive skin.

A key appeared in his hand. It wasn't there before, and I didn't see him reach into any pocket, but the rusted iron key was suddenly in his grasp. He unlocked the cuffs in one swift movement. I gasped at the sudden weight lifted off me. My arms fell to my sides, and I immediately looked down at my swelled wrists.

The Reaper's gloved hand grasped my shoulder and pulled me to my feet. He helped me steady myself when my legs nearly gave out.

I wondered whether it was the exhaustion, the cold, or the hunger that calmed my mind enough to let the Reaper lead me upstairs without asking any questions. I followed him toward warmth without complaint.

He took me to a bedroom on the third floor. He unlocked the door and waited for me to walk inside. I was hesitant to brush past him. My eyes never left him, and his didn't leave me, until I passed through the threshold. Only then did he follow me inside.

The room was equipped with a narrow bed and a fireplace, which housed a small flame. Not much, but all I needed to survive. I noticed quickly that the room had no windows, and the only other door led to a small bathing chamber. The only exit was the door to the corridor.

He gave me a room with no escape. He took off my chains, but I was still a prisoner.

"It's been three weeks now. How long do you plan to keep me imprisoned here? I thought we'd be working together," I said as I turned to face him.

He gave me no response, but beneath the shadow of his hood, I thought I saw his brow arch up. I waited a few more seconds before I continued, "there's a lot of rumors about you, you know. About why you don't speak."

Again, no response. I sank down on the bed. "One woman told me that if you hear the Reaper's voice, it's only because he plans to kill you afterward. Another man said that you were born mute. I even overheard a child bet his buddies that your tongue was cut out."

He didn't so much as blink.

"And that mask," I added, waving a hand. "The number of stories I've heard about that mask could fill a book. You have scars too hideous to show. Beneath it is the face of the Accuser. You suffered from the Great Epidemic all those years ago, and still wear the mask to this day. Oh, and my personal favorite, that you are an anonymous mercenary hired by the king himself to clean up the city."

I leaned forward, searching his eyes to see if any of those rumors sparked anything. I got nothing. The Reaper's expression was as blank as ever.

I shook my head. "Who are you, beneath that mask?"

He reached for his pocket. I tensed, preparing for him to draw a blade. Instead, he pulled out a small piece of paper and a quill. To my surprise, he scribbled something onto the paper and offered it to me.

Who are you beneath yours?

I must've read the words ten times over. "I don't know what you're talking about."

He took the paper back and scribbled some more. *You are the shadow of a great name. What else?*

What more than a Vermillion? Did I need to be more? My father always said that family is

69

what's most important– that honor in the family name is most important. Being a Vermillion is all I am. I never even considered that there should be more.

The Reaper moved from the doorway toward the fireplace. He knelt and stacked a few logs on the glowing embers to keep the fire from going out.

I studied his every movement. There had to be something that I could see from the outside. Some part of him that I could crack.

"How can I prove that you can trust me? How can I become more than just a prisoner?" I asked.

Time was of the essence. I needed his trust. I needed him off his guard so I could lead him to the vault unsuspecting.

"When you fulfill your promise, and help us kill your father," Ryder's voice called from the doorway. I turned to see him leaning against the wood frame with his arms crossed over his chest. His silver eyes moved over to his brother. "I didn't realize the prisoner would get the spare room."

The Reaper stood and walked toward his brother. I expected him to stop short, and exchange some sort of communication, but instead he brushed right past Ryder and left the room entirely. Ryder glanced after him, but otherwise seemed unphased by his abrupt exit.

He chuckled at what must've been my surprised expression. He pushed off the wall and turned away from me. "Use the bathing chambers.

There will be a meal waiting for you once you're done."

He began to walk away, but I stopped him. "The season has nearly changed. When do we move on the vault?"

"We were waiting on the Reaper's signal. He's decided that tonight is the night. So, get a bath and a meal. Tonight, you'll start being useful." With that, Ryder closed the door, locked it, and walked off. I listened to the sound of his footsteps fading before I bothered going into the bathing chamber.

I may have been in there for hours. The hot water was a welcome sight after weeks of cold. Just as Ryder said, there was a steaming meal of biscuits and stew, as well as a new set of clothes, waiting for me once I returned to the bedroom.

I'd been given a black tunic, black breeches, and a large black cloak. A laugh of disbelief left my lips as I shoved them on. Not once did I think I'd be dressing like one of the Reaper's henchmen and leading them directly to my father's emergency vault. The only thing getting me through it all was knowing that it would be over tonight.

Even if I should fail, my father owns several "emergency" vaults around the city, all hidden in strange places. Destroying one would do little harm to him. It would only succeed in annoying him further. But if that should happen, my father would never forgive me for it. It's either capturing the Reaper tonight or living in exile for the rest of my life. It was an easy choice.

The door to my room opened, and Bryce stood in the doorway. She looked me up and down with a wicked grin tugging at her lips. "It's your time to shine, pretty boy."

She chuckled at her own comment as she waved me along. She wanted me to walk in front of her, still not trusting me enough to turn her back to me.

I stepped out into the narrow hallway. The dim light of the candles reflected off the smooth stone walls. The corridor was short, with only two or three doors leading to the spiral staircase. As we walked toward the stairs, the sound of laughter echoed through the tower from somewhere below. I've come to recognize the voices of each person in the Reaper's small group, and I could tell that the laugh belonged to Ace. It was too boisterous to be Ryder's, but far too deep to be Quinn's.

I learned a lot about the four henchmen in the weeks I spent with them. For instance, Ace isn't his true name, it's Aerin. They call him Ace because he's a hand-to-hand combat expert and has never lost a fight. What's worse, he earned that name fighting in the underground rings on the East Side. I learned this fun fact when Bryce threatened to unleash Ace on me after I told her that no man would be happy marrying a war deserter like her.

That was what I learned about Bryce. Ryder and the Reaper found her very much alive after she faked her death to escape the war. She was the most feminine assassin I'd ever met. She could slit a man's throat and then be disgusted about the blood, and how it may have stained her perfectly new designer dress. I'd heard of the difficulties that women soldiers go through in their time in the army, so it was remarkable to me that she managed to keep that delicate part of herself through it all.

Maybe that was why Ryder was absolutely infatuated with her. He might not say it aloud, or confide in any of his teammates, but it was obvious. I'd never seen a man stare longingly after a woman as much as he did Bryce. How Bryce managed to convince herself otherwise was beyond me.

Then there was Quinn. The kid was a teenage genius. He had a temper though, as most kids his age do. His attitude often had Ryder biting his tongue. A few times, I had to hold back a laugh at his sarcastic comments that ruffled the whole team.

The Reaper remained a mystery. He didn't speak once nor did he remove his mask or cloak. He seemed to always be watching or listening, always in the room with the others. Almost like an otherworldly presence.

Bryce's voice broke through my thoughts. "Do you plan to go down the stairs?"

I hadn't realized that I'd stopped walking when I reached the landing. I glared back at her before continuing on.

My boots made a loud scuffling sound against the ironwork of the stairs. It alerted the others of my approach. Their laughter stopped, replaced by an eerie silence.

We rounded the last set of steps and entered the front room where the others were waiting. The Reaper stood in the shadowed archway that led outside. Ryder stood to his right, while Quinn and Ace stood to the left.

Bryce stepped down behind me. She was dressed in her finest beneath the cloak she wore. The dress was a bit long for her, however, which told me that she stole it. If she bought it, it would've been tailored to her measurements. The corset tied tightly around her midsection doubled as armor, and its crimson red color paired well with the black of her dress. She had her hair pulled away from her neck in a braided crown around her head to show off her bare collarbone, seeing as the dress's straps wrapped around the sides of her arms. She kept her head held high as she walked past me and went to stand beside Quinn. All the others stared at her for a moment, but it was Ace who said, "By the Kings, Bryce, we're going to raid a vault, not to impress a prince."

Bryce rolled her eyes and tied the cloak closed all the way, hiding the dress from view. "Any opportunity to leave this tower is an opportunity to dress to impress."

"I hope you don't plan on going out afterward," Ryder said darkly.

Bryce's head snapped toward him. "So what if I was?"

The second Bryce and Ryder's eyes met, the tension in the room reached a new level. Ace and Quinn shifted uncomfortably on their feet. I had to fight instinct to do the same.

The Reaper placed a hand on his brother's shoulder. Ryder tensed, his nostrils flaring, before he shrugged away from the Reaper's grasp and walked outside. The Reaper went next, followed quickly by Ace and Quinn. Bryce waited until everyone else was outside before finally relaxing her shoulders. She sighed and rubbed her face. She must've forgotten I was standing only a few feet away, because when her eyes landed on me, she gave me a questioning stare. "What are you standing there for, Vermillion? Go follow the others."

I started to walk toward the archway, but I stopped short. I don't know why I felt like I had to comfort her. She meant absolutely nothing to me, and I would betray her trust soon enough. I chalked it up to the fact that spending the entire autumn season around her skewed my judgement a bit. Whatever the reason, I stopped and turned back. "He just hates the thought of you with someone else."

I could tell that her first reaction was to be angry with me for saying anything. She gave up on that rather quickly. She nodded her head and looked to the floor. "I know that."

I felt my brows pull together. Before I could think about what I was saying, I pushed a little further. "What are you so afraid of?"

The sadness began to fade from her eyes. Anger hardened her features. She clenched her jaw. "You should ask your father," she said, her lip curling up in disgust as she spoke.

I hadn't expected that response. Curiosity drove me to pry. "What are you talking about?"

I could see in her eyes that she had no intention of explaining. But I knew that the anger within her stemmed from something more than an imagined grievance. In fact, it wasn't anger at all. It was rage. Deep, hungry rage that blazed in her soul like a fire, begging to be let loose on the world– to devour everything in its path. I could see it all in the vast, dark green forest that made up her eyes. That forest itself was on fire, with glowing orange strands branching out through the green of her irises.

She shoved me forward. "Walk," she commanded, her voice deeper than usual.

I decided it was best for my well-being if I did what she asked. The thought of being incapacitated by an angry woman didn't feel appealing to me at this point in time.

We walked out together, with Bryce only a step behind me. The others waited for us in the alleyway just outside of the tower. The Reaper narrowed his eyes at us as we made our way over to them, and even Ryder eyed me up and down suspiciously.

"Alright rich boy, where's this vault?" Bryce asked. She crossed her arms over her chest and added, "you better not be leading us straight into a trap."

My heart faltered, but I showed no emotion on my face. I tilted my head. "I've been stuck inside with the five of you for an entire season. When, exactly, would I have set up this *trap*?"

She arched her brow, saying nothing.

It was time, then. The Reaper would meet Death tonight. And the others, unprepared for my trap, will be put in chains and tried for their crimes. My father will decide what to do with them in the end.

They all looked at me expectantly. I turned around, taking in my surroundings in an attempt to decipher where we were in relation to the vault. There were many throughout the city, but only one was in the South Side. My father didn't like to hide his money here, it was too great a risk. Too many thugs resided in the South.

The vault was hidden in the basement the local Vatra inn. My father used an alias to buy the property and paid a few southerners handsomely to keep the place running for him. No one would think that a disgusting, rotting inn in the heart of the South Side housed millions of gold marks.

I turned north and started to walk toward the main strip of road. "It's this way," I yelled over my shoulder. I didn't turn to see if they followed. I kept walking until I reached the main road, looking both ways to try to jog my memory. After a long moment, I decided that the strip of road to my right looked more familiar.

I walked for a moment before I realized how awfully quiet it was behind me. I whirled around to find that I was completely alone. The others, no matter what direction I turned, were nowhere to be found. I almost thought they'd left me. My heart began to pound at the thought of it.

A low whistle sounded from above, then a chuckle. I looked up to see the others looking down at me from the rooftop of a random house.

Bryce laughed at me. Ace shook his head, walking off. Quinn motioned for me to climb up the fire escape and join them. The Reaper didn't even look at me. His eyes were on the horizon, where the sun was just beginning to rise.

My eyes lingered on the Reaper for a second longer than I intended. I was transfixed by the way he held himself. He had such confidence and authority in his posture. He could cut down a single blade of grass across a vast field with his throwing knife if he wanted to, but in the three weeks I'd spent with the group, I'd only seen him use his skills on the first night we met.

I never thought about the fact that the Reaper was never spotted walking the streets of southern Shadieh. He had to keep hidden. What better place to hide than right above everyone's head?

"Quit drooling over the Reaper and get up here!" Bryce called.

I cursed them all under my breath as I climbed the fire escape. It was five flights to reach the rooftop. By the time I made it, I was breathing heavily, thanking the King above for the cold morning, otherwise I might've broken a sweat.

"Glad you could join us," Ace mocked.

The smirk on his face angered me enough to snap back, "Funny. That's exactly what your parents said to me the other night."

Bryce burst out laughing. She threw her head back and clutched her stomach tightly as her laughter echoed through the morning sky. Quinn turned his head away from Ace so he couldn't see him smile. Even Ryder's lips twitched up into a smirk.

Ace, however, did not find it funny. His eyes narrowed at me, and he drew one of his twin axes from over his shoulder. "You think you're hilarious don't you, Vermillion?"

"Only when I say something funny."

Ace took a step forward. The Reaper whirled around and caught him by the arm, holding him in place. The two of them exchanged a knowing glance before Ace relaxed and sheathed his axe. The Reaper let him go. Ace glared at me and said, "Don't worry Vermillion, you'll spend a night with my parents after I've killed you. They'll be sure to get their own revenge on your family in the afterlife."

The smirk fell from my face.

"That's enough," Ryder spoke up. He pushed off from where he sat on the edge of the rooftop. "Take us to the vault, Kalieth."

It took me a second to shake off the chill that settled in my bones. I reluctantly brushed past Ace. The group fell into step behind me.

I never hopped rooftops before, and quickly decided I wouldn't do it again. I wasn't a fan of the heights. I simply refused to look down as I leaped from one building to another, not thinking about how many stories I'd be falling with one misstep.

The first rays of sun rose over the horizon as we bounded across rooftops, setting the sky on fire. The Reaper stuck to the shadows as best he could, while the others soaked up as much sunlight as possible.

The natural, warm light made Bryce's blonde hair glow. The darkness of the tower seemed to drain all the color from her, but out here, exposed to the rays of the sun, she truly was a sight to be seen. Color flooded her cheeks and tanned her skin. She practically glowed.

The others seemed to be averse to the sun's effects. Nothing changed about them. They lived in the dark with no particular hardships, but aside from the Reaper, they did not shy away from the light.

We landed on the Vatra inn's rooftop with such loud thuds, I feared that any guests on the top floor would come investigating the noise. I waited for my father's guards to come out of the shadows. I waited for arrows to fly or for bullets to be shot. I felt no fear. I was ready to show my true colors to my new *friends*.

But there were no arrows, no bullets– just silence.

"The Reaper shot down your raven before it could even leave the South Side. There is no help coming for you," Ryder said, clasping a hand over my shoulder. His grip was rough, punishing. His eyes met mine, and I saw the rage within them. He pushed me forward, hard enough to throw me to the ground. "Take us to the vault."

I bit my tongue as I picked myself up. There was no time for fear or hesitation. My mind raced to think of a new plan. The table had flipped, and now I truly was their prisoner.

I tried the rooftop door, but it was locked. I thought we might have to descend to the street and try to go through the front entrance. But the Reaper wasn't going to let a lock slow us down. He pushed me aside and kicked down the door in one swift movement.

It flew off its hinges entirely, landing somewhere beyond in the darkness with a loud bang. Dust clouded the entryway. We waited for the dust to clear before entering the stairwell. I was forced to follow. I couldn't bring myself to be fully present, however. Not when I knew my father would hear of this and think the worst of me. I might as well put a knife through my own heart if reports get back to him, detailing my part in this.

"I'll evacuate any residents. The rest of you, raid the vault," Ryder said. He slipped through the doorway and disappeared into the darkness.

Evacuation? They didn't bother with that when my sister burned.

When I didn't walk forward, I was shoved by Bryce. We followed a few steps behind the Reaper as he picked his way through the dark stairwell, leading us into the top floor's corridor.

All the doors in the hall were left ajar, the rooms vacated. The doors swayed in the morning wind from the open windows at the end of the hall. I wondered if it was the breeze that had blown out the torches, or if the inn had gone dark long before we arrived. The corridor was narrow, with barely enough room for Bryce and me to walk alongside one another; her dagger pressed to my back, as if I had anywhere to run to or anyone to ask for help. The building was utterly empty.

In fact, each level we passed through was vacant. The entire building was eerily silent, which had the hairs on the back of my neck rising. Something felt very off about the inn since the last time I'd visited with my family. Back then, it was bustling with workers and customers. Now only our footsteps and the sounds of mice scurrying across the floorboards echoed through the space. By the looks of the empty rooms, with no traveler's bags or personal items to be seen, it seemed as though no one had been inside the Vatra inn for several seasons.

When we finally got down to the main floor, they all turned to me expectantly. "Alright Vermillion, where is it?" Ace asked.

I turned slowly, scanning my surroundings. It all looked exactly as I'd last seen it, and yet it still felt wrong. The top floors were rooms for travelers to rest in, but the bottom floor was a tavern for everyone to come and enjoy themselves. I remembered the front room filled with laughter, music, and cheers. Now the furniture was covered with sheets, and everything else was coated in dust.

"Well?"

I cleared my throat. "This way."

The door to the basement was behind the bar. I knew it would be locked, as always. But I grabbed the old brass key from its hiding place beneath the counter. I slid it into the rusted lock and turned it swiftly. A click sounded just as the door creaked open.

I led the group down the old stone stairs and into a large underground meeting room. This was the location of many of my father's high-profile, private meetings. Not even I knew who he met here.

Just beyond the meeting room, through a narrow archway, was the vault. Even with the dimmest bit of light, the gold exterior of the vault glistened for all to see, as if announcing its own presence. I noticed, for the first time, how arrogant it was of my father to place the vault there. It was almost as if he was boasting. He wanted all his associates to sit on fine leather couches and stare at the pure gold vault in the corner.

But the group at my back did not come to sit and stare. Ace drew his axes with his eyes set on the lock. He meant to try to break it open.

"It's spelled, genius," Bryce told him, her tone laced with sarcasm. "I can feel the primal magic from here. You need Vermillion blood to open it."

The Reaper stepped away so that I could come through. I looked into his eyes as I walked past, seeing suspicion swirl within them. He stayed close behind me, likely expecting me to pull something as a last resort. He was shorter than me, though, so I wondered how much he could really see over my shoulder.

Opening the vault was simple. All I had to do was prick my finger and smear a bit of blood across the locking mechanism. The magic instilled into it recognized my family blood and the entire wall moved to the side to reveal another room, furnished, decorated, and filled with marks, gold pieces, and family heirlooms. It was probably enough to buy the entire South Side of the city.

Bryce, Ace, and Quinn nearly knocked me over as they all rushed forward to stuff their pockets with my father's money. I followed them into the room, but I did not touch a single mark.

Ryder joined us in the basement just as the vault opened. He approached the Reaper and stood beside him. The brothers made no move to enter the vault. They only watched the other members of their team steal as much as they could carry. They couldn't look more uninterested.

I came close to asking why they wanted to raid all my father's vaults if they wanted nothing from them. But I became distracted when my eyes landed on a golden locket across the room. The air was knocked straight out of my lungs at the sight of it, and I nearly tripped over an ottoman on my way over to it.

It sat in a decorative bowl on top of a chest of drawers, amongst many other pieces of jewelry. It was a beautiful heart-shaped locket, with the Vermillion family crest decorating both sides within a large 'O'. I wouldn't dare open it here, but inside I knew I would find pictures of my sister and me, along with a picture of the whole Vermillion family. I should know, I got her the locket, and she never took it off. She was wearing it the last time I saw her. The night she died. My father said it was lost in the ashes, which begged the question, how did it get into a vault that could only be accessed by a Vermillion?

Bryce came to stand next to me. She took a few of the pieces she liked before she caught onto my sudden change of demeanor. She peeked over my shoulder. "What is it?"

I shook my head, slipping the locket into my cloak. "It's nothing."

Not another word left my lips as the others finished stuffing their pockets. I kept my hands in my cloak, fumbling the locket around, nearly expecting it to disappear into thin air if I let it go.

Someone in the Vermillion family was working with the Reaper. That was the only explanation for this. They aided in Octavia's death and returned her locket here to be forgotten. A traitor lies amongst my brothers.

My mind cleared temporarily when someone set fire to the vault. The marks caught fire instantly, burning away in seconds. I watched in horror as the thin, golden colored papers were reduced to ash. I was prepared to see them steal everything my father worked for, but not for them to burn it, erasing it along with all my father's years of hard work within mere seconds. My eyes found the Reaper's. In complete shock, I watched the reflection of the raging flames in his eyes.

"The two of them never take anything," Bryce told me. She must have read the confusion on my face.

"Why?"

She shrugged. "The only answer I ever got from Ryder was that the Vermillions' money is dirty, earned from blood and chaos. He and the Reaper want nothing from Xaphan Vermillion, not even a spare coin. They just want to see his empire fall. They want to bring an end to his tyranny."

Surprise coursed through me. All this time, I'd never given much thought to why the Reaper was doing this. I figured that like many others, he wanted what my family had– the money, the power. But learning that he wanted nothing, well, somehow it made everything worse. It only spiked my curiosity. What could my father possibly have done to these people to make them do something like this?

"But you'll take some?" I asked Bryce after another moment of watching the soaring flames.

"I don't have quite the same restraint as they do. I want to destroy Vermillion, yes. But taking what's his doesn't seem so bad to me," she said with a shrug.

I turned away from the fire to face her completely. She must've been surprised by the sudden movement and the intensity in my stare, because she stepped back.

"What did we do to you?" I asked.

The crackling of the fire concealed the sound of my voice breaking. The question hurt to ask. I was truly afraid of what her answer might be. My entire life, I looked up to my father. I thought he was the smartest, bravest person I knew. He taught me to take pride in our family name. I never doubted my family. I never doubted my upbringing. But the heat of the fire matched that of the rage burning in the hearts of each person in the room. There was no deception here. Their hatred was more real than anything I'd ever experienced before. In fact, it was so real and so potent that they were all willing to risk their lives if it meant taking another step toward destroying what my father built. I needed to know why. I needed to know the truth.

I saw rage flash through Bryce's eyes again. She opened her mouth to respond, but she was cut short when Ryder yelled, "The fire's spreading. Time to go!"

The others ran upstairs while Bryce and I stared at each other. A soft, half-smile played on her lips. "I guess it's a story for another time," she said. She whirled around and sprinted toward the stairs, leaving me without answers.

I was right on her heels when I heard the fire pop behind me. Ryder was right. The fire was already spreading up toward the higher levels. The entire building would come down in a few short moments, and if we didn't leave, we'd be buried under the rubble.

Our footsteps pounded against the floorboards. I took the steps two at a time in my rush to make it out. The smoke blurred my vision as I stumbled out the front doors. Bryce and I were the last out. For a moment, all six of us stood in a close circle, doubled over, coughing and wiping tears from our stinging eyes. I was so focused on catching my breath, I failed to notice the armed soldiers surrounding us.

I wiped my eyes one last time and realized what was truly happening. The six of us stood outside on the open street. There were enemies waiting for us, but they were not soldiers.

All six of my brothers surrounded us, swords drawn.

CHAPTER
6

Kalieth

I should've felt relieved to see my brothers. I should've thanked the King above that I could finally take the Reaper to my father and be finished with this mess.

But I only felt fear because I knew that I wasn't done yet. It was about more than my father now. I needed to know why the Reaper and his henchmen sought to destroy my family name. I had to find out if I'd spent my entire life fighting for a lie. I needed to know which of my brothers aided in the death of our sister. One of them was working with the Reaper and finding out which one meant staying with the group a little longer. With a heavy heart, I closed ranks with the Reaper's team.

Ace practically whooped with joy. He flipped a pair of daggers between his hands, a smirk lifting his scars. "Fuck yes," he sneered. "I've been waiting an eternity to make a Vermillion bleed."

The others weren't as thrilled. "I knew you'd betray us!" Bryce hissed at me.

"He's been chained to a wall, Bryce. He couldn't have set us up," Ryder told her.

"Well, someone did," she spat back.

Ryder was about to respond when a shaky voice said, "Alastor?" Quinn took a small step back, his chest rising and falling fast. A stricken expression overtook him as he stared at my youngest brother. The hurt in his eyes went deep, as though he'd been betrayed by a good friend.

Bryce's accusing gaze snapped from me to Quinn. Even Ace looked shocked. The only person appearing unphased was the Reaper. His gaze was as blank and uncaring as always.

"Quinn? You did this?" Bryce asked, her eyes wide.

Quinn shook his head vigorously. "No! No, it wasn't like that. He said he wanted to join us. He said he hated his father like we did." His hands shook as he spoke. There was a tremor to his voice. He knew deep down that he'd been wrong. For his own sanity, he was trying to convince himself otherwise.

Alastor laughed. "You're even more naïve than I thought. I heard you were supposed to be some sort of genius, how disappointing to find another sheep herded by a wolf. The only reason I didn't kill you the second I saw you was because I knew you'd lead me right to the others."

Quinn lowered his head, ashamed and hurt. He wasn't the first to fall for Alastor's tricks. Of

90

all the team members, I was surprised Quinn fell for it. Then again, Al was good at finding a weakness and exploiting it. My youngest brother was a master of deception.

"Enough, Alastor. We're not here for that," Azazel, the oldest, said. He stood in front of the Reaper, and he took a step forward to get a better look at what lay beneath the hood. "I thought you'd be... bigger."

"He compensates," Bryce said from behind us.

Az hummed his consideration. "You're coming with us." He raised his sword, putting it against the Reaper's throat. The Reaper raised his chin, letting it cut deeper. His blood slickened the blade. He didn't flinch or cry. He didn't even blink as he held my brother's simmering gaze.

Ryder snickered. "Yeah, I'd like to see that."

Az's eyes shifted over to me. "I see you've chosen the wrong side, brother."

"That remains to be seen," I said. By the disgust in his gaze as he stared at me, his own sibling, I wondered if Az was the one responsible for the death of Octavia.

Az looked me up and down once more before nodding to our brothers. "Leave Kalieth and the Reaper. They will answer to father himself. Do as you wish with the rest."

The order was met with smirks and snickers from my brothers. My siblings stepped forward, herding us into a tight circle. They sneered and taunted, trying to intimidate us. They reeked of confidence. My brothers lived their whole lives being told that they were the best, and they were arrogant enough to believe it, just as I had believed it. I already saw the end of this story. I lived it. I pitied the family doctor. He'd be putting in many hours tonight.

In numbers, we were evenly matched. In skills, however, some outweighed others. Bryce stepped forward to face the second-born, Eligor. It was strange to see her pitted against him. He was the biggest and strongest of all my brothers. I thought Ace would've taken him on. But Bryce did not balk from him. Instead, she shed her cloak and drew two daggers from her sides. Eligor took one look at her and flashed a wicked smile. "Don't worry, love. I won't scar that pretty face of yours. I'd miss it too much."

Bryce spat at his feet. Pure disgust was written on her face. "I'm honored. Maybe I'll grant you a quick death in exchange."

Eligor lashed out first. Bryce avoided his sword easily with a jump to the side. She blew out a breath, twisted her blades in her hands, and launched herself at him with an enraged cry.

The others followed suit. Ace attacked my third-born brother, landing a blow to Tynan's jaw, snapping his head to the side. They were fair opponents. Tynan had the same height and build as Ace, but when it came to experience and expertise, Ace excelled. I watched, awed, as he landed each punch that he threw Tynan's way. He dodged all my brother's counterattacks with little effort. Within seconds, I understood how Ace earned his name.

Ryder fought Alastor and Nox, the seventh and fourth-born, simultaneously, while Quinn cowered behind him.

That left Darcel, the sixth-born. He was younger by a mere two years, and yet we were complete strangers to one another. He twirled his sword between his hands as he circled me. "I never liked you, but I never thought you would betray the family," he said.

I realized quickly that I couldn't win this fight. Not because he was the better fighter, but because he had an advantage. He had an entire belt full of weapons while I had nothing but my fists.

I had to stall for time. "I'm just trying to find answers."

Darcel laughed. "Try explaining that to father when he hears of this."

From the corner of my eye, I saw a shadow move toward us. No, not a shadow. The Reaper. With the sun hidden behind the buildings across the street, he was able to move through the darkness unseen by those who did not think to look for him.

"Get on with it then," I snapped at my brother.

Darcel raised his sword and aimed for my midsection. I jumped back just in time for the Reaper to slide between us. Their blades clashed. Darcel reeled back in surprise before he caught himself. He tried to go for the Reaper's legs, but the assassin was far too quick on his feet. He dodged Darcel's strike and drove my brother backward. He raised his sword above his head and brought it down on Darcel as hard as he could. Darcel deflected. The blades passed only inches from his face. The Reaper didn't miss a beat. He moved to deliver the same attack again, his silver eyes trained on my brother's head.

Darcel raised his sword to meet the Reaper's, but in the last second before the blades collided, the Reaper sidestepped, dropped to his knees, and went for Darcel's leg.

Unfortunately for Darcel, the Reaper hit his mark. My brother went down hard, clutching his leg to his chest. He was no match for the Reaper. The cloaked assassin aimed better, moved faster, and hit harder.

I heard a groan of frustration to my left and turned to see Azazel coming toward us, sword raised. The Reaper took one look at my eldest brother and unsheathed his obsidian dagger. A single second of hesitation passed before he placed it in my hands, and with it, his trust.

An ultimate decision lay in my hands. I had a choice to make, charge Azazel and turn my family against me, or exact my revenge on the the Reaper and return home with no real answers.

Octavia's name was a whisper on my lips, a reminder to try for answers. I gripped the dagger in a tight fist and charged my eldest brother.

Az was a formidable opponent, but he stood no chance against both me and the Reaper working as a team. I went low when the Reaper went high. I went right when he went left.

Together, we were able to knock Azazel to his knees.

I turned away to see how the others faired. My heart sank in my chest.

Eligor had Bryce pinned down on the ground. His hands were wrapped around her throat, squeezing hard. The pale skin on her face turned blood-red. She clawed at where his hands gripped her throat, but he didn't let up.

All it took was one glance in her direction to make Ryder falter. He let his guard down. Nox and Alastor seized the advantage. They surged forward to drive him back. Alastor took his legs out. Ryder's knees hit the cobblestone *hard.* He didn't seem to notice. His mouth opened to call out to Bryce, but Nox punched him in the face. He fell to the side. Nox and Alastor turned away from Ryder to close in on Quinn.

But then Ace was there. He emerged triumphant from his fight with Tynan. His knuckles were cracked and bloody, but still, he raised them to defend Quinn.

But while Ace defended Quinn, that left Bryce at Eligor's mercy. She was thrashing in his grip, gasping for air. Her eyes started to roll back.

I moved to help her. I took one step toward her when the hilt of a sword came down against the back of my head. Spots of light blurred my vision as I fell to the ground. My ears rung at a painful frequency. For a few long moments, I couldn't move. The throb spread from my head to my neck and shoulders, beating like a second heart. The pain was unbearable.

It felt like eternity passed before I managed to blink away the fog in my eyes. Everything seemed to move in slow motion as I watched Ryder get to his knees, fighting with everything he had to get to Bryce. Her hands fell away from her neck. Her head tilted upward as she took what would've been her last breath.

Quinn was pinned against a wall by Alastor, and Ace dropped his axes to the ground while staring down the barrel of the gun that was suddenly in Nox's hand.

"Kill them," Az commanded from somewhere behind me.

Rays of sunlight finally hit us as the sun rose above the buildings across the street. I relished its warmth, turning toward it as I fought to stay conscious. The light reached toward me like outstretched hands, beckoning to me with the promise of a warm embrace. I wondered if it was the King of Stars, come to take me away.

The warmth was gone as quickly as it came.

It was replaced by cold. A cold so frigid that I might've thought I was in the Northern Kingdom. It sank beneath my skin like a thousand claws and scraped over my bones.

Was this the embrace the light promised? Was this what the King of Stars had to offer me?

I stilled on the ground, in a state between sleep and consciousness. My head was spinning, yet my thoughts were clear. As I watched the sunlight fade, I watched complete, utter, terrifying darkness surround me. All I thought about was the two Kings. The King of Shadows. The King of Stars. I watched light and dark battle, and I wondered why the King of Shadows was feared, when it was the King of Stars who could only thrive in the dark. Shadows exist even in the light, but without darkness, the stars would be nothing.

Night won. The sunlight was gone. Black mist surrounded us. It enveloped the entire street. I raised one of my hands, watching the strange darkness weave through my fingers. It wasn't mist at all. It was shadow. Tendrils of shadow that curled and swirled through the open air.

There was nothing. I was sure of it. Nothing existed anymore. I couldn't feel the ground beneath me. I could hardly feel the cold anymore. I was floating, numb. With each second that passed, I strayed farther and farther from– something. Was it life? Was I fading from the mortal realm entirely?

Had Death come for me? Did Az smash my skull in? Maybe the shadows came to take my soul. They enveloped everything within seconds. They created a pocket of darkness impossible to see through. They brought the temperature down until my teeth chattered and shivers racked through my body. This was the Shadow Realm. I would spend eternity here, blind and cold.

I was convinced of my own demise until I felt arms snaking under my shoulders, lifting me. "Get up," a hoarse voice croaked. Bryce.

With her help, I got back to my feet. I gripped the back of my neck, feeling a thick, warm substance trickling down from where Az hit me. I kept pressure there for my own comfort, knowing it didn't help much.

"We have to move. He can't keep this up for long," she whispered.

I was trapped in a dark abyss. I looked around, trying to glimpse anything that might help me piece together what was happening. That's when I saw it. A gleam of light broke through the dearkness and reflected off the Reaper's mask.

That's how I saw his hands. They were open, palms facing upward. Shadows poured from his fingers like fire would from a dragon's mouth.

The Reaper was an *azkriva*, an *abomination*. A rank in the army that was only a myth.

The Reaper was a shadow-bender.

CHAPTER
7

Ryder

I searched for Bryce first, but she'd already gone. I prayed to the Kings that she was okay and grabbed Quinn instead. We ran for the nearest alleyway without looking back, using the shadows for cover before they dissipated. He didn't bother fighting against my hold. He let me drag him along. He was in enough trouble already. I assumed he didn't want to add to it.

We split up to lose the Vermillion brothers. Luckily, they were just as confused about the shadows as we were, and they refused to follow us through them. But even though they retreated, it wouldn't be long before they came after us again. We needed to be long gone before then.

Our group had a plan set in place for this exact situation. If we were ever split up, we would go to Nero Village, just one day's journey outside the city. The others would already be on their way, but Quinn and I had some talking to do first.

Once I was sure that we'd put enough space between us and the Vermillion brothers, I slammed Quinn against an alley wall. I had to fight my own desire to strangle him right then and there. Because of him, the Vermillion brothers nearly killed us all. We would've been locked in the cold embrace of coffins, dropped into the ground to be consumed by worms.

"What were you thinking?" I yelled. My anger was so overpowering that my hands trembled with restraint as I held him there.

Quinn wouldn't look me in the eye. His lip shook as he stood there quietly, his head lowered towards the ground.

"Do you realize that Bryce nearly died? That would've been her blood on your hands. Do you realize that? I thought you were smarter than this!" My voice continued to rise with frustration.

"*I'm sorry, I'm sorry, I'm sorry...*" He said the words over and over again until their meaning melted away. It sounded like the words meant nothing to him. His frantic whispers wouldn't be enough to assuage my wrath.

"I'm not the one you should apologize to. It's Bryce. If she can speak, that is."

The sight of Bryce pinned beneath Eligor– his hands squeezing the life out of her– her nails slashing through his skin to get free– it killed me. For a split second, I thought I'd lost her. I thought I might have to face a world that didn't have her in it, and that wound dug deeper than I ever thought possible.

I pushed Quinn away from the wall and shoved him forward. "Walk."

"I just wanted to live again," he whispered. He stumbled forward, nearly falling on his face before he caught himself. I almost felt bad for him. Almost.

We walked in silence for at least an hour. We crossed over the southern bridge into Center City. We had to weave through the crowds of locals doing their morning errands. Shops were opening their doors and vendors were setting up their stands on the sides of the streets. Their promises of cheap prices and good products fell flat to my ears. I didn't care for enchanted gems or powder that kept you from sweating all day.

It was the smell of freshly baked goods wafting from the open doors of the bakery across the street that had my fingers itching to spend my marks. They smelled just like the ones Ma used to make at the end of every week. Our family would sit in the fields and savor them as we watched the sunset. My stomach rumbled at the thought of those memories. It would be easy for my feet to carry me there, easy to survey all the choices and pick whichever pastry had a beautiful, flakey golden crust.

Instead, I pulled Quinn along and worked our way through the crowd.

Center City was the best place to lose a tail. The main strip was bustling with shoppers, vendors, merchants, shopkeepers, and nobility. The streets were especially busy on this particular morning because it was the last farmer's market of the season, seeing as winter was upon us. I could disappear into the throng of people with ease to become just one in thousands, another unknown face in the crowd.

I knew Quinn wanted to explore. Beyond a writer, he was an explorer. But I could sense his fear. I could feel the tension between us, still crackling and raging like a wildfire. Guilt doused the light in his eyes. They looked utterly empty when I caught a glimpse of them.

My anger toward him diminished as the hours went by. He betrayed us, yes, but it was an accident. The brightest student in Shadieh was fooled by the deceptive Vermillion brother. And, if we were honest, the Reaper and I knew that we were walking into a trap one way or another. The Vatra inn had been evacuated long before our arrival, and it was simply too easy. Even Xaphan Vermillion was too smart to leave a property housing a hidden vault unprotected.

The Reaper assured me that no matter what, we would all evade capture. At the time, I didn't understand his certainty. Now I did.

As if on cue, Quinn spoke for the first time since sunrise. "Did you know the Reaper could do that? Control the shadows, I mean."

I took a deep breath. I knew that question was coming. I also knew that the others would be hounding me for answers the second we met at the rendezvous point. I wished I could take herbs to prepare for the inevitable headache.

"No."

"He didn't tell you?"

"No."

"You know what this means, don't you?"

"Yes."

Quinn looked up at me expectantly. "What will we do?"

"I don't know yet." The words came out sharper than I intended. Quinn snapped his mouth shut and shied away from me. Any other day, I would expect him to have a sarcastic remark at the ready, but he was smart enough not to push his limits with me today.

Quinn stayed silent for the rest of the trip. We took the long way through Center City. Then, we crossed to the West Side of Shadieh, the mainland, and hiked through the Sombra mountain pass. The trail took us deep into the forest, climbing up the mountainside until we reached the other side of the mountain range. We would reach Nero Village by sun-down. That left plenty of time for my mind to wander and assume the worst about Bryce. Anxiety formed a tight ball in my chest. It weighed down my heart not knowing what happened to her.

I thought of Ace too. Last I'd seen, he was taking on two Vermillion brothers. He never lost a fight, but only the Kings knew how he faired in the darkness.

The Reaper would be okay. My sibling, even before the shadow-bending, was too tough to be brought down by the Vermillion brothers. The only way they'd capture the Reaper would be if the Reaper wanted to be caught. That day would come. Soon. But I couldn't quite think past the fact that I was not told about the shadow-bending. I had no idea the Reaper was an *azkriva*. We'd never kept anything from one another before, even as children, so why start now?

Kalieth Vermillion surprised me. I expected him to stand with his brothers the second things escalated. But he stood by us to fight his own kin. I didn't know whether he'd find his way to Nero Village. If Kalieth got there, it was because the Reaper chose to show him the way.

By the time the sun reached the western horizon, my feet ached, and my knees were ready to give out entirely. I wanted to rest and continue in the morning, but that changed when the faint sounds of music reached us in the forest. Heavenly voices, like whispering gods, sang of peace and dreams. Their music weaved through the trees, echoing through the forest and up into the stars that were beginning to appear in the evening sky.

My entire body relaxed. Quinn and I took one glance at one another before we broke out into a run, following the sound of the music.

We ran up the steep incline of the last mountain in the range. At the top, we looked down at a welcome sight. The large village of Nero celebrated below us. The flames of the large fire at the village center soared high into the night. The voices of the singers carried on the wind, telling our story. The drums, fiddles, and guitars worked together to create a rhythm for the villagers to dance to– and they did. They danced through the streets. Even from atop the hill, I could see them moving to the beat and reaching toward the stars.

There'd be ale awaiting us down there, lots of it. A night of laughter and storytelling was in our near future. What we saw now was only the beginning of a celebration that would last long after moon-high.

"Is it a holiday?" Quinn questioned, his eyes full of wonder.

A knowing smile lifted my lips. "No. They're celebrating the Reaper's return."

I felt his eyes on me. "Return?"

I chuckled as I met his curious stare. I nodded and began to descend the hill. "Come. You'll see."

We rushed into the valley, toward the village. It sat between the two mountain ranges that separated Shadieh from the rest of the kingdom. It was truly a beautiful place, but almost completely isolated from the rest of the world. The people were able to provide for themselves with no help from trade. Or, should I say, no help from the Vermillions.

The northern side of the valley consisted of farming fields and training rings, where they taught young warriors to hunt. A small stream ran through the length of the valley to empty out into the Atris Ocean beyond the mountains. The entire valley was surrounded by forests. The tree line gave way to the tall, soft grass of the valley that pressed to the ground beneath our boots.

The village itself was on the southern side of the valley and as we approached, I could feel the beats of the drums in my chest. I felt the warmth of the fire even from the outskirts of town. I drew in the scent of acrid smoke laced with something sweeter; some sort of delicacy that they cooked in the flames. The delicious smell quickly made me aware of my utterly empty stomach, which began to growl in reaction.

Quinn and I stumbled down the dirt road toward the village center. We almost collapsed to the ground with exhaustion when we finally made it. I did not fall to my knees, despite my desire to do so. I did not want to give out until I saw the rest of our group. Until I knew that they'd all made it here safely. That *she* made it here safely.

Our entrance drew a crowd. Many of the locals recognized me and rushed to help us. We had to politely push our way through, ignoring their greetings and questions.

All the other villages and cities in the Southern Kingdom were run by Duke's or Lords who answer to the King. But not in Nero. The King didn't care about this place. He probably had no idea it existed. The villagers used that to their advantage by establishing their own leadership. They recognized their chief as the sole authority and the only woman to lead a village in the kingdom. Her name was Chief Amirah Kamiyama, and she happened to be the one to approach me first.

"We did not expect you and your friends on this night," she said with a smile, outstretching her hand in greeting. Her valley-folk accent weighed down the vowels of her words, and it took me a second longer than usual to comprehend her statement.

We grasped each other by the elbows. "We did not expect to be here, but it seems your people are always ready to dance around the fire."

Her smile widened. "It is good to see you, Ryder."

"And you, Chief Kamiyama," I replied quickly with a bow of my head. The last thing I wanted to do would be disrespect her. "Where are the others?"

She pointed across the open square, through the ring of dancers and the fire. I followed her gaze to see the Reaper sitting on the wooden railing of a front porch, back leaning against the supporting beam, sharpening a sword with whetstone.

Ace stood on the ground in front of the railing. He laughed at something the woman clinging to his side said. He gladly accepted a second ale from a barmaid who passed by. But I couldn't care less how Ace spent his free time. It was when my eyes met familiar emerald green ones that I froze.

Bryce spotted me first. She sat on the steps leading up to the front door. The village healer sat by her side, one hand rummaging through a bag of herbs while the other pressed a cold compress to Bryce's neck. Her hand instinctively went to her throat, to cover it from my gaze. She knew that I would want to see the wound. She read it in my stare.

I don't know when I started walking. I shoved through the crowd to get to her. Flashbacks to this morning clouded my mind, of how I clawed, punched, and kicked anything I could, and yet I couldn't make my way to her. I watched her eyes roll back into her head, watched her take what I thought was her last breath.

I failed to protect her. I failed to protect them all. I refused to let it happen again.

When I reached her, I realized I had no idea what to say. I wanted to be angry at her for choosing to battle the only brother capable of defeating her. I wanted to hug her close to my chest and never let her go. I wanted to fall to my knees and thank the Kings that she's alive.

I could see the hideous blacks, blues, and purples that covered the skin of her neck. I saw the way her eyelids drooped low, and she leaned her head against the step behind her. Exhaustion weakened her. I was surprised she made it to Nero in one day given her condition.

She read all the questions in my expression. "Ace brought me here. Wouldn't let me rest, the bastard. Said he'd carry me if he had to. That wouldn't do. I couldn't very well let him gloat about it for seasons to come," she said in an attempt to joke. Her chuckle came out as more of a choked sound caught at the back of her throat. Her voice sounded hoarse and weak, too breathy. Her words ended in a coughing fit.

"Why would you choose Eligor? You knew he'd overpower you."

The remaining light drained out of her eyes. Her features hardened to turn her face emotionless. "I just wanted..." she trailed off. She stared off into the distance, unseeing. After a few seconds, she shook her head and cleared her throat. Her lips twitched up into a smile that didn't reach her eyes. "I wanted a challenge."

"You're lucky. If it weren't for your mystic blood, you'd be dead," the healer told her sternly. She closed her bag of herbs and walked off.

"Mystic blood?" Kalieth stood in the house's doorway. He stepped toward the porch stairs. His brows were bunched up in confusion as he looked down at us. "That's not possible. The mystics went extinct decades ago."

Bryce turned her head as much as she could to raise a brow at him. "Who told you that?"

"My father."

Another choked sound left her. "Well, my kind is very much alive, and your father is well aware of it."

He narrowed his eyes and crossed his arms over his chest defiantly. "He had no good reason to lie about it."

"But he did." Bryce winced in pain as she moved her body to raise one of her hands. Once it was close to her chest, she let fire flow from her palm.

Kalieth reeled away in shock. He knocked over an old rocking chair in his sudden episode. He stumbled over the furniture and fell on his back. He got to his knees and watched through wide eyes as fire crackled in her hands. He began to feverishly shake his head. "You could do that the whole time and you didn't burn my brother to ashes?"

"Believe me, I tried. It's hard to call to the flames when there's no oxygen flowing to my brain."

He shook his head. "I don't understand."

"That makes two of us," Quinn spoke up from behind me. We all turned to see him, and despite knowing that we were all angry with him, he stood there defiantly. He looked at us as though *we* were in the wrong. "I want to know what we're doing here. What is this place? How do the villagers know about us? And when exactly was the Reaper going to tell us that he happens to be a shadow-bender?"

"I'm sorry, you think you get to ask questions after the stunt you pulled?" Bryce asked.

"Don't act like you don't want answers," he countered.

She narrowed her eyes for a second, but then shrugged. "He's got a point."

"You mean none of you knew about this?" Kalieth asked.

"No, we didn't, and I think I know why," Quinn said in a matter-of-fact tone.

The Reaper arched a brow.

Bryce rolled her eyes. "Do tell."

Quinn looked to the Reaper, his eyes narrowing. "The Reaper didn't tell us because he knows exactly what this means. Haven't any of you read the Accuser's Last Testament? It clearly states that whoever shall hold the power of shadow in their hands, no matter their background or heritage, will be the rightful ruler of all the lands. By the most ancient law, the throne belongs to the Reaper."

We all went silent, even as the party raged on around us. All eyes turned expectantly to the Reaper who focused only on the sword in his lap.

"Well then," Ace said, raising his ale. "Drink up friends. Tonight, we're in a king's company."

CHAPTER

8

Bryce

Ryder approached his brother angrily. He clenched his fists with each step, his muscles tensing. "How long have you known about the shadow-bending?" he demanded. I flinched at the sound of his voice. I'd never heard him so–furious.

The Reaper did not look up from his sword. He continued to pass the whetstone over the blade. *Once. Twice.*

"Two?" Ryder asked. "Two what– days? Weeks? Seasons?"

He drew the stone across the blade again. *Once. Twice. Three times.*

"Two *seasons*?" Ryder's voice cracked in disbelief.

I stopped listening the second I saw a barmaid making rounds across the square. The burning desire to forget the entire day by chugging a few ales seemed very appealing, despite the second heartbeat I felt in my throat. I tried to ignore the pain as I waved her over.

"Really?" Quinn whispered; brows raised.

I gave him an incredulous look. I took an ale from the barmaid's tray, thanking her kindly. I directed a hateful side-eye glance his way. "Oh, he'll pay," I said with a nod in Quinn's direction. "After all, he is the one that almost got me killed today. Keep them coming, please."

Quinn grumbled something under his breath before handing the woman a bronze mark.

I looked down at the pint of ale in my hands. I suddenly wondered how I'd be able to get the stinging liquid down my injured throat. I could choose to put the ale down and focus on something else, like the way Quinn glared at the woman clinging to Ace's arm, or I could listen to the riveting interrogation Ryder was conducting with his brother. I could ponder why my power faltered today, but I already knew the answer to that. I would rather endure the sting of the alcohol down my sore throat than admit to Ryder the true reasoning behind my choosing Eligor.

If there was ever a night that I needed to cloud my head, it was tonight. So, I tipped the glass back and drank it without stopping. I tried not to taste it as I gulped it down, because I knew that the revolting flavor would make me stop. I finished it as fast as I could, ignoring the way it stung. I had to try my hardest not to cough or gag, but I could not stop my face from contorting in distaste.

I set the glass down on the stair beside me. The foam of the ale stuck to my lip, forcing me to breathe in the pungent smell. I used my sleeve to wipe it off, and that's when I saw a group of men staring at me from across the square. They all held ales of their own, but none made a move to sip from one. They only stared with slacked jaws. They'd witnessed me tossing back my drink, and it shocked them. They'd never seen a woman chug an entire ale without spewing. They must've been impressed. We truly weren't in Shadieh anymore.

I was vaguely aware of Ryder still yelling at his brother somewhere in the distance, but after the barmaid brought me my second ale and I drank it as fast as the first, his voice faded away. I couldn't concentrate on their quarrel any longer. I was too absorbed in the celebration around me.

The band was one of the largest I'd seen play here. I counted thirteen musicians. The voices of five singers echoed through the streets. Three men and two women made up their ranks. Their voices combined in a perfect harmony. They sang in the first language, the language of the Kings, which I did not know. It didn't matter. I found the tune beautiful either way.

The singers swayed with their song, and the musicians tapped their feet to the upbeat rhythm. The tempo was fast and heavy, my favorite kind.

It didn't take me long to lose myself in the dancing crowd. I pulled the hood of my cloak down, letting my hair tumble down to rest on the lower portion of my back. A smile tugged at my lips as I ran my fingers through the waves, shaking them out. My feet moved to the beat of the drums.

I weaved through the other dancers as I let my body go.

It had been so long since I'd done this– too long.

The skirt of my dress lifted as I twirled around and around. My hair tickled my back as I moved. I lifted my face to the sky and bathed in the moonlight.

I grabbed another ale from the barmaid, drinking it with the same vigor with which I drank the first two. The alcohol warmed my stomach and scattered my brain further. The rational voice in my head suddenly went very quiet. I could hardly hear it anymore and I *loved* that.

Closing my eyes, I lifted my arms and launched into another dance with my entire body.

The sounds of celebration around me faded away as I danced. Soon, I could only hear the music ringing in my ears. I felt nothing but the vibrations in the ground beneath my feet and the warm air of the night.

I forgot about the people surrounding me. I forgot about the Reaper's watchful gaze. I forgot about Ryder. I forgot about the nightmares that kept me from sleep. All I knew was this song and the next. They drove me forward and fueled my soul.

A magnificent violin solo left my heart aching for more. I twirled on my feet again, propelling myself into another turn. That's when a man's warm, strong arm wrapped around my waist. I was too intoxicated from the music, not to mention the drinks, to question his embrace. I only felt joy at the fact that I now had a partner.

The villagers clapped to the tune, stomping their feet with the drums. I felt the beat in my chest now. I jumped up and down with it, letting my partner swing me around as the music continued to build toward its climax.

I decided not to question the stranger's hands that crept up my waist. The small voice in my head might've warned me, but the alcohol brought only silence to my mind. I carried on with the dance because I didn't want anything to ruin this moment, this one precious moment of freedom. I assured myself that the time to confront my partner would come soon enough. For now, I just wanted to finish this song. I convinced myself that it was Ryder who held me as we continued our dance.

The music grew faster still. My partner and I didn't miss a single beat. We drew a crowd. They cheered us on, clapping with the drums and smiling at us with light in their eyes.

The singers strained to hit the high notes of the song, but no one noticed the few who went flat. The main focus was on the instrumentals, which did not disappoint. The song came to an end with an abrupt halt. On the last beat, my partner dipped me low to the ground and held me there as everyone cheered and clapped.

I waited there, panting in a stranger's arms, eyes staring up at the night sky. I was terrified to shift my gaze to my partner, not because I feared meeting him, but because the time I spent in his arms allowed me to come down from the high the music provided me. He wasn't Ryder.

His warm breath, reeking of alcohol, fanned across my neck. He held me to his chest, with one arm banding around my waist and another snaking its way toward my chest. "Why don't we find somewhere more private?" he groaned into my neck.

My heart started to pound wildly in my chest. My hands shook as I tried to push him away. He clicked his tongue at me, smacking my hands away. "Don't be like that."

Words eluded me. I couldn't remember a single one. Memories flashed through my mind. I saw a table and straps that held me down. I heard the screams coming from all the rooms around me. I saw the man that walked in, the evil glint in his eye as he stared down at me like a predator would its prey.

I couldn't breathe and this time it had nothing to do with my throat. I was back in my nightmares.

I was powerless again. I was just a girl, nothing more. I was back there, in that dark place. I had to face the truth. They were never nightmares at all. They were memories. The painful memories I tried so hard to suppress.

The man was steering me toward one of the many stone buildings. I was retreating into my past. I was going back to my hell. This was my punishment. I deserved this.

I deserve this.

117

"Get your fucking hands off of her," Ryder said from somewhere behind us. I couldn't see him, but I knew he was the one to tear the man off me. I looked over to see the stranger's body hit the ground a few yards away. He was older and fatter than I imagined. He got up quickly, ready to fight. But the second he saw Ryder's face, he ran off. He knew not to mess with the silver-eyed ones. Everyone did. Not just because of what they can do, but because the entire village will shun them.

Ryder gently placed his hands on my shoulders to spin me around. He cupped my face and searched my eyes. "Bryce?"

I couldn't speak. That room was still fresh in my mind. The man just opened a chest full of memories that I'd buried so deep inside myself, I nearly forgot they were there at all. But while the memories may have faded over my time with the group, the pain never lessened. I felt it now. I was paralyzed by it.

"Bryce?"

His voice brought me back. His gentle, caring touch reminded me where I was. I was not in that horrid room. I was with him, in his arms. I lifted my gaze. The sight of his silver eyes gave me something to focus on.

He slid an arm beneath my weak knees and picked me up. We set off in the direction of our safe house. I was still shaking, and I knew that he felt it. I could tell by the way his hold on me tightened, as if to tell me that he wouldn't let anyone near me now, to reassure me I was safe.

I rested my head in the crook of his neck as we reached the foot of the porch steps. Ryder turned, eyes searching.

"Ace," he called. "Take care of him."

Ace smirked before trudging off in the direction the stranger ran.

Ryder didn't stop to speak with any of the others even though Quinn and Kalieth both stood, asking questions. He walked straight through the front door and kicked it shut after us.

He took me upstairs to the same room we shared the last time we journeyed here. It warmed my heart to think of the memories we made here. My favorite was waking up one morning to Ryder gently brushing his fingers down my back. I looked up into his loving eyes and asked how long he'd been staring at me like that.

He'd smiled down at me with an emotion in his eyes that I knew, but refused to acknowledge. "Not nearly long enough," he'd whispered.

I'd blushed. I said something along the lines of, "seems like a foolish way to spend your time."

Nothing could change the look in his eye that morning. "No amount of time would satisfy me when it comes to you, not even forever."

The memory eased some of my pain. I swore that when I peered into his eyes now, I saw that same look.

I wanted to tell him. I wanted him to know everything.

He placed me on the bed with heart-breaking gentleness. I hated to admit that the second my head hit the pillows, sleep called to me. Between the traumatic events of the day and the alcohol, my body begged for rest. But I couldn't let myself succumb to it yet.

Ryder went to move away, but I caught him by the wrist. "Ryder, I have to tell you something."

He smiled softly and kissed my hand. "No, you don't."

"Please, I want to explain. The truth this time."

He shook his head. "You didn't want to tell me before the drinks. I don't want you to tell me now."

"Wait—" I began.

But he'd already slipped from my grasp. "Sleep," he whispered. "I'll be here when you wake."

I didn't want to. I wished I could stand and demand that he listen to what I had to say, but my body refused to go on. My eyelids felt too heavy. I convinced myself I was only closing them for a second. I slipped into the dark depths of unconsciousness faster than I ever had before.

CHAPTER 9

Kalieth

Quinn and I watched the villagers dance from the porch steps. Everyone clapped and cheered. They had no cares in the world. I couldn't echo their joy. I was worried about Bryce, and I had no idea why. I didn't care about her, or whether she was okay. At least, that's what I told myself. It just irked me to see her so utterly broken, the one person in the group who always had a joke to share or a smile to offer. The toughest woman I'd ever met, who would take three grown men down instantly if they offended her in any way, was just carried into the house a trembling mess. I wondered what caused her to weaken. I wondered if my father had anything to do with it.

"She'll be okay, don't worry," Quinn said. I watched as he brought a glass of ale to his lips and sipped at it slowly, either too afraid to take a larger gulp, or too proud to admit that he hated the taste.

I scoffed. "I'm not worried."

Quinn gave me a look that said he knew otherwise.

I meant to drop the subject entirely, but curiosity had become an itch in my side that I just had to scratch. "Do you know what happened to her?"

Quinn took another sip of his ale. "No. She won't tell anyone. Not even Ryder."

My eyes shifted to just over Quinn's shoulder, where the Reaper still sat on the porch railing. His silver eyes watched everything from afar. Like a panther, quiet and observant, but deadly. I nodded in his direction. "What about him? Does he know?"

Quinn followed my gaze, then shrugged. "How should I know? You think he'd say anything if he did?"

"Why doesn't he speak?"

"He took a vow of silence about a year ago, before he came to Shadieh. Ryder says he'll speak again once he kills Xaphan."

His words hit me like a rush of cold water. It awakened me to a hard truth. I'd let the rumors whispered in the night seep beneath my skin and chill my bones. There were no scars or burns beneath the mask, no missing tongue. His voice did not promise death. The Reaper simply took a vow of silence.

The thought of all the rumors branching off one another in a search for an answer nearly made me laugh, because the truth was so simple. A vow of silence. It was so obvious, so evident.

I felt brainless. The feeling only got worse as I watched a young girl, half Quinn's age, approach the Reaper. She walked barefoot across the dirt road, the skirts of her dress barely dragging on the ground. The fire cast a warm glow across her dark skin, and added an orange tint to her golden eyes.

She approached him shyly with a raised hand, offering him a small, white flower.

I tensed when the Reaper looked down at her through narrowed eyes. Horrible thoughts went through my mind; scenarios that I made up to guess how he would react. Would he kill her, just as he killed my sister? I half expected him to strike his sword clean across her throat.

The Reaper, as graceful as a prairie cat, hopped down from where he perched. He kneeled in front of the girl.

My heart thundered in my chest. I reached for my side, where I strapped the Reaper's dagger. I would kill him with it here and now if he harmed that girl.

I watched him look into the girl's eyes. I watched him raise a fist. He leaned forward. By the Kings above and below, he was going to snap her neck. I was sure of it. I stood, adrenaline striking a fire beneath my skin.

But the Reaper uncurled his fingers. He gently took the girl's flower into his hand. He stared down at it for a moment, then lifted it to her hair and tucked it behind her ear.

The girl giggled and held out her hand. I watched the Reaper hesitate for a second; just a second. Then he placed his gloved hand in hers and let her lead him into the dancing fray.

My jaw dropped to the ground when the Reaper started dancing with her. The deadliest assassin in the kingdom was dancing. The most feared man in Shadieh twirled around a fire with a child, and yet the child did not cower. She smiled and laughed along with all the villagers around her– villagers who rejoiced in the fact that the Reaper now joined them.

"They don't fear him?" I asked no one in particular.

From the corner of my eye, I saw Quinn shake his head. "They have no reason to. He saved them all. He sent them here to keep them safe. Almost everyone in this village was helped by the Reaper in some way. That's what Ryder told me, anyway."

I sat down, still unable to pry my eyes away from the scene in front of me. "How?"

"Many of them were slaves to your father. Others were his prisoners." He pointed to a woman across the square, sitting on her porch. "She's the only mystic to escape his prison, and she won't speak of it."

Each statement brought on another load of questions. My father didn't have slaves, I'd never heard of any prison, and he was the one to tell me mystics went extinct. Now I learn that he had held one captive?

"The Reaper really isn't the monster you think he is. He's just trying to help people," Quinn added, his jaw clenching.

I gulped down the lump in my throat. "Yeah? How can you trust him to do that? How can you trust him at all? You've never even seen his face. You've never even heard his voice."

Quinn turned to me, drawing my attention away from the Reaper for a moment. He looked into my eyes for a short eternity, his lips tipping up into a smirk. "Your family is rich, right?"

The question caught me by surprise. "Yes?"

"So, do you have a personal chef? Someone to cook all your meals for you?"

"Yes."

The thought of dinner at our Vermillion Estate had my mouth watering. I missed that the most, the delicacies that our dining table had to offer.

"Have you ever spoken to this chef? Have you ever seen his face?" I didn't need to respond. He read the answer in my expression. Quinn nodded. "And yet you still trust him to do his job well? To satisfy you? Not to poison you?"

I left him with no response again. I didn't want to give him the answer he was waiting for.

"You're asking the wrong questions. You ask about his silence and his mask but never once about his motives."

My brows pulled together. "What motive could possibly justify what he's done? He burns down properties and kills who he pleases."

Quinn's eyelids drooped lower than usual as he shook his head. His entire body swayed with the gesture. I wondered if he'd had too much ale already. "The only properties he's burned belong to your father. The only people he's killed are loyal to Xaphan."

"So?"

"So, what do you call a good man who does bad things to protect the people?"

I couldn't stop the chuckle of disbelief. "You're defending an *azkriva*, Quinn. The Accuser was an *azkriva* too. He brought the Eternal war onto us. Do you not think that the Reaper's actions will have similar damning consequences?"

Quinn shrugged. "Call him an abomination if you must. I understand it must make you feel better, to belittle the one man in this world capable of challenging your family's power. But legend states that *azkrivas*– the *abominations*– the *shadow-benders*– they were more than monsters in the night. They were *gods*."

I stared at him through raised brows. "That's enough ale for you tonight. You're talking rubbish."

Quinn grumbled something under his breath, took one last swig, and hesitantly handed over the rest of his drink. I put the glass down on the stair beside me. Once I was sure Quinn wouldn't make a move to grab it behind my back, my eyes roamed back to the dancers before us.

The Reaper weaved through everyone. It seemed they each wanted a chance to dance with him. Even the chief of the village joined in to celebrate.

"Of the people in this group, I didn't expect you to be defending him," I said.

Quinn grimaced. "Showing gratitude is... hard for me. I'm not where I want to be, and so, my first response is to blame the Reaper for getting me into this mess. But I don't truly blame him. He's good in a strange, bad sort of way." He looked down to his hands, rubbing them together. "He and this group are all I've got now. They're family."

Words eluded me as I watched the celebration. I watched villagers smile and laugh in the Reaper's presence. There was no fear– no intimidation.

I knew for certain in that moment that I'd misjudged the Reaper. I was too quick to believe rumors and lies. I let arrogance steer my path. If he truly was the monster people whispered of in the dead of night, how could the kind, innocent people of this village treat him as a king?

My father lied to me about many things, and while the extent of his deceit was unknown to me, I was getting closer to the truth. The truth was drifting me farther from home, from my father, and closer to this group.

The Reaper's silver eyes met mine from across the square. The reflection of the fire in his irises made him look all the more menacing, but for once, I didn't fear whoever may be behind the mask. His gaze induced something else, a different emotion. It was curiosity, and something more. It might have been awe. Maybe it was respect.

I was staring into the eyes of a killer. I knew that. But I wasn't so sure that he killed the innocent girl who was my sister. All I knew was that as the Reaper and I stared at each other through the fire, I made a decision that would change everything.

As if he knew exactly what went through my mind, the Reaper left the dancing circle and approached us. He stopped at the foot of the steps.

I stood, towering over him with the added height of the stairs. We stared at one another in silence for a long moment. I stepped down the last few stairs to bring our faces only inches apart. I unsheathed the dagger on my belt and placed it in his hand.

"Train me."

It was meant to be a question, but it came out as a demand.

He said nothing. He didn't break eye contact with me, even as he placed the dagger back in my hand. Once he curled my fingers around its hilt, he brushed past me and disappeared into the house.

I stared after him, unsure of what that meant. But when I looked down at Quinn, he smirked up at me, raised the glass he somehow stole back without my noticing, and cheered to, "welcome to the team."

CHAPTER 10

Bryce

I jolted awake with a pounding headache. For a long moment, I couldn't piece together where I was or how I'd gotten here.

It all came crashing back in flashes. The Vermillion brothers attacking us. The Reaper's shadow-bending. Our escape to Nero. All the ale I drank to forget the events of the day. The creepy man who'd put his hands on me, and of course, Ryder chasing him off.

My eyes snapped open once the images faded. And there he was. Asleep, slumped over in a reading chair. I could tell by the dark circles under his eyes and his ruffled hair that he did not have a good night's sleep.

But he stayed. He stayed through the night in case I had need of him.

I suddenly couldn't remember for the life of me why I chose to push him a way. I cursed myself for thinking he'd run the second I told him the truth. I knew now that he'd never turn away from me.

He loved me. I could admit that to myself now. He loved me and– and I loved him too. I'd fallen in love with him on the very first day we met. I'd been a coward, too afraid to admit it to myself. Terrified of what that meant for my future.

We loved each other. But I couldn't let him love me without knowing my past. He needed to know me, needed to know who it was that he wanted to give his life to.

I left the bed and walked to the reading chair. I sat in his lap and took his face into my hands. As my thumbs brushed over his cheeks, his deep breaths turned shallow.

His eyes slowly fluttered open. They were glazed at first, but they soon focused on me. I smiled at him as my thumb brushed over his chin, catching on his lower lip.

He raised his hand to push mine away, but I froze him with one look. "The ale doesn't affect my mind anymore," I assured him.

He reached around me and softly braced my hips. His eyes searched mine, trying to guess what I might be up to.

My heart pounded in my chest like the hooves of the fastest horse, so hard that I wondered if he could hear it. I ignored the constant thud and took a deep breath. I traced one of the scars along his shoulder as I began. "I was sent to the Mystic

Academy at thirteen. I trained with all the *elemefnis*, but the masters picked me out quickly."

The knot in Ryder's throat bobbed nervously. I had no doubt that he realized the weight of the confession that was to come.

"All mystics manifest their power in different ways. Some can shapeshift, others can shake the earth. Some are mere witches that can only perform simple spells to make hair grow longer or stop an infection from spreading. But I was the only fire-bender. Until me, there hadn't been one in centuries. They explained it to me as some sort of dormant gene in the family line or whatever."

"It was hard to master fire with no teacher to demonstrate for me. It had its own will. To control it, my will needed to be stronger. I found control with rage. I had a lot of it to spare. I was abandoned by my parents and raised in a group home. When I tested positive for mystic blood, I was sent to the academy straight away. I had no choice in any of it."

I fiddled with the amber ring on my finger. "Rage made it easy. I graduated from the academy at seventeen. I was immediately sent to the front lines, as all mystics are. I used my rage to burn the Northmen. I earned the call sign 'Harbinger.'"

I paused. My breath hitched in my throat. This was the part I feared talking about. "My unit was captured during my second year. I thought our attackers were Northern soldiers, they dressed like them, talked like them. They were mystics too. That's how they bested us. They injected us with something that dampened our power, put us in chains, and loaded us into a carriage. I thought they were taking us somewhere to kill us. Sometimes I wish they had, or that I was smart enough to do it myself, because when they opened the doors again, we were at the Vermillion estate."

Ryder's grip on me tightened.

"I don't remember the walk to the dungeons, honestly. I just remember the fear, and how I trembled so horribly that our captors had to drop their whips and drag me along."

I looked down at my shaking hands. I went to bring them into my chest, to hide them, but Ryder quickly interlaced our fingers and gave me an encouraging squeeze.

I took another deep, shaky breath before I continued. "They threw me into an old cell. It had no window, or bed, or toilet. Only three walls, a floor, and a ceiling, all made from stone that retained no heat. I sat there for at least a month before they came back for me."

I stood, unable to sit still any longer. Ryder stood with me, staying close. I began to pace the room in short strides.

"Xaphan came with two other men. They weighed me, took my measurements, and..." I shuddered. "Ensured my overall health. Once they were satisfied, they left."

I blinked back the tears. "They returned only a day later. They dragged me out of my cell and took me to a different room. There was nothing in it. Just a healer's bed. They relieved me of my clothes, and then they strapped me down–"

I choked. I couldn't hold the tears back any longer. I heard the haunting screams of the past, still ringing in my ears. I felt the pain of it all over again. I was falling once more into the darkness I'd succumbed to in those seasons. I felt it rising over me like a tidal wave ready to crash. It would drown me this time. I was sure of it. I leaned against the bed post for a moment. My fingernails dug into the wood, scratching off the finish.

But then there was a hand on my shoulder. There was an arm banded around my waist. There was a warm chest pressed to my back. The scent of cedarwood and sage. He feathered kisses along my shoulder but said nothing. He wouldn't say anything, not yet.

I straightened and squared my shoulders. I stared off into the distance as I said, "They sell us off. Xaphan Vermillion captures mystics, then sells them through the underground market to a buyer in the Northern Kingdom. He doesn't care what happens to them as long as he gets paid. He doesn't care what his sons do to us in the meantime. The unlucky ones became favorites, and we were kept there."

I broke away from Ryder's grasp to face him. I met his eyes to find hatred simmering in them. Not for me, but for the Vermillions. For what they did to me and continue to do to others.

My voice had grown quiet. Tears slipped silently down my cheeks. "You asked me why I chose Eligor as an opponent. Well, Xaphan picked the strongest, most powerful mystics for his own sons' pleasure. He said that we had a *duty* to strengthen their bloodline with mystic children.

His two oldest, Azazel and Eligor, got to take their pick of us."

"Bryce–" Ryder started. He took a step forward to console me, but I stepped back and shook my head.

"No, wait. I have to finish." I waved him off. "I only got out because of my sister."

Ryder stopped, his brows pulling together. "Sister?"

I nodded as more tears slipped down my face. "When we were abandoned on the doorstep of that group home, she made sure we stayed together. She's older by one year, and she never let me forget it, not even in our last moments. She was always driving me forward. Always protecting me. We have different mothers, so she isn't an *elemefnis* like me. She's a *shifklov*. She comes from a very powerful bloodline. She's one of the only shapeshifters ever recorded who could not only shift bodily forms but faces too. Her unit wasn't captured with mine, but she heard of my disappearance. To this day, I don't know how she tracked me back to the Vermillions. I guess it doesn't matter. She found me. She shifted faces to look like one of Vermillion's guards, learned their routine, and when she felt the time was right, she broke me out."

My knees felt weak, so I sat down on the edge of the bed. Ryder came to kneel in front of me, placing his hands on my knees in a gesture of reassurance. He even went as far as to brush his thumb over my cheeks to wipe away my tears. I gratefully leaned into his touch.

"We only made it down the hall. The other prisoners started screaming and begging for us to let them out too. The commotion alerted the guards. They saw my empty cell and sounded an alarm. I still couldn't use my magic from whatever injection they gave me, so I couldn't defend myself. I couldn't defend either of us."

I exhaled in a shuddering breath and continued. "So, when I rounded the corner, and heard a shot fired, there was nothing I could do. I stood there like a helpless idiot and watched my sister fall to the floor. I turned back to see her blood splattered across the stone. But the eyes I looked into were my own. In her last moments, she'd changed her face again. She shifted into a new appearance. My own. It was my own face that I saw. She knew that the guards only saw one empty cell. They'd only be looking for one prisoner. She decided to take my place." I reached back for her, but she shook her head. She told me to go– that I had to get out while I could.

The memory was still clear as day in my head. I'd lost count of the number of times I replayed it over the years. I memorized the way her eyes flew wide, and her mouth parted in a pained scream that never sounded.

Her breathing turned fast and shallow, her skin pale as moonlight. She fell back against the floor. Her eyes looked up toward the ceiling, but they had a strange, cloudy glaze over them.

I heard the guards drawing closer. I had to go. If I stayed, she would have sacrificed herself for nothing.

"I thought she died that night," I whispered. "It haunted me, all this time. I sank so low, Ryder. So low. I almost didn't make it out of that dark, isolated void within myself. I had to live my life like a criminal after that, using fake names and hiding in the shadows. All so that Vermillion couldn't find me. It felt like I had died with her. Each day I thought about joining her in the afterlife. The only thing stopping me was the thought of her death having no purpose. I couldn't join her in the Shadow Realm after she sacrificed herself to save me."

"The pain never left. It dulled a bit over time, I suppose. But I used it. I started to train myself in combat, without the use of my powers. That way, I would never feel weak and helpless again. They would never be able to take me back there again. I didn't call to the flames for almost two years, and I grew weaker for it. A mystic who rejects their gift grows sick, both physically and mentally. I only made it worse, without knowing."

I met his gaze with a soft smile. "I lived off dreams for so long. Fantasies I created just to keep myself going. I told myself that I deserved it. I deserved to live off the lies I whispered to myself in the last few moments before sleep. It was my punishment for losing her. For being stupid enough to get caught in the first place."

"It was like that for two years. I lost myself in the grief. The rage. I thought I'd never find my way out of it," I continued. "But then you came along."

Ryder stiffened, and I took his hand in mine. "You came along, and it felt like I'd been struck by lightning. I felt drunk. For the first time in ages, I felt fire stirring inside me again. I felt it igniting my soul, and this time, it wasn't because of rage. It was something else entirely. I was burning again, burning for you. For us. For a future. I burned like a newborn star, and I never wanted to stop."

"But night would fall, and while you slept, I would lie awake, too scared to fall asleep and dream of the past. I thought of Alina, and what she would think of me if she saw me now. It all felt wrong because I was happy again. It felt wrong to be happy after all that passed. How could I be happy when Alina was dead? How could I feel joy after I got my sister killed? How was it fair for me to smile when she would never be able to again?"

I looked down at the ring on my finger. "I pushed you away because I needed to. I had no right to happiness. You made me happier than ever, and if I had to live with Alina's death, than I needed to feel miserable. I had to hate myself, because I didn't deserve to have something so good, after I did something so horrible."

"But then the Reaper gave me this," I held up the second amber ring that matched my own. "Alina's ring. She's alive. I don't know if it makes it better or worse. On one hand, I didn't get her killed. But on the other, she's been living a life worse than death for over two years, all while I've been cowering in the shadows."

I hooked a hand around his neck and pushed his chin up with the other so that he looked into my eyes. "I know one thing, though. I want to keep burning with you, Ryder. No more running. I want to get lost in this fire. I want to dance in the flames and disappear in the smoke. Will you do that? Will you burn with me despite everything?"

Ryder touched his brow to mine. His answer was so soft that I nearly mistook it for a whisp of wind.

"*Always.*"

He kissed me. It was gentle, slow. The kiss I dreamt of in my darkest days. I melted into his arms, relief consuming me.

The kiss grew in intensity. His arms snaked around me and pulled me close. We were both burning then. Together. Forever and always. He was my kindling. He was the oxygen I needed to thrive. Without him I was nothing but a dying ember in a dark world, constantly fighting to keep the demons at bay. But in that moment, we were an inferno. Our light cast all the shadows away.

Our love had become an eternal flame, burning for all time. A blaze that could never be destroyed, no matter what or who tried. Forever awaited us, and for once, I could look forward to a future beyond the darkness.

CHAPTER 11

Ace

The bed I woke in was not my own. I was definitely not in the safehouse. The room was too-clean. Too furnished and decorated.

There were two women draped over me, one on each side. Another man slept on a nearby sofa with his back facing me, his soft snores filling the air. We all lacked any garments of clothing. For the life of me, I couldn't remember any of their names.

The roar of rain drifted through an open window beside the bed. Only the faintest bit of light filtered through the silk curtains, and there were no sounds of villagers roaming the streets, which told me that it was still early in the morning. I still had time to return to the others, possibly before they even wake to find me missing.

I slipped out from beneath the ladies. Careful not to trip over the many empty liquor bottles, I picked my scattered clothes off the floor, and left as quickly as I could.

Finding my way back to the safehouse was easy. It was a small village. But I realized on the way, as I stumbled over my own feet, that I might have still been a bit drunk, something I knew the Reaper would not approve of. Not that he approves of anything, really. He just gives everyone annoyed, judgmental stares. If he was truly the wise man he thinks himself to be, he would know that his disappointment and distaste would only make me want to do it more. I get bored rather easily, and annoying the others is the only way to make the hours go by faster.

I cursed my own weight when I climbed the creaky, old porch steps. I staggered through the front door only to see everyone sitting in the common room. Silence fell over them. All heads turned to face me when I walked through the doorway. I found myself wishing I'd tied my tunic closed all the way.

I was surprised to see them all, especially Bryce. I couldn't remember the last time I saw Bryce awake at dawn. I was tasked to wake her up once, and she nearly stabbed me in the eye. But there she was, sitting comfortably in Ryder's lap on a reading chair. If my head weren't already pounding, I'd attribute the pain to those two and their tendency to change their minds about one another every five minutes.

Quinn and Kalieth sat on an old couch, both watching me skeptically. It was Quinn's stare that caught my eye. He looked me up and down, but there was more than judgement in his eyes. If I didn't know any better, I'd say there was a hint of jealousy in his brown irises. I pretended not to notice, as usual. I'd known about his feelings for a while now. He never said anything, but I knew. I refused to address it. I'd rather weather his anger than have to reject his love.

The Reaper stood, as always, in the corner of the room, leaning against the wall. His eyes narrowed on me, but he did not move.

The way his silver gaze looked me up and down with some sort of consideration, as if he was trying to make a big decision, reminded me of the day I met him. He'd given me that same look when he approached me in a pub on the East Side of the city, where the burly pirates liked to hang around. I made a living by taking wagers on my own fights. I made quite a name for myself that way, and not in the best way.

The Reaper found me bruised and bloody, but still a victor, after a match. I'd just ordered my second ale when two hooded figures joined me at the table. One on each side. I put down my drink and prepared myself for another fight.

"Ace Taziri, we saw your match. Impressive." It was Ryder who spoke, but I didn't know his name at the time. He sat to my right; his hands clasped in front of him. He obviously didn't belong here. Everything about him was too perfect, from his straight teeth to his ironed clothes. He wore a tight black jacket and dress shoes to an East Side bar. It seemed like he *wanted* to get punched.

"What of it?"

He shrugged. "I have a proposition for you. One that will earn you a lot more money than the few silver marks you just earned for that fight."

I looked down to my bloody hands then back to him suspiciously. My gaze swayed from Ryder to the figure beside me. That's when I noticed the silver eyes. The Reaper looked me up and down and cocked his head to the side.

I'd never seen silver eyes before. Greens, blues, browns, purples, golds, and blacks were all common. But silver? Never.

"Allow me to introduce–," Ryder said.

"I know who he is. What do you want?" I snapped.

Ryder straightened. "We want you to join us. Help us take down the Vermillions."

I laughed dryly. "No one can take down the Vermillions." I made to leave.

"We can," Ryder said confidently. "And even if we can't, what do you have to lose? You're a homeless drunk. You have nowhere else to go and no one to go to."

The words sparked an anger through me that I hadn't felt in a long time. I stood abruptly, knocking over our table and drawing everyone's attention. The comfortable chatter in the bar faded as I raised my fists, ready to break Ryder's nose. But when I turned, the Reaper was there. He stood one stride behind me, and he caught my fist with ease.

Ryder stepped forward to stand beside his brother. "You grew up on these streets. You lived in an orphanage for your first years of life, until Xaphan Vermillion bought it and all the surrounding buildings to make his trade center in the Northern part of the city. He left you and all the other children out on the streets. You came to the East Side because you knew the pirates would be easy to steal from. You'd take something, and they'd be back out at sea long before they noticed it was gone. You fought and stole for every meal. That was until the vikings picked you up. They hardened you into a real warrior. You stayed with them for the better part of your teenage years before you realized you could make good money off your combat skills."

"I know what happened. I was there," I snapped.

Ryder sighed. "Come with us. Be part of something bigger than yourself. Help us take the Vermillions down so that more children don't have to suffer like you did."

They really must've been desperate to have me if they had to add the children guilt trip. I thought about it for a minute, only because it was fun to see Ryder's confident demeanor fade as he shifted uncomfortably in the silence.

In the end, I really had nothing better to do, and bringing down the Vermillions would leave me with enough gold marks to drown myself in.

I was torn away from my memories when Bryce said, "You look like shit."

If looks could kill, I'd have her lifeless on the ground by now. She didn't have much room to judge given her bruised neck and ruffled hair. "Really? Have *you* looked in a mirror recently?"

Ryder cut us off before our little dispute could intensify. "Ace, the guy from last night– has your shadow grown?"

Did you kill him? That's what Ryder really meant to ask. I wondered if he danced around the words for Bryce's sake. Everything about last night had been fuzzy until he said those words. The memories came rushing back to me. So, *that's* where the blood staining my hands came from. I raised my hands for all of them to see. "He's not dead, but I think he knows that he will be if he ever shows his face again. I reckon he'll be spending a few weeks at the healer's cottage before he's even back on his feet."

I caught the small twitch of Bryce's lips, even though her face remained blank. Ryder, however, flashed me a wicked grin with a curt nod. "Thank you."

I returned his nod as I sank into the second reading chair across the room. Another long silence ensued before I spoke again, "anyone want to tell me why we're all up so early?"

"We were just discussing the consequences of the Reaper's shadow-bending," Quinn answered.

I met the Reaper's stare again. Now I understood why he looked particularly irritated this morning. He hated it when we tried to offer up our thoughts on his actions.

"And?"

It was Ryder who spoke next. He looked to his brother with a weary expression on his face. "And I think it might be time to end this. I know

145

you want to kill Xaphan and avenge our father, but don't you think it's a bit-- I don't know--childish to keep fighting this *battle* when you can ascend the throne and end the *war?*"

A strange snorting sound came from the Reaper. He pushed off the wall and walked across the room to look out the front widow, lightly smacking his brother upside the head as he passed him. Ryder gasped and raised a hand to rub the hurt on the back of the neck. He narrowed his eyes at his brother, clenching his jaw. "Do that again. *I dare you.*"

The Reaper rolled his eyes and turned away. He crossed his arms over his chest, looking out the window to watch the rain.

"No," Bryce said suddenly. "We can't get sidetracked. Not now. The Reaper will still be a shadow-bender after we kill Xaphan. I say we table the issue until we finish what we started."

"How can we *table* this *issue?*" Quinn asked.

Bryce opened her mouth to respond, but she stopped short to glance back at Ryder. There was some sort of message passed wordlessly between them. Ryder gave her a soft smile and nodded, squeezing her hand. Bryce took a deep breath before turning back to the rest of us. "I want to tell you all what we're really up against. We're not just fighting for revenge or vengeance. We're fighting for the lives of hundreds of soldiers."

We listened silently as Bryce told us her story. I always respected Bryce. She never failed to put me in my place if I overstepped, and I appreciated her strength and skill. But after listening to everything she went through, the torture she endured, I felt more than respect when I looked at her. I felt awe, inspiration.

I found myself watching Kalieth's reaction throughout the story. I expected him to jump from his seat and call her a liar. I thought he might argue with her and say that his family was not capable of such evil.

He didn't.

Kalieth sat up straight, his body tense. Not once did he interrupt her or flash a skeptical expression. He respected her in his silence, but he did bounce his leg nervously. When she brought up his brothers, Azazel and Eligor, and their role in her torture, Kalieth's face went white as snow. I thought he might be sick. Luckily, he kept his breakfast down and listened intently.

Once Bryce finished, a silence fell over the room. She looked toward Quinn. Anger simmered in her eyes. "Do you still think we should drop everything and head to the Capital? You want to let Xaphan get away with all he's doing and let innocent people suffer?"

Quinn said nothing. The floor suddenly became very interesting to him. He refused to meet Bryce's fierce stare.

Kalieth rose from his seat. "Two years ago, Az and Eligor started disappearing at night. They started talking about their *big choice* at dinner. I always wondered what they meant, but I never cared enough to ask. Now I know." He came to kneel in front of Bryce. "I want to apologize for all my family's done to you. To all of you. I knew we weren't perfect, but I never thought... I never could've imagined–" He shook his head. "I'm so sorry."

Bryce's eyes narrowed. "You mean to tell me you didn't know?"

He shook his head. "Az and Eligor are the oldest and closest to father. It makes sense that they'd be the first to know. I was the only one of my brothers to leave home and find my own profession, so my father would trust me least with that sort of information. But with the attacks and threats they've been facing from you and others, it wouldn't surprise me if father clued all my brothers in by now. But I will fight them all if that is what honor demands."

"If you're truly with us now, tell me what the symbols mean," Bryce said, her voice wavering slightly.

Kalieth's brows drew together. "Symbols?"

Bryce nodded. "It was too risky for Xaphan to call us by our names or write messages with words. He feared word getting out to the public. So, he used symbols instead. There was an empty cell across from me, but there was still a symbol to label it. I would trace it into the stone floors to pass the time. It was two palms holding up the moon."

Quinn's gaze flew wide. "I saw it," he whispered. "It was carved into a dedication stone in the library. Busiris Vermillion's dedication stone."

Kalieth nodded. "It's my grandfather's symbol. He created it when he ran the city. He said it represented a new world. A world that would be shaped and defined by the Vermillion family."

Bryce rolled her eyes.

Kalieth shrugged. "It's nothing important."

"No. No, you don't understand." Quinn became frantic. He trembled in his seat. His eyes flew wide, but they were unseeing. "I was researching that symbol when Xaphan put a price on my head. It was just a side project, so I never brought it up. I saw it on the dedication stone and decided to investigate it. It wasn't mentioned in any book or record. I asked the scribes about it the same night Vermillion tried to have me killed."

Ryder's features hardened. "Whatever Vermillion's hiding must have something to do with that symbol."

"So, we go to the library?" I asked, unimpressed. I wasn't a fan of libraries. Why read about great achievements when you can go out and accomplish more?

"We can't go back, not yet. Winter is here, and if we go back to the city, we'll likely starve," Ryder said. "We'll wait until the season passes, then we return, and we search the library. Let the Vermillions think they chased us off. Then we return with a vengeance."

"What are we meant to do for an entire season here?" I couldn't keep the annoyance out of my tone.

"Get drunk and sleep with women. Isn't that your go-to free time activity?" Bryce shot back.

"And men," I corrected. "I don't discriminate."

Bryce met my smirk with her own. "Oh, so it's not a stick up your ass then, it's a–"

"I have one question for you in return," Kalieth said, interrupting what would've been a horrible comeback. His features were taut. Tension coursed through his entire body as he stared at the wall beyond Bryce and Ryder.

Bryce leaned forward, curious. Even Ryder straightened in his seat. It wasn't often that Vermillion interjected. But he was still fighting to find his tongue, it seemed. He opened his mouth to speak, closed it, and tried again. His eyes found Bryce's and he sucked in an uneasy breath. "Were you the one to light fire to the warehouse in the North Side? The one on the corner of King's Street and Main?"

I remembered that fire. It was the same night we burned two other properties on the East Side. We watched it from the tower. Bryce had been right beside me the whole time, and it was long before she decided to use her power again.

Bryce leaned back into Ryder. Her brows drew together. For a moment, she said nothing. She could see, as the rest of us could, the pure anxiety that the question brought Kalieth. He bounced his leg and rubbed his fingers together. The answer meant something to him, for whatever reason.

The Reaper turned. Not all the way. Hardly at all. But he tilted his head toward the conversation.

"We were in the East Side that night," Bryce answered.

"All of you?" His eyes glanced to each of us. His eyes found the Reaper. "Then, who burned it down?"

"The same person who framed us all for the many casualties of the working men inside. He wanted the public to see us as the enemy who would burn their families," Ryder muttered, his fists clenching.

It was Quinn who answered. "Kalieth, your father burned that warehouse down himself."

CHAPTER 12

Quinn

I hate the Reaper now more than ever before. I didn't think it was possible to hate someone so much, especially after never having seen his face. But I hated him with the force of a thousand fires.

I felt bad when I brought the Vermillion brothers onto us. Guilt consumed me completely for the first week or so. If I didn't know better, I'd think that the Reaper was making this training my punishment.

He decided it was in my best interest to train alongside Kalieth. He forced me to run around the perimeter of the entire valley. *Three* times. And when I finally got back, on the brink of collapse, he'd have me hold buckets full of water in outstretched hands until my muscles couldn't stand it anymore. He considered those things our *warmup.*

Once, the Reaper committed an entire training day to teach us how to breathe. Apparently, it was important to control your breathing during combat, so we had to sit there for hours, inhaling for four counts, and exhaling for four counts.

Kalieth and I had been training with the Reaper for half of the winter season already, and we still hadn't even touched a weapon. Admittedly, Kalieth was in much better shape than me, so he blew through the warmups with ease. Still, I could tell he was growing increasingly frustrated with the pacing of our training.

But it wasn't just training. He was especially irritable lately, ever since the first morning of our stay in Nero Village. I wondered if he simply hated it here. I wondered if he missed his family. For the first week, he would leave his room for training, and promptly return to it afterward. He hardly spoke to anyone. He never ate with us. It was only in the following weeks that he started to move on from whatever fog he'd been lost to.

In recent days, he's seemed more like his old self. He complains constantly, which had me mistaking him for Ace on a few occasions, but it was better than his miserable silence. If I knew no better, I'd think that he too was writing records on the Reaper, because Kalieth was always watching the masked assailant. I often caught Vermillion studying the Reaper's every move, as if he planned to become as well-versed in the assassin's language as Ryder. Until he could translate every glare and flick of his fingers.

His studies didn't seem to pay off in training. The Reaper always bested the both of us, even when we worked together against him.

On this particular morning, Ryder sat perched on the nearby fence, watching our warmups in the snow-covered field. "The Reaper has decided it's time for you two to begin training with swords."

"Finally," Kalieth muttered under his breath.

Ryder smirked. "Don't get too excited." He dropped down from the fence and approached us. The snow made an audible crunch beneath his boots and his breath billowed out of his mouth in small clouds. He had a large duffle bag slung over his shoulder, which he dropped in front of us. He opened it up to reveal fake, wooden swords within.

Kalieth let out a dry laugh. "This is a joke, right? You've got to be kidding."

The Reaper stood beside his brother, and I could've sworn I saw something like amusement flash in his eyes.

"We only have a few weeks left until we go back into the city. You're going to waste my time teaching me basics, which I already know?" Kalieth continued. The anger made color rise to his cheeks.

The Reaper ignored Kalieth completely and leaned down to pick up one of the wooden swords. He threw it into my hands without warning, and I nearly fell over. I wasn't expecting it to be as heavy as it was. Its weight might've equaled five of my textbooks stacked on top of one another.

Kalieth saw how my arms sank down once I'd caught the sword, and his brows drew together.

He didn't have much time to ponder it before the Reaper threw him his own sword.

"Are all swords this heavy?" I asked, suddenly reevaluating my fantasies of being a knight in shining armor.

"No," Kalieth answered for me. He was examining the wooden sword, turning it over in his hands. "They're weighted practice swords."

"If you train with these swords first, you'll build muscle strength. Then, when it comes time to use a true sword, it will feel weightless in your hand," Ryder explained further.

"It's an old tradition," Kalieth told me. He glared between Ryder and his brother. "One proven not to work. It will only confuse you more."

"You clearly know nothing. Now I know why the Reaper was able to take you down within two minutes," Ryder said with a chuckle.

Kalieth narrowed his eyes. "I was trained by the best swordsmen in the kingdom."

"You were trained by arrogant men who taught you to give away your next move and plant your feet in one spot," Ryder shot back, his own frustration rising. "Either go on through life with those skills or pick up the damn weighted sword and stop whining."

For a moment, I thought Kalieth might drop the sword and walk off. But he clenched his jaw, grabbed the sword in a white-knuckled fist, and waited. Ryder looked to the Reaper with raised brows, as if he'd just won a bet that we didn't know about.

Ryder put an arm around me and turned me away from the other two. "Since Kalieth knows the basics already, he'll train with the Reaper. But you'll be with me, and I'll catch you up."

I couldn't see Kalieth's face, but I heard him uneasily ask the Reaper, "you're going to enjoy this, aren't you?"

Ryder walked me across the field, far away from the other two. He started our lesson by showing me defensive and offensive stances. I practiced moving the sword in one fluid motion. Ryder showed me how to properly grip the sword's hilt and put my weight into my strikes. He spent the rest of the day teaching me the eight-point star of sword fighting. Each angle of the star made up an attacking strike. Straight up and straight down. Horizontal to the left and right. Diagonally up and down to the left. Diagonally up and down to the right.

We went on for hours. By sun-down, my arms shook terribly each time I lifted the sword. Ryder called it when I finally dropped the blade. The second he said we could be done, I sank to the ground. My body was too exhausted to care about the harsh, cold bite of the snow against my skin.

I couldn't remember what it felt like to wake up comfortably. For weeks, I'd been waking up unable to move. My muscles were stiff and sore. Each day without fail I wanted to stay in bed. The Reaper always came for me, and he would drag me back out to that field to do it all over again.

But all the work was slowly paying off. I no longer lost my breath within the first lap around the valley. I could see the muscle building along my arms and legs. I was able to hold up the buckets of water for a few seconds longer each time I tried.

I still hated them all for making me endure this torture, but it might be nice to not feel pathetic and helpless the next time we face a fight.

Ryder would go easy on me in comparison to what the Reaper put Kalieth through. The two of them stayed out long after Ryder and I went back to the house. I couldn't help but watch from the window.

Kalieth would attempt to strike or jab, but it was obvious that the weight of the sword was throwing him off. The Reaper dodged every single blow Kalieth threw his way. He moved like a shadow avoiding the light, quick but graceful, as if nature itself controlled his movements. Kalieth couldn't catch up, couldn't anticipate where the Reaper would go. With the added weight of the practice sword, each jab Kalieth aimed hit lower than he meant it to. At least, I assumed he meant to aim for the Reaper's abdomen when he hit him below the navel. The Reaper didn't so much as flinch before side-stepping and landing a punch to Kalieth's stomach. It knocked the breath out of him, and he hunched over as a result, which allowed the Reaper to bring his knee up and strike Kalieth right in the nose.

He fell back, holding his nose as blood gushed out. I saw his mouth move frantically while his arms waved around. I couldn't hear what he was saying, but I knew he was infuriated.

Ryder and Bryce, who watched from the kitchen, both laughed. "That's why you don't piss off the Reaper," Bryce muttered. "Serves him right for complaining constantly."

"You should go out there now. Save Vermillion from more pain," Ryder said.

"Can I not?" Bryce asked. Ryder gave her a look. "What? He deserves it."

"You have every right to hate the Vermillions, but you cannot blame a son for his father's mistakes."

"You have a severely annoying moral code."

"One of us has to."

"Good. So, I stick to burning things. You stick to being Ace and Quinn's babysitter."

I stiffened in my seat. They couldn't see me from where I sat in the common room, but Bryce knew I was there.

Ryder glared at her. "I am not their babysitter."

"Babysitter, busybody, cockblock, human shield, whatever you want to call it," Bryce said, waving him off.

"Someone has to keep them from tearing each other apart."

Bryce laughed. "Oh, my darling, the only thing they want to tear apart is their clothing."

I choked on my coffee. Heat rose to my cheeks until I thought I might have sunburn. I prayed to the kings that Ace couldn't hear this conversation from his bedchamber.

Ryder went rigid. His head swiveled on his shoulders to look into her green eyes, which were shimmering with humor. "*What?*"

Bryce laughed again, the sound echoing through the house. She patted his back and turned toward the back door. "I'll tell you when you're older."

Without another word, she left to relieve Kalieth. As the only other mystic in the group, she'd been training the Reaper to control the shadows every night. They always waited until after dark, given the fact that people in the village might start talking if they saw an *azkriva* practicing openly.

She sent Kalieth back into the house with the rest of us while she stayed outside with the Reaper. By the squealing I heard only seconds later, I assumed that the Reaper presented her with her nightly reward. In exchange for training him, he would give her a variety of gifts. I walked by her room once a week prior, and with the door cracked open, I could see the pile of earrings, rings, necklaces, shoes, and gowns on her floor. It explained her unusually cheerful attitude over the past few weeks, and the elegant outfits she'd been sporting lately.

Heavy footsteps thudded down the stairs, drawing my attention away. I could hardly meet Ace's eyes as he descended into the common room, but I had to. I had to know if he heard what they'd said.

But the Ace I saw was the same as always. His features were the picture of boredom dancing on the edge of annoyance. He hardly glanced at me as he passed, and I didn't know whether to be joyed or disappointed. By the weight in my chest, I knew which one my heart chose.

Kalieth stomped into the house and immediately poured himself a glass of liquor. He plopped into one of the reading chairs, glass in hand, and towel in the other. He dabbed the blood away from his face as he took one long sip.

Ryder, Ace, and I all watched him closely. He didn't so much as glance our way. The three of us looked between each other to decide who would speak to him. Ace and I looked to Ryder, who recoiled and shook his head. Ace rolled his eyes and stepped forward.

"Tell me, where did your father find the *great swordsmen* that trained you?" Ace asked. He folded his arms across his chest. "You know, you're supposed to dodge the blows, not take them like a punching bag."

Prick.

Ryder and I both rubbed a hand over our faces. We should've known to stop Ace before he even opened his mouth.

Kalieth didn't respond. He glared daggers toward Ace, though. He gripped the glass so tightly, I thought he might break it.

"I'm sorry for my brother, Kalieth. He just knows we're running out of time, and he wants you to be ready. I'm sure he just got frustrated," Ryder said. He walked over with the liquor bottle and refilled Kalieth's glass for him.

"Breaking my nose will ready me faster?" Kalieth muttered under his breath.

"Actually, statistically speaking, you're more likely to perform well if you believe that performing poorly will result in a negative outcome like pain," I said, remembering a book I once read regarding human instincts.

They all stared at me.

"Really? Does that mean if I punch you each time you run your mouth, you'll stop doing it entirely?" Ace asked, taking a step toward me. He cracked his knuckles threateningly.

I glared at him. A hundred different retorts scorched my tongue.

"Ace," Ryder warned.

Ace mumbled something under his breath before he lost interest in us and left the room.

Ryder chuckled, deep in thought. "You two better follow his lead and get some rest. Tomorrow, the real work begins."

CHAPTER 13

Kalieth

The more time that passed with our *training,* the more I felt like an idiot.

Once I finally got used to the weight of the practice sword, the Reaper decided it was time for target practice. So, he had Bryce sit there and blow bubbles. *Bubbles.*

"I know it seems ridiculous, but it improves your hand-eye coordination skills like you wouldn't believe," Ryder explained.

Quinn and I were forced to strike and jab at the small pockets of air floating on the breeze. I refused to let myself admit that it was difficult. If I swung the sword too hard, the wind would catch the bubbles and they'd gravitate away from my blade. If I slowed down my strike, I'd miss entirely.

We practiced with bubbles for another two weeks. The weighted sword didn't seem so heavy anymore. The task of slashing through bubbles became easy. I was able to maneuver through them and strike each one without missing once. Just before sun-down one day, Quinn and I both managed to strike each bubble before they popped. We moved through them gracefully and dodged them as though they themselves were fatal blows. Not one touched either of us, and not one escaped our blades.

It was then that the Reaper stood. Ryder stayed sitting behind him, but a smile played over his face. "You're ready," he called out.

The Reaper parted his cloak to show us the two broadswords sheathed to his belt. One a bit longer than the other, to compensate for the height and weight difference between Quinn and I.

He unsheathed the longer one first, and gently handed it over to me by the hilt. The sword felt surprisingly light, but I knew that was only because of all the time we spent with the weighted sword. "Just as I said," I told them. "It will take us an entire week to readjust to the weight."

The Reaper ignored me. He unsheathed the second sword and handed it to Quinn, who stared at it through wide eyes, as if it were an alien object.

"Your training will be considered complete once you hold your own against the Reaper for five minutes straight, or if you can knock him on his ass, whichever comes first," Ryder told us.

I went first. I used every technique they taught me. I stayed light on my feet, dodging each blow the Reaper sent my way. I controlled my breathing and put my weight into each swing of my sword. None of it seemed to make a difference. The Reaper still managed to anticipate every single move I made. I lasted two minutes. Then Quinn tried his hand. He could barely keep it together for thirty seconds.

The Reaper decided that Quinn and I would spar with one another one last time, and then training would be concluded for the day. But Quinn was exhausted. I could read it in his expression, even though the way he dragged his sword on the ground didn't need much of an explanation.

"Why don't we call it now?" I asked for his sake. "We can pick it up with sparring tomorrow."

The Reaper's eyes slid to me, narrowing. I felt my heart slow in my chest, as it always did when those silver eyes settled on me. But Quinn didn't realize that my attention was directed elsewhere. He took a swing at me. I was a hair's breadth away from being sliced open. He grazed my arm with his blade. A few drops of my blood tainted the snow, causing steam to rise from the ground.

I stared down in shock, my jaw hanging open. Quinn gasped when he realized what he'd done. He made to apologize, stumbling over his words like a drunk man, but I acted quickly. I crouched to my knees, scooped up the blood-stained snow, and packed it together into a tight ball. Before he could react, I hurled it at Quinn's face with all my strength.

I hit him directly on the nose. The impact sent snow spraying everywhere. It melted into a thousand tiny droplets that slid down his cheeks. His mortified expression was enough to have me sitting back on my ankles, clutching my stomach as laughter, deep and true, tumbled out from a place a warmth.

Quinn narrowed his eyes. He clenched his jaw before stooping low to grasp at the snow. He hurled his own snowball at me, but he was far too slow. I moved to the side, dodging his blow. I was still laughing, but at the sight of Quinn's face blanching, I turned.

The Reaper stared down at where the snowball hit his chest– at where the clusters of tiny snowflakes slid down his armor, falling back to the ground. His silver eyes slowly raised to Quinn. The fires within his irises blazed brighter than ever before. They stared at one another as tensions rose.

Then all hell broke loose.

The Reaper was ducking to the ground, chasing after Quinn, pelting snowballs at his back. Quinn was laughing, kicking snow up as he sprinted across the field toward the cover of the treeline.

Before I could think, I was following.

The snow made an audible crunch beneath my boots. Every step was an effort in the thick white blanket. The breaths I drew were so cold that they felt heavy in my throat, in my lungs, and left a burning sensation in its wake. Heavy exhales left my nostrils in billowing clouds.

My entire body went numb long ago. My clothes were soaked through from the snow, the chill was starting to seep beneath my skin. It felt like the shivers wracking through my body were shaking my very bones.

But still, I ran toward the treeline. I looked across the field and took in the beauty of winter. I noted the way the light reflected off the snow, sparkling like millions of tiny stars fallen to earth. It covered everything in sight– the roofs of homes, the branches of trees, the ice of the stream. The entire world glowed brighter. Even the sky above seemed to be mocking the earth. It was so full of clouds that it was milky white in color, forcing the sunlight to reach the mortal realm in an evenly spread layer. The air was crisp and fresh.

The smooth, open field quickly gave way to the uneven terrain of the forest, where the snow thinned at the roots of the trees. A thin layer of ice coated everything in sight, giving the forest a blue tint. Leaves, twigs, branches, and even the entirety of the shrubs were caught in the clutches of last night's freeze.

Utter silence filled the absence of bird calls or rustling leaves. The birds had flown south, and the leaves had fallen to the ground and deteriorated long ago. But the lack of bird song wasn't what bothered me. It was the lack of *anything.*

The Reaper and Quinn were nowhere to be seen. I no longer heard the heavy footsteps of the Reaper, or the high-pitched squeals of Quinn.

Wind whipped and howled through the bare trees with no leaves to slow it down. The cold blast of air was like a stinging slap in the face, causing my jaw to throb. My ears ached and my fingers trembled. My entire body begged me to turn back and walk toward the warmth of the safehouse, but I didn't. Not yet.

From somewhere to my right, Quinn's yelp carried on the wind. "Okay! Okay, I lost! Go get Kalieth!"

Oh, I don't think so.

It may be something as insignificant as a snowball fight, but I didn't plan on losing to the Reaper.

I pressed my back to the nearest tree, crouching low so I could prepare a trove of snowballs. I didn't stop, didn't let my aching fingers rest, until I had a small pile of them by my feet. I rose from the ground, clutching one in my hand, and waited.

When the Reaper drew close, I knew it. I felt it. It was an indescribable electric charge in the air. It was the way the trees groaned and swayed, as if trying to get away. It was the winter's icy chill. It was autumn's ominous fog. It was spring's sweet silence before summer's storms. That was the Reaper's presence.

I closed my eyes. They couldn't aid me in finding him. I had to rely on my other senses. I listened for the crunch of boots in the snow. I breathed deeply, searching for the scent of leather and rain. I felt the tension in the air, following to where it beckoned.

Then I heard it. The smallest shift in weight. I homed in on it, springing out and flinging the snowball. He ducked behind a tree. The snowball hit the damp bark with a thud. I sucked in a sharp breath, looking to where my pile of snowballs sat a few feet away. I dove for them.

The Reaper was quick. He met me halfway, tackling me to the ground just as my fingertips brushed the cold orbs. We fell together, rolling through the foliage. Then his weight was over me. His knees pinned my thighs to the ground while one of his hands held my wrists together.

My head kicked back. The snow acted like a soft pillow, holding my weight as I relaxed into its cold embrace to get a good look at my opponent.

Despite the winter winds, my soggy clothes, and the snow surrounding us, I only felt heat as I stared into the Reaper's eyes, as if the fire within them was warming me. I lost myself in that raging inferno. I wondered if he truly controlled the shadows, or if the darkness was simply the smoke from the fires of his rage.

My skin flushed and tingled beneath his gaze. He looked at me through the same entranced stare. The world around us was suddenly lost, faded away into shadow. There was only us, only our stares and the breath that left us in two clouds of condensation that swirled through the air and mixed with one another.

Octavia. I had to remind myself. *He killed Octavia.*

The words didn't affect me as they once did. They sounded softer in my mind, more like a question than an accusation. I couldn't be sure if what Quinn said was true. I couldn't believe that my father started that fire. For my own sanity, I had to believe that Quinn and the others were lying to me. The thought was enough to snap me out of the trance.

One of the Reaper's small, gloved hands was hardly enough to keep my wrists bound. I easily broke through his grip and flipped us, pinning him down in the same way he had me.

I could end it here. I could slide my hand down to the Reaper's belt, unsheathe his pretty obsidian dagger, and glide it across his throat. He knew it too. Maybe he was testing me. He didn't fight in my hold. He relaxed just as I had, staring up at me through ever-narrowed eyes.

Those eyes. They haunted my dreams. So strangely familiar, as if I knew them in a past life. I looked into them, and I saw nothing and everything. No emotion but countless thoughts. No feeling but calculations and judgements. I could kill him. But beyond Octavia's mysterious death, there was an issue.

I didn't know whether I'd be killing the hero or the villain. I couldn't be sure of anything anymore.

So, I dug my hand into the ground beside him. He didn't flinch or glance. He stared straight into my eyes as I clawed at ground beside his ear. I withdrew my fist with a ball of snow in my hand, and I hit him right in the mask.

With a smirk, I climbed back to my feet. I offered him a cold hand. He took it, and I helped haul him to his feet.

Brushing the snow off my breeches, I called, "I win."

CHAPTER 14

Kalieth

The icy winds of winter made way for the warm breeze of spring. It felt like only days had passed since we first stumbled into this village, and yet the leaves fell and regrew in our time here.

The snow melted away, and from the damp ground grew spring flowers. The city of Shadieh would soon be preparing for the annual spring celebration, the Dragon's Feast. It started when a great fire, caused by a dragon's breath, swept through the lands and destroyed everything. But despite the devastation, rebirth and regrowth came with the spring season.

The Vermillion family always hosted a ball on the night of the Dragon's Feast. I looked forward to it each year, but this time, things would be different. I didn't know if I'd be able to attend. I didn't even know if my father would be alive to host it. The future was more uncertain than ever before.

Everything changed after Bryce's story. I wouldn't dare think that she lied. I heard the truth in the tremor of her voice. I saw it in the shaky breaths she took as she spoke– in the hatred in her eyes when she spoke of my brothers. My family tortured her, and possibly many others, but why?

Her story proved that none of my brothers were working with the Reaper. Bryce would never work with them after what she'd been through. Her story did raise other questions. If my father had been doing this for many years, could he have started the practice long before my brothers and I were born? Could it explain why my brothers' and I share very little physical traits? And then there was the issue of the warehouse. Could it be true that the Reaper had nothing to do with my sister's death at all? Could it be possible that my father was behind it? That he framed the Reaper because it was the easiest course of action?

After an entire season, I was left with more questions than answers.

I tried not to think about my complicated situation much. I took each day like a step. I was walking on a winding path; I just didn't know where that path was taking me. I couldn't be sure how far it stretched on. So, after the initial shock, I made the best of my days. I sparred with the Reaper. I laughed with Bryce. I debated with Quinn on stupid topics. I drank with Ace, and I shared stories with Ryder.

This team changed me in a short time. The Reaper was right, all those weeks ago. I'm nothing more than the Vermillion name. But I wanted to be more. They were teaching me to be more. Before stumbling upon this group, I'd never known such loyalty. My brothers and I were raised to stick by each other for sake of the family. We fought for our father's attention and pride because it was all that gave us purpose. All I'd known was the fighting and competing. All I could remember was living in the shadows of my siblings. We felt loyalty to each other only because we sported the same family name. There was no other bond between us. I never knew family could be anything more.

But the Reaper and his henchmen protected one another like a tight pack of wolves. An attack on one of them was an attack on all of them. Despite their constant bickering and teasing, they would die for one another. They'd become more than an assembled team. They'd become a family.

A family that wanted to kill my father. No amount of time I spent with them could blind me to that fact. After all I heard about him, maybe I wanted him dead too. A part of me still wanted to believe that he was innocent of all the crimes they accused him of. I'd want to hear a confession from his own lips. I'd want him to tell me why he did all of it. What could he possibly have to gain from all their suffering? What could he have to gain from burning his own warehouse, and his daughter with it?

I wouldn't have to wonder for long, because even though my training wasn't complete, it was time to leave Nero Village. Ryder announced just last night that we'd be leaving for the city today. We'd go back in teams, to avoid drawing any

172

attention to our return. Ryder would go with Bryce. Ace and Quinn would go together, and that left me stuck with the Reaper himself. We would rejoin the others again at the university library, where we'd investigate my grandfather's dedication stone and try to find more information on the history of the mysterious symbol.

We left at sunrise to be back in the city by sun-down. Ryder and the Reaper said their goodbyes to Chief Kamiyama before we set off. Ace and Quinn went first, followed by the two lovebirds. The Reaper and I were the last to leave.

As expected, the trek back to the city was– quiet. All I could hear was the squish of mud beneath my boots and the faint call of phoenix birds. After a while, the silence became maddening. The Reaper and I had been in each other's presence many times since the snowball fight in the woods, but ever since then something had changed between us. It was subtle, hardly noticeable, but it was there. Like a spark, it erupted in a burst of energy only to be gone the next second. I felt it each time he walked into a room. Each time we locked eyes. An electric shock that spread through my every cell. It was slowly driving me insane, wondering if he felt it to, or what he was thinking when our gazes locked unexpectedly.

"I know I shouldn't bother to ask questions, because you won't answer them, so I'm just going to start talking," I said aloud. The Reaper didn't even bother glancing my way.

"You're not what I thought you'd be, you know. I expected... well, I don't know exactly

173

what I expected, but you're not it. I thought maybe you'd be a deranged veteran or merciless killer. Actually, I still you think you might be a bit of both. But not entirely one or the other."

The Reaper continued walking. For all I knew, he couldn't even hear me. He gave me no hint to tell me he was listening.

"And the others, well, I didn't even know that you had a team at your back when I first searched for you. But they're everything I never had in my brothers. Everything I would want in friends. I wish we all could've met on different terms, maybe even in different lives, so that we might've been able to trust each other."

I kicked a pebble between my feet, looking up to see nothing but forest stretching on for as long as the eye could see.

"I never thought I'd end up training with you. *You.* Of all people. The man who wants to kill my father more than he wants to live his own life. I wish I could say I can't blame you, but I know nothing about you. There are a few questions I want to ask my father once I see him again. Not that I don't believe your stories, it's just that I need to hear it from him."

The Reaper threw his head back in annoyance. His fists clenched tightly at his sides as he whirled around to face me. A throwing knife whirled through the air only to be embedded in the soft soil between my feet. I stared down at it through raised brows.

"Is that supposed to be a warning to shut me up?" I kicked the blade back over to the cloaked assassin. "It won't be that easy."

I walked past him, feigning boredom by dragging my boots and admiring the surrounding forest. "I wish you could speak. There are still so many questions I have for you." I turned on my heel; my face only inches away from the Reaper's. "Are you afraid to face my father?"

I expected a mere shake of his head, but the Reaper didn't move. We stared at one another for a long moment with nothing but silence to fill the time. Despite the tension, I refused to look away. Even as he raised his hands, palms facing the sky, I did not look away. I could not look away. I was lost in a sea of silver fire, the flames like crashing waves that continued to rise and ripple.

The darkness surrounded me. Engulfed me. The ice-cold tendrils of shadow wrapped around me like long, freezing fingers. They gripped me and held me in place. Suddenly I was frozen; paralyzed. I could feel the weight of my own body slowly fading away. The darkness was trying to take me from the mortal world. I don't know where I'd go if I let it sweep away. I could see nothing. I could hear only whispers of a life beyond the void, but strangely, I felt a sense of tranquility. Peace awaited me in the realm beyond. All I had to do was let go.

The Reaper was my tether to this realm. I could no longer see him through the dark, but I could feel his presence beside me. He was the only thing keeping me from disappearing into the abyss of the unknown. Ordinarily, the thought of that would terrify me and yet, I felt no fear. He had no intention of letting me go. He did this for another reason.

The incoherent whispers grew louder. They continued to get closer until two voices rose above the others. It was the deep, steady voice of a grown man, contrasted by the high-pitched voice of a child.

"You know, one day, you'll have to fight in that war," the older man said.

"Should I be afraid?"

"Yes, but only because fear gives us strength. Never let anyone convince you that fear makes you weak. Only cowards say things like that," He paused. "But fear is a beautiful thing. It is a reminder of our humanity. The only thing that matters is how you react to your fear. If you let it paralyze you, you have failed. But if you use it to your advantage and learn to dance with demons instead of fighting them, then nothing in this realm can stop you."

The cold gave way to warmth as the shadows rescinded. The mortal world flooded my senses. The smell of the pine trees seemed more pungent than before. I could've sworn that the phoenix birds sounded closer and louder. I came back to my senses with my eyes closed. Opening them left me blinded by the sun-high brightness.

The Reaper had to catch me because my knees gave out the second the shadows disappeared. He steadied me until I felt the ground beneath my feet again.

176

I had to gulp down the lump in my throat. "Those were wise words. Was that your father? Are you the little boy? Or is there an old man under that mask?" I meant for the words to sound sarcastic, but the haughtiness just wasn't there. I was still in shock after what just happened. My body was still processing the effects of wherever I travelled to.

The Reaper gave me a weary look before he brushed past me. I didn't miss the way he looked down at his own gloved hands. He looked down as if he'd never seen them before. I wondered if he even knew he could do that– whatever it was he just did.

I don't know if he meant to scare me into silence, but it worked. I walked a few paces behind him for the last few hours without saying another word. Well, for the most part.

CHAPTER 15

Ryder

I'm not one to fear, but I grew concerned when the moon reached its peak and the Reaper and Kalieth still weren't with us. It wasn't like the Reaper to be late. I worried that the Vermillions caught them trying to re-enter the city.

Bryce ran a hand over my tense shoulders. "They will come," she assured me.

Ace and Quinn sat just behind us on the library steps. Ace twirled a dagger between two fingers, his face the epitome of boredom. Quinn, on the other hand, looked rather nervous. He wiped his sweaty hands on his breeches and bounced his leg anxiously. His eyes darted over the distant rooftops and alleyways, searching for any movement. It made him nervous to sit out in the open with a bounty still on his head. He jumped at even the slightest of sounds, which Ace was having a field day with. Every time Quinn's attention went elsewhere, Ace would lean forward and yell indistinct words or blow air across his neck. If Quinn was capable, he probably would've strangled Ace by now.

Quinn wasn't the only one on edge. It felt foreign to be standing in the moonlight on an empty street. Without the Reaper, our best weapon, I felt like an exposed wound.

Our group would normally stick to the shadows, but tonight, depending on what we find, might change that. For the first time since my father's death, we had a hint. A path to take. A single light after a year of darkness. We couldn't afford to lose it. It was our chance to stay one step ahead of the Vermillions, while they still assumed we were on the run. Every minute we spend waiting outside for the Reaper chipped away at our advantage.

Bryce ran a finger across my cheek. A soft smile crossed over her lips as she scanned my face. "I don't like when you worry. It gives you frown lines."

I chuckled and pulled her close. "Well, we can't have those, can we?" I kissed her softly.

She kissed me back instantly. She threaded her fingers into my hair and pulled me against her. The warmth of her hands on my skin compared to the cold kiss of the night's air sent a spark through my entire body. A shudder worked through me when her tongue brushed against mine. With her mystic power growing once more, I could feel the heat radiating from her, like fire burning just beneath her skin. It flowed into me and settled in my chest, not just warmth but light. A weightless feeling beyond relief.

A faint gagging sound came from behind us. Bryce broke away from me to whirl around and glare at Quinn. She ripped all the warmth right out of my skin when she turned away. The icy sensation set in so quickly that a choked sound escaped my throat, and I instinctually brought my hands close to my chest. The utter cold was like nothing I'd ever felt before. My teeth chattered so harshly I thought I might chip one. Shivers racked through my entire body to make me weak in the knees.

Bryce was too busy snapping at Quinn to see the sudden change in my demeanor. She didn't see that I was about to fall, and I would have, if it weren't for the hand that grasped my forearm. I fell back into steady arms. Suspicion fell second to fear– fear that sparked from the fact that my fingertips were turning blue.

The gripping cold only lasted one long moment. The color gradually came back to my skin. The shivers subsided on their own, and although the goosebumps refused to fade, the cold turned to a slight chill until it vanished completely.

Bryce's power never did this to me before. The fire within her made her skin warm. She could summon the flames whenever she wanted, and she could even light a torch with a mere look in its direction. But she never ripped the warmth right out of me.

I was pushed back to my feet when the shivers stopped. I went for my dagger, but another hand grabbed my wrist to stop me. This time, I recognized the smooth feel of leather. I sheathed my dagger and turned to face the Reaper.

Dressed in the usual, I saw nothing but silver eyes. Upon first glance, they betrayed nothing, but when I really looked, I saw worry within them. Worry for me.

I pushed out of the Reaper's grasp, waving him off. Though I was vaguely aware of Bryce continuing to chastise Quinn behind me, I ignored it completely. I crossed my arms over my chest and looked the Reaper up and down. I felt inclined to do my own bit of scolding. "You're late."

"My fault. I saw a family of chimeras and chased them down. Did you know that their tails are live serpent heads? Well, I didn't," Kalieth said. He walked out from the alley behind the Reaper with a spring in his step.

My gaze reverted to the Reaper. With raised brows, I asked, "you let him drag you around the Sombra mountains to hunt for chimeras?" The one person in the group who had no tolerance for delays.

"He didn't have much of a choice. I chased them for about two minutes before *they* started to chase *me*. He took on three of them for me, but I got one!" He proudly held up a long, curved tooth.

The Reaper rolled his eyes and held up his own trophy. A claw as long as a dagger.

Bryce came to stand beside me. She took one look between the two chimera hunters and rolled her eyes. "If you two are done comparing, I'd like to find whatever it is we're looking for in this library before the Vermillions come to kill us all."

"What is a chimera?" Ace asked.

Quinn looked at the warrior as if he just asked what color the ocean was. "You don't know what a chimera is?"

Ace glared back. "I raised myself on these streets. I didn't exactly have the means to explore the Sombra mountains, or the money to buy a book about the creatures roaming the forest."

Bryce chose to answer before the two of them got into it. "It's a creature with three heads. One of a goat, one of a lion, and one of a drake. They usually leave people alone–" she glared at Kalieth. "Until they're *provoked.*"

"Blame the Reaper. Maybe if he talked, I wouldn't have been bored enough to provoke a chimera," Kalieth said with a shrug.

The Reaper stopped in his tracks, sending a look to Kalieth as if to say, *really?*

"Fair point. I probably would've done the same," Ace said, still twirling his dagger.

Kalieth spun on his feet, his eyes wide. "Did you just agree with me?"

"No."

"I think you did."

Ace stared at him blankly. "Of the two of us, which one could actually take a chimera in a fight, and which is just an overconfident, presumptuous ass?"

Quinn raised a brow. "I can't believe you know what presumptuous means."

"I may be a brute, but I'm not an idiot," Ace said.

Kalieth considered them both for a moment. "One of these days, Ace, you and I are going to have it out."

Ace's dagger fell into his hand. He glared toward Kalieth. "Is that a bet?"

I rolled my eyes, but it was Bryce who said, "please, for the love of all things good in this world, stop this now, before I have to light a fire under all your asses."

The Reaper cut the conversation short by brushing through everybody to walk up the front steps. His brief pause and glance over his shoulder was our cue to follow.

He stopped at the large double doors that marked the library's entrance. The inscription along their wooden frames was in a language long forgotten, and the faces carved into them were withered beyond recognition. But the doors were made from drearwood, a tree believed to originate from the Shadow Realm itself, and so its presence in the sacred places is believed to ward off all shadows and evil, like obsidian stone.

The Reaper raised his hand to the door. Shadows poured from his palms, but they recoiled and retreated into his sleeves once they touched the dark wood.

"What is it?" Bryce asked. She jumped to try to see over my shoulders. I would've chuckled at her cute attempt if I wasn't so mesmerized by the shadows. Hundreds of years could pass, and I still wouldn't get used to the sight of them spilling from my brother's fingertips.

I didn't know what to think of the fact that the Reaper's shadows shied away from the drearwood. It meant that the Reaper's power came from the Shadow Realm. That not only was it otherworldly, but it was an evil power born from the Accuser himself.

"Bryce, burn the doors down," I muttered. It was the only way the Reaper would be able to enter.

She gaped at me. "What?"

"Burn the doors down," There wasn't a hint of humor.

If a stranger saw the look on Quinn's face, they might've thought I threatened his mother. Everyone in our group knew that the thought of putting one book on the wrong shelf in this ancient library would have him in a frenzy. But he used his wit and kept his mouth shut.

The Reaper stepped away to let Bryce through. He tucked his hands beneath his cloak, his eyes clouded. Ace and I exchanged a knowing glance over the Reaper's shoulder. Something was changing about our fearless leader, beyond the power. He'd been acting strange ever since Kalieth joined us, and it was past time we asked why.

Bryce stepped up to the doors and gently ran her hands over the carvings. I knew that she didn't like the thought of destroying something so rich with history, but we had no choice. We didn't have time to carefully take them off their hinges.

Bryce pressed each of her palms flat against both doors. She closed her eyes and tilted her head. An orange glow shined beneath her eyelids. The same glow warmed the veins of her arms, moving in the very cells of her blood toward her palms. Once the brilliant light reached her hands, fire erupted from them. Her eyes flew open, glowing a mixture of orange and red from the flames crackling deep within her irises, the green hardly noticeable beneath it.

The heat radiating from her seemed to warm the entire city. It came off her like the rippling waves of humidity visible on a hot summer day. With each passing second, the light beneath her skin grew brighter, until she was a newborn star, casting away all the darkness in the world.

The fire that sprang from her palms was so hot, it disintegrated both doors in mere seconds. There wasn't even a single flake of ash left on the ground to commemorate them. One moment they were there, and the next, only the scorch marks on the marble threshold served as a reminder that they ever existed.

Bryce stepped away once the job was done. She shook out her hands while she walked. The glow gradually faded from her skin, but the small strands of flame that blazed in her eyes did not.

A low whistle sounded from Kalieth. He stared at the doorway through wide, unblinking eyes. Just one season ago he believed mystics went extinct, and seeing Bryce use her power never got old for him.

The others walked through the smoke without hesitation. Quinn waited a moment. He stared at where the doors just were with a pained expression. He shook off whatever thoughts kept him in place and walked through the threshold, brushing his fingers over the scorch marks as he went.

I waited for Bryce. She walked out to the top of the steps and looked over the city. She glanced down at her hands, turning them over to inspect them. "I haven't felt like this in a long time," she said. Her back remained turned to me, but she knew I stayed with her.

"Like what?"

Her hands dropped to her sides. "Strong. Like I could chase off all the shadows in the realm. When a mystic doesn't use their power, they grow weak. Before I joined this group, it had been two years since I'd used them. The physical toll it had on my body almost became too much. But I couldn't call to the fire, because I controlled it with rage, and my rage was suddenly overpowered by guilt."

She turned to face me. She cupped my face in her hands. "I don't control it with rage anymore, and the flames burn differently because of it. They're stronger, and it's all because of you."

I wanted to tell her about what happened a few moments ago, when she ripped all the warmth right out of my body. I wanted to ask if she'd ever done anything like it before. But I didn't because she seemed so happy. She had more color in her cheeks and light in her eyes than I'd ever seen before. I didn't want to ruin her joy. But I still worried. She felt stronger than ever, and if she truly hadn't used her power in years, who's to say that it was me who changed it? Maybe she was just destined to be powerful.

I pushed the thoughts to the back of my mind as I kissed her fingers and took her hand in mine. "Come. Best not to keep the others waiting."

The air of the library was cold and dry, enough to make my nose sting when I breathed in. The large, dark chamber was only lit by faelights and a sliver of moonlight filtering in through the stained-glass window high above us. Though the faelights cast an eerie blue tint through the space, it wasn't enough to see any defining features in our surroundings. I could barely see the silhouettes of my companions through the darkness.

"Bryce?" I called softly.

Her steps faltered when she looked my way. Realization flashed across her face. "Oh, right, sorry."

With one flick of her fingers, all the torches around the room lit up simultaneously. The flames came to life with a loud hiss. The crackling echoed through the space. The warm light of the fire contrasted with the blue glow of the faelights, driving the shadows back to the corners of the room.

Vines stretched across the walls, fanning out from the giant, ancient oak tree that the library was built around. Its thick roots breached the tile floors. Weeds and flowers grew through those cracks. Beautiful night-blooming flowers grew all over, but they instantly retreated from the light. The vibrant petals rolled into themselves and left dull, white buds.

I caught Bryce before she tripped over one of the many roots sprouting up from the floors. The growth was beginning to overtake the bookshelves and statues. The running fountain in the middle of the room was almost completely covered in foliage. The sounds of the falling water and popping fire were interrupted occasionally by the scuffle of our footsteps.

Ace walked over to a random bookshelf and picked up the first book he saw. He blew on the cover, and a cloud of dust whirled through the air. He raised his brows and leafed through the first few pages. "The Origin of Irrigation in the Farmlands." He immediately slammed the book shut and put it back on the shelf. "I will never understand how Quinn spends entire days here."

Quinn scoffed from somewhere within the rows of shelves. "That's because you're an imbecile with no appreciation for history."

"Why would I waste my time reading about things that I can see for myself in the real world?" Ace shot back. "If anything, you're the imbecile for locking yourself up in this musty place instead of experiencing the world."

"Really? Are you going to go see the dragons in the real world? Or the strategic tactics of King Judriel II?"

The Reaper paid no mind to the conversation at hand. He brushed past Ace and walked through one of the many archways that lined the room.

Most of them led to study rooms, but the first two archways led into narrow corridors. The halls were lined with dedication stones, and they eventually reached the offices of the head scribes.

While the Reaper disappeared into the shadowed hall, Quinn remained hidden between the stacks of books. Bryce and I walked down the room, looking through each aisle to search for him. We found him looking through the ancient history section.

"I thought we were looking for a stone, not a book," Bryce chided, putting her hands on her hips.

Quinn glared at her. "If you never let me leave the tower, at least let me pick up a few of my favorites."

"You know, every time you talk, I think, 'no way he could be any more dorkish,' but then you go and say things like that," Ace said.

"Ace, I swear to the Kings above and below, I'm going to punch you in the throat," Quinn grumbled.

Ace's eyes lit up. "Promise?"

"That might have to wait," Kalieth called from across the room. He leaned against the wall beside the archway. He gestured for us to come see for ourselves.

Quinn dropped the books and followed behind Bryce and me. Ace beat us to the corridor. The tensing of his shoulders was our only warning. He stepped out of our way to give us a look. I peered in to see the Reaper standing beside

Busiris Vermillion's dedication stone. Carved into the stone, beneath his name, was the symbol of two palms holding up the moon.

"Well, we found what we were looking for. Now what?" Bryce asked.

No one answered her. No one knew the answer. With the exception, it seemed, of the Reaper. He turned away from the stones, and when his eyes fell on Kalieth, they narrowed. He grasped Vermillion's arm and yanked him into the corridor. Kalieth barely had time to react before the Reaper had a dagger in his hand and sliced through Kalieth's palm.

Kalieth grimaced, clenching his teeth. He opened his mouth to snap at the Reaper, but no words came out before my sibling slammed his palm against Busiris's stone. Kalieth's blood smeared over the symbol and covered it entirely, in the same way it covered the lock to open the vault.

Once the Reaper was satisfied with the amount of blood on the stone, he ripped off a piece of his own cloak and wrapped it around Kalieth's hand. He pushed Kalieth away afterwards, his eyes focused on the wall.

We all waited, tension thick in the air. The silence between us was deafening. Each crack of the fire or trickle of water from the fountain made one of us flinch. Each second felt longer than the last.

Nothing happened.

Ace pushed off the wall and clapped his hands together. "Well, I think I've wasted enough time here tonight. Drinks, anyone?"

Before we could answer, a rumble sounded from deep within the walls. The stone wall in front of us started to shake. Dust fell from the ceiling, showering down on us. Two cracks formed through the middle of the wall. They continued to grow larger and more defined until the entire portion of the wall with Busiris's name retreated and moved to the side, leaving enough room for an extremely narrow corridor.

Ace frowned. He took a step back, shaking his head. "My ass is not going to fit through there."

Quinn crossed his arms over his chest. A mischievous smile crossed over his face, and his eyes lit up. "Are you– you're claustrophobic!"

Ace whirled around. "I am not!"

"Oh, you so are," Quinn said, laughing. "Hey, no worries, big guy. Everyone's afraid of something."

"I am *not* afraid of walls," Ace practically growled.

Quinn shrugged. "Whatever you say."

Ace took a step forward, But Bryce halted him with a hand on his chest. "Ace, you can and will come with us. Quinn, stop provoking him, don't make me lock you two in a room, *again*," she called over her shoulder.

That was not a good day. The two of them had been bickering like an old married couple, so we locked them together for twelve hours. Neither of them speak of it. In fact, they didn't speak to each other, or anyone else, for two days afterward. Bryce and I never found out what really happened in there. Her threat worked, though. The two of them straightened up and faced the passage without another word.

Dust clouded the corridor. It was clear that this passageway hadn't been used in a long time. I could barely see the Reaper's black cloak as it disappeared into the opening. I hurried to follow directly behind him. None of us knew what was on the other side of the wall, but I refused to let my own blood face the unknown alone.

Ace grabbed me by the collar and pulled me back. I swatted his hand away and made to bark orders at him, but he stopped me. "Don't you think it would be wise to let the one who can actually light the way go first?" he asked as he nodded in Bryce's direction. She patted Ace on the shoulder and brushed past us without a word.

Ace winked at me, just because he knew it would annoy me, and followed her in. I was only a step behind him, and Quinn a step behind me. Kalieth brought up the rear. The entryway closed behind us, leaving us in the complete and utter darkness. Bryce held out her palms, and fire sprang up from both. With the faint glow of the flames to guide us, we felt our way along the walls and followed the Reaper.

A gradual decline in the floor made it hard to keep our balance. Quinn would've slipped once or twice, if it weren't for Kalieth reaching out to steady him. The stone was damp, as if water ran through here not long ago, maybe when it rained. We were headed downward, underground. It wasn't an easy hike. We walked for a few minutes before the cold stone walls opened into a chamber of some kind.

Sparks flew from Bryce's hands. They went in a dozen different directions, finding torches and oil lamps. The room came alive with light. It looked to be just another records room. Dusty bookshelves and yellow-paged books filled the space. The shelves were full, and so books were stacked in piles on the floor or shoved into every nook they could fit.

Quinn picked up one of the books. He wiped the dirt away from the cover and squinted at the title. As he explored the records, the rest of us looked around. Bryce and I marveled at the detailed statues that sat on polished pedestals. Not one had a chip or crack. It was almost like they were frozen in time– incapable of decay. The faces and names were ones that we didn't recognize.

Ace went straight for the ancient swords on display. By the markings on the wooden sheath, I guessed they were from a time before the war. The Reaper watched us, keeping to the shadows.

The grimace on Kalieth's face still hadn't left. He flexed his fingers and clenched a fist. When he was satisfied that he still had full use of his hand, he began to investigate for himself. He touched nothing. Maybe he was worried about his bloodied hand. He stepped lightly as he walked through the narrow aisles.

"There's something strange about these records," Quinn called. He lifted a book for all of us to see. He held open the front cover to display the year, bolded and large. It was dated back several centuries ago. "They were written before the war began."

Bryce went still. "I thought all the records from before the war were lost or destroyed."

"They were," Quinn said darkly. "Or so we were told."

"Why would my family want to hide away history?" Kalieth asked.

"And so, you have come. As I had seen it. As I foretold it," a deep voice drawled from the shadows.

All six of us had our weapons drawn in an instant. We closed ranks, forming a tight circle. Fighting stances were taken. Breaths were held. The air turned thick with tension.

A cloaked figure stepped into the flickering light of the fire. Half of his face was concealed in shadow, but the other half showed a man just past his middle years. He shared a similar skin color with Quinn, not pale like the moon's surface but not dark like my own. It was slightly tanned, in a birth-given way that the sun had no part of. He had long black hair that fell to his shoulders, half of the curls were tied back somewhere behind his hood. His silver eyes were narrowed, as though years of suspicion and deception made them permanently so.

His black cloak moved as if it were alive. Upon further inspection, I realized that it wasn't made of cloth at all. They were shadows that surrounded him. They swirled, whispered, and dissipated, acting as a layer of protection between him and his surroundings.

Ace was the first to speak. "Who are you? Why do we care?"

The man ignored Ace entirely. He stepped toward the middle of the room, staring down at his own black boots as he did. "I heard your story like a song at dawn. A hope after centuries of darkness. A harmony after a lifetime of silence," he said. He stopped abruptly; his boots made a scuffling sound on the stone. His head snapped up, and he took a long look at each one of us. "Six companions, brought together to change our course. Each one fighting for a different purpose. One for terror. Two for rage. Three, a murder. Four, a cage. Five for answers. Six for gold." A pause. "And all part of a story to forever be told."

He raised his arms in a triumphant gesture. The sleeves of his tunic fell with the motion, and for a brief second, before the shadows could cover them, I saw the glint of the shackles on his wrists.

He stooped low into a bow. "I am Eichi, God of Time and Wisdom. You will find all the answers you seek in me."

CHAPTER 16

Kalieth

For the first time, all six of us were rendered completely speechless. We glanced around at each other through narrowed brows and wide eyes. Tension crackled through the air like the fire blazing from the torches. No one moved. No one made a sound. It seemed like no one breathed.

Ace smirked, ready to finally pummel someone into a bloody pulp. His gaze found the Reaper, and he raised a fist. "Please tell me I get to knock his brain back into sorts."

The Reaper held up a gloved hand. *Stand down.*

Ace's entire body slumped in annoyance. "You people suck the joy out of everything," he grumbled, turning away.

"I don't understand," Bryce said, shaking her head. "There are no gods. There are only the two Kings."

Eichi straightened back to his full height. He towered over all of us by a few inches. A solemn look passed over his face as he slowly tossed his head from side to side. "That is a deception. A lie told by a tyrant so that he may retain his power."

"My father?" I asked, my voice low.

Eichi met my gaze. I could see rage, suspicion, and pain in his stare. His eyes held such age and wisdom, gained through a period of time I could hardly begin to comprehend. I saw eternal torment in his stare. A god, an all-powerful being, an omniscient entity, suffering all the same.

"Your father, his father, and his father before that. A hundred generations have ensured that the lie continues," he replied after a moment.

"Why?"

"They do not wish for the war to end. They created the fiction of the two Kings to guarantee that the Southern Kingdom remains fighting. When a tyrant has disposed of all other enemies, then he will always stir up some war or another so that the people require a leader. As long as the war continues, the Vermillions wealth grows, and they remain the true power in Shadieh."

"How did the Vermillions convince people to start a war in the first place, if there were never any kings?" Quinn asked. I'd never heard him sound so small. He even appeared to shrink back into the shadows when the god turned his gaze upon him. The boy who loves history, cowering in the face of limitless wisdom.

"Quinn Chinen, he who grew old too fast by seeking knowledge, I wondered when you would find me. You were so close before," Eichi said as he bowed his head.

Quinn's lips parted. His eyes darted around as he tried to think. "The Vermillions wanted me dead because I nearly found you?"

"You grew too curious, and you questioned the fabricated history, did you not?"

All eyes were on Quinn now. He stared down at the floor, but that wasn't what he saw. He was searching through his memories, trying to uncover the truth. After a moment, his head snapped up. "I asked my professor about the Accuser. I didn't understand why there was no record of where his body was buried."

Eichi nodded. "The scribes are paid by Vermillion to write whatever he desires. They report to him, and so in questioning his history, you questioned his power. Then, you searched for the meaning of the ancient symbol. You were getting far too close to the buried truth. Xaphan ordered your execution promptly. To resist he who is in power is evil."

The god's words hit me like a blow. For over a season, I'd listened to horror stories about my father, and all the other members of my family. But there was still room for doubt in my mind. I could still hear a small voice whispering words of hope in my ear. Hearing it from a god, however, felt different. It felt real.

"Answer the question. If there were no kings, how did the war start?" Ace asked with eyes narrowed on Eichi.

Eichi took a deep breath. His eyes darted around the room as though he expected someone to jump out of the shadows at any moment. "There is no time to discuss the past. They are coming. We must focus on the future." His eyes went back to the Reaper. He stepped forward; his hand raised. His fingers hovered mere inches away from the Reaper's face, and I couldn't believe that the Reaper allowed him that close.

The god closed his eyes as his head fell back. His fingers twitched and his hand shook. For a long moment, the two of them stood there in a tense silence. Eichi broke it again once he opened his eyes and met the Reaper's gaze. "She has touched you," he whispered, breathless. "She comes to you when you sleep. She has given you power, I can feel it within you. It wishes to be let out; to finish what it started. Your power is like the ocean. It's vast and goes to great depths. It evolves and changes with you as you grow. But if you continue to fight it, it will drown you."

The shadows that rested on Eichi's shoulders flared. They reached out farther than ever, as if they could sense the Reaper's presence. As if they knew that they belonged with the assassin. The god did nothing to stop them when they curled down his arms and crossed over to the Reaper. He only watched them move with a smile on his face. "She gave me a touch of her power too, long ago, so that I may recognize it when it comes."

The Reaper said nothing. He tilted his head and narrowed his eyes.

Eichi smiled. "You refuse her offer, but it is not to be refused. I have seen your future, Reaper. This power was destined for you alone, it will not answer to anyone else."

Bryce looked between the Reaper and Eichi. "Is anyone else completely lost?"

Quinn raised his hand like a schoolboy. Ace and I nodded. But Ryder didn't seem surprised at the sudden turn of conversation.

Eichi ignored Bryce entirely. He refused to look away from the Reaper, and the Reaper would not break eye contact with Eichi. It was as if they were having a conversation without words. All that needed to be said, they could read in each other's eyes.

I quickly grew bored of whatever it was that the two of them were doing, and I walked further back between the shelves. I skimmed my hand over all the volumes there. I flicked off the dust that accumulated on my fingers and read the titles. The voices of the others grew fainter the farther I walked back, until I could hardly hear them at all.

I doubt they heard the scuffling sounds of my boots when a hand came down over my mouth and an arm snaked around my neck. I struggled against my attacker, but he had the advantage, and I was dragged backwards into the darkness.

He took me through a small passageway in the wall, so narrow and curved that it was impossible to see without prior knowledge to its existence.

I was finally pushed into a small chamber, the size of a small bedchamber, and I fell to the ground. I rolled to my feet and whirled around to face my attacker, sword drawn, only to see one of my brothers. Alastor watched me with hate and disgust in his eyes.

"Al?" I asked, surprised. "What are you doing here?"

"Watching you betray our family, and risk everything our ancestors worked to achieve," he spat. His upper lip curled in disgust as he looked down on me. He drew his dagger and pressed it to my throat. "I should kill you now and take your head to father."

"Alastor, I thought we discussed patience," a deeper voice drawled from behind me. A familiar voice that made the hairs on my neck rise and brought forth a sensation of pins and needles along my arms.

A knot formed in my throat as I turned to see my father sitting in a reading chair, book in hand, with his legs crossed. His eyes crossed over the words on the page. He didn't care enough to see if I was alright after an entire season away from home. He looked well. His dark hair was slicked back. His stout body was completely covered in the finest clothing on this side of the sea. He picked at invisible lint on his breeches while his icy blue eyes skimmed over the pages of his book. His sharp features appeared menacing in the dim light of the chamber. The torches cast shadows under his eyes and somehow made his pale skin look inflamed.

Alastor immediately dropped down on one knee behind me. He raised a clenched fist and pressed it to his chest as he lowered his head. "Forgive me father, I only meant to express my anger. I would have done no such thing without orders from you."

My father's piercing blue gaze lifted from the pages and lingered on Alastor for a moment before it rested on me. He slammed his book closed, tossed it to the table beside his chair, and stood. "My son, you've been away from home for far too long. It appears you've already forgotten your manners."

The realization was sudden, like a switch had been flipped in my head. I forgot to address my father properly. We were meant to kneel before him, a fist to our chest, and our heads lowered, and stay that way until he allows us to stand. It had been that way my whole life, and I never questioned it. But after being away for so long, it seemed odd to address my father the same way I would address the king, if his majesty ever came to town.

Without a word, I sank to one knee and greeted my father properly. It seemed to please him. He waved his hand to tell my brother and me to stand. We glared at one another as we got back to our feet.

"Your brother wanted to kill you for this betrayal, Kalieth, but I stopped him. You've always been loyal to this family, and I want to hear your reasoning for bringing the enemy here, to your grandfather's private collection, before I decide your fate," my father told me.

I struggled to find a lie. So, I started with the truth. "You sent me on a mission to bring you the Reaper. I originally set out to do exactly that, but I quickly realized that it wouldn't be that simple. If I wanted to outwit this group, I had to do it from the inside. I've spent the past season gaining their trust. Now, I wait for the perfect moment to strike. We're here because the group discovered grandfather's symbol, and I couldn't blow my cover by refusing to allow them access. They would've killed me and left me in an alleyway."

My father was silent for a long moment. He rubbed his chin in a pondering manner. The tension in the air weighed down my chest as I waited for his decision. A smile broke out over his face. "I knew you wouldn't betray me. You've brought them straight to us. We can kill them here and now."

I was relieved that he believed me, but panic gripped my chest at the thought of my brothers ambushing the group any minute. My head and heart pounded in unison. My father would kill me now if I sided with the Reaper. The Reaper would kill me later if I sided with my father. Death was a promise either way. But I'd been flirting with Death my whole life. The beginnings of a plan came to mind.

"No more waiting, Kalieth. They've done enough damage already. It's time to tear them apart, starting with the Reaper," Alastor said.

"Al is right. You've waited long enough," father added. My brother seemed to lift his chin with the praise.

The beginnings of a plan quickly turned into the first few steps of a great one. A plan that could go wrong in hundreds of ways. It was risky, and I could get killed by my family or the Reaper at any point, but it was the best way to find the truth, one way or another. Plus, if I did it right, I'd get to keep my head, which seemed like a positive.

I looked to my brother, forcing a wicked, evil grin to come to my face. "I know exactly what to do."

CHAPTER 17

Bryce

The Reaper and Eichi stared at one another for a long time. I couldn't tell if they were sizing one another up or simply too proud to be the first to break eye contact.

"We should go," I told Ryder. "The Vermillions may have someone watching the library. We've been here too long already."

Ryder nodded. He looked around, and suddenly his expression turned fearful, and he spun around on his heel. "Where's Kalieth?"

The Reaper's eyes snapped away from Eichi for the first time since we entered the chamber. He spun on his heels, scanning the room for any sign of Kalieth. We all did the same. Eichi was the only one to look to the floor. The god simply walked to closest bookshelf, picked up one of the volumes, and handed it to Quinn. "You will need this, if you are to defeat the evil that is to come," he said. Quinn took the book into his shaking hands. I watched his shoulders twitch as he took in a breath.

Ace took a threatening step toward Eichi, his patience and trust depleted. He held his dagger to Eichi's throat and grabbed the extra cloth of his tunic. "Quit speaking in riddles and tell us what the hell is going on."

"Ace!" I yelled. I knew he could be idiotic and impulsive, but I never thought he would stoop so low as to threaten a god.

Eichi smiled down at Ace, as if he expected him to act that way. He leaned forward and said, "You only have the war to fear now."

"I don't fear war," Ace said, his words short and mean. "I happen to enjoy violence quite a lot."

"You should. War does not spare the brave or the young, the warriors or maidens; it spares the cowardly."

Anger made Ace tighten his hold on both Eichi's tunic and the dagger in his hand. "This one comes with us," Ace said to us all.

Eichi shook his head. "I wish I could go with you. Truly, I do. But I cannot leave this place. I am but a fox confined to its den."

"Can't leave? Why the hell not?"

He nodded toward the bookshelves and held up his shackled hands. "Drearwood trees grow where gods' blood has spilled. It weakens the magic of the gods. They've used it to lock me here. Everything you see is carved from it."

I looked down to my hands. I could still feel the flames beneath my skin, begging to be released. "I still have my power."

Eichi didn't bother to look my way. "You are not a god." There was a bite to his words.

I looked to the Reaper. "Well, neither is he and the drearwood doors..." My eyes flew wide. "Wait, is he?"

Eichi followed my gaze. "A god, no, not yet. But created by one. The silent one is, what we once called, a champion. Chosen to carry a kernel of a god's power. When that god dies, he will inherit all their power and replace them."

Ace dropped him then. His words took us all by surprise. And as Eichi brushed the wrinkles out of his tunic, my gaze flew to the Reaper. He met my stare with a challenge in his eyes, daring me to say something.

"Guys, Kalieth is gone," Ryder said as he approached. In the time Ace threatened the god, Ryder had gone searching through the aisles.

"He's probably wandering around in one of the corners. We all know the man *loves* to go looking for trouble. Just fan out and we'll find him," I said. We made to each walk off in a different direction, but Eichi stopped us.

He spoke only to the Reaper, but the rest of us stayed to listen. His words were too intriguing to ignore. "The mask will come off soon, and your voice will be heard, but you must remember that there is worth in your silence that brings no risk. Regret comes from the speech, not the silence.

Know when to speak your truth, and when to hold your tongue."

The Reaper turned to meet Eichi's stare once more. The god took a long look into the assassin's silver eyes. "You exile yourself with your silence, and men in exile feed on dreams. Do not waste time thinking of what might've been. She's told you what you are. She's told you what you will become. And now, I am here to warn you. Beware lest you lose the substance of yourself by grasping at the shadows. Your physical self will be lost if you let them consume you. No matter how grim the circumstances may seem, the six of you each have a role to play in the games to come."

Eichi turned to Quinn. "Read," he said, nodding to the book. "All will be revealed."

With that, the god turned on his heel and disappeared into the darkness once more. The rest of us were left standing there, staring after him. Quinn clutched the book close to his chest while Ace sheathed his dagger. The Reaper did not move. He stood there like a lifeless statue with his eyes glued on the spot where Eichi walked off. The shadows that once belonged to the god now swirled through the Reaper's fingers.

"Alright then," Ryder said after clearing his throat. "Find Kalieth, and let's all get the hell out of here."

We each chose a different aisle to go down. It would cover more ground. I cursed Kalieth under my breath for always bringing a new level of difficulty to any task. The other Vermillion brothers would be on their way by now, and if I had to tear another one of my nice dresses while fighting that family– there'd be hell to pay.

The aisle of bookshelves didn't appear to be too long when I stood at its end, but once I started to walk through, it seemed to stretch on forever. I wondered if the chamber was spelled to look small, so anyone to stumble upon it unknowingly would be fooled into believing there wasn't much here. It would be a smart move on Busiris's part. How they got a hold of that sort of primal magic was beyond me. Even the spell to lock the door, relying on specific bloodlines, was a primal spell. Primal magic once filled the world, because there were beings, like dragons, powerful enough to harness it. Only a handful of beasts and men could still manage to manipulate even small bits of primal magic. The thought of Xaphan having one of those sorcerers under his influence was deeply disturbing.

"Kalieth?" I called. It was my last attempt to find him before I rejoined the others and left him here. I got no response. So, I spun on my heel and made to return the way I came. I stopped dead when I saw Alastor Vermillion standing in my way; his sword drawn, with an evil smirk stretching across his face.

Fire instantly crackled to life in my palms. The glow provided me with the light to see the fresh blood splattered onto his shirt.

My mouth went dry. "What have you done to Kalieth?"

Alastor's smirk turned into a genuine smile. A smile that had my stomach turning over. It made everything seem wrong. He looked down at his shirt and then back to me. "Made you look."

Something pricked my neck.

The fire in my palms fizzled out. I tried to summon it again, but I could only get sparks, and seconds later, nothing. I started to lose feeling not just in my hands, but in my entire body. The constant fire that burned with my soul was no longer there. Without the flames, I became paralyzed. There was nothing left of me.

I fell back into awaiting arms. I could hear, see, and feel everything, but I couldn't move no matter how hard I tried. I felt cold– frozen. Like a block of ice.

"I'm sorry," Kalieth whispered into my ear, so quiet I wasn't sure if my mind tricked me into hearing it.

"We should've gone for the Reaper," Alastor hissed. "We have no use for this one."

"You don't know this group like I do. The Reaper has a brother who happens to be in love with *this one*. The second he realizes what happened, he'll come after her. The Reaper won't let him go alone. The others will follow the leader. With this one, we'll have all of them coming to us. There will be no need to fight," Kalieth explained. "Now, go with the others. Deliver my message. Hurry, before they realize she's missing."

Alastor grumbled something and stomped off.

My eyelids felt heavy. I couldn't resist the pull of unconsciousness. Right before I drifted off, I felt Kalieth's warm breath fan across my neck as

210

he leaned down. "No harm will come to you, I swear it."

My mouth still felt dry, and my tongue like sandpaper, but I still managed to say, in a hoarse, weak voice, "I trusted you."

I held onto consciousness long enough to see the hurt pass through Kalieth's eyes before everything went black.

CHAPTER 18

Ryder

Bryce was gone.

She didn't come back from our search for Kalieth. I knew immediately that something was wrong. I could feel it in my gut. We didn't bother looking for her in the aisles. We knew that someone took her, and whoever it was took Kalieth too.

Quinn tried to talk to me; to calm me down, but I wouldn't listen. There was a roaring in my ears that drowned his voice into nothing. Ace didn't even try. He just followed me, ready to fight whatever battle I was headed towards.

They followed me back out into the street, and they all ran with me as I sprinted back toward the bell tower. If Bryce escaped or went off on her own, she would be there. I ran faster than ever. I could feel the burn in my calves. My body begged me to stop. But I had to push forward. I had to keep going.

The Reaper was right on my heels.

Heat rose to my face. Sweat creased my brow. My hands felt strangely numb. I ignored it all. None of it mattered. The only thing that mattered was getting to Bryce. I promised myself I'd protect her, and if I failed– if the Vermillions took her back to that torture chamber–

I shook the thoughts away. She would be waiting for us at the bell tower. The old building loomed in the distance. The sharp spires impaled the dark clouds above, reaching toward the stars. Through the clouds, the moonlight made the grey stones glimmer. I could see a faint glow coming from the windows of the upper levels. It dimmed and brightened just as ocean waves pull and roll.

I stopped dead in my tracks and stared up at the building, because once I got a closer look, I realized that the bell tower was on fire.

Ace and Quinn ran inside to put out the flames before they spread further. But I didn't care about the fire or the tower. It was barely a thought in my mind once I saw the message written across the stones of the outer wall.

Tomorrow night. Where we first met. The Reaper for Bryce.

~K

The message was written in a red substance that dripped down through the cracks of the stone. I stepped forward to touch it, finding it warm and thick. "Blood," I said. The word sounded choked.

The Reaper stepped forward and put a hand on my shoulder. I looked into the silver eyes beneath the hood; the ones that looked just like my own, and just for a moment I could see the person behind the mask. I could remember what everything was like before the vow of silence. Before the alias of the Reaper was created.

"I have to get her back," I whispered. My voice sounded weak and hoarse, because it pained me to even think of what Bryce was feeling. I couldn't imagine the fear and betrayal. But mostly I thought about what the Vermillion brothers planned to do to her. But I met the Reaper's eyes again. "I have to get her back, but I won't lose you too." My sibling, younger than me by a few years, was still my responsibility. I had to protect them both. I wouldn't choose between them.

The hand on my shoulder squeezed down slightly. The brows beneath the hood raised in offense, as if I'd insulted the Reaper by suggesting he can't handle himself.

"You heard Bryce's stories. You know what they'll do to you," I said, my voice growing softer still. The thought of Xaphan or his sons touching the Reaper–touching Bryce–

My fist collided with the stones just as thunder rumbled in the distance. Pain burned my hands through cracked knuckles and bruised fingers. I couldn't stop myself, though. Even as I spilled my own blood, I continued to pummel the stones. Normally, some part of me would care that I was staining my clothes red. But not tonight. I kept pushing. I made no dent or chip in the rock. The hard surface did not bend to my fists. In fact, it almost felt like it pushed back against me.

The Reaper pulled me away before I could beat my fists into a bloody pulp. I tried to fight against his pull because I didn't want the pain to fade. I needed the distraction to keep me sane. It gave me something to hold onto, to remind me that this is my reality.

Ace and Quinn came back outside once the flames were put out. They saw the message, and they saw my bloody hands. Ace came forward to help the Reaper drag me away. I fought against him, but he got my arms pinned to my sides.

"Calm down. You won't help Bryce by breaking your fingers and being unable to fight for her. The stones would win this fight," Ace hissed into my ear.

He was right. I had to stop. I needed to keep my sanity for her. I needed to be able to bash a few Vermillions' heads in. That sounded good. That sounded really good. I nodded to the others to tell them I was okay. They could let me go. Once the pressure of their grip left my limbs, I stretched my arms and rolled my shoulders. Ace was able to take another look at the message just before the rain started to fall and wash it away.

"Kalieth did this?" Ace asked. His face hardened, and his voice was a promise of death.

"I'll kill him," I vowed.

"What are we going to do? We can't hand the Reaper over. That's exactly what they want," Ace said.

I smiled, because he didn't understand that the Reaper was not a person who we could hand

215

over. The Reaper would make the decision to go or not, it would not be possible to dissuade him once he made up his mind. And despite the hard, cold person everyone assumed the Reaper was beneath the mask, I knew that he would hand himself over to the Vermillions to save Bryce. He would rather sacrifice himself than know that someone else was suffering in his place. He wouldn't think twice.

The Reaper said all of that and more in the annoyed glance he directed toward Ace. He shook his head to himself and looked down at the many obsidian blades on his belt. I had no doubt that he was thinking of all the ways he might be able to fight his way through this situation, just as we had fought through all the other ones. But this time was different because the Vermillions have the advantage. They have one of us, and they won't hesitate to kill her if we step out of line.

Nothing could be done tonight. The Vermillions would have Bryce smuggled onto their estate by now, and there is no getting past their defenses when the guards are on high alert. So, we fled from the bell tower, even as the rain put out the last of the embers. We ran through the winding streets and alleys like three snakes wiggling across a forest floor until we reached our second safehouse. It used to be a teahouse, but the owners fell ill two years ago. They went west for rest and healing, and never returned. The shop, and the apartment above, were frozen in time, as if the owners simply stood up and walked out without any prior thought. Only the ghosts of the South Side stayed here now.

The tile floors were cracked and covered in grime. Shards of porcelain snapped beneath my boots; the remains of expensive dishware. Many chairs were overturned, sporting worn cushions and broken legs. The little round tables that once sat the finer side of the lower class now stood eerily empty. Old teacups remained out on their saucers, as if the spirits of the dead communed here to reminisce. If I strained, I could almost hear their whispers and mournful wails, reaching out to beg me to bring them back to life, only to pass straight through me and leave the echo of an icy spider crawling down my spine, sending a shiver in its wake.

I didn't like this place.

No one else appeared to be bothered. Quinn didn't waste a second. He sat himself down at one of the many tables, set Eichi's book on the counter, and started to read. Nothing could break his focus from the words on the page. Not even the clanking of dishes or scraping of chairs as the Reaper, Ace, and I tried our best to clean up and make some space.

Quinn only read the first few pages before he was jumping from his seat, pointing at the book, waving us over. Ace stood over his shoulder, peering down at the yellowed pages. The Reaper, to my surprise, did not stay leaning against the wall in the shadows. He went to stand beside Quinn, crouching down in front of the table to get a closer look.

"What's going on?" I looked down to see the book open on a picture of a woman. She had silver eyes that glowed like starlight. White, textured

217

hair tumbled down to her shoulders in tightly coiled curls. She had skin even darker than mine, so dark that it nearly blended in with the black background of the drawing. But her face was covered in freckles that glowed white like the infinite stars in the night sky. The galaxy lied within her, and at her heart was the full moon. But what stood out the most was the charm that hung from her brow. It took the shape of the moon, and two cupped hands held it up. It shined bright with silver starlight, as though the entire soul of a newborn star was cast into it.

"The symbol never belonged to the Vermillions; they stole it. They wanted to make a mockery of it and all it once stood for," Quinn said. He was giddy with excitement. I'd never seen him so stirred. "And the story of the two kings? It was based off small parts of the true history, but they weren't kings. They were gods and primals."

He picked up the book and shoved it toward my face. His finger tapped against the charm which rested against the goddess's brow. "This symbol stood for peace and unity. It stood for creation relating to life or death, womanhood, and empowerment. Before the Vermillions, it was associated with Cheusi, the Goddess of Creation. She was the first god."

The information came too fast. It brought an ache to my head. I had to make Quinn stop. "What does all of this mean?" I asked.

Quinn gulped and looked to the Reaper. "It means that your brother has the power of the first god in his hands. He's the Champion of Creation, and he's destined to end the war, and maybe the world with it."

Ace snorted. "*That's* the prophecy? I thought they were supposed to rhyme."

"That's not the prophecy. This is." He drew in a sharp breath. "*When the wolf howls, the pack awakens. The call of rage and sorrow will sweep across the lands, stoking the flames in the North. The red eyes set upon the last dragon, who awakens in the face of Death. The battle of light and shadow will remake the realms even after the sun falls into darkness, and the Long Night arrives.*"

The page was ripped down the middle. The prophecy was unfinished.

"It still doesn't rhyme," Ace muttered.

I scanned the words ten times over, but my mind still couldn't catch up. "That makes no sense."

Quinn gulped. "I can't make sense of all of it, but I know that if the Reaper accepts this power, he will eventually replace Cheusi as the God of Creation. He will be the King of Gods."

CHAPTER 19

Quinn

An indescribable sensation spread through my body when everything I once believed was revealed to be a lie. It was an unnamed emotion that danced on the line between anger and shock. It froze the blood in my veins. My pulse hammered so forcefully, I could feel my own heartbeat in my fingertips. And yet it was nothing compared to the pure terror I felt when Bryce was taken.

We were balanced, and without Bryce we would fall into chaos. I couldn't let that happen, not yet. Not when we just started to get along, to see one another as more than teammates. The Reaper may have brought us together, but he was not the only thing binding us to one another anymore. We evolved from a group of rage-filled amateurs into something else– something more.

I didn't have words to describe it; the bond we formed. It was stronger than what I had with my parents, my only blood family. My parents are wealthy, and they own a large estate in the farmlands, where servants do anything and everything they desire. I was meant to inherit it all. That was until my mother discovered my lack of interest in the village girls, and my notice of the stable boy. After that, they disowned me.

The family mansion suddenly became a prison. I was not permitted to leave. My father enforced that rule, afraid that if I went into the village, or even stepped foot outside, my *disease* would spread to others in town. He feared that I would *convert* someone else, and word would get out, and I would be the Chinen that tainted the family name.

I tried to negotiate through my mother, but every time I walked into a room, she would look right through me. When I spoke, she would find a way to steer the conversation to the common, easy topics. The weather, the war, and once she even tried to talk about the horrible season of crop we were having. I became invisible to them.

The books were my escape. I discovered that everything became easier in the library. I could leaf through the pages of a good book, and my own harsh reality would fade away. There would only be one string of words leading to another, painting new worlds and old worlds; fantasies and histories alike. Soon enough, I only felt at ease when I had several books open in front of me. Several other realities to jump into at any given moment.

A few months passed and I became so unbearable to them that they shipped me here, to the city of Shadieh. They expected the change of environment to *fix* me, and it did, but not in the way they wanted. It made me realize that I wanted to be a scribe. I wanted to write history in a way that represented others like me.

I never told the group any of this. But I would like to, one day, because a part of me knows that they'd understand. Especially Ace. I envied his openness about loving both men and women. I could only hope to achieve his level of confidence. To have that chance, I had to save Bryce. I needed to keep this group together. So, I opened Eichi's book and started to read. I stayed up through the night reading. I couldn't put it down. Not when I discovered a new lie in the taught history with each page.

The gods and the primals were born from a burst of energy that exploded across the universe. There are many metaphors relating the two powerful species to the moon and the sun. They were at war with one another long before they found physical forms. In fact, one theory from an ancient scribe suggested that the very explosion of energy that created their physical forms was a result of their power clashing together.

The gods were not short in numbers. They were the embodiment of the universe's magic. Their power stemmed from aether, the element of the moon. Many of them perished in the Eternal War when they fought against the primals. When killed, the power of a god is passed down to their strongest child, or, if they have no children, their power searches the world and makes its own choice. The gods that weren't killed found their resting places eons ago and have not woken since. To this day they lie within their temples or valleys, their tombs like a cold embrace, and sleep as we slaughter each other above them.

The primals were born from the sun. Morrighan, the Primal of Destruction, reigned over the primals. There is no record of her going to rest or perishing. In one of the last records written of the war, it states that Morrighan took up residence in the Northern Kingdom. She whispered lies into the ears of greedy human kings and practiced the darkest of magics. She slithered her way into the position of Queen of the Northern Kingdom and commanded her troops from within her ice fortress.

Cheusi fought honorably with her troops, but she was feared for her power. Some witnesses stated that falling into her clouds of shadow was like stumbling into the afterlife. Their senses were stolen from them, and suddenly they were stuck between a time when there was nothing and a time when there was everything, a place outside of the chain of cause and effect. Whispers of souls long lost or never born reached to them, convincing them to join the endless void of nothing. An invisible force pulled them toward something, but to find out what meant surrendering to darkness and Death.

Cheusi went missing centuries ago, assumed to have gone to rest with the other gods. Morrighan turned to even darker ways to gain power. The last record of her, dated back a few hundred years, states that the Primal of Destruction feeds off live mystics, drawing out and consuming the essence of their power.

I read the book cover to cover within a few hours, but now the candlelight was fizzling out. I turned the last page to find a hand-written note from Eichi himself.

Your group is the key to the end.

Beware the orange flames. They burn in the eyes of the Primal of Destruction.

The last sentence sent my heart to the floor to shatter into a million pieces. I slammed the book shut, instantly on my feet. I was moving before I knew where I was going. My legs took me out of my own room, down the corridor, until I stood before Ryder's door. My fist was banging against the old wood before I could think twice.

The groan of a bedframe sounded from within. Heavy footsteps thudded toward the door. He would not be happy with me for waking him. Not when he needed to be rested and ready for a fight tomorrow.

The door flew open, so fast that the breeze from it had a few stray hairs on my head flying in all directions. Ryder appeared in the doorway, squinting in the light of the corridor. I honestly felt sorry for him. He looked *defeated.* His hair was in a ruffled mess. The bags beneath his eyes told me that even if he was sleeping when I knocked, it wasn't true rest. The hand he gripped the door with sported chewed fingernails and cracked knuckles. His skin even looked a shade lighter than its usual deep brown color.

"What?" he croaked. Even his voice sounded monotone and drained of life.

I wondered how many scenarios he envisioned to keep him from sleep. I had no doubt he was imagining every single thing that the Vermillion families could be doing to Bryce this very moment. After hearing her story from her first time there, I didn't want to know.

"I know why the Vermillions want Bryce," I said quickly.

A spark of interest lit up his eyes. His hooded gaze became attentive. He opened the door a bit more, leaning against the threshold. "Go on."

"She's an *elemefnis*, but she's a fire-bender."

He raised a brow. "I noticed."

"They're rare."

"Indeed."

I realized that I hadn't yet said anything he didn't already know. "They will sell her to Morrighan, the Primal of Destruction." I gave him a short summary of all that I'd read. I made sure to include Morrighan's habit of capturing mystics and absorbing their power. Then, I told him the last bit. Orange flames burn in the eyes of the Primal of Destruction.

"When Bryce calls to the flames, do her eyes glow?"

Ryder rubbed his eyes. "This doesn't make sense."

"Ryder, do her eyes glow like a fire burns within them?" I asked, my voice raising.

He drew his hand away from his face. With an uneasy look in his eye, he nodded. I felt the breath leave my lungs as I took a step back. "Then she's a descendant of Morrighan. She was born from the power of destruction. The Vermillions will sell Bryce to the primals, and Morrighan will take Bryce's power before killing her."

Ryder was quiet for a long moment. He looked me up and down, considering. His eyes shifted to look over my shoulder. "This must've been what father knew. They will do the same to you," he warned.

I turned to see two silver eyes staring at me through the darkness, and I jumped out of my skin. "By the Kings!" I screeched. "Can't you ever announce yourselves? All you have to do is cough or scuff your boot or something."

"I think it's 'by the gods' now," Ryder murmured.

The Reaper ignored both of us. He walked forward to stand beside his brother and placed a gloved hand over Ryder's calloused ones. Ryder searched his sibling's eyes. I watched, bewildered, as Ryder read everything the Reaper wanted to say in his eyes. "You say you can handle yourself, but you've never faced something like this before," he said.

The Reaper's hand tightened over Ryder's.

"I refuse to let you surrender yourself to this. There has to be another way."

To my absolute shock, the Reaper raised his hand to his face. He had his back turned to me, and his hood up as always, so I couldn't see his face, but I watched as he lowered his hand again. A hand that now held a mask. Ryder was looking down at his brother's unveiled face.

If I took two wide strides to my left, I'd be able to see what Ryder saw. I'm not sure what stopped me. I stayed put.

Ryder's eyes widened. It seemed that he too didn't expect to see his brother's unmasked face tonight. A few second passed, and then the Reaper's free hand wrapped around the back of Ryder's neck. The brothers pressed their brows together. Ryder closed his eyes, his expression pained. I realized that this might be the last time they embrace one another.

"This is heartwarming," Ace drawled from beside me, causing me to jump once more. He wasn't even looking at me or the brothers before us. Instead, he inspected one of his axes, watching the tip of it glimmer in the torch light.

"Does anyone around here announce their presence when they walk into a room?" I grumbled.

"But it's so fun to see you riled."

"I'm trained now, so maybe riling me is a poor decision."

Ace looked up from his blade. His lips tipped up into a smirk. The intrigued, determined expression that settled on his face sent a shiver down my spine. "Is that a challenge?"

I gulped down the knot in my throat. "A warning." The words sounded softer than I intended.

His smirk widened into a wicked grin. He took another step closer, until his face was only inches away from mine. "Do it again." His voice

227

deepened with the words. It had goosebumps rising over my skin.

My focus was drawn away, however, when the Reaper brushed past the two of us, his mask covering his features once more. He glanced at us, and something like humor glistened in his eyes. Still, he did not falter as he made for his room. The shadows of the hall reached out for him as he went, as if they were comforted by his presence.

The sound of his boots scraping against the floors soon faded away. He disappeared into the dark corridor, and the faint click of a door shutting echoed through the hall. Ryder, Ace, and I stood together in silence, watching the shadows return to their place.

"I'm surprised he took off the mask with us so close," I whispered.

Ryder's expression was grim. "He did not take off the mask."

My brows drew together. "But I saw it. He–"

"He took off the physical mask, but that is not the only mask my brother wears. When all the masks come off, that is when we should run. That's when the power he's been given will ravage the world."

Ace and I exchanged a glance.

Ryder nodded. "When our Da died, the Reaper did not grieve for him. He put on the mask the same night. He let rage steer him, forge his path, ever since. When the mask comes off, the façade will crumble with it. With this new power that he can hardly control, I worry for anyone who might be near when it all comes crashing down."

"I think I'd like to see it," Ace murmured. "Think it will happen tomorrow night?"

I rolled my eyes. *Adrenaline seeking brute.*

Ryder's gaze returned to us. "I don't know. But I do know that the Reaper plans to kill every single member of the Vermillion family." He clenched his jaw. "Even if that means getting himself killed in the process."

CHAPTER 20

Bryce

I woke gradually. Each of my senses came back one by one. Touch was first. I knew my back was pressed against something cold. I knew I was in an uncomfortable position, standing, with my arms stretched over my head. My toes barely able to touch the ground.

Sound came second. I heard distant wailing, and the maddening rhythm of consistent droplets of water, as if someone left a faucet on just enough for a drip. I could hear the scuffling of boots against stone. It was close, only a few feet away.

As I drew in a deep breath, I inhaled anything but fresh air. It was cold enough to dry out the back of my throat. It smelled of mildew, earthy and damp. There was another stench in the air, but I couldn't quite place it. I only knew that it had my nose scrunching up in distaste.

I tried to open my eyes, but my eyelids still felt too heavy. I needed another moment before I would be able to force them open. Besides, I wanted to stay in the darkness for a little while longer.

Ryder's warm lips pressed against my neck. He must've woken before me. A soft smile graced my lips, and I tilted my head to give him more access.

He smiled against my skin, and it–

It felt *wrong*.

The lips pressed to me were dry and cracked. The breath smelled of ale and something worse, like garlic or onion. There was nothing gentle about the teeth dragging over my skin, or the fingers digging into the bone of my hip.

"Welcome home, love," his gravelly voice drawled.

That voice.

I knew that voice.

It haunted me in my sleep. I heard it on the darkest of nights. It made me tremble. It had bile creeping up my throat, and my stomach turning over as my heart dropped.

Eligor.

Last night's events came flooding back to me all at once. Too many emotions clawed for my attention. Sadness, anger, shock, and fear. Fear won, as it always managed to do when Eligor was around. I tried to summon the fire to my palms, but nothing came. I felt cold, empty.

"There is no fire. There never will be again. I hope you like the cold. I asked my father to close the vents to this room, just for you."

I could pretend all I wanted to be a warrior. I could play dress-up, and wish to be a lady of the court, or a princess who lost my way. None of it mattered, though. At the end of the day, I was nothing. Nothing but a girl who was too weak to fight for herself when it mattered most. I let him win, and I would never be able to change that. The walls I put up, the icy exterior of sarcasm and banter, it all melted away in the presence of Eligor.

With him, I was a hollow shell of a person. I had no voice, and I certainly had no fight left in me. He made my knees weak and my skin numb. I hated him more than I hated dry blood beneath my fingernails, or turtlenecks, which says a lot. But I couldn't bring myself to fight him. He broke me already.

I couldn't let him know how he made me feel, however. So, when my eyes flew open, and I saw him standing before me, I willed my expression to remain completely blank. I retreated into my mind, becoming something, *anything*, other than myself.

He was the largest of the Vermillion brothers. He had a bull neck and a solid build. He had more muscle than anything else, including personality and intelligence. He also happened to have the largest hooked nose I'd ever seen. It must have been broken before without healing correctly, judging by its odd angle. His dark hair was slicked back with so much gel that it looked *wet*. The pungent smell of spice instantly put an ache in my temples.

He pulled away from my neck, but his hand remained on my hip. I tried to keep my lip from curling in disgust when I caught a glimpse of his yellowing teeth. You'd think that with all the money in the world, the guy would be able to keep up with basic dental hygiene or pay someone to do it for him.

I pulled on the chains that shackled me to the wall, but it was no use. Each time I thrashed against them, they stretched me farther. My back was arched against the stone wall to the point where each movement was pained. My entire body ached, with all my weight now reliant on the chains. My wrists felt like they might break off at any moment. I had no idea how long I'd been hanging from the wall, but by the ache in each of my limbs, I knew it was at least a few hours.

"I got these just for you," he said. He reached up and pulled on the chains. They stretched me again, forcing a cry from me as my arms were jerked even further apart. It felt like they might be ripped from my body with one more movement. The sound of my pain made Eligor's smile grow. "Each time you struggle, they pull harder. The cuffs on your wrists will squeeze down more and more, until your blood flow is restricted, and you dislocate both of your arms."

I instantly relaxed in the chains as best I could and leaned my head back against the wall.

"If you're good, I'll think about letting you down."

"*Fuck* you."

"I hoped you'd say that." He turned his back to me, walking off toward the shadowed corner of the cell. With his attention directed elsewhere, I surveyed my surroundings. We were in the same cell I'd occupied last year. I recognized the scratches on the wall. I carved into the cobblestone walls with a rock I found on the floor. Each vertical mark counted for one day I spent in this prison.

An arched door of iron bars locked me in, and allowed me to see into the dim hallway, lined with more cells going back as far as the eye could see. The rest of the cell was nothing more but four stone walls. There was no window or natural light. The little light we did have came from the torches in the hall.

Eligor turned back to me. I looked past him and saw that he had a tray of knives, varying in shapes and sizes, sitting atop a small table in the corner. He held a scalpel in one hand, tapping it against the other.

He cocked his head, looking me up and down. "Tell me, what kind of woman leaves her own sister to die?"

A wave of crippling fear swept through me, bringing a chill to my bones. I couldn't keep the tremor out of my voice. "What did you do to her?"

"I did nothing. Azazel, on the other hand..." A dark chuckle left him. "He had his fun."

My fists clenched beneath the cuffs. "I'm going to kill you all. I'll watch you burn."

He groaned, his eyes falling closed. "I love it when you do that. Makes me want to skip all the foreplay and get straight to the best part." He took another step forward. "Want to know the funniest part?" he whispered into my ear, pressing himself against me. His fingers snaked into the golden locks of my hair and pulled. My head was jerked back, exposing my neck to him. "She said the exact same thing."

He raised the scalpel, dragging it along my arm. "Her screams were so pretty. Almost as pretty as yours. But I loved it when she begged him to stop. And on the best nights, she'd call out for you. She truly believed you'd come back for her."

My entire body shook. I don't know if it was from rage or guilt, but either way, it pleased Eligor.

"She lasted longer than I thought. It took Az a few months to break her. After one, she stopped fighting. After two, she stopped screaming. And after three..." he bit down on the shell of my ear, hard enough to draw blood. I had to bite my tongue to keep from crying out. "After three she gave up all hope that you'd return for her."

I said nothing. I had no witty comeback this time.

He smiled again, pressing down on the scalpel a bit harder. Blood dripped down my arms. "Az did all sorts of things to her. Things I'd never even dreamed about before. What do you say we try some out, love?"

Prick.

"Where is she?"

"Az enjoys a good hunt. He let her go before he killed her. He found her in the South Side. She was causing a scene trying to find you. But he drove a dagger clean through her heart, and we left her body in an alley, hoping you'd find her."

I couldn't breathe. My lungs refused to take in air. The lump in my throat grew to be painful as I held back tears. I finally had my answer to the question I'd been too afraid to ask aloud. My sister was dead. They killed her and– and it was my fault. Now, I'd be punished by meeting the same fate. I was going to die here, just as I should have the first time.

"The Reaper will come for me. Ryder will come for me."

"We're counting on it, love."

If he called me *love* one more time...

"Is that his name? *Ryder?* Do you honestly think he can protect you?"

I opened my mouth to say something– anything. But I snapped it shut. There was nothing I could say that would end this. I would only make him angrier, and that would only bring me more suffering. But maybe the suffering and pain is what I deserved. If I'd accepted it the first time around, Alina would still be here.

"Oh no, don't go quiet on me now, love," Eligor purred. His hold on my hair tightened, making the throbbing pain in my scalp more prominent. "You've always been my favorite. You could never hold that indecent tongue of yours.

You had such a spark in you." He laughed, drawing away from me. "Maybe that was the wrong choice of words."

I refused to meet his eyes. I stared down at the stone floor, expressionless.

"Don't fret. We're going to have so many good times together. Don't you remember all the fun we had?"

He licked away the tear that slid down my cheek. His tongue pressed against my chin and followed the tear's salty trail up to just beneath my eye. I gagged at the touch and tried to squirm away, but his hand left my hair and came to snap my chin into place, his fingers digging into my skin. The fiery pain sank into the nerves of my jaw. My eyes watered in answer.

Cold metal pressed against my cheek. I glanced down to see the scalpel he pressed into me, hard enough to sting but not to draw blood.

He saw the way my chest caught. One side of his lips curled up in a revolting half-smirk. "I'll carve you up real nice and then maybe I'll let you run back to him, so you can see the revulsion on his face once he sees you, sees what I've done to you. When he rejects you, you'll have nothing left, no one to live for. Only me."

The scalpel trailed down my cheek, across my jaw, and down my neck. The touch of the cold tool was so light that it nearly tickled. He wanted it that way. He wanted to toy with me.

"Where should I begin? Here?" He used the blade to slice my tunic open, and he glided it over the smooth skin of my breasts.

The scalpel continued its path downward. "Or maybe even here?" He slid it over the inside of my thigh. He drew it in a circle, bringing it back up. "Or–"

"Eligor," a hardened voice called from the hall. Kalieth stood there, his face twisted with quiet anger. He surveyed the scene in front of him with a clenched jaw. "Enough."

"Is it, brother?" Eligor asked. He dramatically dropped the scalpel back on his tray and faced Kalieth. He crossed his arms over his chest, his eyes narrowing. If looks could kill, Kalieth would be limp on the ground. I decided I wouldn't mind that much. But the younger brother remained breathing, staring down Eligor, whose lip curled as he said, "If I didn't know better, I'd say you've gone soft. Why should you care what I do with my pets?"

Kalieth stood firm. "If the others see one hair misplaced on her head, the trade will go sour. She remains unharmed in her *temporary* stay here."

Eligor rolled his eyes. His gaze travelled back to me, however, and another wicked grin displayed his yellowing teeth. He adjusted my tunic and winked. "Don't worry," he whispered into my ear. "I will have my fun with you, today, tomorrow, or a decade from now."

With the words still hanging heavy in the air, Eligor left my cell. He bumped shoulders with Kalieth as he went. The brothers exchanged a heated glare before Eligor finally left the corridor entirely. Kalieth remained standing outside of the cell. He didn't move for another long moment. When he was sure his brother was far away, he came inside.

The second he stood before me, I spat on his face. Admittedly, it was a childish move, but with my hands chained above my head, and my feet barely touching the floor, it was the only thing I could think to do to accurately express my anger.

He had the audacity to look shocked. With raised brows and wide eyes, he lifted two fingers to his cheek and wiped my saliva away. He looked down at his glistening fingers, his nose scrunching in disgust before his gaze met mine again. "That was rude."

A rush of air that might've been a shocked laugh left my throat. I *knew* he did not just accuse *me* of being rude.

He studied my face. "You're angry with me?"

Angry? I was furious. Enraged. Infuriated. If steam could come billowing out of my nose, it would.

"Why don't you let me out of these cuffs and then I'll tell you whether or not I'm angry," I suggested sweetly.

He narrowed his eyes. "That seems like it would end badly for me."

"I'm not inclined to disagree."

"So, for my own safety, I think I'll leave the cuffs on."

An inhuman sound, almost like a growl, left me as I thrashed against the chains. I even went as far as snapping my teeth at him in hopes I could catch his nose or ear. Kalieth quickly jumped back before I could grasp any part of him. My body was jerked back against the wall as the chains tightened once more.

"Would you like to hear my explanation, or would you rather continue to act like a savage?" He had the nerve to look *bored.*

"I will get free of these chains one way or another, and then I'm going to use that scalpel to carve out each of your eyes. Then I'll feed them to you as I carve my name into your chest, so that even in death your soul will be branded. Once I've had my fun, I'll cut off each of your limbs and leave you to bleed out, alone."

Kalieth arched a brow at me. "Are you done?"

Shock coursed through me at how unaffected he seemed. It was enough to have me pressing my lips together in confusion.

"While all that sounded like joyous fun, I think you might like my plan a bit better. It involves you returning to the group, the Reaper taking your place, and then me setting him loose so he can tear this place down from the inside. Are you interested?"

"You... you brought me here just to *trade* me back?"

He pressed his lips into a thin line. "Yes. I'm sorry it had to happen the way it did. I never wanted to blindside you."

240

I shook my head. "I'm more determined to kill you now than I was two minutes ago."

"If you listen to my explanation, I'll buy you the entire contents of one of the stores on market street," he offered.

I narrowed me eyes. "Which store?"

"The Royal Court's Boutique."

I paused. "Fine."

"Will you behave if I let you out of those chains?"

"Did you really just ask me if I'll *behave?* I'm not a Kings' forsaken animal!"

He shot me a disbelieving look. "You just tried to bite me."

Oh. Right.

"I'll behave if I like what I hear."

The answer must've been good enough, because although he approached me cautiously, Kalieth withdrew a key from somewhere within the folds of his cloak. He watched me closely as he reached up to unlock the chains. I wondered if he feared that I might try to bite him again. I'd be lying if I said the thought didn't cross my mind.

The cuffs on my wrists popped open, and I immediately fell. Kalieth caught me before I could hit the floor, and slowly placed me down, where I slumped against the wall. I quickly realized I wouldn't be able to fight him if I tried. I couldn't feel my arms, except for a dull pain in my muscles. My legs were too weak to stand on. I'd need a few minutes– maybe even an hour before blood crept back into all my fingers and toes. Until then, I was helplessly crippled.

"Why? Why did you do this? If it was truly all part of your plan, why didn't you clue us in?" I asked.

"There was no time." His eyes met mine, the blue of them shining and rippling like sunlight reflecting off the sea's surface. "And would you really have agreed to it if I asked? Would the Reaper?"

"Would I have agreed to being abducted and taken back to the literal root of all my trauma? Hmmm..."

"Yeah, that's why. My father and Alastor were in the library last night. They pulled me away while you and the others were occupied with Eichi. They would've killed you all then and there if I didn't come up with something. So, I made a plan."

"Drugging me and taking me prisoner?"

"*Temporarily* using your presence to observe my family's behavior. I now know that my father lied about you, the mystics, and this prison. Probably about everything else too."

"And if you'd discovered that I was the liar? Would you have let them torture me? Kill me?"

Kalieth met my gaze again. It took him a second too long to answer. "No."

"Why didn't you take all of us prisoner? You had us trapped in that library."

"I convinced them that the Reaper was too powerful, too cunning. I told them this plan would ensure his surrender."

"So, you've chosen your side then?"

He gave me a curt nod. "I won't let my family hurt anyone else. The trade will go down tonight. The Reaper will come, I will let him go, and I'll find out who killed my sister."

As the last words left his lips, I straightened against the stone. "Sister?"

I couldn't help but think of Alina, and the fact that she would not be one of the refugees of this place. She never left this hell. She died in it. I would never be able to change that.

Kalieth nodded. "She died in the warehouse fire here in the North Side. Someone left her there to die. My father told me it was the Reaper, but now I know it wasn't. The Reaper will kill my father, and before he dies I'll hear the truth."

"Does the Reaper know of this plan?"

"I didn't exactly have time to tell him."

"So, you just assume that he'll let you live long enough to explain? That Ryder will?"

"Ryder doesn't scare me. The Reaper may have once. But now..." he shook his head. "I don't know."

I laughed. I couldn't stop myself. It sounded strange, even to my own ears. But that look in Kalieth's eyes– it was the same one I would see in my own reflection during the dark period with

Ryder. Loneliness, confusion, and something more. Another emotion that overpowered the others. "What's the next step in your brilliant plan?"

"To keep you and Eligor far away from one another. Whatever he drugged you with really took its toll. You slept a long time. The sun is setting. It's nearly time for the trade."

"Kalieth, if this ends the way we want it to, you'll lose everything. Your family, your home, and your inheritance. Are you ready for that?"

A soft smile tipped up the corners of his lips. "They aren't my family, and this was never my home," he said. "I didn't know it until I met the five of you. I didn't know that siblings were meant to protect and support one another, like the Reaper and Ryder do. I didn't know that a family could transcend the idea of shared blood. I– I don't know. Suddenly I'm a part of this group that I can rely on. That I can trust. So, yes, the Reaper will kill my father, and maybe even my siblings, but he won't be killing my family."

Alina came to my mind again, but I willed the memories to stay in the locked chest in the darkest part of my mind. I reached down and squeezed Kalieth's hand, at least, squeezed it as much as I could with the little feeling I had in my arms.

"Right," he said, clearing his throat. He stood and walked to the cell door. "Try not to die before the trade. Eligor's feeling touchy today."

My lips twitched up. "Death is not here for me tonight."

CHAPTER

21

Kalieth

My father refused to come with us for the trade. He locked himself in his office and sent all six of his sons out to do his dirty work for him. But he'd taken the time out of his busy schedule to see us off, and demand that we bring the Reaper back alive. My father told us that he wanted to be the one to end the Reaper, and if any of us killed him first, we'd meet the same fate.

My siblings, Bryce, and I made it to the South Side of the city, to the rooftop where I'd first met the Reaper, without exchanging a single word. I don't know why I assumed something would be said. After all, we have nothing in common. Only this. The mission.

We reached the rooftop, and my brothers fanned out along the far railing. Eligor and I stayed in the middle, holding Bryce, who was gagged and blindfolded. To discourage the Reaper from trying anything, I held a syringe to the inside of Bryce's wrist, and Eligor pressed a gun to her temple. The fact that the syringe was filled with a placebo, and I emptied Eligor's gun prior to this would remain unknown to everyone except for Bryce and me. She was in no danger, but I needed the others to believe that she was. Otherwise, they'd fight, and my plan would be ruined.

We waited in silence. The tension in the air was thick enough to be crushing. It felt like I dove too deep into a body of water, and the pressure was building by the minute. The only sounds were muffled music from bars and distant clicking of hooves against stone. There were a few instances of my brothers reaching for their weapons when a group of companions passed by on the street, their shouts and laughter carrying through the night. We waited for nearly an hour and still no one came.

"You were wrong. They don't care about her enough to walk into this trap," Alastor spat at me. "We've wasted precious time."

"Hear that, love?" Eligor muttered into Bryce's ear. "No one's coming for you. You're mine now."

A whimper sounded from Bryce, muffled by the gag. I couldn't tell whether she was acting, or if she was genuinely scared that this plan would fail. I was starting to lean toward the latter myself.

"They will come." The words rang out with confidence, but I honestly didn't know if I was trying to convince my brothers or myself.

The minutes continued to pass by. The temperature dropped as the moon rose higher in the sky. The chill began to seep through my cloak, into my bones. I could feel it like a spider made of pure ice crawling across my skin. With each touch of its legs, goosebumps erupted across my arms and back. It wasn't until I started to shiver that I realized the cold was not from the weather alone.

Thunder rumbled in the distance, coming closer. The ground shook in its wake. Winds swept through us, weaving through my fingers, and pushing my hair away from my brow. My brothers, confused and weary, reached for their weapons. But it wasn't thunder at all. It was the sound of power– a power that had grown and evolved since I'd last seen it. It shook the ground. It shook the very earth beneath the stone roads. It could level the building I stood on, disrupt the waves of the Atris Ocean, or even cause an avalanche far into the Northern kingdom.

Even with the moon shining down on us, I had to squint to see my brothers in the corners of the rooftop. That all changed when shadows, rising from the ground like a tidal wave from the sea, took away all hope of sight. The rippling wave towered above us, lingering for a moment before it came crashing down.

The shadows enveloped us, bringing freezing temperatures and haunting whispers with it. An overwhelming feeling of despair gripped me when the black mist surrounded me– once I breathed it in. I felt fear, pain, and hopelessness. It was paralyzing. It felt like a crushing weight on my chest, seizing every cell in my body and making me want to collapse to my knees. It forced the air out of my lungs, and even though I wasn't physically suffocating, I felt as though I couldn't breathe.

Fuck. We're dead.

Despite everything, I kept a firm grip on Bryce's arm. The shadows were so thick, that I couldn't see her through the darkness, but I felt her relax in my hold.

"What the hell is this?" Eligor yelled. He had to be close. Only a foot away at the most.

"He's here." It was all I could say.

"Show yourself!" Eligor yelled into the endless night. "Recall your power or I'll decorate the roof with her brain!"

"Consider me shaking in my boots," someone called to our left. I recognized Ace's voice.

Someone else called from the right, "why don't you at least let them *think* we're intimidated. We might get Bryce out of this *alive.*" Quinn. It was Quinn.

"We'll get her out alive. It's *this* one I'd worry about," Ryder said, his voice guttural. He sounded close. Too close. As the last word left his mouth, I felt a curved dagger slide across my throat. A warning. He was behind me, but I was too focused on the pair of silver orbs in front of me, drifting closer, like twin stars in infinite night.

My nose scrunched with effort as I squinted to see better. But I froze at the sound of a gun being cocked.

"I mean it," Eligor warned. "Pull your power back, or I crack her skull open."

There was a pause, then the shadows whispered and sighed as they drew back. They wisped past me. I shivered as they brushed over my skin and drifted through me on a cool breeze. The dagger at my throat lowered. The presence at my back left.

It took a moment for my eyes to adjust once more to the moonlight. It glinted off Ryder's dagger, and it had their black cloaks glimmering. The twin stars, glowing silver, were the Reaper's eyes. I'd never seen them so bright.

Both sides closed ranks. My brothers formed a semi-circle around Eligor, Bryce, and me. Ryder stood to the right of his brother while Ace and Quinn came to stand on either side of the pair. Silence ensued.

"You threatened?" Ace said, rocking on his feet. He was more enthusiastic than normal, probably because the idea of breaking my brothers' noses or cracking their teeth gave him more joy than anything else.

"You know how this goes. The Reaper for this one. Step out of line, and I pull the trigger. If you kill me before I can shoot, Kalieth will inject her with that poison, and she'll be dead before she hits the ground. Kill Kalieth, and I pull the trigger, either way–"

Ace tossed his head back and blew out a breath that had his lips audibly smacking together. "Gods, I'm bored already. We get it. We move and Bryce dies. Let's all move on."

Eligor's grip on the gun tightened.

249

Ryder's eyes narrowed on my brother. "If there's a single mark on her, there's nowhere you can hide from me."

"Marks?" Eligor repeated, a smirk snaking over his face. "Like these?" He twisted Bryce to her side and ran his fingers over her arm, where several gashes were already scabbed over.

Ryder took a menacing step forward, but the Reaper pulled him back before he could do anything he'd regret.

"*This* is the team that's been terrorizing us for the past year?" Alastor scoffed in utter disbelief. "You've got to be joking."

"You want a review card?" Ace grunted.

Bryce, unable to say anything through the gag, groaned in annoyance. The sound snapped everyone back into their right minds.

"Let's get this over with. Reaper, walk forward with your hands where we can see them. Once you're chained, Bryce goes free," I said. All my focus went into keeping my voice steady and convincing.

"And *you*," Ryder added, his gaze moving to me. "I'm going to–"

I nodded. "You're going to kill me? Believe me, Bryce already gave me the talk." My eyes travelled to the Reaper, who watched me intently. When our gazes collided, a spark of something flashed through his eyes. He walked forward with his arms raised.

I nodded to Alastor, who took my place by Bryce so that I could approach the Reaper with great caution. I disarmed him first, fastening his belt around my own waist. The obsidian blades were far too valuable to be lost in the Vermillion family treasury. Once they were in my possession, I chained the Reaper's hands together behind his back.

As I walked him behind the line my brothers formed, I pressed a thin piece of wire into his gloved palm, a tool he could use to pick the lock later. He gave no reaction other than closing his fist around the metal and sliding it up the inside of his sleeve. We walked to the edge of the rooftop as my brothers closed in, forming a circle around us, trying to keep the Reaper contained while also forming a defensive line against the rest of his team.

Once we reached the edge of the rooftop, I turned, keeping a firm hold on the Reaper's arm. I looked to Eligor, who was glaring daggers at Ryder. "Let her go Eligor," I warned.

My older brother hesitated, and I thought he might try to go against my plan. But he ultimately thought better of whatever it was he wanted to do. He practically threw Bryce to Ryder. She fell to the ground hard, a gasp escaping her lips. Ryder was there instantly, untying her gag.

"I'll be back for what's mine," Eligor warned.

Ryder glared at him with a fierceness in his eyes I'd never seen before. It was a look I would've cowered from. When he spoke, his voice turned low and menacing. "Good. It will be the day you die."

251

"You sure that can't be tonight?" Ace asked as he cracked his knuckles.

I didn't stay long enough for Ace to get bold and attack. Three of my brothers came with me to escort the Reaper back to the estate. Az and Eligor, the oldest and strongest, stayed behind to make sure we weren't followed.

The Reaper walked with wide strides; his chin held high. I wished I could read his thoughts. After all, tonight was the night he'd been waiting for. Tonight, the Reaper would face my father. One way or another, all of this conflict would come to an end.

CHAPTER 22

Kalieth

We crossed into the North Side of the city, toward the family estate. It was quite a hike from the South Side but taking horses would've drawn too much attention. I didn't mind the walk much. It gave me time to think about everything.

I found myself continuously glancing at the Reaper. I tried to discern an emotion from his hooded gaze, but I saw nothing. He walked at a leisurely pace, keeping his chin up high. I wondered how he planned to kill my father. I wondered if he was prepared to die trying.

He endured my brothers' taunts and jabs. He did nothing when they pushed him down or punched him in the gut. He simply picked himself up and continued to put one foot in front of the other, with his eyes fixed on the Vermillion family estate in the distance.

Children. My brothers were children. I nearly cringed at the fact that there was a time when I would've acted this way. I would've beat an enemy down after their capture and taunted them for coming after my family. It's dishonorable behavior, and I was blind to that until the Reaper. I was blind to a lot of things before the Reaper.

As if sensing where my thoughts had gone, the assassin looked away from the looming mansion. His gaze of silver flames turned to me, and I *felt* warmth pass over my skin. I saw no fear within his eyes. I only saw hunger, a need to unleash the power he'd been hiding for so long. His gaze left as quick as it found me, and the loss of it felt like leaving a warm bath on a cold night. A chill crept up my spine, pricking my skin with thousands of invisible needles.

We drew closer to the estate. It brought a strange feeling to my chest to walk through the iron gates again. I used to nod to the guards and stride through them with pride. But now I felt anger and shame when I glanced at the family crest carved into the stone wall surrounding the gates. It stood for oppression and lies, nothing more.

The guards saluted us as we walked through the gates. Some of them broke formation to try to get a good look at the Reaper. Others seemed to shy away, as if they knew what he was capable of. My brothers remained oblivious to all around them, laughing and cheering amongst themselves. We waited by the gates for Azazel and Eligor to rejoin us. Luckily, they were only a few minutes behind.

"Were we followed?" Alastor asked.

Eligor snickered. "Would we be here if you were? Those four will be too preoccupied to come after us."

The words, and the twisted smile Eligor wore on his face, put a sick feeling in my stomach. Even the Reaper seemed to still. "I thought I told you to leave the others be," I said, my voice lowering in warning.

Eligor looked me up and down suspiciously. "I don't take orders from you, Kal. What I do with my pet is none of your concern. It never will be," he spat.

"What did you do to Bryce?" I asked again, taking a step forward. Consequences be damned.

"Catch feelings in your time with the misfits?"

I matched his wicked expression with my own, lacing my voice with as much arrogant confidence as I could muster. "I wanted her alive to bring back when all this is over. I'm still a bounty hunter, Eligor, I need *something* to hunt. What else am I meant to gift to you for the Dragon's Feast?"

Eligor watched me closely. Tension was thick in the air as my other brothers waited. After a long moment, a feline smile broke out over Eligor's face. He took another step and clasped my shoulder. "Not to worry, Kal. The poison I injected won't kill her... hopefully. Although, I did give it ample time to work into her system before we let her go." He laughed at his own words and then continued on his way, leading the group toward the main house.

255

I fell in line beside the Reaper. I kept an arm at the Reaper's back, occasionally pretending to drag him along as we walked up the drive. Our estate was known for its eerie feel, with black oak trees planted on either side of the main path, their branches twisting sharply into the night. A slight fog was setting in, dampening the grass and my boots. The horses whinnied and stamped from somewhere within the large stable directly to the right of the main house. The animals could sense the dangerous power that drew closer with each step. Their instincts told them to run from it. If I listened hard enough, mine might've told me the same.

The moon broke through the clouds from somewhere behind the estate, casting its shadow over all of us. The sharp spires and snarling gargoyles didn't aid the house in appearing welcoming, nor did the chipped obsidian stone columns or the numerous statues of armed soldiers that towered over our heads. Each one was placed on a pedestal between the trees along the drive. They were carved from marble with their swords hugged close to their chest and heads bowed. Their features were so realistic that they looked like they would come to life at any moment. It wasn't the statues with faces frozen in battle cries that irked me, it was the one's with expressions of utter despair and longing. If they were to come to life, I imagined they would wail and weep. They'd roam the grounds like lost spirits, searching for something. I had a nightmare about it once as a child, and I avoided looking at them for an entire season afterward. The thought had the hairs on my arms rising. I picked up my pace.

The entire estate stretched over one hundred acres. The main house stood before us. It was built by the same architects who created the king's castle in the Capital. Looking at it with a pair of fresh eyes, it's nothing more than a gross waste of space and resources. My father demanded to be addressed as a royal, and he built himself a castle. I wondered if he also had a crown to wear when he stared at himself in the mirror.

Guards were stationed by every door and window. Each one armed with two broadswords, one on each shoulder. My father would not risk losing the Reaper. He hired extra help just for tonight. Some of them wore the Vermillion family crest, but others wore cloaks and tunics. Those not dressed in uniform were hired mercenaries and thugs. We called them sellswords. Normally, they were despised for having no honor or loyalty. They traded themselves to whoever paid the highest price. My father was either very desperate or expecting war to come to his doorstep.

The guards opened the large set of double doors for us. The warm air of the house, and the scent of the Vermillion family, hit me immediately. The scent of our estate, like citrus, was overpowered by bleach and polishing chemicals. The marble floors and stone columns of the front room were freshly cleaned. My father was preparing for the annual Dragon's Feast ball. It typically occurred before the first bloom of spring, but this year it was late. I assumed that was also thanks to the Reaper. It took time to convince the Vermillion family associates that their travels to Shadieh would be safe.

A fire crackled in the hearth between the two twisting staircases leading to the upper levels of the house. A balcony, decorated by stone bannisters with intricate patterns and symbols carved along them, connected the two stairwells and formed a corridor. The corridor, adorned with portraits of each of my family members, stretched in both directions. The bedchambers were found up there, but that would not be a part of the Reaper's tour tonight.

On the first floor, a set of doors sat to the left and right. One led into the ball room. The other led into my father's private office. A large statue stood in the middle of the foyer. It was a beautiful carving of a young woman dressed in royal attire, holding a torch high. The torch she held was made of true metal, and within it a real fire burned to light the room. It was meant to represent freedom and light our way through dark times. As long as the fire burned, the Vermillion family would be enlightened to truth and justice.

Whatever the hell that means.

The Reaper eyed the statue with raised brows. He gave me a side-eye glance as if to say *"Really?"* I had to hide the twitch of my lips.

Once all of us were through the front doors, the guards immediately escorted us into the ball room. They swung the doors open with a bit too much force. They hit the walls with a loud bang. The sound echoed through the entire house. It also drew my father's attention away from the cloth samples he studied. His gaze settled on our prisoner. His lips stretched into a wide grin. He lifted his arms in a prideful sweeping gesture.

258

"Welcome Reaper. It's an honor to finally meet you. I dressed my best for you." And he had. He wore an expensive, gold-threaded tunic, made by the king's tailor, no doubt. He also wore tight dress pants and a blazer that sported the Vermillion family crest.

The Reaper said nothing. By my brothers' hands, he was forced to his knees in front of my father as the servants in the ball room scurried out, closing the doors behind them.

Xaphan glanced at my siblings. "Well done, my sons. I trust you didn't have much trouble?"

Darcel and Tynan both jumped at the opportunity to tell dear old father what happened. "Kal's plan worked like a charm, but you'd never believe it!" Darcel exclaimed.

"It was like the night itself came alive. It surrounded us, and we couldn't see a thing!" Tynan added.

"It was suffocating," Darcel said.

Then chaos ensued. All of my brothers began to speak at once. Their voices rose higher and higher as they tried to be heard by my father.

My father listened intently. How he deciphered a single word from the jumbled mess of voices, I had no idea. But he understood a good amount, judging by the change in his demeanor. The smirk faded from his face. His jaw became set, his brows pinching together with unease and irritation. His gaze settled on the Reaper as his eyes narrowed suspiciously.

His eyes suddenly flew wide. His lips parted on a gasp. "You fools!"

He didn't have time to say anything else before night burst through the room. The last thing I saw was the Reaper snapping the metal chains that bound him in half with nothing but force. He didn't need the lock pick I'd given him; he only took it to show me that he understood my intentions.

Shadows exploded from the Reaper's palms. They shot in all directions, aiming to douse the torches first. All warmth in the entirety of the estate was stolen away. If I could see, I'd bet condensation poured out of my nose and mouth with each breath I took. The sudden change in temperature had pins and needles piercing my skin all over my body. It physically *hurt* to stand in the shadows, to breath them in.

Just an hour ago, despair weighed the shadows. Breathing them in meant feeling sorrow and isolation. Now, something else laced the tendrils of darkness. It burned the throat. It ran through my veins and tensed my muscles. It stirred deep in my chest.

Rage.

It was rage. Absolute. Undeniable. It festered and burned. It gave the shadows a painful edge, and beneath it, below the surface of anger, there was still despair. It seemed that the sorrow was always there, faint but present.

My brothers screeched and bumped into one another. The called to each other, trying to find their way in the dark. I heard the slide of metal as they drew their swords. I opened my mouth to tell them to keep quiet, but I snapped it shut again when I was faced with two stars shining in the darkness. Two stars I now recognized as the Reaper's eyes. They drifted toward me through the void of nothing. They never faltered or slowed, which made me wonder if the Reaper could see perfectly well.

He approached in a few smooth strides. His eyes searched mine, and a cold talon of fear tore through my stomach for a split second. I thought he might kill me here and now. He reached forward and curled one of his hands around the hilt of my sword.

His sword. I realized. I took his belt on the rooftop. He was drawing his own sword.

The waxy feel of leather slid across my open hand. The Reaper put his hand in my own. I felt my brows pull together, looking into the twin stars in the endless night. They burned bright with determination, and after a long second, they turned away from me. He pulled me along with him, ignoring the fact that I was blindly tripping over my own feet.

We walked a fair distance across the room before he released me. He shoved a hand to my chest to steady me, and let it linger there for a moment.

Stay.

I obeyed. There wasn't much else I could do in the dark.

"Is this how the Reaper faces an enemy?" my father yelled into the darkness. "How dare you hide in the shadows like a coward! It seems the townspeople spoke lies when they said you fight with honor. I've been deceived!"

"*Lies.*"

The word was short. It came from somewhere to the left. The voice it was born from sounded guttural and raspy. It sounded like a thousand sicknesses infected the throat and the voice left behind did not match anything I knew to be human. It sent a wave of fear through me capable of weakening my knees and twitching my fingers. It seemed that the Reaper had a tongue after all.

"*Deceit.*"

The word sounded from my right this time. I squinted my eyes, straining to see in the dark, but it was no use. I could only listen, and what I heard was the voice of a grown man. It was strained and breathy from months of no use, but it belonged to a grown man. The same voice the Reaper shared with me in the Sombra mountain pass.

"*Honor.*"

A low chuckle followed. "Xaphan Vermillion, he who deceives an entire kingdom, speaks to me of lies and honor." The sounds of boots scuffling against the floor, and a door opening and closing echoed through the ball room. A silence followed before a snicker. "It seems two of your sons have abandoned you. Four to go."

"Cowards!" My father cried; his voice laced with rage. I couldn't be sure which of my brothers

262

fled, but I knew that they'd better keep running until the city is far behind them. The only place they could escape my father's wrath now would be the Northern Kingdom.

The shadows slowly began to recede. The smallest bit of torch light from a single source cast a warm glow across the stone floor. A bubble of light formed around my father. I stood just on the border, where my body was hidden in the swirling mist of black smoke that was the shadows. It was in a constant state of motion. It dissipated and thickened all at once. It whispered and circled.

My father stood in the center of the bubble. He stayed light on his feet with his sword drawn. The long blade of nyx steel had a hilt made from obsidian stone, with a gemstone of polished onyx at the top. Etched into the blade itself were ancient symbols from a foreign language. The first language.

Laughter and snickers came from all directions. The Reaper was everywhere at once. His voice echoed in an eerie, haunting sort of way. He planned it that way, though. I knew that somehow. I'd spent over a season with the Reaper, and so I knew that everything he did had a purpose. It was his first tactic for taunting my father.

"I've spent a year tearing your empire apart. I burned your warehouses. I sunk your ships. I set your money aflame. I estranged your associates, and I killed those who remained loyal to you. All of which I accomplished without uttering a single word." The Reaper finally stepped out of his sea of night. His hood, mask, gloves, and cloak remained intact.

My father stared at the Reaper through lowered brows. The dark circles beneath his eyes made his glare seem all the more menacing. "Who are you?" Each word was drawn out, spoken through clenched teeth.

His question went unanswered.

"They whisper of me in the streets. They tell tales of scars and burns, of a cut tongue and a sewed mouth. They say that if my voice is heard, it is because Death is near." The Reaper paused his circling. He tossed his obsidian blade between his hands. He cocked his head to the side. "They say all of this, and yet I never spoke once."

My father gripped his sword in a white-knuckled tight fist. "Who are you?" he repeated.

"Always the same question. *Who are you?* It's the wrong question to ask."

"Why have you done all this?"

"That's a better one. It has a simple answer. I've come to kill you because you killed my father. He discovered your secret, so you had him *silenced.* You cut out his tongue. You left him in a pool of his own blood to die on his farmlands." The Reaper spat the last few words out as though they tasted foul in his mouth.

Xaphan responded with a laugh. It was a joyous sound born deep in his chest, and it was loud enough to shake the skies. His head tossed back, and his arm relaxed so that his sword touched the floor. Once he was finished, he raised the blade to point it at the Reaper's throat. "You've done all of this for a dead man?"

"For him. For those who came before and after. For those still to come because of your deception."

"It's a cute story. I would say you could write a children's book about it, but it would not be appropriate. The ending is awfully violent," Xaphan replied. He lifted his free hand to grip his sword properly. He took up a fighting stance.

The Reaper squared his feet. "You're right. Children would be scarred to read of how I turned you inside out with your own sword. The sword you pried from my father's cold, dead hands and kept as a trophy."

The determined expression on my father's face was wiped away with the Reaper's words. His eyes flew wide. He looked down at the blade as though he saw it for the first time. "Your father's sword?"

The Reaper remained in his defensive position. "Starting to remember?"

My father's eyes darted between the Reaper and the swirling mass of shadows behind him. His parted lips slowly stretched upwards until his porcelain teeth showed in an evil grin. "I told myself it was a trick of the light. An illusion created by a talented enchanter. But it's true. You are the champion."

The mischievous light in the Reaper's eyes faded. There was no more amusement in them. He said nothing, but he kept his sword raised.

Xaphan laughed again. He threw his sword at the Reaper's feet. "Take it, then. I thought I might kill you with it tonight. Now I know that is impossible. But I'd like to see you try to drive it through my own heart. See what happens."

The Reaper did not move. His eyes did not leave my father. He did not dare look to the blade at his feet.

My father narrowed his eyes and cocked his head. His smile faded into a bold smirk. "You don't even know what you are, do you? What your father was?"

Again, the Reaper said nothing.

"Good. That will make this easy," he added. Xaphan smoothed wrinkles out of his tunic and picked an imaginary piece of lint off his sleeve. "Tell me, young assassin, do you know how to kill a god? Do you know how to inflict an injury on one?"

The Reaper became very still.

"No? Allow me to enlighten you."

White light lashed out from my father's hands. It was a dry, blinding light. I had to shield my eyes beneath the shade of my arm. Instinct told me to turn away, but I forced myself to look on as the light cast away all the shadows. Several long strands of it wrapped around the Reaper like the fingers of a hand. The light sank into him, and he went rigid.

When the light faded, and my eyes adjusted to the dim torchlight again, I saw the Reaper on his knees. His sword clattered to the ground beside him. His previously dark skin appeared white and pale as the light continued to swirl within him.

"I was going to kill you tonight. I planned to scatter pieces of you around the South Side to make an example of those who rise against me. But it seems my plan needs altercation. After all, there is a certain Queen in the North who would have my head if I don't hand you over," Xaphan said. He stood over the Reaper with his back turned to me. My remaining brothers, Nox, Alastor, Azazel, and Eligor, stood behind the Reaper.

Darcel and Tynan were the ones to run. My father surveyed his remaining sons before nodding to Az and Eligor. "Find your brothers. Bring them to me. In chains if you must."

Eligor and Azazel bowed their heads before turning on their heels and leaving the ball room.

My father's head turned to Alastor. "Send a raven to the Northern Kingdom. Tell the Eternal Queen that I've found her prize."

"Yes, father," Alastor murmured. He sent one more glare in the Reaper's direction before heading off toward Raven's Keep.

Alastor's footsteps echoed through the empty ball room before finally fading off.

"What did you do?" I found myself asking aloud. The cold shock of surprise faded into a numb sensation in my chest.

My father straightened. Slowly, he turned. His gaze found mine, and I stared into glowing

267

silver eyes, just like the Reaper's. He smiled at me, and strands of white light crackled in his irises. "I only paralyzed him. It won't last long. Be a lad and fetch the drearwood chains in my study. They're in the largest drawer of my desk."

I did not move. "H–how?"

My father looked back down to the masked assassin. Pride lifted his chin. "The Reaper may be a champion, but *I* am a *god*."

CHAPTER 23

Kalieth

My father used the drearwood chains to hang the Reaper from the ceiling. His boots hung nearly a foot off the ground while his arms were stretched over his head, angled away from his body on either side. He was confined to a small cell with stone walls and a single iron-barred door. Etched into the stone walls of his cell was a symbol. Two hands holding up the moon. The symbol of the gods. As if my father saved this cell for the Reaper– as if he knew all along.

I held the key to his chains in my hand, as well as the rusted brass one that opened the cell door. I watched closely from the hall as his chest rose and fell. He clutched the drearwood chains tight to try to take some of the pressure off his wrists. His neck was too weak to hold up his head. It rested uncomfortably against his chest. But relief coursed through me with each breath he took.

Breath in.

Breath out.

As long as the rise and fall of his chest continued, hope for the city would live on. Hope for peace lived on.

My father stood within the Reaper's cell. He looked up into the Reaper's eyes with curiosity. His hands were crossed behind his back while he paced the short length of the cell. "What do you think, Kal?" he called. One hand slowly reached for the Reaper's face. "Is it time to see who lies behind this mask?"

"No." The word left my mouth before I could stop it. I knew it was not the answer my father wanted to hear. Even the Reaper raised his head to look down on me, knowing that I'd just made an idiotic mistake.

I couldn't explain what I felt in that moment. But seeing my father's hand reaching to rip the Reaper's mask off his face... it sickened me. I couldn't bear to see it. I wanted nothing more than to know the face under the mask. But I wanted the Reaper to show me himself. I wanted the trust that would come with the reveal.

"No?" my father repeated as his brows knotted together.

I shifted uncomfortably on my feet. "I only meant that unveiling the Reaper alone in your dungeon would not be nearly as satisfactory as doing it in front of the whole city."

My father cocked his head. I'd gained his interest.

"If you wait for tomorrow, we can do it publicly. Unravel everything the Reaper has worked for by showing his true face. Show the people that they cannot hope to defeat the Vermillions, that the Reaper is nothing more than a vengeful man who failed."

An inhuman sound came from the Reaper as he thrashed against his chains. A sound that brought a smile to my father's lips. There was nothing more satisfactory to him than having control over others. He would do anything if it meant breaking the Reaper's spirit before his execution.

"Very well. You'll see to the preparations?" Xaphan asked. He turned away from the Reaper and left his cell. He walked down the hall and disappeared without another word.

My eyes found the drearwood chains once more. They would keep the Reaper powerless as long as they were in contact with his skin. Drearwoods, trees which grow where gods' blood is spilled, weakens their power until they're almost mortal. Almost.

The sight of the Reaper hanging helplessly affected me more than I ever thought possible. I was sent to kill him all those months ago. I was taught to hate him because he fought for the people, taught by the tyrant who kills and lies to keep control of an entire city. Now I was told to keep him in chains so that my family could keep their façade and offer the Reaper to the Queen in the North who would use his power for greater destruction.

Everything I'd ever done was for my family. I killed. I lied. I fought and I hunted. All along I did it so that I might gain my father's praise, so that I would bring honor to the family. But what honor was there in slavery and executions? What would I be fighting for?

I ripped the embroidered patch of cloth off my sleeve and tossed it to the ground. The Vermillion family crest landed in a small puddle a few paces away. It turned wet and dark, and then it sank beneath the water's surface until I couldn't see it anymore. When I threw down the crest, I rid myself of something else too. Something deeper. Something I couldn't touch or see. But it was gone. I felt the lightness in my chest; in my soul, and I knew something was gone. A darkness that plagued me for longer than I knew.

I walked forward with the rusted key in hand. I unlocked the cell door and stood before the Reaper. He narrowed his eyes at me, and for the first time since he'd been put in chains, I got a good look at his eyes. They didn't glow like they usually do. Their shining silver color turned to a deep grey, like the clouds of the worst sea storms. They held nothing in them. No hint of fear or anger. No emotion at all. He'd made himself numb. He had to. If he let himself feel, he'd be overcome by it. He would not spend his final hours cowering or begging. He was too proud for that.

I did not look away from him as I reached over to unlock his chains. He narrowed his eyes as the brass key scraped against the lock. When the key finally slid home, and the cuffs clicked open, the Reaper fell to the floor with a thud. But he reached into his boot, withdrew a hidden dagger, and had it pressed to my throat within the blink of an eye. I felt his other hand snake around my neck, grip my hair, and yank me back to further expose my throat to his blade. Still, he said nothing. The silence allowed me to hear the roar of blood in my ears and the tremor in my breath.

I felt my lips press into a firm line; a wave of throat-tightening adrenaline pumped through me. "Do it then," I said. I practically spat the words into the Reaper's face.

He wanted to. I could see it in his gaze. There was a burning desire to draw that blade across my throat and watch me choke on my own blood. But he couldn't do it, and that angered him more than anything else. Just like how I couldn't kill him when the opportunities presented themselves. There was a force that crackled between us. A force beyond our control. It drove the world forward, ancient and eternal. It whispered in our ears and influenced our actions without our knowledge. It interfered even now, to keep me alive.

No. It seemed to say. *It is not to be.*

The Reaper's hold on my hair tightened. His breathing deepened. He seemed to be willing himself to do it. Trying to force his hand into motion, but the blade did not move. He finally let go of me, cursing under his breath. He turned away from me and kicked the cell door with all his might, sending it flying off its hinges and clattering against the opposite wall. The sound was loud enough to make me flinch and worry that my father heard it from the floor above. It was the thought of guards rushing into the corridor to find the origin of the sound that had me jumping into action.

"Down the hall and to the right. There will be four doors. Go through the second on the left. It will lead you into the servant's lounge. There will be one door that leads out to the Southern gardens. It will be the least guarded exit of the estate. Through the hedges, there's a small gap in the wall that was never repaired. You can get out that way. There will be guards, but nothing you can't handle." As I spoke, I pushed the Reaper out of the cell and urged him down the hall. I made sure to pick up the drearwood chains as we walked.

The Reaper spun on his heel to face me. "I will *not* leave here until Xaphan Vermillion is dead," he said. I would never get used to that horrible, damaged voice.

"Then you will die. Here in the Vermillion family home. Is that what you want? Everything you've worked for will be for nothing. Your father will receive no peace if it ends that way. No justice." The Reaper's knotted brows loosened just a bit, and I knew my words hit home. I gave him a final push towards the exit. "I'll buy you time."

He hesitated. It was just a split second of indecision. The spark of an inner debate radiated through his eyes before it was gone. He turned away from me and disappeared into the shadows of the corridor beyond. I was left to stand alone in the dungeons, peering into the darkness for any sign of movement. I saw nothing, but I heard the retreating footsteps of boots scuffing against the stone floor.

I walked the long way to my father's study. Each step I took felt heavier than the last. A weight settled in my body, one that came with the realization that I would likely never step out of the Vermillion family estate again. I would die here tonight. Without question, my soul would descend before the rise of the sun. At least I would die an honest man. My death would come from doing something I believed in, for once. But I would not let Death come for me before learning the truth about my sister. I would avenge her. I swore it to the gods and the kings, whichever would answer.

I climbed the spiraled stairs from the dungeon to the first floor. I faced the door to my father's study. There were a few feet of corridor between my feet and the door, and yet I still stood frozen.

This is it. This is it. This is it. The words rang through my head repeatedly. My muscles tensed in fear, making it impossible for me to move. I stood there, staring down my imminent death, for many long minutes. The fear soon subsided to anger. Anger at my father. Anger at myself. I was about to die at the hands of the man I'd idolized for decades. I would die for the same family I served to protect and honor. The irony burned.

I took one step forward. Then another. And with each step I forced a small part of myself to break away. I didn't want to be myself when I faced my father. I wanted to be nothing. No one. I wanted to be a canvas wiped clean of all paint. It would make it all easier in the end.

My fingers nervously scratched at the drearwood chains in my hands as I walked forward. I unfastened a single cuff from the chain and let the rest fall to the floor. Someone would find them later, but it would be too late. I slid the cuff into the inner pocket of my cloak.

I raised my fist to knock on the door, but my hand only thudded against the wood once before the door creaked open itself. My father sat at his desk, feather quill in hand, scribbling away at a small parchment, one I was sure he meant to roll up into a scroll and send off to the Northern Kingdom.

He glanced up at me through lowered brows, noted my presence, and returned his gaze to his paper. He continued to write as though I never entered at all. The sound of the quill scraping against the paper echoed through the chamber.

A tense silence ensued. My father did not look my way, and the continued scratching sound of his quill was slowly driving me mad.

"Did you honestly kill the Reaper's father?" I asked.

My father dipped his quill in the ink again. He put aside the paper he'd been writing on, now filled with words, and grabbed a second page. He answered my question as though it was obvious. His tone of voice implied that he was irritated by my presence, and answering my question was nothing more than an annoyance. "I've killed many men."

And lied to your own sons, posing as an innocent tradesman.

"Why?"

"It had to be done. For the better of the family."

I felt my throat constricting with the flood of emotions coursing through me. I wasn't sure if it was the tightness of my throat or the heavy, sandpaper sensation I now felt in my tongue, but I struggled to say the next few words. "Is that what you told yourself when you killed *her*?"

An annoyed exhale followed. "Who would that be?"

I tossed Octavia's locket onto his desk. The metal bounced and rolled until it fell right across his paper. The ink tainted the gold.

The scribbling of the pen stopped abruptly. My father froze, his grip tightening on the quill. After a second, he audibly sighed and sat back in his chair. He folded his arms over his chest while he continued to stare down at his papers. He had nothing to say to my accusation, and that *hurt.* But the worst part was his *annoyance.* The question meant nothing to him. The only emotion he could muster was annoyance at the interruption to his work. If he refused to speak, I would continue.

"When you told us that she burned in one of the Reaper's warehouse fires, I believed you along with the others. But then I lived with the Reaper and his henchmen. I ate with them. I trained with them. I laughed, talked, and fought with them. I know them well enough to know that they would *never* kill an innocent girl like Octavia simply because she shared our name." My voice started to shake. My hands wanted to tremble with it, but I curled them into fists so he would not see.

After another moment of silence, I walked forward and slammed both my hands down onto his desk. The sound echoed through the study. My father finally looked up into my eyes, but there was still no emotion in his gaze. "I took them to the vault in the Vatra inn, and I found the lcoket there. Only a Vermillion can get into that vault. At first, I thought one of my brothers betrayed us." I laughed harshly. "But Bryce, Ace, Quinn, and Ryder told me their stories. I know what you did to Bryce. I know what you let Eligor and Azazel do. I know how you gain your wealth."

I leaned forward, my knuckles pressing against the wood of his desk as I clenched my fingers into fists. "But I don't know where Octavia fits into all of this. What the hell did you do to her?" My lip curled up as I spoke the words.

My father drew in a long breath through his nose. He leaned forward to put his elbows on the desk, close enough that our faces were only inches apart. He looked straight into my eyes; straight into my *soul,* and said, "Your sister was too weak of heart to be a part of this family. She discovered my operation and betrayed us by threatening to expose it to the public."

The answer punched the air out of my lungs. It stabbed my heart and caused it to falter. All this time, he'd been deceiving a kingdom, a city, and even his own family. He killed is one and only daughter for the lie. I stumbled back from the desk, shaking my head. "She was a child!"

He twitched a shoulder in something like a shrug. "I have others."

278

His nonchalant attitude and quick remarks were enough to send me into shock. He spoke of his own daughter as though she were another item for him to buy or sell. Like her life meant nothing to him.

Because it didn't. She didn't.

I forced myself to relax. I decided to remain calm, because I would get no more answers if I succumbed to my own blind rage.

"Yes, you have six sons. Six sons who share no features. We share nothing but blood. *Your* blood," I said "Tynan has straight hair. Darcel has the soft jawline and heavy-set body that only inherited genes could cause. Eligor has the biggest hooked nose I've ever seen, and–"

My father waved me off. "You've made your point. Ask what it is you want to know."

The rapid beat of my heart synced with the rush of blood in my ears. I tried to keep my voice steady, but even with all my focus, it proved difficult. "Who is my mother?"

A smile snaked across his face. "Meaning you haven't figured it out yet?"

"Did you kill her too? Like Octavia?"

"She was far too valuable for that. She served her purpose to me and then I had her shipped off. She fetched a decent price if memory serves."

So, I was right. My brothers and I were bastards born from slave mothers. My hands itched to draw my sword, but I fought the urge. "Then you will give me all of your sale logs."

"You think a man in illegal trading keeps sale logs?"

"Then you will give me every one of your clients' names–"

"And you will– what? Go to each estate and knock on their doors? What will you say? You don't even know her name. I know I don't remember."

A shaky breath left me as I ran a hand through my hair. I couldn't fathom what I was hearing. "I don't understand," I whispered after a moment. I cleared my throat and met his gaze. "I thought you were an honest man. I killed for your praise. I lost myself for your pride."

"An honest man gets his pick between Death and poverty. I veered off that path long ago, and I found wealth and power. It would do you well to do the same."

"You taught me that a good reputation is worth more than money."

"You understand little about the age we live in if you believe honor is sweeter than cash in hand."

I threw up my hands in frustration. "Then what is left when honor is lost? What are you fighting for?"

My father arched a brow. "Am I meant to be insulted? Can you truly question my honor? You fight for criminals."

"Crime is honest, for a good cause."

"How long do you tell yourself that before you are no better than I am?"

Hatred put a bitter taste in my mouth. My lips parted, prepared to fight, to shout or scream, when the sound of running footsteps approaching cut me short. I stepped to the side of my father's desk so that we could both see the newcomer. While his focus was on the guards in the hall, I reached into my pocket, grasping the cuff.

Alastor led a group of four guards. He strutted down the hall with a wide stride. With his slicked back hair and sword swaying at his side, he looked like a war commander headed for combat.

"The Reaper is gone," he said. He held up the drearwood chains I discarded for emphasis, unaware that a piece was missing.

Xaphan's head snapped over to me. His nostrils flared and his lip curled up with disgust for me. "You did this?" He stood up abruptly, knocking over his chair in the process. "Where is he?"

I feigned innocence, cocking my head to the side. "Meaning you haven't figured it out yet?"

A deep grumbling sound came from the back of his throat. He made to take a step toward me, raising his arm to strike a blow. I was quicker. I withdrew the drearwood cuff and clapped it over his wrist, squeezing until I heard a click. It locked into place. The only way for him to get it off would be to find the key I'd already tossed from the east window. Before he could react, I raised my other hand to land a blow to his throat. He reeled away, coughing and gasping.

I didn't have time to revel in my achievement. Alastor was quick to draw his sword and approach me. I finally understood why the others were always mocking my family's fighting skills. Alastor truly *sucked* at hand-to-hand combat. He was slow. He stepped into each move he made. I could anticipate and block every punch. First, I disarmed him of his sword. I dodged the jabs he attempted, grabbed his arm, and twisted it backward. He cried out in pain and dropped his weapon. I kicked it to the opposite side of the room and used the hilt of my own sword to knock him out cold. I didn't kill him. Despite everything, I didn't have the heart to kill my youngest brother.

All four guards rushed at me at once. The first raised his sword over his head. I raised my own and met his blade hard, forcing his entire arm to jerk to the right. As he side-stepped in the direction I led him, I spun around and drove my sword straight through his throat. The light left his eyes before he hit the ground.

The second guard tried to swipe me across the abdomen. I jumped ahead of his sword, grabbing his arm and jamming my blade into his side. If I remembered correctly from my childhood instructor, I'd hit one of his major arteries. He would bleed out on Xaphan's newly polished floors. Something about that made me feel a bit better.

The third guard was bigger than the others. He raised his broadsword with a battle cry. He waited for me to make the first strike, so I aimed for his head in a downward strike. He deflected my blow easily. I quickly adjusted and came back for a second strike to his side. He deflected and met my blade once more when I tried a secondary blow to his abdomen. But he was overconfident. He smirked at me when he blocked my third blow. That split second of his guard being down allowed me to embed my sword in his sternum. His eyes went wide. He looked dumbfounded at his own defeat.

The final guard ran at me. He jabbed for my face. I twisted out of the way just in time to avoid a hideous scar. Before I could right myself, he swiped again. I ducked to save my throat from being sliced. He twisted around and came at me a third time. I had the second I needed to raise my sword. I deflected his blow. He had the advantage of momentum, though. He was driving me backward. He twisted again. This time, he fell to one knee and tried to get one of my legs. I planted my sword on the floor to stop his strike, then raised it above my head. The guard picked himself up and our swords clashed a few inches away from his face. We withdrew and clashed again. I was able to drive him back against the wall. He bared his teeth with exertion, putting everything he had left into keeping my sword from reaching his neck. Unfortunately for him, I had a dagger in my other hand, and when he looked down next, it was embedded in his gut.

I withdrew both my blades, cringing at the blood dripping from them. My eyes found the guard in front of me again. "Sorry about this," I muttered as I wiped the blades off on his tunic. "But to be fair, you won't be needing these clothes again."

I froze at the sound of boots scuffling against stone behind me. Xaphan rose to his feet, his hand still clutching his throat. "Plan to kill me too?" he spat.

I looked down at the blades in my hands, then to the cuff still fastened to his wrist. It was a trick, I realized, to get me close. He wanted me to try because he knew I couldn't kill him. I didn't know how to kill a god, and I assumed that something as simple as a sword wouldn't do the trick.

"Your life is not mine to take," I said. I sheathed my sword and turned away. I walked to his desk, picked up the locket, and placed it back into my pocket.

Xaphan watched it all through narrowed eyes. "I always liked you, Kal, which is why I'm letting you leave here alive. You have until the Dragon's Feast ball to return to me. After that, I'll consider you lost to us, and you will die with the rest of them."

I did not give him the satisfaction of looking back. I stared forward at the wall as he spoke. When the last word left his lips, I left. I walked away from the man I once called father. Away from the people I once called family. Away from the place I once called home. I thought it would sadden me. To my surprise, I felt liberated. For the first time in my life, I was walking toward an uncertain future, and it was *amazing.*

My brothers would come for me. Xaphan would never stop hunting me down. But none of it mattered anymore. I found my purpose. Nothing they could do would be able to take that away from me.

I marched forward. Out of the Vermillion estate. Past the gates and into the city streets. I drew cloak's hood over my face, and I let the shadows swallow me.

Chapter 24

Ryder

Bryce didn't need to speak for me to know something was wrong. The second I had my arms around her, I felt her burning skin. I watched her hands shake and her muscles give out on her when she tried to pick herself up.

"What is it?" I asked, brushing the hair out of her face. "What's wrong?"

She opened her mouth to speak, but only a strangled sound escaped her throat.

"I say we follow them," Ace said. He stood at the edge of the rooftop, staring in the direction the Vermillions disappeared to. He drew his sword and held it out in front of him. The moonlight hit the blade perfectly, reflecting onto his face and highlighting the scar through his eye.

"No. We're outnumbered, and Bryce needs a healer. We must trust that Kalieth won't have the Reaper killed before the sun rises," Quinn said.

"Trust Kalieth?" Ace repeated, stepping closer to Quinn. "He served Bryce up to Eligor like a fine meal, and he's bringing the Reaper back to Xaphan in chains. Why would we trust him?"

"Eichi is a *god.* The God of Time to be exact. He knows what will happen *before* it happens. He told us that each of us would have a role to play. That included Kalieth. Do you think you know better than a *god*, Ace?" Quinn asked. Their faces were only inches apart now, both fuming.

Ace looked Quinn up and down, head cocked. "I'm starting to think you might."

"Only the ignorant despise education, but I would expect nothing less from someone who values brawn over brain."

Ace scoffed. "At least I'm capable of being something. You, on the other hand, read about the accomplishments of better men because you know you'll never measure up."

Quinn's eyes flared wide. "Better men? Is that what you are? All you do is drink and fuck anything that walks. The only thing honorable about you is your sense to spare your conquests from waking up beside you and realizing their mistake."

Even Bryce, in her weakened state, cringed at that.

But Ace only clenched his jaw. "You sure you want to go down that road? Let's not forget who nearly got us all killed last time, all because you wanted a Vermillion between your legs."

"That is *enough*!" I snapped as I got to my feet. I held Bryce in my arms, her body limp. She was going downhill fast. She could barely hold up her own head.

The second the other two got a look at her, their argument was forgotten. Ace was itching to chase after the Vermillions, but he would stay for Bryce. They both would. We were family now, for better or worse.

"Where will we go?" Ace asked.

"She needs more help than we can give," Quinn added.

There was one person I knew who could fix something like this, but it was risky. Not because of the procedure, but because of the person. She's, well... unpredictable. My feet started to walk before my mind remembered the way.

Ace and Quinn fell in step behind me, giving each other one last side-eye glare. They asked no questions. They followed in tense silence as we made our way down to the street. I led us through the bad part of the city. The healer I knew also lived in the South Side. All I had to do was follow the sounds of the night. She liked to help her patients in the loudest parts of town, because no one would hear their screams over the other sounds.

Trying to listen to Bryce's labored breathing over the noise proved difficult. Her chest would rise and fall in short, shallow breaths. I feared that she might stop breathing completely before I could find the healer.

I practically sprinted toward the Snaka Tavern and Inn. It was a bad place to be if you weren't local to the South Side of the city. The tavern sat on the corner of the street. Across the cobblestone road was nothing but construction sites that had been sitting there with no real progress for over three years.

Above the tavern were rooms for travelers or drunk men who would rather stay the night than go home to their wives. *She* would be up there, accepting patients in secret because the other healers disapproved of her ways.

I stopped short just before the entrance to the tavern. It was so abrupt that Quinn walked straight into my back, reeling away in shock. I faced them and gave them both a stern look. We could not afford to offend this healer. "Listen well, both of you. You will *not* look her in the eye. You will bow your head in respect when she greets us. You will *not* stare at the markings on her skin or ask about them. You will *not* speak unless spoken to. Do you hear me?"

They nodded their agreement.

I wasn't convinced, but I had no time to continue schooling them. I had to trust that they would behave appropriately.

Gods, we're dead.

I led the way into the tavern. I'd never been more grateful for our reputation, and the way people stepped aside when they saw us. The barmaid had her hands full with ales. As she handed them out to her regulars, a few guys who had a few too many started to approach her.

"Ace," I said with a nod to the barmaid.

He was already redirecting himself. "Yeah, I'm on it."

"And get a room for us once you sort it out," I called after him.

With Quinn still a step behind me, I aimed for the stairs to the back of the tavern. Another barmaid stopped me from going upstairs. She looked down at Bryce with an arched brow and wagged a finger in my face. "Don't think so. Why don't ya leave her with me and get on home?"

I shook my head. "We're here for Artemis. The Reaper sent us."

Her face paled. She pointed a stiff finger upwards. "Second door on the left." She promptly hurried off to serve another table, whispering a prayer under her breath.

"Who's Artemis?" Quinn whispered as we took the stairs two at a time.

"A very skilled healer," I said. "Don't say anything now. Remember what I said outside?"

Quinn nodded just as we reached the door. I raised a fist, took a deep breath, and knocked three times. Bryce stirred from the sound. She struggled to open her eyes, but even when they settled on me, it was like she looked straight through me.

I raised my fist to knock again. The door flung open before my knuckles hit the wood. A young woman stood in the doorway. At least, she *looked* young. I knew better. I immediately looked away from her eyes, but I knew what they looked like from past dealings. They were almond-shaped and a vibrant, unnatural shade of brown– like molten bronze. Her pupils were narrowed into slits, like a lizard. She had long black hair woven into many braids and skin with a warm hue. She wore a hooded cloak made entirely from the orange scales of reptiles. It covered nearly all her skin, which brought me a bit of relief, because I knew that if Quinn could see markings that littered her arms, he would ask questions.

I bowed my head in greeting. I could only hope Quinn did the same.

Her eyes narrowed further when they scanned over my face. "We have no appointment." Her voice was coarse and scratchy.

"Please, Artemis. She's dying." My voice broke over the words. I dipped my arms low so she could get a better look at Bryce.

Her eyes flicked down for a fraction of a second. "My debt is to the Reaper himself."

"If you help us, consider it paid."

Her skeptical gaze scanned over my face one last time. I tried to show her how serious I was, but it was hard to convey such emotions while staring at the bridge of someone's nose. She said nothing more. She stepped aside and opened the door wide enough for us to pass. I stepped through the threshold and nodded for Quinn to follow.

The small room could barely fit a bed and a chest. Still, it was one of the nice rooms, because it had a private bathing chamber the size of a closet.

Artemis closed the door behind us and motioned to the bed. "Put her there."

I lowered Bryce onto the furs as gently as possible. I tried to keep the panic out of my expression as I spoke to Artemis, but I never felt fear like this. Fear that seeped into my very bones and chilled me to the core. Fear that made me want to run a mile and collapse to my knees all at once.

Her blonde hair was plastered to her sweaty brow. Her fair skin was a few shades paler than normal. Her eyes, though rarely open, had a cloudy film over them that told me she could see nothing. Her breathing gradually became more labored as time passed. It was to the point that I feared she'd stop breathing all together in mere minutes.

Artemis stepped up to the bed and surveyed her patient. She shrugged out of her cloak, holding her bare arms out over Bryce. There, covering her the skin of her forearms, were intricate tattoos of twin snakes that wrapped around her arms and disappeared into the loose sleeves of her tunic. The golden scales of the snakes, while they looked to be the fine work of a talented artist, were very real. They grew straight from Artemis's skin in rough patches that hardly blended in. The snakes' eyes began to glow as she summoned her magic.

Heilaris– healers– syphon magic from the world around them and direct it into the injured body. For most, that is the full extent of their power. Not Artemis. No one knows her limits.

She's considered the most powerful healer to walk this mortal soil. No one truly knows how she got her magic, but rumors suggest that she found primal magic that did not want to be touched. It lashed out and tried to consume her. Artemis fought back, and though she lived, she was forever scarred with scales. But she got to keep a piece of that primal magic. I could see it swirling between her fingers like sparks that fizzled and popped. She lowered her hand until it hovered a hair's breadth away from Bryce's brow. Artemis closed her eyes and tipped her head back, slowly dragging her hand over Bryce's body, never quite touching her.

Artemis moved her hand all the way from the top of Bryce's head, down to her toes, and back again before she finally stepped away. She opened her eyes and shook her head, scattering a few stray hairs. "The poison is almost to her heart. If it reaches, she will die. That doesn't give me much time to work with."

Panic had thoughts racing through my mind. I wanted to rush her. I wanted to yell at the top of my lungs and ask her what she was waiting for. But I didn't. I knew that would only get me kicked out of this room, and Bryce's fate would be sealed.

Artemis looked to Quinn, who gasped and averted his eyes. She pointed a rigid finger at him. "You," she hissed. "Help hold her down."

Quinn launched into movement, walking to the other side of the bed. He pinned Bryce's arm down. I held her other arm while Artemis stood by her head. She hovered a hand over Bryce's mouth and began mouthing words beneath her breath.

"You know the first language?" Quinn asked excitedly. "I've never heard it outside of the university, besides the songs."

I shot him a reprimanding look. He snapped his mouth shut and looked away shamefully. We could not risk breaking Artemis's focus as she summoned her magic. He was right, of course. Artemis *was* whispering in the first language.

As Artemis repeated her whispered words, Bryce's veins slowly started to turn black. From her face to her arms and legs, a black glow spread through her skin like ink on paper. Artemis was making it so that she could see the poison before she tried to extract it. Once the poison was visible to us, Artemis raised her voice and changed her words. She chanted the same phrase over and over while holding a tense hand over Bryce's mouth.

"Ne'expean ëa copandan thrándas. Miythran ëa periel demorvir," Artemis chanted over and over.

Quinn leaned over Bryce. "Expel this bodily evil. Heal this unnatural ill," he whispered in translation.

I tried to give him a look that told him if he didn't stop talking, I'd kill him myself. I found that I wasn't as good as the Reaper in communicating with my eyes.

Artemis continued to chant. Her words got louder and more commanding each time. While she kept one hand over Bryce's mouth, the other circled over the black veins of her forearm.

The twitching of Bryce's fingers was the first sign of her struggle. Sharp inhales came next.

294

Then, her whole body started to convulse, fighting against our hold. It took all my strength to keep her down. But the worst part was when her lips parted, and a scream tore from her throat. It was an ear-splitting sound born from pure pain. It echoed off the walls, only drowned out by the music blaring below.

As the minutes passed by, she fought harder and screamed louder. We managed to keep her pinned down, but that was only until I felt her skin heating up. Dread climbed up my spine as I looked to her open hands. Fire burst from her fingertips and caught on the sheets.

Quinn gasped and jumped back before he could get burnt, releasing Bryce. She thrashed around and spread more fire until I had to dodge a streak of flames myself.

Artemis stepped back, shaking her head. The entire bed went up in flames, and Bryce laid in the middle of it, relentless in her writhing and crying.

"This won't work. There's one more method I can try, but you're not going to like it," Artemis said, her voice lowering.

I already knew what she meant. I'd seen her do it before. Subjecting Bryce to something like that was not an idea I was fond of, but if there was truly no other way, I would not hesitate. I nodded for Artemis to proceed. While she stepped forward, her arms raised and palms up, I grabbed Quinn and backed away from the bed.

"Velenen   œndir   a   helmîel," Artemis commanded.

295

"Come alive and aid me?" Quinn asked. "What is she doing?"

The snakes' eyes tattooed into her skin glowed a bright gold. They got brighter as she spoke. We watched the sparks swirling between her fingers retreat down her arms and feed into the serpents. The rough patches of scales embedded in her arms began to move beneath her skin. The very ink of the tattoos started to shift. Soon enough, the snakes were rising from her arms and dropping down into the bed.

Both snakes had to be at least three feet in length with sharp fangs. Their sleek, gold scales were unaffected by the fire. Their orange eyes held strands of gold within them and reflected the warm glow of the flames.

Quinn released a shuddering breath. "What are they doing?"

"They'll suck the poison out," I said, unable to hide the tremor in my voice.

"I've never seen–" Quinn gulped. "I didn't know healers could do this."

I glanced between him and the bed before muttering, "they can't."

The snakes slithered across Bryce's legs, wrapping themselves around her limbs until she couldn't shake them off. Each one reached up to one of her wrists and bit down into the soft, veinous part of her inner arm. The scream that left Bryce's lips as the snakes' fangs pierced her skin was bone-chilling. I forced myself to turn away, so I didn't have to watch the way she writhed through the pain.

"It's working," Quinn whispered.

I looked back to see the black substance in her veins retreating from her other limbs. The last of it was moving through her arms, straight into the snakes' awaiting fangs. She stopped writhing, and her screams turned to low groans. The fire that raged seconds ago dwindled down into embers.

As the last of the poison left her, the snakes slithered away and returned to Artemis. They coiled themselves around her forearms and sank back into her skin until they were nothing more than tattoos once again.

I jumped into the bed with a racing heart. I brushed a hand over Bryce's cheek, glad to feel her temperature returned to normal. "Bryce?" I called gently.

She opened her eyes slowly. When she saw me, a soft smile lifted her lips. "Ryder."

I wanted to collapse with relief. Instead, I climbed to my feet and turned to find Artemis. "Thank you." The words were breathy and raw. "You have no idea how much I–"

She grabbed my arm, her nails digging deep. I made to look at the bridge of her nose, but she shifted so that I stared directly into her eyes. My heart lurched into my throat, but it was too late. I was already staring into the reptilian bronze irises. Her magic was sinking into me, keeping me in place and slowing my mind enough for me to process her words as she leaned forward and hissed, "When the wolves start guarding the dragon, no one is safe."

She was forcing me to pay attention, but I still couldn't make sense of her words.

"What–"

"My debt is paid," Artemis said, pushing away from me. "Keep the room." She threw on her snake's skin cloak and gave us each a nod before heading toward the door. When she pulled it open, a bored-looking Ace stood in the threshold, his fist still raised to knock. Artemis slipped past him without a word.

Ace watched her go. He looked back into the room and surveyed Quinn's pale face and the scorch marks on the ceiling. His brows pinched together as he cocked his head. "For fuck's sake, what did I miss?"

CHAPTER 25

Kalieth

As a bounty hunter, I often pursued targets that required me to drop off the grid for long periods of time. To do that, I needed a place of my own that no one else knew about. So, I saved the markings I'd earned on previous jobs and bought a one-room space on one of the less prestigious blocks of the North Side.

The North Side was known for large estates with vast lands and fertile grounds. The property I purchased, however, was on King's Street, just one block away from the northern bridge into Center City. It sat on the busiest road in all the North Side, and therefore it had no land. It was a narrow building nestled between two others, short in width but it towered high into the sky.

All the businesses, taverns, pubs, and theaters worth visiting in the North Side were located on this road. We referred to it as the main strip, or the King's strip. Live classical music played for several different businesses, enticing shoppers to enter their establishment. The idle sound of water moving and trickling in the nearby river paired with the instruments would've made a beautiful, calming duo, if it weren't for the drunken fools belting lyrics for all the North Side to hear. Laughter, cheers, dishes clinking together, and loud chatter all disrupted the peaceful night. Somewhere off in the distance, I was sure I heard swords clashing. I had no doubt that another brawl broke out in one of the pubs. It was a regular occurrence in these parts. The rich were easily offended, and quick to defend their honor.

The pungent scent of baked goods and spices drifted on the breeze. The sun hadn't risen yet, so I assumed the bakers were just starting their first batches.

Faelights cast a blue glow over the streets. In the rare moments that the moonlight broke through the clouds, the silver and blue hues mixed together to create an eerie luminescence. I tried to stay in dark alleys and shadowed corners as I made my way down the street. Horse drawn carriages flew past me. The enthusiastic laughter of the rich snobs within echoed through the night. The click of the horses' shoes against cobblestone quickly became a welcome constant variable in the chaotic jumble of sounds.

My boots dragged audibly over the stone as I shuffled hurriedly into the threshold of my building. I took one last look over my shoulder to ensure I wasn't followed. I searched for even the smallest flick of movement in the shadows. Satisfied that I wasn't being watched, I moved through the courtyard and made for the staircase.

The iron staircase was an exterior feature. The steps were rusted and falling apart. I didn't expect them to hold my weight. Unfortunately, there was no other way to my room, so I took a chance on the first step. I hesitated when it creaked beneath my boot. I tried it again. This time, I put all my weight down on it. Still, it did not give way. Slowly, I climbed the stairs to the third level. I crossed a narrow catwalk that acted as a makeshift corridor that stretched across the entire building.

The metal catwalk groaned beneath my feet as I approached my own room. My door was once yellow or orange, but the paint chipped away over the years. Now, all that remained of the door was decaying oak wood, an old doorknob, and a lock that would probably slide straight out of the door if I pulled too hard. It still worked well enough, though, so I reached into my pocket to find my key.

Just as my fingers brushed my silver key, I noticed that the door was cracked open. The wood around the doorknob was split up the sides, with entire chunks missing in a few places. The room beyond seemed dark and empty, but I refused to take a chance. I drew my sword and used the blade to slowly push the door open. It creaked louder than chalk against a blackboard. I cringed at the sound, tightening my grip on the hilt of my blade. I squinted, but still saw nothing in the darkness.

I took one step forward, reaching toward the table beside the door. There was a gas lamp sitting there, and just by turning one knob, the entire room was instantly lit up.

I had no time to even look around before something whirled past my face. I felt it brush over the tip of my nose in the faintest touch. It hit the back of the door beside my head with such force, the door flew back into the wall with a loud thud. Through wide eyes, I looked to see an obsidian throwing knife embedded in my door.

My head snapped around to see the Reaper leaning against the far wall. He tossed another throwing knife up into the air, letting it twirl before he caught it again with one hand.

I felt the searing heat of adrenaline creeping up into my face and neck. I knew my mouth was gaping, but I couldn't seem to shut it. I could only stare, my gaze flying between the knife and the Reaper several times before my brain could summon words.

"You could've killed me!" I exclaimed, my voice high and defensive.

The Reaper shrugged as though he had no care in the world. As though he didn't just throw a knife at me in my own home. "You didn't announce yourself."

"This is *my* house! I shouldn't have to announce myself! *You* should be the one doing the announcing."

His bored gaze met mine. "I just did."

"By throwing a knife at my head?"

"It worked. You became aware of my presence."

302

"Did you plan to lacerate anyone who walked through the door?"

In an instant, he was before me. His callused hands wrapped around my neck and slammed my head into the wall behind me, right beside the knife. His brows were lowered, and his eyes narrowed in anger. He leaned forward to speak into my ear, his voice low. "You will start talking now, or the next one goes between your eyes."

"You have– you have small hands," I said between gasps of air.

He dug his nails into my skin. Pain tore through me. Strangely, I wasn't afraid. "I know you're angry–"

"Anger is felt when the King raises taxes. You endangered my friends and nearly got me killed tonight. I've surpassed anger." He tightened his grip on my throat. My breathing became labored. My own hands flew up to try to loosen his hold, but it was no use.

I shouldn't have opened my mouth. But I was never good at self-control. "Technically, I nearly got you *sold.*"

The Reaper pulled me forward and then slammed me back against the wall again with all his strength. Pain exploded from the back of my head. Spots of light clouded my vision. An inhuman growl sounded from the back of the Reaper's throat. His nails dug further into my neck. "No jokes. No witty remarks," he warned. "The time for that has passed. We're at war. Whose side are you on?"

The pressure he put on my throat muffled my voice. "Yours. I just needed to see it all for myself first. I needed to hear it from my father's lips."

My answer must've surprised him. His grip on me loosened. After what felt like an eternity, he released me and took a step back. "You made your choice when you let me go."

I took my first deep breath of air, massaging the sides of my throat. "Yes."

"You had everything you ever wanted. You had your father's pride, and you had me in chains. Why would you give it all up?"

Because you and this group are all I have left.

"My whole life, I've done my father's bidding without question. I was taught from a young age that honor and family come before anything else. The Vermillion family name was something to be proud of," I said. I shook my head and looked to the floor as memories of my father's speeches flashed behind my eyes. "I hunted my father's enemies with pleasure. I thought he was a decent man, and anyone who challenged him was challenging the authority of the Vermillion name. My pride couldn't allow that."

"What changed, then?"

A quick wave of anger had bumps rising across my skin. Disbelief came next, at the fact that he honestly had to ask me that. "You did. You and the others. You changed everything."

"You might see how tonight's events would bring me to question that."

"I needed answers from my father, and you needed a way in."

The Reaper's questioning expression quickly turned cold. "Was it worth it then? Did seeing me on my knees and having Bryce poisoned finally convince you of the truth we've been telling you for weeks?"

I shook my head. "I know that what I did was wrong, but I don't regret it. Now, I know the truth, I know that there is no honor in the Vermillion name. I know that my destiny is to restore it. I know, undoubtedly, that I'm meant to help you fix all the wrongs Xaphan has caused."

The Reaper took a threatening step closer. "You nearly got me killed tonight."

I felt a lump gathering in my throat. "I–"

"You nearly got me killed tonight, *but,*" he continued. "You learned the truth and you saved my life, knowing that you would never be able to go back to your family. For that, you have my trust."

My breathing was still labored, but I straightened, staring at the Reaper. I inhaled sharply through parted lips when his hand started a slow journey upward. My heart thundered in my chest as his fingers slid over his chin.

I watched, paralyzed by shock, as the Reaper took off the mask.

CHAPTER 26

Mara
One Year Ago

I had a shadow long before I served my term with the king's army. The five other soldiers in my squad would devise tall tales about the origins of my shadow in the rare moments when we weren't about to die.

Lucian joked that I wasn't human at all and therefore I was born with a shadow. Lucian was an idiot though, so none of us ever bothered to disprove his theory.

Enzo told the others that my mother conceived twins, and I killed my sister in the womb, earning me the beginnings of a shadow before I could step foot on the mortal soil. Enzo and I never like one another. I think he made up the tale to have my fellow soldiers look down upon me. His plan didn't work, and he died only three weeks later. I didn't pity him.

The only other soldier in my squad that I admired, Tihana, typically kept to herself. I admired her simply because she was one of the few women left in the king's army, and while she spoke few words, she used silence as her strength. People assumed that because she remained silent, she was weak or afraid, but in truth, she was stronger than most. When it came to questioning my background, she'd put the others in their place. She'd tell them to keep the fairytales for their wives and children at home, if they ever made it back there. She'd pretend like she wasn't curious, but in the dead of night, silent as a shadow, she'd come to me. She didn't ask about my shadow, but about my skill set. Where did I train? Which great swordsman taught me?

The only soldier who knew that I came from an underwhelming family farm, Silas, assumed that I lied about keeping crop to myself, and with each lie my shadow grew. He was the only soldier in the squad I had lain with, but to be fair, we all thought we were going to die that night with the Northern forces closing in on us. Reinforcements arrived just in time to save our sorry lives, but not early enough to spare me from the shame I felt after being with Silas intimately.

I never told anyone the true origin of my shadow. Most of my colleagues would be disappointed to hear the story. I didn't kill a twin or lie about crops. I wasn't born a murderer. I wasn't bred to be a monster. My first kill was my childhood dog.

Despite how it may sound, I didn't act maliciously. Orion was our farm dog. He spent the nights out by the chicken coop, protecting the livestock from predators lurking in the forest beyond our property. One morning, I woke earlier

307

than my siblings. It was the job of the earliest-waker to feed Orion.

I remember the walk to the coop so vividly, even ten years later. I went without shoes. I used to like the chill that went up my spine when my bare feet touched the cold morning dew on the grass. Pheonix birds called somewhere in the distance, and goosebumps rose on my arms when I stepped into the cool air of the autumn morning. The bowls of feed felt heavy for my young arms, but I knew Da wouldn't wake to feed the animals for another hour or so.

The long grass tickled my legs as I made my way down the unkept path toward the coop. I thought it was strange that I couldn't hear the chickens from the yard, but I brushed it aside. It wasn't until I emerged from the wheat field that I understood why it was so quiet.

The chickens were nowhere to be found. Bunches of feathers remained scattered across the ground, slowly drifting off with the wind. A dark red substance covered the coop. It was splattered onto every surface. The wood sported deep scratch marks from whatever animal attacked it. Beyond the coop, I saw a bundle of pink fur– fur that used to be white, before blood stained it. My heart dropped to my stomach when I recognized Orion's crumpled form.

Our dog's body lay in an unnatural position. His legs were twisted beneath him. Bite marks and gashes littered his body. There was a deafening silence where his happy good morning barks would be. But soft wheezes left his muzzle while his chest rose and fell at a slow pace. The poor thing lived through the attack.

I set the bowls of feed down before I picked my way through the blood, splinters, and feathers to get to Orion. I could see the glaze of exhaustion coating his eyes, but I knew he still recognized me when he tried to stand to greet me. It broke my heart to see him struggle.

I'm ashamed to admit that Orion's struggle was not the first thing to come to mind when I grabbed the shovel. I did it with the thought of my brother, who would be distraught at the sight of him. I wanted to protect Ryder from that pain.

So, I grabbed the shovel beside the coop and lifted it well above my head. The sound of bone cracking against metal was forever engraved in my mind after that morning. The scavenger birds circling overhead screeched and scattered at the gut-wrenching sound that tore through nature's illusion of a peaceful morning.

Though the memory would haunt me forever, Orion was instantly relieved of his pain. That morning, a shadow formed at my backside, and it's followed me ever since.

I was never inclined to tell my fellow soldiers the anticlimactic tale. I rather liked the idea of them wondering about me, fearing me. I rested assured that it drove men away.

Even if the rumors about me didn't scare them off, my kill count did. In the Southern Kingdom, we have a tradition that for each kill, a soldier earns a bead of obsidian stone which is then sewn into the back of our armor. With only one year of my service complete, my back was completely covered in obsidian, which only emphasized the size and darkness of my shadow. It intimidated the men, and it made the few other women envious.

I trained with every weapon, but sai and throwing knives were my specialty. I never missed a target. I most definitely never hesitated. Both happened to be skills that my father taught me. He trained me since the day I was strong enough to hold up a sword. When my time came to go to an army training camp, it felt like just another day on the farm, throwing knives at bags filled with hay.

The other soldiers preferred rifles. I found them merciful. Too quick for my taste. When given the choice, I stuck to my knives. It gave me the satisfaction of knowing that my victims knew exactly who brought them down. That they tasted their own blood before Death claimed them. In that respect, I built myself quite the reputation on both sides of the war. That was why I would've been promoted to a Captain's position. Would've—if not for my father's untimely death.

The raven came one week before my squad was sent to the front lines again. My mother sent it to inform me of my father's passing and explain that the farm might be lost to us. I wasn't meant to leave; I could've been killed if they caught me deserting. I suppose it wouldn't have mattered, seeing as my squad died on that last tour to the front lines just days later. For all anyone knew, I died with them.

I returned home for the funeral. Walking toward our run-down old farmhouse through the wheat fields, with the stalks crunching beneath my blood-stained boots– it felt wrong. Hundreds had died by my hand by that time, and to return to the farmhouse I once slept in as a shadowless child...

Part of me wanted to feel ashamed. To feel remorse. To *feel.* Despite everything, I held my head high, knowing that my father would be proud. I used what he taught me to fight for my kingdom. What more would he have wanted?

The old wooden house came into view just over a small hill. The sun set behind it, painting the sky in pastel pinks, oranges, and yellows. Tendrils of smoke flowed out of the chimney and swirled through the air before dissipating into the sky, like a whisper fading into wind. All this made the decaying farm seem flawlessly beautiful. The destination of dreams. Somehow nature managed to hide all the land's flaws, even just for a moment. The warm light concealed the house's chipping paint. The smell of smoke covered up the livestock odor that drifted in the breeze.

I stopped for a second, at the edge of the field, to simply take in the view before me. To silently wish that I could be a kid again, running home into Da's arms. I could stand there all night, sifting through memories to relive them once more before they fade into nothing. But it was painful to think about my younger self. To wonder what she might think of me now.

It seemed that reality always found a way to break through a façade. So, broken free of my nostalgia, I continued on my way. I stopped dead at the rotting porch steps, at the sight of small flowers and incoherent shapes drawn onto the deteriorated wood. Innocent sketches two children drew together in the boredom of a summer day.

My brother.

He would be home from service by now. What would he think? What would he see when he looked at my back; to the stone and shadow gathered there? A murderer? A monster?

I took a deep breath and reminded myself not to think of such things. War changed me, as it changes every soldier in one way or another. It is not something to be ashamed of. Everyone knows that you wear battle scars on the outside while you host deeper wounds within, silenced by fear and pride. I was no exception to that.

One step at a time, I ascended the stairs and stood in front of the door. My armor felt too tight on my body. My boots felt too heavy. My skin heated with the force of a thousand fires. But I still raised my fist. I knocked once. Only once. She would hear it. The woman had inhuman hearing.

Ma opened the door within five of my thundering heartbeats. Dark circles weighed down her eyes. Her black hair sat at the top of her head in a frizzy, tangled bun. Her dark skin, normally sun-kissed and unblemished, looked pale and dry. She was thin and frail. Wrinkles I didn't remember seeing before proved that age finally caught up with her. I supposed grief did that to people.

Her golden eyes landed on me, widening instantly. She put her hand on the door to push it open further. I didn't miss her bloody, chewed fingernails. She must've followed my gaze, because she jerked her hands behind her back, out of my vision.

We stood in silence for a long moment. I wanted to say something. Anything. But my throat tightened, and my mouth went dry. My tongue felt like sandpaper.

She cleared her throat and shifted her weight between her feet before she addressed me. "You deserted?"

I shook my head. "They think I'm dead. I wanted to pay my respects to Da. Then, I'll be on my way."

She nodded, more to herself than to me.

"Am I too late for the ceremony?" My voice broke on the words. I'd never forgive myself if I missed it.

"No. We wanted to wait for nightfall. You're just in time." She pushed the door open the rest of the way and ushered me inside.

The house was filled with warm candlelight. The only sound was that of Ma's shoes scuffling across the floorboards. She gestured for me to follow her as she walked toward the sewing room. The floorboards creaked under my weight. For once, I was grateful for the old house. I wasn't sure I could bear utter silence as I approached my father's body.

He was laid out on the sewing table. Ma dressed him in his Captain's uniform. The black jacket with silver embroidery on the shoulders fit him tight after his years of retirement. The silver metals pinned to his chest shined in the dim light. His once black hair was white with age. His sunken skin was grey from Death's touch.

As I surveyed Da's body, I caught a flash of silver eyes in the corner. Ryder sat in the shadows. His disheveled hair fell partially over his brow. He clutched a half-empty bottle of liquor close to his chest. His silver eyes met mine, widening with shock.

Ma joined us. She looked between Ryder and me and nodded. "Carry him outside."

Ryder stood, towering over me at his true height. He'd grown stronger and thinner since I saw him last, over a year ago, when our squads were deployed to two different stations. He lost the round face of boyhood. Now, he was all taut muscle and sharp features. He looked me up and down without saying a word. We both stared for a moment, scoping out what changed in a year, and wondering what might have stayed the same. We were silent as we each took an end of the table. Together we lifted, Ryder at Da's shoulders and me at his feet, and carried him out the back door toward the creek.

Ryder and I placed Da's body into the small stream. I tried not to look at the deep gashes torn through his throat, surrounded by burnt flesh. At the lack of a tongue through his parted lips. At the bruises and welts that tainted his skin.

We placed his body into the water, submerging him just enough for his eyes to go under, but for his nose and mouth to remain above the surface. The full moon above reflected light off the water's surface, creating a shadowless space. It was there, in the absence of shadow, that the Kings would judge him, and his soul would reach its final destination.

I stood between my mother and Ryder. "In the letter you sent, you said Da died in an equipment accident."

Ma didn't even blink. "He did."

"I've never heard of an equipment accident that cuts a man's tongue clean off."

"Hush. We will speak of this after the ceremony," she said as she waved me off. Just as the last words left her lips, coils of pure light streamed from Da's nose and mouth. His soul. Brighter and larger than others I saw in the past.

We all kneeled in unison, bowing our heads in respect. I watched through my brows as Da's soul slowly ascended toward the sky. Relief warmed the blood in my veins when I saw his soul travel toward the stars. That relief morphed into frigid horror when his shadow emerged from the water. Tendrils of darkness reached out from the creek as if Death himself returned to claim Da's soul. The shadows wrapped around his soul, consuming the light.

The full moon disappeared behind a cloud, plunging us all into utter darkness. The creek, which shimmered in the moonlight just a moment ago, turned black and murky. The swirling mass of shadow slowly fell beneath the surface of the water and vanished into the gloomy depths. Da did not ascend to the Land Above the Stars. His shadow dragged his soul downward, to the Shadow Realm.

Something within my chest ached and burned, stealing the air from my lungs. Anger clawed its way from somewhere deep within me, ready to kill. Instinct had my fingers reaching toward the hilts of my throwing knives. In the distance, thunder rumbled as if in answer to my pain. "I don't understand." My voice no longer sounded like my own. It was low and hoarse. "He was a good man," I whispered, shaking my head. "What did he have to be punished for?"

"He was a soldier. A Captain," Ma replied. "All soldiers have blood on their hands. But your Da had more than most."

"So, he will be punished for fighting for his country? His people? His family? He'll spend eternity in shadow because he did what was expected of him?" My voice rose with my anger. My nails dug into my palms so hard, blood seeped through my fingers.

A warm hand found my shoulder. I looked over to see that Ryder's gaze was still fixed on the creek, where Da's body now faded into shadow that drifted off in the wind. The knot in Ryder's throat bobbed before he spoke. "He always knew where his soul would go. He was content."

I shrugged out of his grip. "I don't care. He didn't deserve it." We watched Da's physical body dissipate into darkness, so that his energy could be reused. When nothing remained, I turned to Ma. "Tell me how he died."

"He urged the Southern Army Generals to call a ceasefire. He arranged a meeting with the Northern Commanders. He wanted to send a message to the Northern Kingdom. He said he'd found a way to end the war–" Ma began.

"But there are many who do not want this war to end. They silenced him quickly," Ryder finished.

We sat outside, staring at the creek where Da's body had just been, for hours. The moon reached its peak when we finally went back inside. We spent the rest of the night sorting through his possessions, deciding what to keep and what to sell.

Ma retired to her room first, leaving Ryder and I in the common space in the early hours of the morning. I opened the lid to Da's last chest. Within it, I found all his weapons and armor. I reached in and grabbed his assassin's mask. Made from the same metal as his ebony blades.

Silenced.

Ryder's words replayed in my head again and again. They thought that they could silence my father, and their problem would disappear.

"I'm not going back to the king's army," I said.

Ryder stopped searching through his chest and sat back on his knees. "What?"

"I'm going to find whoever did this. I will make them pay."

A pause.

"Then I'm going with you."

I barked out a short laugh. "No. Ma needs you here."

Ryder waved me off. "I'd step on her toes more than help her. She's already sick of me being here."

"You don't know what you're walking into. We don't even know who killed him."

"Yes, we do," Ryder said. At my confused expression, he sighed. "Ma dressed him up before you got here. But on his chest–" he paused, shaking his head. "It was a brand burned into his skin. The Vermillion family crest."

Just the sound of that name was enough to have my lip curling in disgust. Everyone knew the Vermillions. They were a bunch of rich bastards who paraded around the city of Shadieh, truly believing that they owned it. They used their money and power to crush those beneath them.

"We'll leave for Shadieh in the morning. I know a few people we can talk to," Ryder said.

Silenced.

That word rang through me again.

"Da talked. He pleaded and begged. We know how that ended. They silenced him. They'll do the same to us. Talking isn't the answer. I'll show them a new type of hell. I'm going to give them exactly what they wanted." I lifted the mask up further to see it in the candlelight. "Let me show them the power that lies in the silence."

That night, I put the mask on for the first time.

CHAPTER 27

Bryce

The water would've turned cold long ago, but I kept warming it up. The tub was small, not big enough for me to stretch out. I didn't care. I wanted to curl up. I wanted to hug my knees close to my chest and stay like that for hours.

It was in times like these that I wished I could burn. I wished I could feel the scorching heat of the water and pretend it was burning Eligor's touch off my skin. But thanks to my power, my skin could not burn or blister. I had to settle for rubbing myself raw with soap and pretending it was cleansing in the way I wanted it to be.

A knock at the bathing chamber door snapped me back to reality. I'd nearly forgotten that I wasn't alone. I knew Ryder would respect my need for space, but I stayed in the bath too long, and he grew worried.

"Bryce?" he called.

"Come in."

The door creaked open. Ryder stood in the doorway, dressed for bed. He wore loose pants that hung low on his hips. His chest was bare, his dark skin gilded by the candlelight. In his hand was a soft, red towel.

"I managed to sweet talk us a new set of sheets," he said. When I said nothing, he continued. "I brought you a towel. Ace and Quinn got a fireplace in their room, so I asked them to warm it for you." He held it out for me to take. I reached out and, sure enough, the cloth was delightfully warm.

I stood up, allowing the night's cold air to caress my bare skin. The water in the tub sloshed and spilled over the edges from the sudden movement. It dripped down my body and onto the floor as I stepped out.

Ryder was instantly there, wrapping me up in the towel. I was perfectly capable of drying myself off, but he insisted. His strong, callused hands used the towel to soothingly stroke my shoulders and back. Once I was dry, he let the towel fall and helped me into a silk robe. He took my hand, led me to the bed, and sat me down on the edge. He knelt behind me, pressing his fingers into the corded muscles of my neck, moving in slow, small circles to relieve the tension in my body. A warmth spread through me that had nothing to do with how hot my bath was. I groaned my appreciation just as his lips brushed over the side of my neck. "Are you okay?" he asked softly.

"I will be," I whispered back, trying my best to smile for him.

One of his hands slid up my chest, coming to rest on my throat. His fingers cupped my jaw. He slowly turned my head to face him. His thumb brushed over my lips, catching on the lower one. His gaze remained fixed on my mouth, as if he could mesmerize every little detail. "I thought I lost you tonight." His voice was so low I nearly mistook the words for a whisper on the wind.

"Death couldn't keep me from you," I told him.

His eyes fluttered closed for a moment before he met my gaze. "No, he couldn't, because I would tear through the very fabric of the realms to get you back. I would douse the stars and set fire to the shadows. And anyone who tries to take you from me will be carved up and left for the wolves."

I shivered at the intensity of his gaze– at the determination in his voice.

"I will destroy whoever would harm you. I would fucking *rip* them apart, because I love you, Bryce Reitenour. Through good and bad, weak and powerful, I will love you. Forever."

My whole body went taut and loose at once.

"I know you've been waiting for those words," he whispered. "I'm sorry it took me so long. I was waiting for the right moment, but I almost lost you tonight. I don't care about perfect moments anymore. Any moment shared with you is perfect. Absolutely, unquestionably perfect. So, will you promise me forever, Bryce?"

Something between a laugh and a sob left me. I leaned forward to press our brows together, closing my eyes. "I love you more than anything, and I promise you forever and always."

Even with my eyes closed, I could *feel* his smile.

Our lips sealed together, and everything else faded away. It was full of both relief and desperation. It was the aftermath of horror—horror of believing we'd never see each other again. One of his hands slid into my hair, tilting my head back to deepen the kiss, while his other slid to my waist, pulling me closer.

I could get lost in him. I ran my hands over every inch of him that I could. Every hard plain of muscle or soft, raised scar. I never wanted to let him go.

We parted for air, and the light in his eyes was enough to cast away all the shadow in my heart and soul. But there was something more. Something awed and fascinated in his stare. He was mesmerized, and his fingers twitched as he fought the urge to brush them over my skin.

Because I was glowing.

Not metaphorically. Literally. There was a faint glow beneath my skin, casting golden light through the room. As if the sun was reflecting off me.

Ryder swallowed thickly, and then said, "I have to tell you something, and you have to promise to stay calm."

I narrowed my eyes. "Okay."

"Promise me."

"I promise."

"That didn't sound very convincing."

"I don't know how I could sound any more convincing," I said, arching a brow.

"You could get back in that tub while I tell you so I know you won't set anything else on fire," he suggested sweetly.

Unease pricked my skin. "Ryder, what is it."

He released an uneasy breath. "While you were gone, Quinn did some reading–"

"Shocking."

Ryder shot me a look. "Anyway, he read all about the gods, and what started the war. He discovered that you, my love, are a descendant of a primal."

The glow subsided swiftly. My body went cold. "*What?*"

"The war started between the gods and the primals, two species of equal power. Gods were born from the moon, and primals were born from the sun."

I stared down at my palms. "So, the reason that I'm the first fire-bender in centuries..."

"Is because the Southern Kingdom hasn't seen a primal in centuries," Ryder finished, watching me carefully.

My body went numb. I fell away from his hold, caught by the pillows. I tried to breathe, but none of the breaths I took seemed to fill my lungs.

"There's more," Ryder said. "You're not just the descendant of *any* primal. We believe you're related to Morrighan, the Primal of Destruction." He took my hand, squeezing it. "Also known as the Queen in the North."

CHAPTER 28

Quinn

The sound of the fire crackling in the hearth was comforting as I leafed through the pages of my book. The warm light cast over the pages and made them look golden. As if the book itself was sent down by the gods. I leaned further into the pillows, wrapping the soft furs tighter around my legs.

It would've been the perfect study environment, if not for the scraping sound of rock against blade as Ace sharpened his axe. He sat across the room, directly in front of the fire, watching the flames intently.

This wasn't the first time Ace and I had to share a room. Still, there was a strange tension filling the space that never existed before. It was unresolved anger from our argument earlier in the night.

Another harsh zing of rock against blade had me shutting the book, annoyance pinching my brows. I couldn't focus with that horrid sound echoing off the walls every few moments.

I made sure to slam the book shut loud enough for him to hear before I spoke. "Are you ever going to put that thing aside?"

I expected him to have a witty remark prepared, for him to flash me that devilish smirk and make my heart skip a beat.

But he didn't.

He didn't look away from the flames. He kept his back turned to me, but I saw the way he straightened. I saw his muscles tense. I braced myself for the worst, but he didn't speak for an eternity. Only when the wood in the hearth popped, sending sparks flying, did he seem to break out of his trance.

"I'm sorry for what I said to you today," he said, his voice low and sincere. I'd never heard him speak like that, not to me.

But that wasn't why my heart lurched in my chest. No, my heart faltered because Ace *apologized.* Aerin Taziri expressed regret toward something. He expressed an emotion other than anger or boredom.

Ace never apologized. Not once in the time I knew him. That was what made me set the book aside entirely. The sheer shock of it had me throwing the furs off my body, sitting up to get a better look at him.

"The last time I saw my parents, we fought. I said awful things, and I could never take them back," Ace went on. "I was angry about our loss today. I didn't mean what I said. But in case the day comes that we can't prepare our last words for one another, I want you to know that the banter is just that. Banter."

My throat tightened. I wanted to ask what he might say to me if that day were to come. I wondered if his words would be gentle, or blunt. Instead, I asked, "You remember your parents?"

He blew out a sharp breath. "Enough."

"Did you love them?"

His chin tipped upward. Still, he did not face me. "Yes."

"Did they love you? Did they approve of you?"

"They never told me otherwise."

I thought of my parents and the words we exchanged when we last saw each other. "Even...even knowing about your–" I paused, searching for the right word. "Preferences?"

Ace finally turned to face me. His eyes were narrowed, stretching the scar that ran through one. He flashed me a cocky grin that threatened to stop my heart entirely. "My *preferences?*"

I lifted my chin, trying my best not to acknowledge the blush tinting my cheeks. "In the bedroom."

Ace's brows flew up. "I didn't make a habit of asking their permission. I was seven years old when they died. But if they still lived, yes, they would approve."

I nodded, fiddling with the furs.

Ace stood then, stalking toward me. "Why do you ask?"

I shrugged. "Curious."

"No need to play coy with me, Quinn," he scoffed. "I noticed you drooling at me within the first two days of meeting you."

My jaw dropped. "I did *not!*"

"You most definitely did."

Yeah, I did.

"There is absolutely nothing drool worthy about you," I retorted, crossing my arms over my chest.

Excitement danced in his eyes. I'd just offered him a challenge. I offered a challenge to a man who loves to gamble. The one person in the group who built his life around bets.

Gods, help me.

He walked alongside the bed until he was standing beside me. Only then did he lean down low, his breath fanning over my face. My fingers shook, so I hid them within the furs. I didn't want to seem nervous. That would make him think he's right.

Ace leaned so far down that his face was only inches from mine. Then, his hand reached out, and I thought it might be coming toward my face. But at the last moment, he veered away and picked up the ale on the nightstand that he never finished, chuckling to himself at my flushed reaction.

He continued to stare down at me with humor glinting in his eye as he took a sip of his drink. The foam stuck to his lip when he finally lowered the cup. I disregarded the thought of licking it away.

"Alright then," Ace said. "How many people have you slept with that were drool worthy?"

I opened my mouth to respond, ready to somehow prove myself right in this scenario, but no words came. I had no idea what to say. I never slept with anyone before. He knew just from the way I stared up at him, dumbfounded.

"So, no one?"

"I've been with plenty of men, thank you very much."

"Sure you have," Ace grunted in response.

I rolled my eyes. "Is it honestly that important?"

Ace smirked. "Let me teach you something you will never learn in one of those books," he said, his voice deepening. "There are only three things of importance in this world. Drinking." He brought the ale to his lips and gulped the rest of it down before setting the cup aside.

I stiffened as he lowered himself to the bed and *prowled* over me.

"Fighting." His fingers threaded into my hair and yanked me back harshly. The burn in my scalp was forgotten when I realized that my lips aligned with his.

I couldn't be sure if he was really going to kiss me, or if this was part of a twisted joke. All I knew was that I wanted him to kiss me. Gods, I wanted it more than anything.

His eyes searched mine before his smirk widened into a wicked grin. "And sex," he muttered before his gaze dropped to my lips. He pulled me forward by my hair and smashed my lips against his.

I was stiff against him, inexperienced and unsure of what to do. It didn't matter. Ace knew exactly what he was doing. He played me like an instrument, knowing exactly where to press and pull. As his lips moved against mine, he ran his tongue along the seam of my lower lip. I parted them for him, and he groaned his appreciation.

That groan set me on fire. It had me running my hands up his chest, fisting the fabric of his shirt. I used it to pull us impossibly closer. He growled his approval of that too.

He angled my head so he could better taste me, explore me. His teeth nipped at my lower lip while his tongue delved into me.

I don't know when I started to kiss him back. Maybe I'd been doing it all along. All I knew was that I never wanted it to end. I wanted him pressed against me, his weight over me, as his tongue battled mine, for all eternity. It was too good. Nothing ever felt this good. Nothing.

He shifted us so that my back was against the headboard. I was trapped between the hard, warm muscle of him and the cool, unrelenting wood of the bed. I groaned when my head hit the hard surface, and the sound snapped whatever restraint Ace had on himself. His fingers curled inward on my scalp, burning my skin as they scraped through my hair and worked their way down to my shoulders. His lips moved faster. His teeth grazed more. His groans turned deeper, richer.

There was nothing slow or loving about the kiss. It was savage and harsh. It was his exploration of me with tongue and teeth. It stole my breath away far quicker than I would've liked.

When he pulled away, that grin was still plastered to his face. We were both panting, just breathing the same air for several long moments. He surveyed my swollen lips and wide eyes and arched a brow. "Well? Drool worthy?"

I could hardly find words. "I suppose it was... adequate."

His answering chuckle was dark and raspy. It rolled along my spine and made me shiver. He noted the movement, his lips tipping up into a smirk. "You infuriate me. Every snarky comment, every history lesson," he said, shaking his head. "And yet every single time you run your mouth, all I can think about is shutting you up just like that."

A wave of heat passed through me. "Oh?"

"I want to show you just how uneducated you are. I want you to know that you might be a genius in some areas, but you know nothing in others. I want to hear you admit that I know more in this. I want to hear you beg for me to teach you in the ways of pleasure." As he spoke, his hands roamed down my body, pulling the furs down with them.

"You don't want to call me drool worthy? That's fine. I have *many* more interesting ways of prying the words from you. Tell me no now, Quinn, or don't say it at all."

I opened my mouth, but the words didn't come. I didn't want him to win, but I wanted this. More than he could know, I wanted to *feel* this, to feel him. For the first time in a very long time, I felt the burning heat of desire. It flushed my skin and coursed through me in waves. He was the only thing that could douse the flames now.

I nodded to him.

Ace's answering smile was a dark, cruel thing. "Good," he whispered. "Now shut your mouth, and keep it shut, or I'll think of more creative ways to keep it occupied."

My jaw snapped shut. He laughed before lowering himself once more.

His lips trailed blazing kisses down my neck as his hands explored my chest. Then his lips followed. His hands slid down past my navel, and I was arching, thrusting my hips toward him, begging for him to relieve me of this pleasurable tension coiling through my body.

Then the door flew open.

Ace was on his feet in an instant. Not because he was ashamed, but because he was caught off guard, and his first instinct was to prepare for attack. But by the way he stood directly in front of me, shielding me from the view of the newcomer, I almost believed that his first instinct was protect me from them if need be.

333

Ryder rushed into the room. He stopped dead in his tracks when he saw us. His face paled, and he glanced nervously between us and the door. "Am I interrupting something?"

Too quickly, I yelled, "No!"

"Yes," Ace said flatly, annoyed.

The sound of footsteps stomping through the corridor stopped Ryder from saying anything further. He spun on his feet and backed up to the bed, standing beside Ace. If I didn't know any better, I'd say Ryder was running from someone, and he chose to burst into our room for his own protection.

Sure enough, a very angry-looking Bryce appeared in the doorway. "You knew I descended from a *primal,* and you didn't tell me until *now?"* She froze in the threshold just like Ryder had. She took one look at Ace and me and smirked. "Finally. Was it good?"

"It would've been," Ace grumbled.

"*Ace,"* I gritted out.

Then Bryce and Ryder seemed to forget about us entirely. He hopped over a reading chair, backing away. "You promised you'd stay calm."

"Do you see anything on fire?" Bryce bit back.

Ryder glanced around as if it were a trick question and he had to make sure. "No?"

"Then I'd say I'm doing pretty good so far."

334

She lunged toward him, and Ryder sidestepped just in time. "Ace!" Ryder snapped. "A little help?"

But Ace was already climbing onto the bed, using my lap as his own personal pillow. There was something sweet in the ease of it. The way it wasn't second-guessed or questioned. He leaned into me and settled himself into the furs, crossing his arms beneath his head. "Nah, this is the most entertainment I've had in weeks."

I snorted. "We just learned that the history we know is a lie, the Reaper is a god, Bryce is a primal, and we met a healer with primal magic, but *this* is the most entertainment you've come across?"

Ace looked up at me through his lashes. "Kings, gods, primals, what does it matter? They're all the same entitled snobs in my book. But this? A passionate fight between an angered descendant of a primal and the brother of the Reaper? Yeah, this is entertaining as shit. You know the best part about it?"

"I'm sure you're going to tell me." My hands slid into his hair, stroking the silky strands back into place after I'd ruffled them earlier.

"Best part is we get to take a bet. Do we think Bryce will win with fire and fury, or Ryder with his annoyingly boring smooth-talking and morality?"

"Oh, definitely Bryce," I said, watching her circle her boyfriend like a shark in open water.

"Yup," Ace agreed.

Ryder shot us a glare. "I appreciate your support."

"Can I have your swords when she burns you to a crisp? I don't think you'll need them where you're going," Ace called.

"I'm going to calm her down, and then I'm shoving one of those swords right up your–" Ryder stopped to dodge Bryce's fist from colliding with his jaw. "Hey! Why are you so upset? When was I supposed to tell you? You were having a fiery seizure literally an hour ago!"

"Fair point," Ace said. Ryder glared at him again. "What? You said you wanted my help!"

"That's not helping. That's instigating!" Ryder shouted back.

"Both of you shut up! I'm upset because you let me sit in a bathtub for eternity wallowing in self-pity instead of informing me that I'm the descendant of the Primal of Destruction who could very well be destroying the Vermillion estate as we speak to help the Reaper!"

"Sounds like a personal problem if someone wanted to have a pity party and lock herself in the bathing chamber," Ace muttered.

Bryce's simmering gaze swung to him. "I'm sorry, did I ask you?"

Ace jolted up, waving his hands in frustration. "You barged into *my* room! You want to have it out in here, you get to listen to my commentary. If not, kindly close the door on your way out!"

Bryce crossed her arms over her chest. "Fair enough, but we're leaving in the morning. We're going to the warehouse on the East Side. If the Reaper survives the Vermillions, he'll know to meet us there. It's our closest safehouse to the North Side." When we all nodded our agreement, she turned to Ryder. She gestured for him to walk out of the room before her. He hesitantly brushed past her. "If you hear screaming," she glared over her shoulder at him, "Don't come running."

Ace smirked. "Likewise."

Bryce's answering laughter echoed through the hall as the door finally clicked shut. Then there was only silence and a whole lot of searing tension as Ace turned back to me.

"One last chance. Am I drool worthy?" he asked as he leaned closer.

I fiddled with the furs. "I don't know. I would have to see again."

He hummed his consideration as he climbed over me. The rest of the night was a blur, but I knew one thing for certain:

Aerin Taziri was undoubtedly, irrevocably drool worthy.

CHAPTER 29

Mara

"Holy gods."

I smiled. "They won't help you."

I'd never seen someone more awe-stricken in all my life. Kalieth's jaw hung open. His eyes widened, pushing his brows upward. Wrinkles stretched across his forehead. After a long moment, he finally cleared his throat and spoke. "But– your voice."

Yes, it sounds like someone tossed my vocal cords into a meat grinder.

"It's a bit rusty from lack of use," I said. Though the sound of my voice changed significantly from taking off the mask. I nodded to it as I placed it aside. "But I had the mask spelled so that if I ever spoke while wearing it, my father's voice would be heard instead."

"Why?"

My eyes flew away from the mask to meet Kalieth's. I couldn't keep the resentment from seeping into my words as I said, "Because he had much more to say before Xaphan cut out his tongue."

Kalieth snapped his mouth shut. He looked to the floor. "I'm sorry for what he did."

"Your words mean nothing to me. They are merely the shadow of action," I told him. "I could care less if you're sorry. All I care about is that you fight with me."

"My sword is yours... um–"

He looked at me expectantly. My ability to pick up on social cues was unpracticed. It took me a moment to realize that he was waiting for a name.

"Mara."

He nodded. "My sword is yours, Mara."

The sound of my name on his lips sent a chill through me. It sounded strange; foreign. No one had called me by my name in a year. It felt good to be addressed again. To be *seen*. It was... humanizing.

"Tell me, *Mara,*" he practically purred my name, as if he knew exactly how it affected me. "How exactly did you know about this place?" He gestured to the space around us. His apartment.

"I know a whole manner of things you might believe to be secret," I said with a shrug.

The truth was, when Ryder and I first came to Shadieh, Ryder was set on forming a team. So, while he went scouting for candidates, I watched the Vermillions. I researched them in the library and followed them around most nights, learning the routines of each brother. But Kalieth was a mystery. There was little record of him in the library, and while his brothers visited brothels or gambled in the underground fighting rings on the East Side, Kalieth was elusive. It took me several weeks to track him down.

The first time I ever saw Kalieth, I watched from a rooftop as he handed a gold mark to a shopkeeper in Center City. It was a small jewelry shop, not one I would expect someone of his status to buy from. In exchange for the mark, she handed him a small paper bag. The smile she gave him was one of pure appreciation, likely because the gold mark he gave her could pay her rent.

He accepted the bag, said something that made her laugh, and then turned around to continue down the street. When he turned, I saw his blue eyes, dark hair, sharp features, and something electric coursed through me. There was a profound difference between him and his brothers. It wasn't just physical. It was in the way he held himself. He was... approachable. Unlike his siblings, who held their chins high and looked down upon everyone else. There was something about Kalieth that felt warm and familiar.

As he walked down the streets of Center City, weaving through the crowds, I walked parallel with him on the rooftops. For the first time since my father's death, I felt something other than cold rage. I felt... curious about Kalieth Vermillion. That curiosity only grew when I followed him back to his apartment and found that he did not stay in the Vermillion Estate with the rest of his family.

That was how I knew to come here.

Kalieth arched a brow at my cryptic answer but didn't push it. "Alright then, keep your secrets. What comes next in your brilliant plan?"

"We rest here. We return to the others in a day or two." I reached up and unclipped my heavy cloak. I shrugged it off and let it pool at my feet before sitting on the edge of the bedframe and reaching to untie my boots.

"As happy I am that you feel comfortable enough to walk into *my* home, throw a *knife* at my face, and propose *staying* here, why wait to regroup with the others?"

"Because I was chained, paralyzed, and nearly unmasked by Xaphan Vermillion tonight. I don't have the energy to face everyone, and I don't need to see their faces when they discover that I failed. Besides, you and I probably have a search party after us." My boots hit the floor with a thud, and I stood barefoot on the cold tile.

The ache in my muscles became prominent in my mind once my eyes found the bed. The thought of sinking into the mattress brought a weight to my eyes. I fought to keep them open.

"And what are we meant to do here for two days?" Kalieth must've followed my gaze to the bed. "After all, this is an awfully small room, along with an awfully small bed."

The bed was wide enough to be four or five soldier cots put together. The wolf furs and blankets spread across beckoned to me with a promise of warmth and comfort. A promise that completely contradicted any sleeping accommodations that I ever found myself in the king's army. Memories of bodies crammed together flashed through my eyes. There was no concept of personal space in the army. The only warmth to be found on the Northern front was the body warmth of those around you. We huddled together, with no regard for gender or decency. The only thing on our minds was survival.

I wondered how Kalieth could worry about such things now, after serving his own time. It was uncomfortable, sure, but it was a necessity. If he wanted to risk roaming the streets after tonight's events, I would bid him good luck, but I sure as hell was not leaving now.

"I'm sure your fellow soldiers appreciated your incertitude in the frigid cold of the Zaverath region," I scoffed. When his brows pinched together, I added, "What? Did daddy make a call to ensure you never had to tour there? I should've known a Vermillion son would never have to sodden his boots in the heavy snows."

Kalieth looked to the floor, his jaw tensing. His lips parted as though he meant to say something, but he thought better of it and sealed them shut once more. He pressed them together into a thin, pale line. When his icy blue eyes finally met mine again, realization dawned on me like the first rays of sunlight cracking over the horizon.

"Good gods," I said, the words born on a sigh of disbelief. "You didn't serve."

The lump in Kalieth's throat bobbed. As it rose back up, I found that my anger rose with it. What sort of *coward* used his status to relieve himself of the responsibilities shared by every citizen of the Southern Kingdom? Why should he have the means to save himself from the sorrow and guilt that a soldier carries for the rest of their days?

My lip curled in disgust. I looked down on him through lowered brows. "I should have known. You would have died within the first few hours of touring the front lines."

"It's not what you think," he said, his eyes still down.

"I think men like you are too cowardly to be willing to undergo severe suffering, because you fear Death and pain, but you highly prize being mentioned as having suffered," I spat. "I thought you might've had potential, but I should've listened to my brother. You are nothing but the shadow of a once mighty name."

Kalieth shook his head, his chin rising once more. "I'm no coward. My father bribed General Verzelli to excuse each of my brothers, but I fully intended to register regardless. I withdrew when someone close to me fell ill. I couldn't leave her."

My anger faltered for a single second. It was not the answer I expected. I knew Kalieth saw the slight change when his lips twitched up into a smirk. "Jealous?" he asked.

Prick.

"It was my sister," he finished before I had a chance to come up with any sort of response. It wouldn't have mattered if I did because his words shocked me into silence.

Xaphan had a daughter?

There was no mention of her in the records.

"I was her protector. We treated each other like siblings would. With sarcasm and crude remarks, but also with loyalty and care. I would've gone to the ends of the world for her." As he spoke, a soft smile graced his lips. Despite that, I could see the sorrow within his eyes. I saw the silent pain in the way his brows knotted together. I knew that sorrow. I felt it each day. It subsided over time, but it never truly left. It sits in my heart, taints my soul, and darkens my shadow.

"What happened to her?" I asked.

He looked to me once more. The eyes I once saw as stagnant ice now seemed to rage like the hottest blue flames of a fire. Hatred burned while disgust simmered. I nearly took a step back from the raw emotion he displayed. I'd never seen him so angry. I'd never felt intimidated by him. But now, as he clenched both his fists in a white-knuckled grip, and seethed with as much hatred as I did, I found myself preparing for a fight. "You killed her." The words were spat at me, laced with rage.

A wave of white-hot shock spread through my body. I racked my brain to try to remember any young girl I might have killed, or who may have been collateral damage in one of my raids. No one came to mind.

"That's what Xaphan told us. He told all of us that you let her burn in one of the warehouse fires. I knew, though, once I started to truly get to know you and the others– I knew you would never hurt an innocent girl like that," he added quickly. Any sorrow I saw in him was gone now. All that was left was rage. "He confessed tonight. He confessed to killing her. She found out the truth about his fortune and threatened to go public. He killed her before she could. He silenced her. So, trust me when I tell you that I seek revenge just as fiercely as you do."

Silenced.

That word again. It had my hands clenching into fists. The need to punch something surged suddenly with the adrenaline in my veins. I lived in silence for an entire year because of that damn word. Much may have been different if I'd never heard it.

His rage and hesitation to believe us made sense now. All this time he'd been grieving. He blamed me for the death of the person he loved most in the world. He plotted my demise as revenge for her. I understood why he confined himself to his bedchamber after Bryce told him we did not set fire to the warehouse he spoke of. I understood why I had to leave food at his door to make sure he ate. It was in that time that he truly realized that all he knew was a lie. The anger I felt rising only a minute ago slowly dissipated.

There was a deep sadness in him. His sister left a void that I could not fill. Both of us had

345

voids. Dark spots that tainted our souls. The shadows of our loved ones whose light once shined upon us, only to leave us with darkness in their absence. We could only hope to relieve the pain by avenging them.

"I'm sorry about your sister, truly. Your father will pay, I swear it. But my plan needs sudden reassessment."

Kalieth nodded. "Did you know what he was?"

I huffed a laugh. "No. If I had known Xaphan was a god, I wouldn't have tried to take him on with a sword."

"Do you know how to kill him?"

"No, but I know someone who will. To speak to her, I must sleep." I didn't hesitate to climb into bed. I'd never felt anything as soft as the wolf furs against my skin. Every muscle in my body relaxed once I sank into the soft mattress. It took everything I had not to groan and stretch out.

Kalieth didn't follow. I felt the heat of his gaze on my back like a brand. "I'll take the floor."

I huffed into the pillow, rolling my eyes. I turned over and glared at him. "Do I look like an insecure damsel who requires six feet of space between myself and a man to feel comfortable? I know every way in the book to kill you before you could put a hand on me. Quit whining and get in the godsdamn bed so I can sleep," I said, my words sharp.

Kalieth arched a brow. "The next time you're trying to convince a man to get in bed with you, I wouldn't start off with threatening murder."

I couldn't stop my lips from tipping up into a smile. I said nothing as he joined me in bed, our backs facing each other. I let myself relax, ignoring the way his warmth beckoned. I cleared my mind of all things, focusing on the vast nothingness behind my closed eyelids. I imagined falling into that darkness. Sinking farther and farther until I was too far from reality to think. Too far to feel the ache in my body. Too far from reality to hear–

"So, you've been a woman all along?"

I rolled my tongue along my teeth in annoyance, drew in a sharp breath, and said, "For twenty-one years to be exact."

I closed my eyes again. I sank into the darkness. I became one with it. I had no thoughts. I had no pain. I was drifting out into a sea of shadow. The waves engulfed me, and I could finally rest–

"My brothers might have a heart attack when they discover they were bested by a woman."

My eyes flew open. "Kalieth," I said through clenched teeth. "What will it take to get you to *shut up*?"

There was a pause as he considered. "Three questions. Answer them and I'll stop talking."

I sighed. "Fine."

"Of all the names in the world, why would you choose to call yourself the *Reaper?*"

I stilled. "I give you three questions and *that's* what you ask me? Aren't you curious about more interesting things?"

He turned over. The mattress dipped with his weight, and I slid back slightly, until I was pressed against his chest. He chuckled then. His warm breath fanned over my shoulder, and it took everything in me not to shiver. It'd been a long time since I let anyone this close. "I'm curious about many things, Reaper," he murmured in my ear. "But I don't think the others are entirely appropriate, though they would most definitely be *interesting.*"

I refused to think about whatever it was that buzzed in the air whenever we were close to one another. I threw my arm back. My elbow made rather harsh contact with his side. He grunted in pain. I smirked and returned my thoughts to his question. "I chose nothing. The citizens of Shadieh started to call me that all on their own."

"Why would they choose that name? I thought a reaper is a harvester of crop."

"It is. But the term has been used to describe harvesters of many things, including souls. The great killers of old were known as reapers. Death followed wherever they went. That's why the people named me as such. Death walks with me."

Kalieth was silent for a long moment. I thought, for a few seconds, that I might finally be able to get some rest. But he thought of his final question. "Why didn't you kill me the second you had me on my knees on that rooftop?"

I missed not having to talk. "I knew you'd be useful."

He drew a finger over my arm. The feel of his feather-light touch had bumps rising across my skin. "That's awfully vague. You would've gotten to Xaphan with or without my help. What exactly was my use to you?"

"That's four questions," I replied, my voice a bit softer than I meant it to be.

Kalieth leaned down. His voice grew deeper as his lips brushed against my ear. "Come on, Reaper. Loosen up. How about I start asking those interesting questions we spoke of?"

I fought the urge to lean into his touch. "Do you want my elbow to go for your face next time?"

"I'll be expecting it now."

I jammed my elbow back again. Instead of going for his head, as I said I would, I went low. I hit him just below the navel. He gasped, curling in on himself as he groaned.

I smiled. "You're right. I do feel better now."

"You are a wicked little thing, aren't you?" he asked through clenched teeth.

I laughed. The sound was strange, coming from my damaged throat. But it was something I would treasure forever. It was the first time I laughed aloud since my Da died. Nearly a year later.

I should've moved away. I should've escaped the finger he dragged along my skin, but I couldn't. It'd been so long since anyone touched me. Not in a lustful way– but in a gentle, wonderous stroke, as if Kalieth couldn't resist reaching out and making sure I was real. It was such an absurd, simple thing. I hardly knew I missed touch until now. Until I felt the pads of his fingertips brush against me. I gave in and shifted further back, further into him. He didn't expect it, but he took the opportunity to band an arm around my waist. I glanced down, surprised at myself for allowing him this close. Surprised by how *right* it felt. "This is all rather sudden," I said, the words quiet. "You weren't clawing at my breeches yesterday, or an hour ago."

His answering chuckle was a dark, breathy thing that skittered over my bones. "I thought you were a man."

"Does being a woman change so much?"

His finger paused its voyage across my skin. "It changed nothing in some ways, and everything in others."

I hid the tremor in my voice as best as I could as I murmured, "Tell me."

"An hour ago, I respected you. I wanted to fight for you and lay my life down if need be because I believed in you. In everything you stood for. But now..." he scoffed and ran a hand through his hair. "Knowing you're a woman, all of that was multiplied tenfold. It would be amazing if we lived in a world where women could casually accomplish what you have, but we don't. You are a woman in a man's world, and you're conquering it all the same. You should be worshipped for it." He paused then, letting me consider the weight of his words. He didn't hold his tongue for long. "I know a few ways of worship, and they include those *interesting* things." He paused again. "Plus, you're not ugly."

I glanced back at him, choking on another laugh. "Thank you?"

"Well, I would've thought that if a woman chose to hide behind a mask for a year, she wouldn't turn out to be the most beautiful woman I'd ever seen."

I raised my elbow again, but he saw it coming this time. He grabbed me and yanked me back until there was no space between us, pinning my arm against his hip. "No more of that," he hissed.

"You were sent to kill me, Kalieth. I'm no fool. How could I ever trust you?" I asked.

"Yes, I was sent to kill you, and you knew that, but you didn't kill me. Not even when I betrayed you. I saw it in your eyes, how badly you wanted it, but you still didn't do it. You couldn't. Just as I couldn't kill you."

"You're right, we didn't kill one another. Should we pat ourselves on the back? Perhaps a celebratory drink?"

"You joke, but I'm serious. My purpose in life was once my family name. You know what I did for that. But now it's you. I'm not entirely sure you know what you've started." I drew in a sharp breath at the sudden feel of his teeth scraping over my neck, fighting the urge to tilt my head. "Tell me Reaper, that day in the snow, did you feel it?

351

When I had you beneath me, did you feel the connection between us? It was like... Like..."

"Like the last lightning strike of a summer storm," I said, so low it was nearly a whisper.

"Yes," he breathed. "Exactly."

I felt it. He rolled on top of me, and that feeling settled in my chest. Lightning struck and my heart pounded in answer. I let him stay there, let him have the power, because I was lost in his gaze. Those blue eyes were a deep swirling sea, and I was drowning. I don't know what any of it means, but I know I can't trust it. I can't trust him.

"Then no. No idea what you're talking about."

He tensed against me. I don't know what he expected. Did he want me to declare my love for him, wrap my arms over his neck and ask him to take me into the night? Was that what the other upper-class women did when he whispered sweet nothings in their ears?

I would not be so easily manipulated.

"One day, Reaper, we will both succumb to whatever it is that lies between us. One day you'll succumb to me."

One side of my lips tipped up. I turned over, facing him completely. Surprise shined in his eyes, but he said nothing. My smirk widened into a grin as I leaned closer. Until we shared breath. Until his lips were only inches from mine. The tension between us crackled and sparked. I could see his pulse as it quickened. I moved forward, glancing down at his lips, loving the way they parted on a sharp inhale. He closed his eyes– waiting. I stopped only a hair's width away. "You'll have me when the sun sets in the east and the moon rises in the west."

I pushed him hard enough to knock him off the bed completely. He grappled with the sheets, but ultimately lost his grip and fell to the ground with a hard thud. "I changed my mind," I said, rolling over once more. "You will sleep on the floor."

CHAPTER 30

Mara

The dreams started over three seasons ago. They began with mere flashes that I'd hardly remember in the morning. I'd see a glimpse of a silhouette, or I'd hear a fraction of a sentence. Weeks passed, and the dreams turned into something more– something real. I was still asleep somewhere in the physical world, but my mind was very much aware in this place.

It was a world of shadow. Burning globes of white fire provided the only light. There were billions of lights, and yet it wasn't enough to quell the darkness surrounding me. It seemed to go on to no end. Nothingness stretched out in all directions for as far as my eyes could see.

It was terribly cold in this place. Not freezing like the Northern regions of the world, but chilly like the winds from the sea after sunset. It was enough to send a shiver up my spine, nothing more.

"You failed," she called. Her voice came from all directions. I couldn't pinpoint it.

"Yes."

"You refused what I offered so that you could pursue your previous goals, and yet my gift was the very thing which would've brought you victory."

I rolled my tongue along my teeth. Annoyance flared within me, bringing heat back to my skin. I was never one to appreciate being told that I'm wrong. "I do not want your power. I want no part of this greater agenda. I do not serve the mighty Cheusi, she who sends innocent souls to the Shadow Realm," I spat, my voice laced with hatred.

Two of the orbs of light in the distance began to move. They got brighter and larger as they approached. Eyes. They were Cheusi's eyes, burning bright like the great suns of the galaxies. It was hard to differentiate her skin from the surrounding darkness. But I saw the glow of her freckles, like stars in the night sky. Constellations stretched over the bridge of her nose. Her arched brows were the tails of shooting stars. Her lips were filled in by the faint white clouds of the milky way.

"You should not be so easily convinced that I am your enemy," she said. Her voice carried through space, travelling on for eternity. "Mortals are quick to believe rumor. Too easily scared of the dark." She began to circle me slowly. "They see the shadows and cower. Their fear convinces them of my vileness. This power is far from evil, Mara, I can assure you."

355

"You want me to believe this is the power of creation? Why would all things, good and bad, originate from the shadows?"

"You believe that only evil holds a place in shadow? What do you think there was when there was nothing? Before the worlds formed and the suns burned? Before life roamed the realms?"

Silence ensued. I wouldn't flatter her by asking her to continue.

"Darkness, Mara. Before the origins, when there was nothing, there was darkness." Cheusi stopped circling and came to stand before me. She searched my eyes. "Don't you see? All things, even the light, had to fight their way through the darkness for a place in this world."

"Fine. You want me to believe you're the good guy? Tell me why you send innocent souls, including my father's, to the Shadow Realm to suffer."

Cheusi sighed, pinching the bridge of her nose. "I did no such thing."

My lip curled up in disgust. "I watched shadow consume my father's soul before dragging it downward."

"Mortals and their tall tales," she scoffed, rolling her eyes. "There is no Shadow Realm, and there is no Land Above the Stars. There is only this place. All souls come here. All except for the souls of the primals." She swept her hands in a grand gesture.

I followed her gaze into the vast emptiness. Millions of lights burning on through the infinite dark.

"You saw a soul leave a physical body. What exactly did it look like? A pure soul is a soft, dry light, which leaves the body like lightning breaking from a cloud. A burdened soul is the dense fog of an autumn morning, pouring out of the body in plumes of mist. But a sinful soul, well, that is like a raging fire of starlight."

As she spoke, I noticed that not all the lights here behaved the same way. Some burned like silver fire, others swirled like mist, and a few shined bright without movement. The souls she described– they were here. The lights surrounding me were resting souls. Millions of them.

"I protect them here, in the shadows. They are not eternally damned to suffer. Souls are made of aether, the essence of starlight. The fuel of our power. Their place is in darkness, because here they can shine bright among the stars," Cheusi finshed, gesturing to the sky around her. That's where we were– where she brought me each night. The night sky.

There are no words to describe the betrayal of belief. To be told one thing your whole life, and to know how the world works, only for it all to come crashing down. No Kings, no Shadow Realm, and now even the concept of the shadows was questionable.

"This power is not evil. *I* am not evil, despite the darkness I walk in," Cheusi said.

357

"And you're a goddess?"

"Yes. The first."

All emotion left me as I asked, "And what does that make Xaphan Vermillion?"

Any softness in Cheusi's features disappeared immediately. Her lip curled up in disgust as she sneered, "a menace."

"What more than that?"

A pause. "A false god. He is not like the rest of us. He was not born from the moon. He was *made* many centuries ago. He does not age, and he's been among mortals for far too long. He calls himself the God of Conflict, Strife, and Contention. He feeds off any sort of conflict. It gives him strength. He haunts battlefields and takes great delight in the act of war. He and Morrighan were said to ride together, in the beginning, crying with glee at the terrible sight of battle. But war wasn't his only outlet. He was often involved in family arguments, blood feuds, and territory battles. He despised the other gods, and vice versa. They often wouldn't choose to interact much with him. They saw him as unnatural. An abomination. Morrighan was his only ally. He was mortal once. Morrighan gave him power. She made him what he is now in exchange for his valued service. They continue to conspire with each other to this day," Cheusi said.

"That's possible? To *make* a god?" I asked.

"It would seem so, though I have no idea how she did it." She paused, shaking her head. "If you want to defeat him, you will need the rest of my power, not just this fraction you seem to be content with."

"Why should I take this power? Why did you give me a taste of it? Because I'm out to kill Xaphan?"

Cheusi narrowed her eyes, losing her patience. "I am dying, Mara. Long ago, a witch took my immortality. Time works differently here. It's like stretching a minute into a million seconds. I've been here, holding on to the few scraps of aether I have left to see my power given to the right person. There are few beings left with gods' blood. You are the only one fit."

My muscles locked up. I stood completely still, unable to move. "What did you say?"

Her brows pulled together. "You didn't know? Have you never questioned your eyes? Never asked why you and your brother are the only people in all the Southern Kingdom with silver irises? Never wondered why they seem to glow like moonlight?"

"What's your point?" I asked, crossing my arms over my chest. The chill of this place was starting to seep into my skin again.

"It's aether, Mara. All who have a gods' blood in their veins have silver eyes. Vermillion is the only exception. His eyes glow solely when he uses his power, because he was not born from gods' blood. But you were. You and I are gods, Mara, because aether flows in our veins, just like it flowed in your father's veins. Do you know who he really was? Why Vermillion killed him?"

I couldn't bring myself to speak.

"When he died, you should have inherited his power, as his strongest child. You were robbed of it because Xaphan took your father's aether when he killed him." Cheusi sighed, shaking her head. "You were *always* destined to have great power. I may not have a bloodline, but when I sent a wave of my power to search the realms for my champion, it found you. The shadows *chose* you."

I knew my father better than anyone else in this world. He would've told me, or I would've figured it out. If this were all true– the man I went to war for– I didn't even know him. I didn't know what he was or who he fought for. The man who raised and trained me, who protected me and told me stories after sunset– he was a complete stranger.

It was too much. It was knee-wobbling, world-shattering information, dumped onto me all at once. The questions I wanted to ask came to me far too fast. I couldn't pick one to ask first. Instead, I stayed silent, going over it again and again in my head.

"Vermillion killed your father under direct orders from Morrighan, because he was one of the few gods left, awake and fighting. You want revenge? Take this power and finish what your father started."

Everything I thought I knew was a lie. But I did know this: my father died. Bryce was tortured. Ace lost his parents. Quinn was forced into hiding. Kalieth's sister was sacrificed. *All* of it was Vermillion's doing. The war he supports separated families and orphaned children. The children he raised trade slaves and torture innocent soldiers.

Cheusi knew despite my silence. She saw the determination in my eyes. The eagerness in my furrowed brows. The passion in my clenched fists.

Her lips tipped upwards into a small smile. "Go then and take it all with you," she said, her voice soft.

"What happens to you when I leave here? When I take your power with me?"

Cheusi drew a long breath through her nose. She closed her eyes, picturing something. "I will disappear into shadow, finally free from any physical form. I will be one of the many voices in your shadows. I will be everything, and nothing. I will die only to be absorbed into the fabric of this universe as something new."

"You want to die?"

"After a millennium, I want nothing more."

I nodded. I'd served in the king's army for a fraction of that time, and I could understand. Countless decades of war and death would take its toll on any being, even a god. I gulped down any hesitation and asked, "What happens to me?"

"A champion turned goddess. The Bringer of Night. The Goddess of Creation reborn. Just promise me one thing, *Reaper,*" she spat the name as if it tasted sour in her mouth. "Despite your rage, never allow yourself to find delight in another's misfortune, that is the beginnings of a tyrant."

Did she honestly think I would follow the same path Vermillion did? No, she couldn't. If she thought for a second I would, then she never would have surrendered her power to me. But she couldn't ignore the influence of rage. It made some people blind to morals.

I kept my chin high and willed my mind to return to my physical body. Over my shoulder, I said, "I kill tyrants."

The words echoed through the stars and beyond into infinite space. Three words to shape the future. A vow taken with souls long lost as witnesses. An oath hidden in the constellations. An eternal promise etched into the night sky.

Chapter 31

Kalieth

My back did not agree with the hard, cold floor. I woke feeling stiff in nearly every part of my body. Luckily, I managed to wake before the Reaper. So, I returned to the bed, careful not to wake her.

Her.

The Reaper was a *woman.*

I had the night to sleep on it, but I still couldn't quite wrap my head around it. A woman beat me in combat. A woman was making my father's life a living hell. A woman destroyed all my family worked for. She was the only one brave enough to stand against him. The only one with the strength to fight for the commoners in this city. The only one with the skill to bring change.

I think I'm in love.

She was, after all, beautiful. In a rare, natural sort of way. The bottom half of her face was littered with acne from keeping that mask on constantly, but her skin was otherwise flawless. I did notice, however, markings on her arms and chest that I'd never seen before. They were like tattoos, but much darker; richer. Swirls and wisps of ink across her skin that looked like tendrils of shadow spread across her entire body. I wondered if the darkness in the room the night before prevented me from seeing them.

Without thinking, I lifted a finger and traced one of the swirls over her forearm. That was when she stirred. I immediately withdrew my hand, inching away.

Her eyes fluttered open, looking brighter and more alive with silver flames than ever. She blinked a few times before finally coming to her senses. Once she did, she looked up at me, shocked, and pushed away from me. She got to her feet. "I thought I told you to sleep on the floor."

"And I did. I was just enjoying a few moments of comfort before a long day," I said, tucking a hand behind my head.

Mara said nothing as her eyes searched for her cloak. My gaze dropped to her tattoos once more. "The markings," I said. "Do they have meaning?"

Mara looked down through furrowed brows to the tattoos on her dark skin as if she were seeing them for the first time. She opened her mouth to speak, but words did not come for another moment. "They're a reminder of what I've become," she said, her voice still hoarse, but slowly getting better.

364

She found her cloak and boots. She fastened the cloak around her shoulders and sat on the end of the bed to fiddle with the laces of her shoes. I sat up and watched her.

"Where are we going?" I asked after a moment.

"*I* need training. *You* will stay here," she said.

"Training?"

She had no response. She stood up, her laces tied, and made for the door, wrapping her weapon's belt around her waist as she went. She stopped short when she saw the mask sitting on the table beside the doorway. She stared silently, considering. She broke her vow of silence, but was it time for the city to put a face to the Reaper?

I jumped from the bed while she was distracted. I pulled my own cloak over my shoulders and slipped into my boots. I was ready to go by the time she stepped forward and tentatively picked up the mask. She raised it to her face and fastened it into place before pulling her hood down to hang over her brow.

She didn't need to face me to know I was behind her, ready to go. "No," she said without glancing my way.

"You never finished my training. If you're going to train, I'm coming. I need to know what I'm doing wrong. I want to be a formidable opponent," I told her, taking another step forward.

She turned to face me, only her eyes visible beneath the hood and mask. She narrowed them on me as her brows lowered. She stepped forward until our faces were mere inches apart and we were sharing breath. An image of last night flashed through my mind, coiling up the tension between us once more. A sudden chill coursed through me. It reminded me of the crisp, fresh air after the first real snow of winter.

"You want to know what you do wrong?" she asked, voice scratchy like stone against iron.

She grabbed me by the collar of my shirt and pushed me out the door. I was suddenly bathed in blinding sunlight. She tossed me my sword, which I caught before it could hit me square in the face. She followed me out, shutting the door behind her. She closed in on me before I had a chance to blink and pushed me over the side of the narrow walkway. I fell one level, grappling with the air and landed hard on my back on the next balcony. The breath was knocked out of me. I struggled to regain it as I coughed and turned onto my side.

"You let your guard down constantly," Mara said.

She jumped from the floor above and landed beside me gracefully. I scrambled to get to my feet, but she was quick to kick me down.

"You don't know how to use your position to your advantage," she sneered.

She made to kick again, but I caught her ankle and yanked. She was thrown off balance. She stopped to steady herself, giving me enough time to get back to my feet.

I drew my sword and lunged forward. She sidestepped before I moved an inch.

"Your eyes give away your every move."

I turned, bringing my sword toward her gut. She spun away before the blade reached her.

"You're arrogant. You wield a sword like you would a butterknife, as if it is another tool that you can inflict your will upon."

I backed away, breathing hard. "That's exactly what it is."

She shook her head, scoffing. "No. You still ignore our lessons."

"Hard to take anything away from them when the instructor doesn't speak."

"Well, I'm speaking now."

"I'm listening."

Mara cocked her head, eyes narrowing once more. She took up a defensive stance and drew her sword. As graceful as a prairie cat, she moved through the motions.

"Do you know why I had you practice with weighted swords?" she asked as she sliced her sword through the air, moving her body through the motions of the eight-pointed star.

"To provoke me?"

"To get you accustomed to the weight so that when the day came for you to wield your true sword again, you would feel no resistance. You would move it as though it were an extension of your own arm. It is not to be waved around; it is to be a part of you. You must be one with your

367

blade if you wish to keep your intentions hidden from me or any other skilled swordsman."

I watched her continue her movements. I watched her advice come alive as she became one with her blade. If I were her opponent, I wouldn't be able to see her moves coming. She moved the sword in a way that allowed her to strike out at any moment. Her enemies wouldn't see it coming.

"Who taught you all of this?"

She stopped and sheathed her sword. Her eyes turned cold; emotionless. "My father."

Of course. I don't know why I expected any other answer.

"He was a master. Unbeatable," she said, her voice softer. Her eyes focused on something unseen. She seemed happy, for all of one second before her eyes turned cold once more. "Until Xaphan."

"Now here you are. A master. Unbeatable, going after Xaphan. Don't you think you've heard this story before?" I asked, sheathing my sword.

She shrugged. "The past always repeats itself. If we learn from it, we can change the outcome."

"So, what steps can we take to change that outcome today? Right now?" I asked as I straightened.

She said nothing. Instead, she turned and walked toward the stairs. I was left standing on the second-floor catwalk, looking like an idiot when an old woman opened her door to see what all the noise was about. I gave her an apologetic glance before hurrying after Mara. She was already across the street by the time I stumbled down the stairs.

"Where are we going?" I called after her.

She walked on without so much as glancing back. "The library."

"Library? Why?"

"Eichi."

I stopped in my tracks. "Why?"

She had no answer for me. She kept to the shadows of the alleys, pressing against walls and kneeling behind dumpsters to keep from being seen. It was the first time I'd seen her walking the streets in pure daylight. Whatever she needed from Eichi had to be significant.

I followed a step behind, taking her cues to kneel or hide in the shadows when needed. "You do know the library will be crawling with people this time of day, right?" I asked.

"The week of Dragon's Feast is upon us, Vermillion. People are celebrating. They're home with their families. The university is closed to the public for the holiday, including the library," Mara said.

I nearly forgot about Dragon's Feast. It would be celebrated each day, with Xaphan's ball being the big finale at the end of the week. Preparations were underway. The entire city, all five sides of it, would participate in the traditions and rituals. All businesses would be closed.

We made it to the West Side, and Mara made a mad dash for the library. I was right on her heels. They never replaced the historic drearwood doors that Bryce burned to ash, so we were able to run straight into the dim front room. Mara immediately went for the secret passage we discovered during our last visit, and it dawned on me that she *knew* I would come with her. In fact, she counted on it, because she needed my blood to get into Eichi's chamber. She just didn't want to admit it. She didn't want me to feel like I had cards in my hand. I didn't realize I was smiling until I sucked in a sharp breath.

That cunning, distrustful woman.

She made to grab my palm, with a dagger in hand, but I smacked her away. I took the dagger into my own hand and dragged it across my palm. I pressed my bloody hand to the stone wall and waited for it to give way. It felt like eternity passed before the passage opened.

Mara brushed past me. She disappeared into the darkness beyond, and though I hated this place, I followed quickly after her before the passage closed behind me.

Eichi was waiting for us amid the stacks of books. His back was turned, but he waved his fingers when we walked in. Somehow, everyone around me suddenly had a sixth sense.

Mara stopped in the aisle between rows, facing Eichi's back. He didn't move for a long moment. Eventually, he raised and cocked his head. "You've taken her power. All of it," he said as he turned, a knowing smile plastered to his face.

"Yes."

"What is it that you desire from me now?"

"Instructions."

"For?"

"Killing another god."

Eichi snapped shut the book that he held. He returned it to its rightful place on the shelf and directed all his focus to Mara. He cocked his head again, looking her up and down. He pursed his lips and clicked his tongue, shaking his head disapprovingly. "The wolves howled for you. They knew the moon changed."

I tried to catch Mara's eye, but she refused to look my way. She had to know that Eichi was unstable. He quite obviously was not of sound mind. Understandably so, given that he saw everything, past, present, and future, and he'd been locked in an underground chamber for centurics.

Mara only took a step forward. "Your power... how do you control it?"

"I do not control it. I simply let time flow through me. It is like a bird singing many different songs at once. I simply learned to listen to one song at a time in the jumbled sound."

"How do I learn to let the darkness flow through me? To let *creation* flow through me?"

I no longer knew what they were talking about. From what I could tell, Mara had no trouble controlling her power before.

Eichi turned away and dragged his fingers along the rows of book spines. The chains on his wrists audibly dragged along the wooden shelves. He stopped at the end of the row, fingers coated in a layer of dust, and slid the last book out of its place. He tossed it over to Mara, who caught it easily.

I couldn't see the title from where I stood a few feet away, but I saw the way her eyes narrowed in annoyance. She held up the book cover for both of us to see. "Really? '*Emotional Intelligence: The Language of Society?*'"

I couldn't stop a chuckle from escaping me. The sound earned me a death glare from Mara.

Eichi shrugged. "Aether is tied to your emotions. If you want to have any sort of sway on the power you hold, you need to be able to let your emotions flow. You're blocking a part of yourself from seeing the light. Without accepting it the power will never course through you like a river. Instead, it will continue to trickle like a stream clogged by a dam."

I looked between the two of them. "What's aether?"

In typical Reaper fashion, Mara ignored my question. Neither of them looked my way.

"I don't take kindly to jokes," Mara warned.

Eichi shook his head. "It's no joke. You never grieved for your father. You chose the mask instead. You grew used to it, you got comfortable. Now you hide everything behind a mask, literal or

372

not. It has taken a toll on you, this weight on your shoulders. It weakens you."

"When you cast your shadows before I felt this... rage. But it was more than that. There was sorrow too. It was heavy– choking, even. It physically *hurt* to breathe them in," I said, drawing their attention.

"Emotional projection," Eichi nodded. "An easy mistake for someone holding in as much as you are. The darkness doesn't like secrets. It *craves* for your truth to see the light."

Mara ripped her mask off and rubbed a hand over her face. She held a hand there as she shook her head. She stood, deep in thought, trying to convince herself that there was another way through this. She didn't want to have to let the emotions in after all this time. She was a soldier, a killer. She was a victim, robbed of her father. To let all of that in at once– it would be crippling.

"I struggled to let time flow long ago. It nearly drove me mad," Eichi said, looking down to the drearwood chains. "I imagine that when these chains come off, and my power returns, I will struggle again."

"How did you struggle?" I asked so Mara wouldn't have to.

Eichi looked to me, then back to Mara. "I told you I found a way to listen to one bird song at a time, but long ago I heard an entire flock. Each of them chirping and screeching. The visions would come every few minutes, to the point where reality and prophecy muddled together. The screams of the past, the prayers of the present, and the whispers of the future all spoke at once. My head was filled with words. *Words, words, words.*" Eichi put his hands over his ears and turned away. After another moment, he seemed to come back to his senses. "I found that giving kernels of my power to mortals helped lift the weight off my shoulders. They got portions of my visions and heard some of the voices. You would know them as Seers."

Mara and I both snapped our gazes up to Eichi. I'd never seen such shock in her burning eyes.

"Seers? You created Seers? Their power is your power?" I asked.

"Yes."

"That's why there hasn't been a true Seer in centuries," Mara muttered to herself.

"The chains quiet the voices," Eichi said, holding up his wrists.

Mara frowned. "How do I get you out of them?"

"They are spelled by an ancient, primal magic. He who put me in these chains would have to die."

"Xaphan?"

"Yes."

"Then consider your sentence in its final days," Mara said, securing her mask to her face again. "Tell me how to kill him."

Eichi arched a brow. "You are a goddess now. Learn to control your power, and it will do

374

anything you ask of it. Listen to your shadows. They whisper the answers. They are the voices of the lost ones."

I didn't know what to make of anything he said. I couldn't tell which parts were real and which were metaphors. Mara seemed to understand, though. She raised her chin and nodded. "You will be free within the fortnight."

She made to turn away, but Eichi called after her. "He knows what you are. You lost the element of surprise. He has the wisdom and experience of a hundred lifetimes. Do you have a plan?"

Mara stopped in her tracks. She wasn't facing us, but I could tell by the way her head raised that Eichi's words hit home. She had no plan– none that accounted for the truth of my father's power.

"I might have an idea," I said. Mara glared at me. I knew she was thinking about what happened the last time I had an idea and acted on it. I couldn't keep a smile from crossing over my face. "You're not going to like it."

CHAPTER 32

Mara

"You're really not going to tell me what this plan is? You realize where you led me last time? If this plan involves chains, I'll kill you myself," I warned. I leaned against the wall, twirling one of my throwing knives over my fingers for added affect. The obsidian stone felt heavy and cool in my hands, but I'd grown used to it over the years. By the way Kalieth glanced at it, he hadn't.

Kalieth laughed from where he sat on the edge of the bed, bent over to unlace his boots. "I'm going to tell you. I'm just waiting until we rejoin the others, for the exact reason of them being able to hold you back when you will most definitely draw that pretty dagger of yours."

I watched his boots hit the ground. Then I watched him stand, stretching out the ache in his shoulders. After the library, he demanded we continue his training. I refused because I feared not knowing my own strength with this newfound power. But Kalieth had no fear for his own life, apparently, because he responded to my rejection by drawing his sword anyway. As we fought, he asked questions. His pestering only succeeded in annoying me, and I stopped pulling my punches.

Now, I watched him wince as he stretched, and I wondered if I might've gone too hard on him today. I had a lot on my mind, and in the past months of my silence, the only way for me to get the tension out was while sparring with Ryder. We were trained by the same man, and so we knew each other's moves and were near equals in the art of hand-to-hand combat. But Kalieth was not trained by my Da. He had no idea how to anticipate my moves.

There was still a voice in my head asking why I was doing this. Why am I teaching him to fight? He is the son of my greatest enemy. Does that not make him my enemy too? He tried to kill me once already. What's to stop him from trying again? Who's to say he isn't going to betray me the second it suits him?

There was a time when I trusted that voice against all else. If someone raised the hairs on my neck, I killed them. If I was unsure of an outcome, I would change the circumstances entirely, by whatever means necessary.

But that voice of reason seemed to fade when Kalieth was involved. I could still hear it, but it was faint, because the shadows spoke instead. They whispered in a way only I could hear. They etched words beneath my very skin. They warmed around Kalieth. They reached out to him and urged me to let them explore. I attributed the strange sensation to the fact that besides Ryder,

377

Kalieth was the only other child of a god, even if his father was false.

It was the shadows that I listened to when I pushed away from the wall. I returned my blade to my belt, freeing my hands to help Kalieth rid himself of his cloak. He wore a tunic beneath it, but it was loose. As I set his heavy cloak aside, I saw the large patch of bruised skin beneath his collarbone. A wound that I inflicted, among many others.

I brushed my fingers over the spot. He flinched away from my cold touch, but after a moment he stilled beneath my fingertips. He followed my gaze. The knot in his throat bobbed. "It's nothing."

He was right. It would heal quickly. But my eyes shifted downward, to the long strip of white flesh. Scarred flesh. I didn't care that he watched my every move. I didn't care that his breath caught in his chest as I slowly untied his tunic and pulled it open.

Scars littered his chest and stretched across his sculpted abdomen. Some big and some small. Some deep and jagged, others barely visible. My eyes wandered over each one. I couldn't pull them away. I never saw him this way, as a warrior with his own scars to carry, both inside and out. I never thought about any of the Vermillions this way. They were the enemy, and that's all they ever were. Until now.

Kalieth's piercing gaze stayed on my face as I looked. It wasn't judging or cold, but curious. He didn't dare stop me. He didn't dare say a thing. He only watched, waiting for me to make the next move.

When I'd gotten a look at all of them; when I finally lifted my eyes to meet his, my words cold as death, I asked, "Who did this?"

"My father," he said, his voice soft.

I jerked away as if someone pulled me back. The intensity of the hatred that flared in my chest stunned me into silence. I should've known. I could've guessed, but I never thought— it just always seemed like the Vermillions were a team. But Xaphan taught them to be that way. He did this to them when they stepped out of line. His own children. It made me sick.

Kalieth offered me his hand. His fingers shook slightly, but that was the only sign that this had any effect on him at all. I looked down at his palm, unsure. He only stretched his fingers, waiting.

Tentatively, I placed my hand in his. His fingers closed over mine, and he tugged me closer. He placed my hand over his chest, right over his heart, where a deep scar flawed his skin. He let my fingers trace over it and met my eyes. "This was for interrupting him during a meeting. I was eight, I think."

He moved our hands. Our fingers trailed across his chest until they were at his side. This scar wasn't quite like the others. It was raised and red. It was a brand. A wound caused by something incredibly hot being pressed to his skin. I traced it to find that it was the letter 'V'. My eyes met his to find him already watching me. "I was thirteen. I'd become close friends with one of the stable hands. He was caught stealing, but I knew it was only because his family was starving. I asked my father to spare him, to just let him have the food. We had plenty. My father agreed, but he said someone needed to be punished in his place."

He led my hand across his abdomen. The muscles beneath his skin felt like steel covered in satin. It was warm to the touch. I could feel him moving beneath my hand. With each breath he took, my fingers rose.

He placed my fingers over the deepest scar. The longest one which stretched across his entire midsection. "My brothers and I were forced to fight one another as part of our training. Eligor did this." He paused. Anger flashed through his eyes. "Most of the others you see were my brothers, or from my father afterward. Punishments for losing."

He let go of my hand. My fingers lingered over the scar for a few more seconds before I pulled away. My eyes scanned over all of them again. Each one a reminder of who Xaphan really was.

I didn't know what to say. I was never one to console people. I wasn't good with emotion at all. But I knew I spoke the wrong words when I asked, "You let them do this to you?"

Kalieth's expression turned cold. "*Let* them?" There was a bite to his words, a harshness I never heard before. "You think I *let* them?"

"They're still living," I said, keeping all emotion out of my voice.

His eyes narrowed to slits. "Must be easy for you to say something like that. I forgot that you've never cared enough about someone to endure the pain they cause. I forgot you're too well trained to be hurt like this. That you know every way to kill a man before they can touch you."

"I do."

Kalieth took a threatening step forward. "I didn't *let* them do anything, Reaper. I was a boy. They chained me down. They beat me bloody. I didn't have a *choice*," he said, his lip curling as he stared down at me.

I weathered his anger. My own was building, boiling my blood. "And yet you *still* fought for him. You were going to kill me for him, the man who chained you down and beat you bloody."

"You're going to stand there and act high and mighty, as if you would've done something differently? As if you would've chosen torture over a bounty?"

"I would've," I said, keeping my chin high.

He sneered, stepping closer. "Then you don't know true pain."

I cocked my head. "Are you so sure?" I spat. In a haze of anger, I ripped my tunic open. Buttons flew off in all directions, but I didn't look. I kept my eyes on his, and he did the same. He waited a few seconds before glancing downward. I didn't follow his gaze. I knew what I would see. The scars and welts. The marks that even the shadows beneath my skin couldn't conceal.

As his eyes wandered over me, I tried my best to keep my breathing steady. I had to fight the urge to look away, to look at anything else.

A small eternity stretched on between us before I said, "You don't get as good as me at dodging blades without getting hit a few times first."

I offered him my hand. He was hesitant to take it, just as I had been. His fingers met mine, and I pulled him forward, pulled him close until his breath fanned over my brow. Only then did I press his hand to the scar across my stomach and look into the blazing heat of his eyes. His blue eyes. Not silver. Not white. Blue. A blatant reminder that though we were both children of gods, we were very different in nature.

"An enemy soldier," I said, clearing my throat. "The first I ever encountered. I hesitated to kill him. That earned me this. I never hesitated after that."

I moved his hand across my stomach, to what was once a deep gash on my hip. "I freed Commander Zeldrien's horse after I saw him whip it half to death. This was my punishment. He died in the field before I could repay him, but I would've."

Our hands moved together. They came to rest in the shadowed curve beneath my breast. "This was an arrow. A bounty hunter shot me in the early days of the Reaper alias. Your father sent him. I sent him back with his entire quiver emptied into his chest."

I took us to the last story I cared to share. His calloused hands skimmed over the sensitive skin of my breast, causing my breath to catch. But we kept moving until our fingers sat beneath my collarbone. "A mercenary. Paid by your father. He was good; very good. I was better." I lowered my hand, even though Kalieth's lingered. "Do you know what all those stories have in common?"

He met my gaze but said nothing.

"They're all dead. I know pain, Kalieth. At times, it was all I ever knew. But I refused to live in the fear of it. I will *not* let men like them stay in power. I will *not* do their bidding." I withdrew my dagger from the belt. I folded his fingers around the hilt and pressed it to my chest, just over my heart, hard enough to draw blood. My eyes did not leave his. Not for a second. "But if you will, then finish it now."

He watched the single drop of blood as it trailed down my chest. Then, he lifted his eyes to mine. He searched my gaze for a moment. "I made my decision long ago, Reaper," he murmured. He let the dagger fall to the floor between us. It clattered to the ground, but we didn't look away to see where it landed. "I can't go back to the way it was before. You changed everything."

His eyes fell to the floor. When they lifted to me again, he arched a brow. "You're bleeding on my carpet."

I looked down and sure enough, I was. I'd ruined my tunic, so it didn't matter when I ripped a piece off and dabbed the rest of the blood away. Unfortunately, I didn't have any spare shirts here, and I didn't plan on sleeping with my chest exposed. I searched the room for anything I could use, but there was nothing. Nothing except for the tunic Kalieth wore.

He followed my gaze and smirked. "I rather like the idea of you going to bed just the way you are."

I rolled my eyes, ripping the fabric off his arms. "I'm sure you do."

I pulled it over my shoulders and tied it in the front. When I was sure the knots were tight enough to stay intact through the night, I made for the bed. I brushed past Kalieth, our shoulders bumping together. He watched me go, the smirk still on his face.

"Will I be allowed on my own bed tonight, your majesty?" he asked.

I settled into the furs, relishing their warmth. "Will you behave?"

He shifted on his feet. "Define behave."

I gave him the best annoyed glare I could muster. He weathered it and answered with an arched brow.

I didn't have the patience for him tonight, and he needed rest if his body was going to heal. So, as I settled amongst the pillows, I nodded to the space beside me. He needed no further confirmation. He slid beneath the furs with ease. He wasted no time in banding an arm over my waist and pulling me against him. His chin settled in the crook of my neck.

I went rigid. "What are you doing?"

"Behaving."

"Definitely not."

"Do you want me to show you what *not* behaving looks like? I'd be happy to grant you a side-by-side comparison," he said, his lips brushing against the sensitive skin beneath my ear.

I grit my teeth. "Would you like me to show you what happens when I let you drown in the shadows?"

He groaned. The sound vibrated against my shoulder. "I sleep better when I'm close to someone."

"That doesn't seem like my problem."

"Well, if I can't sleep, we'll have to play our questions game again," he said, humor laced in his sated voice. "And trust me Reaper, I have many more questions."

That does seem like my problem.

"I hate you," I breathed into the sheets.

He huffed a laugh. "If only you could."

Silence ensued for a few moments. Beautiful, uninterrupted silence, and yet, I couldn't quiet my mind. I couldn't fade into the darkness and slip into unconsciousness. The voices in my head wouldn't stop chattering. The shadows wouldn't rest. Not with Kalieth so close. They begged me to let them loose.

I couldn't stand the tension. It was making it hard to breathe, let alone sleep. A frustrated sigh left me. "I never asked *my* three questions."

I felt Kalieth smile against my neck. "Go on, then."

"Your sister– what was her name?"

He stiffened against me. That smile faded and his voice softened when he murmured, "Octavia."

A fitting name for the eighth child of a god. "What was she like?"

"Gentle. Kind." He drew in a long breath. "She was generous. She would give what she had to those who were less fortunate, uncaring about what father had to say about it. She was smart too. Smart enough to figure out the truth before I could."

"There was nothing about her in the library records."

"As Eichi told us, my father had the head scribes under his thumb, and he was ashamed of Octavia from the day of her birth. I'm sure he expunged the records."

I recognized sorrow in his voice. The utter grief in his tone. I knew it better than most. I hated that he felt it now, and I was the one to cause it. I didn't mean to bring him grief. I wouldn't wish that sort of pain on anyone undeserving– the pain caused by the absence of a loved one. I wanted to fix it if I could. The only thing I could think of was what got me through that pain. The desire for vengeance. "We will avenge her," I assured him.

"I know, but that won't bring her back to me."

My heart faltered. It was a simple truth, but it was a truth I'd been avoiding. They were words I refused to acknowledge because the same was true of my Da. Killing Xaphan wouldn't bring him back. I wouldn't think of that now. That was the reality I'd face after.

I must've taken too long to consider his words, because Kalieth murmured, "You still have one question left, Reaper."

But my Da was in my thoughts now. Fear of the uncertain future gripped my mind. I didn't have any more questions. "I'll save it for later."

I couldn't tell whether he was disappointed or relieved. He only pulled the furs over our shoulders. I expected him to talk, to say something sarcastic or snarky and keep me from sleep, but there was only silence. It was grief, really. We remained in mutual silence, occupied with our own thoughts, until we drifted to sleep. He went before me, his breaths turning deep and steady. It took me a while longer, because I could only think of him, and the arm he had around me. I imagined what Da might say if he were here, if he saw it. I wondered what Ryder would say.

But I would allow it this once. I would give myself this one instance of weakness, alone in the darkness. I leaned into him. I relished the feel of his skin against mine, and I relaxed into his warmth. I turned my head slightly, so that I could hear the beat of his heart, and finally drifted into sleep to the steady rhythm.

CHAPTER
33

Mara

I'd been dreading rejoining the others. They would look upon my face for the first time, and hear my voice, only to hear me admit my failure.

Even as I stood outside the warehouse doors, on the East Side of the city, I wondered if I could put it off another day. But with Kalieth beside me, waiting, I refused to show any sort of fear.

I kicked the doors open with enough force to have them slamming back against the wall. The sound echoed through the empty warehouse.

"Ryder!" I yelled, walking forward into the dim room. The warehouse was taller than it was wide, with many rooms stacked on top of one another, housing the personal belongings of sailors out at sea, including furniture that we arranged into four makeshift bedrooms. We switched our housing arrangements every season as to not be tracked, so we stayed here before. It made everything easier to be able to switch between locations on a moment's notice.

I was caught off guard when I was slammed back into the wall. I raised my arm to break my attacker's hold, but I stopped when I looked into golden eyes. When I saw the scars flawing his eye and jaw.

Ace held a dagger to my throat, pinning me to the wall with an arm to my shoulder. His eyes were narrowed on me, cold and suspicious.

Kalieth was saying something, trying to get Ace to let me go, but neither of us were listening. I met his gaze, just as cold, just as unwavering. I refused to back away, refused to let him think, even for a second, that this display of intimidation was going to work on me.

Ace searched my eyes. Seconds later, his brows drew together, and he surveyed my entire face. His eyes came back to mine, though, and he pushed away from me, lowering his dagger. He knew. He continued to stare, his face blank, as I circled around him, walking toward the stairs without turning my back to him.

Quinn was coming down the stairs. He looked between the three of us, having no idea who I was or why Ace let me pass. He was asking questions, but I didn't hear his words.

"Ryder!" I called again, louder this time. My voice may be improving with each day, but it still sounded like nails against a chalkboard. "RYDER!"

Unfortunately, it was Bryce who descended the stairs next. I knew, just from the judgement and disgust on her face, that she thought I was here, calling her boyfriend's name, for a completely different reason. She cocked her head, her eyes zeroed in on me. "I don't know who you think you are," she started, pointing a flaming finger at me. "But I suggest you–"

Ace grabbed her and held her back when she tried to take a step closer. She fought against his hold, cursing and shrieking.

"The eyes," Kalieth whispered to her and Quinn. "Look at the eyes."

I'd already turned my back to them, though. With one hand on the railing and one foot on the first step, I finally came face-to-face with my brother.

He stood at the top of the steps, frozen in his descent, as we stared at one another. His lips parted on a sharp inhale; his eyes widened.

For a long moment, all we could do was stare. We were frozen, seeing each other, truly, for the first time in one year. I felt different beneath his gaze. Words wouldn't do justice to how it felt, but the closest explanation would be simply *human.* To have connections, family, and be loved by someone all seems to fade away when you lose the ability to speak to them. You feel alone in this world, left to your thoughts for far too long. To be seen again by someone who knew and loved me before the mask and the killings... it was a breath of fresh air I didn't know I needed.

A short eternity later, when Ryder overcame the initial shock of it all, he practically leapt down the stairs and gathered me into his arms, twirling me around in his embrace like a giddy schoolboy. I chuckled into his shoulder, holding him just as tightly as he held me, even though we might release each other with broken ribs.

When we parted, he still held fast to my forearms, looking me up and down to scan for injury. His eyes met mine with something like worry. "Has your shadow grown?"

Did you do it?

My eyes found the floor, and he needed no further explanation. He leaned away, drawing a long breath. His hands squeezed mine, and when I looked back, he stared right into my eyes. "It's not your fault. You hear me? You were outnumbered and unprepared. We'll get that son of a bitch. We'll do it *together.*"

A curt nod was my only response. He knew admitting defeat was difficult for me, so he asked no further questions. He drew me closer and touched his brow to mine. A common gesture in our family. Whenever one of us was hurting, we'd touch brows as a reminder that we were in it together.

Ryder withdrew after a moment, and his gaze finally left me. His lip curled up when his eyes landed on Kalieth, standing a few feet away from the others. Kalieth weathered the pure hatred in Ryder's eyes. The promise of death that burned within them.

"*You,* on the other hand," Ryder said, stepping forward. "You'll die for what you put Bryce through. For what you put Mara through."

I reached out and grabbed Ryder's arm, holding him back. "Don't," I muttered. "He saw his mistake. He saved my life. He ensured Bryce's safe return."

"Being poisoned isn't a safe return," he snapped.

I opened my mouth to respond but stopped when I saw the look on the others' faces. Ace with his typical bored expression, but Quinn and Bryce stared with dropped jaws. For a moment, I wondered if I had something on my face. I soon realized it was the lack of something covering me that brought on this reaction. In turning to stop Ryder, I'd given them a good look at my silver eyes.

Bryce was quick to snap her jaw shut and clear her throat. "She's right, Ryder. Kalieth acted like an idiot, but he didn't intend for me to get hurt."

"I'm sorry, who cares about Kalieth right now? Am I the only one seeing this?" Quinn asked, gesturing to me. His wide eyes surveyed the others. "*That's* the Reaper!"

Bryce's lips tipped up into a triumphant smirk. "I am *so* going to enjoy it the next time one of you makes a sexist joke."

"Why make us believe you were a man? What was the point?" Quinn asked, his forehead creased with confused wrinkles.

I shrugged. "I didn't make you believe anything. No one disclosed my gender. You assumed I was a man."

"But Ryder always referred to you as his brother," he pointed out.

"That was long after the rumors," Ryder said. "We figured it would be best to keep you thinking of the Reaper as a man. That way, if we ever needed to split and run, and one of you was captured and questioned, you would give all the wrong answers."

"Speaking of answers," I said, stepping down the last few stairs. "I'm calling a meeting."

In an attempt to be transparent and trusting, I told them everything. I told them about the dreams with Cheusi, the lies about the Shadow Realm and the Land Above the Stars, and her decision to choose me as the new Goddess of Creation. I explained that my father was a god, though I don't know which one, and that Vermillion was too, made instead of born.

Over the course of three or four hours, I told them everything I'd learned in the past few days. In return, Quinn told me everything he'd learned about the gods, the primals, and the prophecy Eichi gave him.

To my surprise, Kalieth stayed silent the entire time. Not a single world left his lips while I told the group about our stay in his apartment, and our journey to the library, leaving out the details of our nights together. He just listened, hands over his mouth and eyes aimed at the floor.

Quinn, on the other hand, interrupted me every few seconds with questions and commentary. He did it often enough to annoy Bryce to the point of leaving the room and returning with tape to seal his mouth shut.

Ryder took the news hard, just as I did. It hurt him to learn that Da was not the man we thought he was. He was quicker to overcome it than me, however. It only took him a few seconds to decide he wanted Vermillion dead now more than ever, for taking away Da's chance to tell us all this himself.

When I finally finished, everyone sat in silence for a long moment. They exchanged glances amongst each other, unsure who should speak first. Unsure if they wanted to speak at all.

"What exactly did you two do for *two* days?" Bryce asked, arching a brow as she glanced between Kalieth and me.

Kalieth smirked and opened his mouth to answer, but I shot him a look and said, "Trained."

Luckily, Ryder took no notice of Bryce's question. "So, you're a *god?*" he asked.

"Goddess," Bryce corrected.

"And the rightful Queen of the Southern Kingdom, since the entire kingdom still believes in the prophecy of the last shadow-bender," Quinn said after ripping the tape off his mouth.

"I don't want any of that. I just want to avenge Da," I assured them.

"Well, what now? The Vermillions pulled back to their estate and *tripled* security. What's the plan?" Quinn asked.

Kalieth sat up and cleared his throat. "I think I have a plan."

Everyone in the room scoffed simultaneously.

"It went *swimmingly* the last time you had a plan," Bryce said, her eyes narrowed. She drew up her sleeves and showed him the bite marks on both of her arms. "I had magical snakes suck the poison out of me while I nearly burned an inn down."

Kalieth sucked in a shaky breath. "Sorry about that," he said, showing his teeth in an uneasy expression. Then, when the words fully processed, his brows drew together. "Did you say magical snakes?"

I leaned forward, examining the marks. I looked to Ryder through lowered brows. "Artemis?" I asked, my voice dropping low.

The knot in Ryder's throat bobbed before he nodded. "Her debt to us is paid."

Risky.

"Does anyone else have any ideas?" I asked, looking between them all. No one spoke up. "Then we'll listen, at least." I nodded to Kalieth.

"My father gave me one last chance to return to the family. He expects me at the Dragon's Feast Ball. Security will let me in without question. My father will be blindsided," he explained.

"*Oh. My. Gods,*" Bryce said, standing abruptly. She stared at Kalieth through wide eyes. "Are you saying you can get us into the ball. *The* Vermillion ball? Do you know how long I've dreamed of going?"

Everyone stared at her unblinking, as if she'd grown a second head. She shrugged, returning to her seat. "What? The guy throws a good party, doesn't mean I like him."

"It doesn't matter. We can't go because Xaphan knows what we look like. If we waltzed into the ballroom, he'd have us killed in an instant," Ryder said, looking to Kalieth. "Right?"

"Yes, but there's one person I can get inside. One who he wouldn't recognize, having never seen her face."

I considered his words for a moment. The realization finally hit me when all eyes turned to me. They watched expectantly, waiting for me to say something. Kalieth stared with the slightest smirk on his face, knowing that I would absolutely *hate* this plan, but that it was all we had to go off of.

I held my chin high. "Absolutely not."

CHAPTER 34

Kalieth

Mara did not speak to me after I proposed her being my date to the ball. She found the idea to be absolutely horrid. I might've been insulted if it were anyone else in the world. I decided to let Ryder do the convincing, however, because the chances of getting her agreement would be extraordinarily slim if I pestered her further. It took him two days, but Ryder finally got to her.

The night of her agreement was the last time I saw her. Three days passed since then, and there was not even a glimpse of silver eyes lurking in the darkness. Not a whisper of shadow swirling through the warehouse. Often, I wondered if she was with us at all. Sneaking off to wander the rooftops of Shadieh alone seemed to be her favorite past time.

We never spoke of our time together. She never sought me out. Quinn and Ace bunked together to give me a room, but she never came. I didn't really expect her to, but a part of me still hoped. It was like our time alone was a break from reality, but when we returned to the others, she returned to her role of our fearless, emotionless leader and whatever happened between us was a distant memory.

Mara wasn't the only one to distance herself. The whole warehouse fell into an eerie silence. I would find the others staring off, deep in thought, or shutting themselves in their rooms for hours on end. As the end of this journey approached, we all had much to consider.

Which was exactly why I suggested spending this last night in the nearest pub, drowning our worries with ale. Ace didn't need to be asked twice. Bryce, Ryder, and Quinn, though hesitant, eventually agreed. Mara, being the joy in life that she is, refused.

Bryce, Quinn, Ace, and I waited on the first floor. Ryder and Mara shut themselves away in her room, but it didn't matter. We could hear their raised voices echoing through the empty warehouse as if they were right in front of us. Bryce picked at her nails as though she were uninterested, even though she was one of the biggest busybodies I ever met. Quinn and Ace didn't try to hide that fact they were listening.

"I don't drink my problems away," Mara said indignantly. "It only brings more problems for the next morning."

"Just come out with us, Mara. This could be our last chance," Ryder said. We could hear his heavy footsteps thudding above us as he paced the room.

"A soldier should not drink before the final battle."

A short silence ensued. "You know what I thought when I saw you walk in those doors without the mask on? I thought maybe– just maybe– I had my sister back. But I think you lost your way long ago and putting on that mask made you forget who you were. There was a time you were more than a soldier ready for battle."

The door opened and closed. Seconds later, Ryder came down the stairs. He nodded to the others. They all stood, heading for the front door. I followed a few steps behind, glancing back at the stairs.

"Don't," Ryder warned. "If she wants to push everyone away, let her."

We walked to the pub without another word. We walked without hoods or cloaks. Half of the men on the streets worked for my father, either sailing his trading ships or handling his cargo, but none of them cared about Xaphan or the Vermillion name once the workday was over. They might care for the bounty on our heads, but without the Reaper's menacing presence, we blended with the crowd easily.

We walked into the nearest pub, the Sailor's Saloon, and found ourselves a table. Ace called the barmaid over to order our drinks. "Five ales. Keep them coming."

"And a whiskey. Neat." Someone called from behind us. Mara stood there, without a cloak or a mask.

While her presence was a surprise to us all, the barmaid thought nothing of it. She nodded and trudged off to the bar, leaving the rest of us to our shock. For Mara to come with us was one thing, but to join us in public without the mask was a different matter entirely.

"Now it's a party," Bryce said to break the uncomfortable silence. Ryder slid over, making room in the booth beside him, and patted the seat for Mara to sit. She nodded gratefully and joined us at the table.

The first round of drinks was downed quickly by all of us. The second round was more of the same. By the third, we were feeling weightless. By the fourth, Ace disappeared, probably picking a fight somewhere, while Bryce and Quinn decided to submerge themselves into the dancing fray that spilled out into the street. All while Mara sipped on the same whiskey that she'd held all night.

She watched the others thoughtfully. I noticed that her eyes never left them. She always knew where they were. One might think it was a bit odd or creepy, but I knew she meant to be protective.

I didn't think about what I might say. I just knew that I wanted to talk to her, so I said the first thing to come to mind. "I know who you are."

Her gaze of silver fire shifted to me. I could practically feel the heat of it as she watched me. But I was in on her game now. I fixed an emotionless expression to my face and narrowed my eyes. "I've been thinking about it for days—why that name sounded so familiar. *Mara.* I'd never met anyone by that name before, and yet I knew it somehow. My father spoke of you."

She tensed in her seat. Her jaw clenched tightly. Ryder looked away from where Bryce danced across the room to focus on my words.

"Yes. He kept records of exceptional soldiers that he may hire once they complete their service. But there was one soldier he spoke very highly of. One whose kill count was higher than anyone before her."

Ryder looked to his sister; brows raised. "Hear that? Vermillion's got a job lined up for you."

"He would, if she were still alive. Reports say you died with the rest of your squad," I said.

Mara remained unaffected by my words. "And?"

"They called you Deathbringer," I said. "Armyslayer. Nightwalker. Shadowcaster."

"I never got that last one," Mara said, looking to Ryder. "That was long before I controlled the shadows."

Ryder shrugged, finished off his ale, and went to join Bryce for the next dance.

Mara looked back to me. A soft smile came to her lips as she took another sip of her whiskey. "It seems I inspired fear long before the mask."

"That's a good thing?"

"In this line of work? Always."

I considered her words. As the Reaper, she used fear as another tool to bring Shadieh under her control. But it was nearly time to put the Reaper alias behind her. What then?

"You're meant to be opening up to people, not making them fear you so you can reign over them like some sort of evil saint."

Mara looked me up and down through narrowed eyes. Eyes that held more judgement than usual. "That's not something I'd like to discuss with others. Especially not you."

"Maybe that's the point. Part of letting emotion out is letting other people in."

Mara rolled her eyes. "And you think I should let *you* in?"

Did I? I guess I did. Not just because the fate of everyone in this group depends on it, but because I wanted her to. Because I admired her more than I cared to admit, and I was dying to know what drove her forward. To know what goes on in her head when she's watching us from the shadows.

"Has there been anyone else? Friends or lovers?" I asked.

Any humor or judgement in Mara's gaze was replaced with something else. Something I couldn't quite recognize. She set down her whiskey and looked off into the dancing crowd. Her silver eyes seemed to become a shade brighter. For a long moment, I thought she wouldn't respond to my question. But in a voice just above a whisper, she said, "I don't hate anyone enough to show them what lies beneath the mask."

"You think they'd run?"

She turned to me, her eyes ablaze. "I think they'd *cower*."

"Maybe they'd fall to their knees in worship."

She huffed a laugh. "I suppose it would be appropriate. I am a goddess now, after all."

I couldn't stop the chuckle that left my lips. "You may be a goddess, but do you feel any better than you did a week ago? Do you feel any more a part of this group? Oh– wait, I'm sorry. I forgot that you don't feel anything at all. Isn't that right?"

Her eyes found the whiskey glass, but she did not pick it up.

"Let me remind you of something, Mara. Lack of emotion does not make you invincible. It doesn't harden your skin from blades or make you immune to poison. It doesn't make you special or unique. It only makes you distant from all who care for you. One day that empty feeling in your soul will bring you an empty life, one of immortality now," I said, my voice raising. "Would you be happy then? When you face eternity with no stupid questions to answer? With no friends or family to fight by your side?"

Mara scoffed. "You'd like that, wouldn't you? To be the one and only person the Reaper confides in. What would they call you? Demonslayer? Cursebreaker? I'm sure you'd revel in that glory."

"If I wanted fame and fortune, I would've stayed with my family. But that's not what we're talking about. What is it that you fear so much? What is keeping you from *living*?" I asked, leaning forward. It was a question that had been burning in the back of my mind from the beginning. There had to be a reason. Something that made her draw back from society. An inner battle that she lost to spur her toward the life of an ascetic.

She leaned forward too, until our faces were only inches apart. I could smell the whiskey on her breath as she said, "Listen well, Vermillion. I fear *nothing*. I will be open to *no one*. I live peacefully in solitude. I *like* it that way."

I slumped back in my chair, defeated. I nodded my head as I raised my ale to my lips. I chugged the rest of it and set it on the table with a loud thud. I wiped the foam from my lips and looked to Mara once more. "It's good to find comfort in solitude. But there comes a point when the voice in your mind turns against you. When the strength falters, that's when you'll need us, and we won't be there."

She leaned back, considering my words.

"That's the thing about being alone against the world, Mara. Unlike illness, there's no cure for loneliness. For the feeling of rejection. For being an outcast. You talk of loving the silence, but really, you did Xaphan's work for him. You silenced yourself. You've brought shame to your father's memory, because while he died using his voice, you will die never having used yours."

The last words seemed to hit home with her. Her lips parted, but no words came. For once, she

404

looked speechless. She sat with her arms crossed over her chest, eyes wide. The shadows rose from her back, surrounded her, and enveloped her. Then she was gone. When the black mist settled, her seat was empty.

I did not see her for the rest of the night. I spent my time arm wrestling, and losing, to Ace, arguing with Quinn about something I wouldn't remember afterward, and dancing with Bryce. We laughed and cheered and danced until dawn chased the night away.

The sun rose over the ocean, casting a warm glow over the waves, as though the sea itself was liquid gold. That was our cue to return to the warehouse.

The Reaper was waiting for us upon our return, standing in the doorway. Even bathed in sunlight, shadows clung to Mara's back. I watched them swirl and curl across her arms, down her spine, and over her boots. I stared in awe. It was a sight that most would cower from, seeing the night come alive. Not me. Not us. It was beautiful. It was a promise of star-kissed wind, of dreams and eternal peace. And the person who wielded those shadows represented all that and more. A beautiful, intelligent woman, a bit murderous and violent, who would fight when no one else would. She who gave us all a new purpose in this world. Who saw all of us at our worst, and knew what we might accomplish together.

As if sensing my gaze, she met my eyes, and I could've sworn that some sort of understanding passed between us.

I couldn't get that glance out of my mind. Even as we all went to bed, though the sun was just rising, I lay awake, considering the look she gave me. The way the fire in her eyes flared. How her chest raised in a quick breath and the shadows at her back reached outward into the daylight, as if ready to envelop me.

I played my last words over and over again in my head. *You silenced yourself. You've brought shame to your father's memory.* I cursed myself for saying it. If I had any chance of getting closer to her, it was gone now. It was the worst thing I could've possibly said to her, but I said it anyway, because the frustration I feel whenever we speak outweighs anything I've ever felt before.

I turned over on the bed. I couldn't seem to get comfortable. I finally stilled when a cool breeze, faint and barely recognizable, brushed across my skin. I realized, in that moment, that I'd somehow gained an awareness to Mara. Like a sixth sense. Like scenting lightning on a spring breeze, long before the storm.

I turned to find her staring out the window, not trying to hide in the shadows, for once. The warm light cast over her dark skin in a warm, welcoming way. It made her look serene, beautiful in the most basic, natural way. She knew I watched her, but her eyes stayed glued to something beyond the warehouse walls. We sat there for a moment, in an oddly comfortable silence.

She drew in a long, shaky breath through her nose, exhaling through her lips. She shook her head to herself, lost in her own thoughts, before she spoke. "I was trained to wield every weapon. To find the weakness in every opponent I face. To survive, and survival meant victory. Every time. No missteps. No hesitation. Kill or be killed." She paused. "I never realized that my need for victory bled into the other aspects of my life. Not until it was too late."

"I learned in my years of service that if you have no one to please, you will never fail. You are free to be your own judge and jury. That mentality led me into a downward spiral. My need for victory; my desire to win... it led me to fear failure," she said, her voice going soft. She looked to me then, and the sadness in her eyes– it shocked me into silence. There was a desperation in the depths of her silver irises. "You asked what I fear. That's it. Failure. I fear it more than anything else in this world. To fail at the one thing that I've trained for my whole life. To disappoint the only people that I care about. To have them see me differently for it. If I can't do this– if I can't defeat Xaphan, then what am I meant to do? Return to my farm? Attend to the livestock and harvest the crop?"

Failure. Of course. I should've known. She was terrified to return to this warehouse and see Ryder, to tell him that Xaphan still lived. Pushing the others away made it easier for her to live with that failure.

She shook her head, turning away. "I never wanted this." She looked down to her hands, turning them over beneath her gaze. "I never wanted this power, or any authority. I just wanted to bring my father's murderer to justice."

407

"And you were given the power to do so."

"But at what cost?" She asked, her voice a mere whisper. She sighed, dropping her hands and looking back to the window. "I can't sleep. The townspeople think I'm a monster who crawled straight out of the Shadow Realm. I wield a power I don't fully understand. I can do this–" she picked a shirt up off the floor, balled it together, and pressed it between her hands. Shadows poured from her palms, engulfed the clothing, and when she pulled her hands away, glittering black dust, like sand, was all that remained. She let it fall to the floor, shimmering in the sunlight as it went.

I stared in shock at the pile of dust that was once my favorite shirt. I couldn't help but wonder if she could do that to people. If she could've done it to me when she engulfed me in shadow in the mountain pass. I wondered if there were more tricks that she knew of but did not care to share with the group. But could I honestly blame her? Was she wrong for thinking they'd run from it? Should I tell her that she just ashed my favorite shirt or just let it go?

She sat at the edge of the bed. Her back was poised, her body tense. She eyed me wearily but did not back away. "Do you know how many Northern soldiers I killed?" she asked, the words born on a choked sigh.

I did not speak. I shook my head instead.

"One thousand two hundred and fifty-seven." Her eyes found the floor. "I was once proud of that number. That was until I discovered this war to be another of Xaphan's great lies." She hid a shaking hand beneath the furs atop the bed. "I

408

killed them all for nothing. And now? Now I will live with that for an eternity."

"All soldiers kill. None of those men and women were innocent."

"They knew no better."

"And neither did you. You fought for the love of your country, your people. Not for the hate of your opponent."

"And yet there will still be children without parents, because of me." A single tear escaped her eye. She was quick to wipe it away, but as that tear fell from her eye, a single strand of her coiled, black hair turned white. Like the purest, innermost part of her irises that burned bright with aether. That's what changed her hair– aether. It seemed to glow and burn like starfire within the very fibers of her hair.

Mara followed my awe-stricken gaze. She looked down to where the small portion of white hair rested on her shoulders amidst the sea of black curls. Her own eyes widened as she picked out the white hairs, holding them closer to her face as if she wasn't seeing clearly. "What is this?" she whispered.

She spoke to herself, but I answered anyway. "I think that means we've made a start."

CHAPTER 35

Mara

The day of the Dragon's Feast Ball came faster than I ever could've anticipated. I woke up that morning with more dread weighing down my stomach than I'd ever felt before, including in my days of service. Not just because I would have to face Vermillion, but because the thought of being in a room with the richest men in Shadieh as they dance and drink while the men and women below them risk their lives for this kingdom– it was revolting.

I'd kill them all if I could, and feel no guilt, because they were behind this war. Their decisions cost thousands their lives. I wanted nothing more than to slice their throats and watch the ballroom floors run red. But I couldn't. I had an example to set now. I had to be better than Xaphan Vermillion.

Not once did I allow myself into a situation I could not control. I never used a weapon without practicing with it first. But it's different now. Anger boils my blood. An infinite rage burns in my very soul and plagues me in the night with violent dreams. Before the power, I did not care what my anger might unleash. But now, with the ability to destroy this world and reform it at will, my anger paved the way for a new fear; the terror of having limitless power with no way to control it. Like living through a short eternity as a mortal and growing wings late into a lifetime. It is a part of me now, but almost unnatural. Something I can always feel but can only call on in times of great instinctual need.

I'd always felt it, though. Like a fish missing a single scale. I knew, in the back of my mind, that a part of me was missing. I feel whole now, finally one with the night. With Death in the palm of my hands, I never felt more alive.

The looming disaster of the Dragon Feast Ball, however, put a damper on my mood. It would prove hard to be intimidating and vengeful while trying to waltz.

The plan was simple. Kalieth and I walk right through the front doors. We mingle while Ace, Quinn, Bryce, and Ryder scope the perimeter, taking out the guards so Xaphan has no backup to call to when we make our final assault. But the guards at the front gate were another issue entirely. There would be too many witnesses if the others tried to take them out. So, Kalieth and I would slip away to distract them long enough to get the others inside. Once we're all together, we attack.

There was one person who was excited enough for all of us. That would be Bryce. The woman practically kicked down my door in the afternoon, squealing excitedly, carrying several dresses over her shoulder. She set the dresses down on the bed and clapped her hands together. "I am going to transform you into the fairest maiden in all of Shadieh," she said, a hint of challenge and determination in her voice. The spark reached her eyes, for the first time in a while, which is why I couldn't bring myself to refuse her.

It took Bryce five trips to bring all her dresses, shoes, makeup, and jewelry into my private quarters. She assured me that she just wanted me to have a selection to choose from, but truthfully, I believe she finally found a blank canvas, and in the art of fashion, she wanted to start painting.

The first dress was a monstrous thing. A behemoth of tool and ruffles. In the sunlight, the bright, yellow color blinded me. Even if it the skirt wasn't five feet in diameter, I would've refused the dress just from the amount of golden beads sewn into the bodice, each one reflecting light onto the floor. Each one scraping against my skin.

An orange dress came second. I'd never seen such a vibrant orange in all my life. It was covered in little flowers, and a veil of thin fabric trailed behind me when I walked. The cut of the bodice was low, showing much more than I preferred. I only had the dress on for a few seconds before I shook my head and took it off.

The only good thing about the third dress was that I wouldn't have to worry about blood stains. The crimson color didn't hurt my eyes like the others, but the lace sleeves did. What's worse, the

412

fabric was thick and scratchy. The entire dress weighed me down. Once I got the horrid thing off, I looked to the pile of remaining dresses. There were at least five more, all in red, orange, yellow, or a single light blue color.

Bryce followed my gaze and sighed in frustration. "It's the Dragon Feast Ball Mara. The theme is fire. These are fire colors. Everyone will be wearing them."

"Not everyone," I muttered. "Dragons are the theme. They always have been. Fire isn't the only thing dragons are known for."

Bryce looked to the floor, shaking her head. She stood, hands on her hips, deep in thought, for a long moment. She went for the door, muttering something to herself as she went. When her hand touched the doorknob she turned, her eyes narrowing when they landed on me. "Do not move," she said, knowing I'd take the first opportunity to run from this dress-up session.

I did as she commanded, though, because she was in her natural element in times like these. For a short while, she could live a normal life, pursuing her interests. I wouldn't be the one to ruin that for her. I didn't want to be the reason disappointment shined in her eyes. So, I stayed put, waiting patiently for her to return.

When she walked through the door again, she carried a dress packaged carefully in a protective plastic covering. She set it down on the bed with wholly gentleness. She took a step back and stared down at the dress, though it was hardly visible through the tinted plastic. She lightly ran her fingers over the covering, seeming nervous.

"This was my sister's," she whispered, so quiet that the breeze nearly carried the words away.

The tension in the air lodged a knot in my throat. I wished I could sympathize with her. I wanted to say something inspiring and reassuring like Ryder always did. But unlike Ryder, I didn't retain the ability to comfort others after my service. It became incredibly difficult to remind people to have faith in humanity after seeing so much of Death, after discovering that the gullible minds of mortals were deceived so easily.

The crinkling of plastic pulled me from my thoughts. Bryce removed the dress unhurriedly, taking care to ensure the fabric didn't snag on the thin wire that kept the plastic bag closed.

An electric charge coursed through my veins when she finally lifted the dress out of its cover. I drew in a shuddering breath and took a step closer, untrusting of my own eyes for what they were seeing.

Bryce held a black dress made of nyx fabric, incredibly rare and one of the darkest substances in this world. But that wasn't what stole my breath away. It was the dragon scales that covered both shoulders.

I moved forward, stretching a hand toward them.

"Dragons scales," Bryce said with a nod. "Don't bother, they're fake."

I shook my head, barely able to find words. "No, they're not. Don't you feel it?"

414

Even with my fingers still a few inches away, I could feel the power emanating from them. Ancient. Primal. Eternal. Strong, even centuries after their extinction. It felt like a thousand fires blazed beneath my palm. All the wisdom of the earth and stars and galaxies was just out of grasp.

Bryce ran her own fingers across the smooth, black scales. She drew in a sharp breath, just as shocked as me. She snapped, and flame burst from her fingertips. She blew the flames onto the scales, and sure enough, they didn't burn. There were no scorch marks or ashes. They were unaffected.

I never thought I'd be in the presence of so much primal magic. I didn't even know it still existed in such quantities. The scales almost felt like an amplifier for my power. Like they unlocked a new level of magic within me that I never knew was there.

"Well, even better then," Bryce said, the words born on a heavy exhale. "Maybe the magic will protect you."

"Your sister had this? She had true dragon scales?"

Bryce lifted a single shoulder in a half-hearted shrug. "I don't know if she knew they were real. But it was my mother's before it was hers. My mother gave it to her before she left us. I think Alina was going to give it to me, but that was before..." she trailed off, her eyes glazing over. "Either way, it's yours to wear for tonight."

She handed the dress over, ushering me to try it on. I took it gratefully. With a nod of thanks, I slipped my legs through and pulled it over.

415

The dress was form-fitting, unlike any of the others I tried on today. It had two thigh-high slits, one on each side, and sleeves from wrist to bicep with the dragon scales covering the rest. It was the perfect dress for an assassin. The slits made it easy to kick out. The sleeves made it easy to conceal blades. The tight fit would allow me to maneuver quickly. It was perfect.

Once I pulled the sleeves up my arms, and the dragon scale patches settled firmly on my shoulders, I felt the warmth travel through my entire body like electricity travelling through water. The scales were a battery, and they were charging me up, making the shadows buzz in my veins.

"Alright. We found the dress. Now it's time for hair," Bryce said waving me toward the desk chair in the corner of the room. There was a mirror beside it, but she turned it away so I could not watch her work. She wanted me to be surprised. I bit my tongue instead of telling her of how I hate surprises.

I did as she asked, smoothing the dress over before sitting down. She took her place behind me, fiddling with my hair as she tried to decide on which style she wanted to do.

She gently pulled at my coiled curls to soften them a bit. She tied my hair back into a low bun, picking out select strands to fall over my brow and rest just above my collarbones.

Next, she reached for her boxes of makeup, opening them to reveal hundreds of bottles of different potions and herbs.

416

Bewitched makeup, expensive and rare. They say it is smuggled to the south from a witch coven in the north. How Bryce got her hands on some, I didn't want to know. They were substances capable of changing someone's appearance for a few hours at a time. The ink could change hair color with a single drop. The nymph's water, when dropped into an eye, would change the eye color to the client's liking. The lotions can make blemished, scarred skin flawless and smooth. Even the dead blood tree leaves, native to the north, would bring natural blush to the skin or color to the lips when smeared across the desired area.

Bryce first picked black squid ink, which she planned to use to dye the single white strand of hair. I shook my head, running my fingers through it. "Leave it,' I said.

She raised her brows but did not question it. She returned the ink to the case and instead picked up a small vile of nymph water. She saw my unease and only had a shrug to offer in return. "Your eyes are a dead giveaway," she said. "What color do you want to go with for the next five hours?"

I took a second to think about it. After a moment, I decided that if I couldn't sport my father's eyes tonight, I could at least have my mother's. "Gold."

Bryce nodded. She used the pipette to suck up two little drops and gestured for me to tilt my head back. I hated the thought of changing my eyes. Changing a part of who I am, even for just a few hours. But I knew I had no choice. So, I put my head back and held my eyes open while she dropped water in each one. I stayed like that, blinking rapidly, until I felt the liquid sink in.

The lotion was next. She applied it to the lower half of my face, where acne and uneven tan lines resulted from the mask. The cool cream felt refreshing on my skin. I felt the magic in it, more so than anything else Bryce used.

She must've seen the confusion in my expression because Bryce said, "It's bewitched healer's lotion. It changes your appearance instantly, but the healer's magic makes the effects permanent. This acne won't return."

When she finally finished, she stepped back to admire her own work. I grew concerned when her expression turned sad. But she shook her head, a soft smile gracing her lips.

"I'm sorry, it's just– I've been thinking these past two days. You're a goddess now, and I'm supposedly the descendant of a primal..." she trailed off. "Does that make us enemies?"

I took her hands in mine, forcing her to look into my eyes. "Not for a second, Bryce. You're my Firemaster. You're my friend. Our ancestry does not change that."

She nodded. "I wish I knew you were a woman all that time. It would've been a comfort. After everything the Vermillions put me through, it's a relief to know that my commander was not just another man seeking my power."

I smiled for her. I vowed to Bryce that she could burn everything the Vermillion's had to the ground. But there was another part of me, deep within, that wanted to see her get her revenge. A womanly understanding of her pain, and maternal desire to help her rip apart the men who did this to her. To reunite her with her sister and relieve her of the guilt that weighs her down.

"I'm sorry," I said, the words foreign to me but genuine all the same.

She waved me off. "I understand. I appreciate what you've done. What you continue to do. It reminds me of Alina, in a way. She was fierce like you. Nobody could give her orders. No one could stop her from doing what she thought was right."

Her eyes glazed over as she spoke. I'd give anything to know what memories she might be seeing within her mind. Her voice was filled with such longing, such nostalgia, that it pained me to listen. It reminded me of my separation from Ryder during our tours in the king's army. How I'd miss him dearly.

She shook herself out of the memories before I could say anything. She plastered a smile on her face, though it didn't reach her eyes. "I wanted to say thank you. For choosing me to be in this group."

The words were a shock. "I brought you nothing but a life in hiding. A life full of fear."

Bryce shook her head. "I had nothing before this. None of us did. Ace lived on the streets, taking punches and splitting knuckles just to make enough markings for a meal of rotten bread. Quinn was hours away from being assassinated by Vermillion's goons. Kalieth– well, he would've gone on the rest of his life believing he fought for the right side. And I lost everything and everyone I cared about."

She took a breath. Tears welled up in her eyes. "You gave me this. A reason to keep going. A purpose in this world. You gave it to all of us. A purpose. A family."

Family. The word skittered over my very bones. I'd only ever had a family in the blood-related sense. I was never close enough to others to call them family. The very concept of family beyond blood seemed futile to me. Without blood, there is no true allegiance. No motivation for loyalty.

I considered it for a moment, though. Why shouldn't I consider them family? They were friends who would follow me to the ends of the world if I asked. Companions that risked their lives to aid my conquest. And I realized that if I were to lose one of them, I would feel the same grief that tore at my chest following Da's death. Is that not family? The people who you could not imagine a life without? Whose missing presence would bring despair?

I'd been blind to the depth of the relationships that I built. But my eyes were slowly opening. I could see their loyalty. I could feel their love for one another. Those bonds could not be taken lightly.

I stood and pulled her into an embrace. "And as a family, we end it tonight. All of it. One way or another."

"And I avenge my sister." Bryce added with a nod.

I squeezed her hands in agreement, pulling away.

"What of the Vermillion sons? What of Eligor? Will you kill him?" she asked, her voice breaking over his name. Her jaw shaking as she spoke.

"Of course not. His fate is to be determined by you, and you alone," I told her.

She nodded silently. I saw her chest lower in relief. She said nothing more of it, though. She stepped away and grabbed the mirror. She turned it over so that I could finally see her work.

I fully expected to hate it. I thought the dress would make me uncomfortable. I assumed the makeup would make me cringe. I honestly thought that all of this would make me feel like a schoolgirl getting ready for a pointless dance. But when I looked in the mirror, I was awed by the woman staring back at me. The golden eyes were strange; a shock at first. After a moment though, I adjusted to the sight and shifted my attention to other areas.

My face was rid of all acne and blemishes. Smooth, soft, dark skin lied beneath my fingertips as I brushed a hand over my cheeks. My hair, free of the hood, and styled accordingly for the first time in ages, complimented my face structure beautifully. The streak of white in the sea of black curls was something unique.

The shoes were black heels covered in silver glitter. Normally, glitter made my stomach turn, but when I looked at these shoes long enough, I saw the night sky.

The dress was the real focal point. It hugged every curve I hardly knew I had. It returned femininity to me while also accentuating the muscles in my arms. It cut low in the front, exposing a bit of cleavage. The back was open, the fabric cutting across the middle of my back. Silver chains hung from the two patches of dragon scales in low arches. The thigh slits came dangerously close to exposing other areas, but there was a bit of fabric built into the interior to keep that from happening. Which was good, because if someone were to see anything more than my thigh tonight, I would have to kill them, and I'd rather not have to bloody this dress. That someone being the fifth Vermillion son.

But I *loved* it. All of it. All of me.

I spent years surrounded by men. I trained with them, fought with them, drank with them, watched them, and posed as one. The part of me that wanted dresses and balls and prince charming died mere days into it. Still, in the darkest hours of the night, in the shadow of my thoughts, a small voice would whisper dreams of beauty and relations. Of leaving the armor behind and returning to the girl I once was, before the stone and shadow. A dream of a world where Da never died, and I was never a soldier.

Bryce gave that to me tonight. A sliver of a dream. She returned a small piece of me, of who I used to be. She reminded me what I was before Vermillion, reminded me why I'm doing this.

"Do you like it?" she asked. She seemed happy, but I saw a hint of worry in her eyes.

I nodded. Words wouldn't come to my tongue, not when all I could think about was how I wished Ma could be here to see this. She always wanted this for me. Not a life of death and ruin.

Bryce smiled. "It's time, then."

A cold chill crawled up my spine. "Have the shadows moved so quickly?"

Bryce walked to the window, peering out. "The sun is nearly set. You should be going if you want to reach the North Side by nightfall."

I dreaded the thought of walking down the stairs in this. It's not the image of a fearless leader that I'd worked so hard to burn into their minds. Would they still see me as their leader? Or would they turn to Ryder now?

As if reading my thoughts, Bryce crossed her arms over her chest, arching a brow at me. "You really think they'll see you any differently? They've watched you bring the toughest men to their knees. Watched you burn an empire to the ground. Watched you bring the night alive. You think a dress will change all that? Hell, I wear dresses all the time, and the boys still know better than to test my patience."

Fair enough.

"You know, I turned out liking you a lot more than I originally planned," Bryce told me with a smile as she linked arms with me. She led me toward the door. The others would be waiting for me downstairs.

I laughed. "You might grow to regret that."

423

She scoffed as she opened the door. The voices of the boys below flooded into the room. They were arguing about something, as usual. I don't know why we left them unsupervised for so long. They always got into something.

"I don't have enough middle fingers to express my feelings to you!" Quinn's voice snapped.

"Do I get bonus points if I act like I care?" Ace called.

"I heard that!" Quinn shot back; his voice distant now.

Ryder sighed somewhere below. "Really?"

"He started it," Ace muttered.

"How?"

"He was practicing his fighting forms."

Ryder laughed. "And that gave you permission to body check him?"

"I was *trying* to teach him to always be alert to his surroundings. He's just... not a very quick learner."

Bryce and I exchanged an annoyed glance. She left me on the second floor as she descended the stairs. She chided the boys for their immaturity and forced them all to start preparing for the ball. Before they could climb the stairs to their individual rooms, she beckoned me down.

I gripped the railing in a death-like grasp as my heels clicked against the steps. I'd worn heels before, of course, but it was years ago, and I wasn't overly fond of the idea of falling on my face in front the others. It would take me a few minutes to adjust to the feel of these shoes. Until then, I would try not to walk too much.

I held my chin high, returning the blank expression to my face as I finally came into view for everyone to see. Bryce stood beside Ryder on the left side of the room. Ace stood in the middle; his arms crossed over his chest. Kalieth and Quinn stood to the right, both distracted as Kalieth tried to bandage a gash on Quinn's arm, getting frustrated with Quinn's jerky movements.

Bryce tried to hide her smile by rolling her lips inward, but it didn't work. She looked to the others with such joy on her face. "Doesn't she look great?" she asked when no one said anything.

Her question drew Kalieth's attention away from Quinn. He'd been smiling at something the teen said to him, but when his eyes landed on me, his smile faded. There was something in my chest that reacted to that, but I ignored it.

I quickly averted my eyes from him. I didn't want to see whatever disappointment or judgement that he would soon show. I didn't need him to ruin this for me.

Ace whistled, low and long. "Looking good, boss."

"I think I'm in love," Kalieth whispered to Quinn, loud enough that he knew I'd hear it. Quinn responded with raised brows.

I shot him a weary glance.

Ryder stepped forward. He offered me his hand to help me down the last few steps. I took it gratefully, keeping my eyes to the floor. I had to watch my step, for fear of stepping on the fabric of the dress. "You look absolutely stunning," he whispered into my ear. "Ma would be so proud."

The words meant more than he could know. It was easy to please Da, but my mother? We never quite understood each other. She and Da did not see eye to eye when it came to my training. She wanted me to appeal my call to service to stay as a farmhand. Needless to say, things did not go as she wished. The thought of having her approval, just once, warmed my heart.

Once I was on the same level as the others, I dared another glance at Kalieth. He wore a black suit. His dark hair was styled nicely, but a few curls still fell over his brow. His blue eyes were accentuated by the dark colors of his clothes.

He stepped toward me, and as he did, Bryce ushered the others upstairs. She winked as she went up last, leaving Kalieth and I alone. Not really alone, though. I had a feeling the others would be eavesdropping from the corridor above, like the children that they are.

"I have something for you," he said. He gestured to a case sitting on the nearby table. I eyed him again, and he rolled his eyes in response. "You flatter me with the idea that any gift I have to offer might be a threat to the all-powerful Goddess of Creation."

I approached the case without a word. I flipped the two latches upward and slowly opened the box.

Inside, three ebony blades sat neatly on a bed of black velvet. Two sleek, small throwing knives, and one short sword, about a foot in length. My hands shook as they hovered over the beautifully crafted metal. I would recognize them anywhere. The pattern carved into the blades of swirls and curves was unmistakable. The hilt of the short sword, adorned with obsidian and real silver, was unique to this one specific blade. I drew in a shaky breath, lifting one of the throwing knives to observe it closely.

"They were your father's, weren't they?" Kalieth asked.

My throat went dry. I nodded.

"Xaphan gifted them to me the same night he returned wielding your father's sword. When you confronted him, and claimed his sword to be your father's, I made the connection. They belong with you," Kalieth explained.

I wished I could've voiced my gratitude. But I couldn't. I just stood there, holding the blade, staring at it with a year's worth of emotion threatening to explode from somewhere deep within me. My attention went toward keeping the lid tightly closed on that chest. The day would come that I would fall apart. But it would not be today. Not now.

Kalieth gently lifted the broad sword and its black leather scabbard. He sheathed the blade and met my surprised gaze. "I have an idea," he told me. "Just– don't move."

He walked to my back. Using the silver chains hanging from the dragon scales, he worked the sword into the dress so that only the handle rested outside of the fabric, held up by the chains. The rest of the blade rested against my back, unseen. He made sure to make it appear as though it were part of the dress. With the black and silver color scheme of the handle, it did.

He picked up the second throwing knife, and gently took the other from my hands, watching my expression carefully. With heartbreaking gentleness, he slid a blade into each of my sleeves. I watched him as he made sure not to nick my skin. My eyes never left his sculpted face. I couldn't draw myself away from his blue eyes that held raging oceans, ancient ice, and bright skies within them.

When the knives were tucked beneath the sleeves of my inner forearms, he let go of my hands. He took a step back and looked me up and down.

"Breathtaking," he said. His voice was so low, so soft that it almost sounded sincere.

I fought to keep my expression cold. To keep a bite to my words. "I don't need your sarcasm."

He shook his head. His eyes continued to roam across my face, as if memorizing every curve and line. "I'm far beyond sarcasm right now."

An invisible knife twisted in my stomach. A strange fluttering sensation echoed through me in answer.

I couldn't stop thinking. My mind refused to still. He returned my father's blades to me. But it was more than just that. He *knew* that going into this ball unarmed would be the equivalent of a sheep walking into a wolf's den. He understood that even though I didn't need my blades to fight anymore, they were still a comfort for me, like a safety blanket. Going anywhere without them made me feel like an open wound, exposed and vulnerable.

He saw all that and more. So, he thought of a way to arm me. A way that would still get me past the guards.

When did he come to know so much about me?

He cleared his throat. Within seconds, that playful smirk was back on his lips. "At least now I know how your shadow grew to be so heavy."

"You mean besides the killing?" I asked.

He nodded. "It's because the real sin was hiding such beauty behind a mask." He winked and offered me his arm.

I took it, rolling my eyes.

The walk to the Vermillion estate was long. The moon rose over the distant mountains just as we reached the bridge to the North Side. We walked in silence, to my delight. There was a small part of me, however, that was worried about Kalieth. Silence was unnatural for him, and I could see the tension in his shoulders. The way his eyes darted to every alley and rooftop we passed. He was just as thrilled about seeing Xaphan again as I was.

When I finally reached the open gates of the Vermillion estate, Kalieth stopped. Swarms of people were walking through, each person being checked by the guards, looking for silver eyes and hooded figures. We stopped a few feet away. I followed his gaze to see that he was staring up at the menacing gargoyles.

"If I die, can you make up something cool I might've said? I really want something meaningful to be engraved into my tomb," he said. He tried to sound humorous, but the haughtiness wasn't quite there.

"Throw your fear to the wind, Vermillion," I said.

"Yes, something exactly like that," he added with a nod.

I drew in a deep breath. "If this is the last time we see one another, just know I always hated you."

A choked laugh left his throat. "Yes, our teaming up was a complete mistake."

We started to walk forward again. The guards nodded to Kalieth, letting us pass.

"I'm glad you realize that," I breathed.

He kept his eyes forward as he said, "A good mistake, though. In fact, the best one I have and will ever make in my lifetime."

We climbed the grand staircase to the double doors of the main house. The chatter of the sea of people filled the night and carried on the wind. The guests surrounding us all wore red, orange, yellow, blue, or white dresses. We were the only ones to wear black.

The color of clothing was hardly what I was concerned about, though. Not when I looked to their faces to see that nearly every guest wore a mask. Each one a near replica of my own.

I yanked on Kalieth's arm, nodding with my head to those next to us. He glanced around, shock rippling through him as it was with me.

"Did you do this?" he muttered.

I shook my head. I definitely did not do this.

We were ushered through the front doors. Everyone turned toward the grand ball room, ready for a night full of music and fun.

I, on the other hand, stayed glued to where I stood in the front room. I refused to move. Refused to breathe. Refused to even look away, because I was now face-to-face with Xaphan Vermillion.

CHAPTER 36

Mara

I stared at him. He stared at me. It felt like an eternity passed before he finally turned his gaze to Kalieth. He smiled at his son; the horrid show of teeth was wolfish, with no love in it. He stood tall over Kalieth, wearing a red and black suit. He had his hair slicked back with far too much gel.

I resisted the urge to reach back for my sword.

"Kalieth, I am glad to see you here," he said. His eyes returned to me. I had to fight to keep my chest rising and falling in a steady fashion. "And you've brought someone."

"Yes, sir," Kalieth said. He bowed his head and pressed a fist to his chest, holding the gesture until his father waved him off. Then, Xaphan's eyes moved to me, and I went rigid. I felt Kalieth squeeze my arm reassuringly as he said, "This is Edana. She's a Healer's apprentice. She patched me up after a rough tavern brawl."

"It's a pleasure, Edana," Xaphan said, offering me his hand.

I stared at his outstretched hand, riddled with disgust. It took everything I had to keep a pleasant expression on my face. Kalieth squeezed my arm again, his nails digging into my skin as a warning.

I forced my lips into a smile and placed my hand in Xaphan's. He returned my smile and brought my hand to his lips.

Gods, I'm going to throw up.

I could feel the bile rising in my throat. I swallowed it down and dipped my head. "The pleasure is all mine," I said, trying my best to make my rough voice sound feminine. I may have sounded like a third decade smoker, but it was womanly enough.

"I'm glad to see you're not participating in this idiocy," Xaphan said as he released my hand. He gestured to those wearing masks around him.

"What's happening?" Kalieth asked.

"It's the commonfolk. They're declaring their support for the Reaper. Apparently, they believe the rich need to start helping the poor. They think they have a right to *my* legacy. To the money *I* earned through hard work and dedication. I suppose they don't think they should have to work. They want handouts. Somehow, their inability to pay for dinner is *my* fault." Xaphan rolled his eyes. "The Reaper is their twisted symbol, because he 'fights' for them."

Say nothing. Bite your tongue. I had to whisper the words over and over in my mind.

"But the real thing is nowhere to be seen. That coward hasn't shown his face around the city

433

since I had him in chains. I think we sent him running."

Bite your tongue harder.

"Where are the others?" Kalieth asked, changing the topic as fast as he could.

"Your brothers are around here somewhere. Probably pestering every fair lady they can find."

"We should be on our way then. I'll have to introduce Edana."

Xaphan nodded, stepping out of our way. "I'm sure we'll meet again before the night is over."

Oh, we'll meet again, I said to myself as I clenched my teeth together.

Kalieth steered us toward the ball room. The large space was lined with torches. Fire was a large part of the Dragon's Feast celebration. The entire room was filled with golden light. It reflected off the polished floors and through the glass dome in the ceiling, into the night. Three chandeliers filled with diamonds reflected small rays of light onto the walls.

Long vines adorned with exotic flowers stretched from one wall to the next above our heads. The columns lining either side of the space also sported vines twisting up their sides. That was the other theme of the Dragon's Feast celebration, the rebirth and regrowth of nature. Of all life, really.

By the end of this night, a feast worthy of kings would be served. At least, that's what happened every year before. Tonight, however, the party would not last to the main course. Which reminded me that we needed to commence with the second part of our plan: getting our companions inside.

"Please tell me you're *not* introducing me to your siblings," I muttered.

"I'm not," he said, searching the crowd. "But I would like to know what you plan to do with them tonight."

"You care?"

"About some."

"Eligor and Azazel must die."

"Agreed. But I think the others can be reasoned with."

I stopped in my tracks. Kalieth turned to face me. We only stared for a moment before I remembered I needed to speak. "They tried to kill us. *Multiple* times."

"Yeah, but so did I. We all have our flaws."

I almost wanted to laugh. Almost.

Kalieth saw the disbelief in my gaze. "They fight for Xaphan's pride and approval. I think they will change sides with the right motivation. Just– just promise me you'll give them a chance."

I considered it. I didn't like the idea, but if I could spare any lives tonight, I would. "One chance. One."

Kalieth's shoulders sank in relief. He nodded, smiling. "So, a dance then?" he asked, offering me his hand.

His words brought the music to my attention. There was a live band somewhere close, but there were far too many people to see through. The dancefloor was only a few feet away. Dresses twirled and feet stomped. People clapped and sang. Watching it almost made me forget why I was here. Watching it made me want to feel the same joy that they did.

"We should continue with the plan," I said.

"Yes, we should," Kalieth said with a nod. "*But* the others won't be here for a while, and this music is calling to us, isn't it?"

I gave him a side-eye glance. "I don't dance."

"I've seen you dance."

"That was different."

"How?"

"That was in my world, where people moved freely and came together with pure intentions. This is your world, with rich snobs prancing around like they have sticks up their asses."

Kalieth looked at me, brows raised, before tipping his head back and laughing. He laughed until he had to catch his breath. I didn't quite understand why it was so funny, but I still found a smile creeping onto my face.

He offered me his hand again. "Dance with me, Reaper. Pretend our separate worlds no longer exist and show these rich snobs what it means to be free."

I looked down at his outstretched hand. I watched the way his fingertips curled inward slightly, as if he already knew I'd say no. I met his eyes again and couldn't bear the hope that shined within them.

"I don't know how to dance like this," I said. My throat felt tighter than usual.

He reached forward and took my hand. "Then let me show you."

He led me out onto the dancefloor. We slid between two other couples, and he took my other hand into his own. He tentatively placed my left hand on his shoulder as his own pressed against my lower back. Our other hands remained joined as he used them to lead us through the motions.

I followed his lead as he stepped forward, so I stepped backward. We went to the right as he turned me, and then he stepped forward again, going to the left this time. The movements had us going in a large circle, following all the other couples around the ballroom.

It only took two or three cycles for me to get the hang of it. That's when Kalieth took it a step further. He released me into a twirl, following me out into the center of the floor.

The music picked up speed, and so did we. Our dance suddenly became a duet with the musicians. We moved to their beat, and they moved their beat to our dance.

When the drums finally joined in, Kalieth let go. We drifted apart, each moving our feet to the rhythm

A few of the couples continued to dance, but many stopped to watch us. We were two coals in a sea of flame, after all, with our black attire. They clapped along to the beat, cheering for us.

The music got faster. The dance became more intense, more frenzied. I returned to Kalieth so he could twirl me once more.

The musicians swayed with their own music, nodding for us to continue. Sweat beaded their foreheads, but they created the beautiful melody without hesitation. And so, the song continued, intensifying even more. The second the musicians played the last beat, the great fires on either side of the room were lit. The flames sprung to life with overwhelming warmth and light. Kalieth dipped me then, as the last note echoed through the night. I closed my eyes, savoring the moment.

We panted together. I could hear his ragged breathing over my own. He held me in that dipped position for a moment too long.

"Is it just me, Reaper, or did you enjoy yourself for a moment there?" he said into my ear over the roar of applause from the crowd.

I had no answer for him.

The musicians changed their tempo and transitioned into a slow dance. I opened my eyes again only to stare straight into Kalieth's blue ones. His eyes widened and he quickly righted us again, swaying us with the music. He looked around, keeping me close to his chest. "Your eyes," he whispered. "They're silver."

"What?" I hissed. The nymph water should've last three times as long as it had. It must be the aether. Maybe I wasn't affected in the same way that mortals are. The magic didn't last as long.

Just seconds after Kalieth uttered the words, I spotted Xaphan through the crowd. He was greeting a few of his guests, but he was headed our way. If he were to see my eyes, he'd know exactly who I am, and this night would be over before it could even start.

He dismissed himself from the guests he stopped for and continued toward us. I had seconds to do something before he'd be close enough to see me. My heart started to beat wildly in my chest. I looked around furiously, searching for anything that could help us. There was nothing. Xaphan was seconds away. A few more feet and he'd be beside us. Panic tore through my every nerve, in a cold, painful way.

Terror gripped me. Thoroughly out of options, I did the first thing that came to my head. Snaking an arm around Kalieth's neck, I closed my eyes, and I hauled his mouth to mine.

For a few short seconds, there was only the warmth of his mouth, his breath. The tension rippling through every muscle in his body. I kissed him in a harsh, savage way, not wanting him to get any ideas from this rare moment of desperation.

I just about pulled away when he finally overcame the shock of it all. He surged forward and kissed me back with more force than I could've expected. It knocked me back a step or two, but he steadied us with a hand on my hip.

I should've pulled away the second I felt Vermillion's gaze leave us. But I didn't. I justified it by telling myself that this was necessary, that Vermillion was still watching. That this was the only way to keep from being caught.

This was all new to me. But almost like riding a horse for the first time, my body knew exactly what to do. Instinct took over, and I let my mind fall into shadow.

I groaned as he scraped his tongue along my teeth; the taste of him like fire to my blood. The feel of his lips moving against mine bringing a new level of sensation to my entire being.

I had to stop this. He was getting far too close. I was feeling far too much.

I pushed off him. I had to rip myself away from his grasp. I turned away, raising a hand to my lips, rubbing a finger over the swollen skin.

"Holy gods," Kalieth said. His words came out breathy as he continued to pant.

I moved off the dance floor. He followed only a few paces behind. When we reached a shadowed corner, I turned and shook my head. "Xaphan was behind us. He would've seen—" I gestured to my eyes. "That changed nothing."

"That changed everything."

"Kalieth..."

"Agree to disagree."

I opened my mouth to say something more, but Kalieth's eyes locked onto someone just over my shoulder. All traces of humor left his face. He pushed me farther into the dark corner and said, "call to your shadows."

I did as he asked, sensing the urgency in his voice. I stepped as far into the corner as I could and willed the shadows to cover my skin. I became one with the darkness around me.

It was Eligor who stood nearby. His eyes hadn't landed on Kalieth yet, but it was only a matter of seconds. Azazel stood beside Eligor, and it was Az who nudged his brother and nodded toward Kalieth. Eligor smiled in the same way his father had. A gesture that promised trouble.

Eligor dismissed himself from whoever it was he spoke to. He and Azazel strut over to us with a disgusting amount of arrogance in their stride. They walked as though they owned the world, having nothing and no one to fear.

Eligor clasped Kalieth on the shoulder. Azazel came to stand on his other side. Eligor narrowed his eyes and cocked his head to the side, flashing his teeth again. "Hello, brother," he sneered. "I must admit I'm surprised to see you here."

"Father told me to return by this night if I still wanted to be with this family. I may have strayed from the path, but I would never turn against the Vermillion name," Kalieth said, wearily glancing between his two brothers.

I watched as Eligor tightened his grasp on his brother's shoulder to an almost painful grip. Kalieth winced, quickly plastering a smile to his face as guests strode by.

"Oh, that's right," Eligor said. "You've missed so much here, Kal, we should catch up." He steered Kalieth away from the corner. They walked toward one of the service doors. I caught a glimpse of a dagger pressed to Kalieth's back.

Their voices faded into the chatter of the crowd. I watched from the shadows as they led Kalieth through a service entrance and turned into one of the many hidden corridors. I held my breath as the doors closed behind them, and Kalieth was out of sight.

I had a decision to make. The others would be here, waiting for me to distract the guards long enough to get them through. But Kalieth's brothers would kill him in there. I couldn't let him die, not after he saved my life the last time we were here. The others would be able to hold their own for a few more minutes.

I stepped out of the corner, keeping the shadows against my skin, and jumped between dancers. I faded so deep into the darkness that I took the place of the dancers' shadows, invisible to all who looked. That was how I made my way across the floor, toward the service doors, curling my fingers into my sleeve to reach for my knives.

The blood bath was about to start, and I planned to be covered in it by the end.

CHAPTER 37

Kalieth

Five of my six brothers were waiting in the corridor. It was Alastor who was missing. Azazel and Eligor slammed me against the wall. My head hit the stone with a sickening thud. Bursts of light burned behind my closed eyelids just as nausea came over me in a swift wave.

"Did you really think you could come back here after all you've done, and be welcomed with open arms?" Eligor asked.

Tynan took his place holding me down so that Eligor could land a punch to my face. My jaw snapped to the side with the force of his blow. I swore I heard something crack. I spit out a mouthful of blood, the metallic taste flooding my senses.

"Guys, you really don't want to do this, trust me," I said between pants.

"Oh, I think we do," Darcel spat.

"She'll come for you," I warned

"Hold him up," Eligor commanded. He threw another punch. Another. Another. The others closed in too. They took turns landing their punches. Their blows to my abdomen stole my breath away. The punches to my face and jaw made me dizzy and nauseous. Someone's kick to my chest certainly broke a rib or two.

They stepped back, letting me catch my breath. "Poor Kalieth," Azazel said, pulling my head up by my hair. "You always did have a bad habit of questioning this family. A bad habit of straying too far."

"Hands. Off." A voice snarled from behind us.

My brothers turned simultaneously. I looked up, a lazy smile on my lips, to see Mara standing in the corridor. She wielded her short sword. Shadows branched out from behind her like obsidian claws poised to strike. Her eyes were on me. I wondered if it was one of the punches to my head making me see things, or if there was fear in those silver eyes of hers. Fear for me.

"What the hell?" one of my brothers said.

I spit more blood onto the floor. "Allow me to introduce you to my new bad habit."

Mara raised her sword. "I don't like it when people take my things."

Eligor looked to me and then back to Mara. He raised his brows in the same moment that a surprised laugh left his lips. He drew his own sword. "You want him? Come get him."

I watched Mara charge all five of my brothers. She could kill them all without lifting a finger, but she didn't touch that power. She fought them with swords, daggers, punches, and kicks. She was honoring her promise to me. She was giving them one chance.

Eligor got to her first. He raised his sword and brought it down for her neck, but she leaned back to dodge it. Once his arm was outstretched enough, she grabbed it and twisted. Eligor cried out, clutching his limb close to his chest. His sword clattered to the ground. Mara grabbed it, threw it in the air, and kicked it so hard that the blade hit Darcel square in the shoulder, pinning him to the wall.

As her leg came down from that same kick, she landed a blow on the back of Eligor's neck with the hardened heel of her foot. He crumpled to the ground instantly. He did not get back up. Still, she did not kill him, because that privilege was reserved for Bryce alone.

Mara turned to my remaining three brothers. Azazel, the oldest and most experienced fighter, drew his sai. Eligor was more outspoken about his strength and power, but Azazel was like silent death. He kept his skills well-hidden so that when he used them, he wouldn't need to do it twice. Even knowing Mara's talents, I still feared for her as she faced off with Az. As children, no one could beat him. I could only imagine what he was like now.

Mara raised her sword and swung with the intent of slicing clean through Azazel's neck. He blocked it with his sai, catching Mara's blade between the tongs. They withdrew, circling each other again. Two predators battling for an apex title.

Mara lunged again just a few seconds later, moving as one with her sword. Azazel struggled to keep up with her quick movements, but he managed to block each strike she planned. He twisted her around, kicking her back so she stumbled straight toward Tynan and Nox's awaiting blades. Mara steadied herself before she fell. But now she stood trapped between all three brothers. She only looked down at her own sword. She stared at it for a long moment before sheathing it into her dress. She then turned to face Azazel again. Her gaze fell upon his sai.

Most sai are blunt weapons, used more for defensive fighting than anything else. They're meant to block, not stab. But not Azazel's. He had them custom made so that each tong was sharpened.

"I have need of those," Mara said. Her eyes were fixed on the silver sai. I remembered always seeing a pair hung on her blades' belt, but I'd never seen her use them.

Azazel scoffed. "You'd be a fool to fight me with no weapon."

Mara's gaze snapped up to meet his. She drew in her brows; her head cocking to the side. "I am the weapon."

Shadows exploded from her back. They spread across her skin and enveloped her completely, until she was lost in a sea of shifting, deepening darkness. Azazel raised his sai, crying out as he charged her. He ran into the shadows, blades extended.

He ran straight through. The shadows dispersed, and there was nothing there. Only empty space where Mara just stood. The shadows moved and twisted, reforming behind Azazel. Mara stepped out of the darkness, a mischievous smirk on her face, and tapped his shoulder.

He turned blades first. She folded backwards to dodge them. Her hands found the ground, and she kicked off the floor, using her feet to land a blow to Az's throat and chest.

He fell back a few steps, catching himself before he fell into Tynan and Nox. He clutched his throat, spurting and coughing. His breaths were gasps of air as he tried to regain control of himself. He glared at our brothers as they help to steady him. He pushed away from their grasp and stalked toward Mara again. She watched every step with a smile on her lips.

She was *enjoying* this, I realized. That's why she let them each try their hand in the fight. She could've ended it the second it started, but she *wanted* to fight. She wanted to show them exactly who she was. More than her power. More than her blades. She needed none of it to destroy them.

The next part was a blur. With shadows still circling around her, she charged Azazel. She engaged him in close range, where the sai could be lethal. She didn't seem worried, though, as she landed punches to his face and abdomen. When he tried to use his sai, she landed a powerful blow to his wrist, forcing his hand to spasm and drop the weapon. She quickly turned and caught his other arm, wrapping her own around it and applying pressure until she heard it crack, and Azazel scream. The second sai clattered to the floor. With her back against Az's chest, she threw her head into his. They connected with a sickening crunch, and Az fell to the ground, clutching his nose.

Mara picked up the sai, twisting them in her hands with expert skill as she faced Tynan and Nox. They exchanged one last weary glance before they both lunged at the same time.

Mara caught both of their swords, one in each sai, and twisted sharply, disarming both of them. Before they had a chance to react, she twisted the sai again so that she held them by the blades and knocked each brother on the head with the hilts, slamming their skulls together. They both fell.

Serene silence enveloped the hall. Mara panted, surveying the bodies of my five brothers. A small smile tugged at her lips as she turned to me, offering a hand to help me up. I nearly took it, but from the corner of my eye, I saw movement. My head snapped to the side to find that Azazel was no longer on the floor. He was lunging for Mara, a sword in his hand. It was mere inches from her skin. For once, she would be too late. There was nothing either of us could do. The Reaper would die by my brother's blade.

But suddenly Azazel was dragged backward. There was a hand on his throat, and he clawed at it, struggling for breath. Nails dug into his neck, drawing blood.

I struggled to see past Mara. Still, I watched Azazel fall to the floor, unconscious. Someone stood over him, fists clenched.

Mara whirled around, sai ready, but she froze. I struggled to my feet, desperate to see who saved the Reaper and put Azazel on his ass.

There, standing over Azazel, shoulders rising and falling with heavy breath, was... Eligor.

Mara and I both looked to where Eligor laid face-down on the floor, still unconscious. But he also stood before us, staring down at Az, uncaring of us watching from behind him.

"You must move quickly. They'll be healing soon. They heal quicker than most," Eligor said. He turned, surveying my bloody face and Mara's defensive stance.

He nodded to himself, as if just remembering that he was our enemy. Before our eyes, his black hair started to grow, turning blonde as it reached his shoulders. His blue eyes changed to a green, almost hazel color. Her skin remained pale, but freckles littered her face.

My breath was stolen always. I'd never seen her before, exactly. But from the resemblance, I knew exactly who she was. We were staring directly at Alina Reitenour, Bryce's shapeshifting sister.

A harsh smile twitched her lips at our looks of shock, but her expression turned serious when her eyes landed on Mara.

"Is that my dress?"

CHAPTER 38

Mara

I lowered my weapons. There were only a handful of moments in my life when I was caught with my guard down. I'd been too confident. Too distracted. It nearly cost me my life.

Alina watched me closely. The way her eyes remained narrowed, her lips pursed, told me that she was unsure, calculating. She had to have been watching us from somewhere along this corridor. Did she make the decision to save my life? Or did she simply decide to put Azazel down herself?

There were more questions I wanted to ask. How long had she been here? How did she roam freely through the estate? Where was she when Bryce was imprisoned here only a short time ago?

There was no time for answers.

"You're here to kill the Vermillions?" Alina asked. She kept her chin high, staring down her nose at me, as if she were establishing herself to be better, higher in authority.

"I'm here to kill Xaphan."

"Good." Her eyes moved to Kalieth. Her lip curled up slightly. Her nostrils flared. "And what of this one?"

"He's with me."

She looked to me then. The hatred in her eyes was unmistakable. "He's a Vermillion."

I took a small step to the side to shield Kalieth completely. I had no reason to distrust her, so I kept the sai down, but I twisted them in my hands as a warning. She noted the movement. "He's with me," I said again, pronouncing each syllable this time.

She looked between the two of us. Her gaze nothing more than a steely, unfeeling stare. Her features set into a hard expression, and then she smiled. A vile, rageful smile that disguised none of her contempt for Kalieth. For anyone with the Vermillion name. Anyone with their blood.

"Then I'm not." She turned, ready to walk off.

"Bryce trusts him."

She stopped. She raised her head slowly without looking back. "Bryce has always been a fool."

"He saved her life. He broke her out of imprisonment here." Best to leave out who got her imprisoned in the first place.

Alina faced us again. She looked to Kalieth. Her stare had no less distaste than it did before. She took a step forward, then another. She walked slowly. Painstakingly slow. She continued to come forward until our faces were inches apart. Only then did she lower into a crouch and grasp Kalieth's jaw, moving his face from one side to the other for a better look.

He winced in pain as her long nails dug into the wounds his brothers inflicted only moments ago. She leaned in close and stared deep into his eyes as she said, "and how does she repay us?" Her voice was a whisper, yet still held so much emotion. Raw and unchecked. Pain, sorrow, hatred, disgust, and even rage. "By leaving us both here to die."

"She's not," Kalieth argued. "She'll be here."

"Don't count on it," Alina countered as she stood. Her eyes found mine one last time before she turned away. She walked a few steps into the corridor, until she was almost completely consumed by shadow. She stopped. I heard a soft sigh, or maybe a sharp exhale of frustration, leave her lips. Without turning, she said, "Vermillion will give a speech in a few minutes. He'll be out in the open. Vulnerable. Unsuspecting. That's your chance."

Kalieth got to his feet, using the wall for support. "You won't help us?"

"I just did."

With that, she disappeared into the darkness of the corridor beyond.

I stared after her. I had many questions itching my tongue, but I couldn't voice any of them. Even if I had, I didn't expect her to give me

452

any answers. I could feel the cold resentment that settled deep in her soul. Like the first crisp winds of winter, it emanated from her, chilling me to my bones. But my shadows, which typically took to the cold, dark places, shied away from her. They couldn't touch her like they could others. It was as though she had built a fortress around herself in her time there. Iron walls that couldn't be seen by a mortal's eye, but was there all the same, protecting her from the evils of this world.

I had a wall of my own. It served a different purpose, however. Because while I created mine for my own desires, I had the feeling that hers was a side effect of whatever tortures she endured here. A subconscious thing she developed to protect herself. A part of her as much as any other.

"Why wouldn't she help us? Doesn't she want Xaphan dead?" Kalieth asked. He pushed off the wall and leaned onto my shoulder. Together, we made our way toward the service door, through which we could return to the ballroom.

"She's still a prisoner here. If we fail, she will have to face the consequences of helping us. This way, she saves herself either way."

"She's not in a cell."

"She doesn't have to be behind bars to be a prisoner."

Kalieth said nothing. I couldn't be sure whether he had nothing to say, or he was in too much pain to focus on the matter at hand. He kept a hand pressed against his ribs as he walked, hunched over like an old veteran.

I stopped before the doors, pushing him to lean against the wall. He went willingly, out of breath just from our short walk down the corridor.

The sight of his pain brought a deep anger to my chest. The shadows reacted to it, reaching out and brushing over his skin. They whispered to me, urging me to let them loose. Like a band of hundreds of ancient voices all chanting at once. *HealHimHealHimHealHim.*

I ripped at his shirt, ignoring the buttons that flew in all directions. He might've made a snarky, suggestive comment about it if he wasn't too busy hissing and flinching away from my touch when I brushed my fingers across the black and blue skin of his ribs.

"You couldn't have come to my rescue two minutes earlier?" he asked, baring his teeth as I pressed harder into his ribcage. They were definitely broken.

I glared down at him. "Remind me to let them kill you next time."

"You'd miss me too much."

This time, I took a bit of delight in pressing my fingers into his ribs. He grunted, fists clenching, as I allowed the shadows to flow through me and seep beneath his skin. I willed them to find what's broken and mend it back together.

The black swirls that covered my skin, the same markings that Kalieth once thought were tattoos, started to move down my arms, through my fingers, and into Kalieth's chest. They'd been

454

shadows all along, covering and protecting me. They hardened my skin and served as a reminder of my connection to another world. A world of peace and whispers; dreams and starlight.

I watched Kalieth's fists clench tighter. His nails dug into his palm, threatening to draw blood, as the shadows tainted his pale skin. They moved within his chest like black ink spreading across wet paper. They made their way to the bruises, cracked skin, and broken ribs, and settled there. They swirled together in a continuous motion. After a few seconds, Kalieth's labored breathing began to return to normal. His clenched fists loosened into tensely curled fingers.

The shadows dissipated, leaving nothing but clear skin behind. Kalieth's body sagged against the wall, relief relaxing his muscles, as the shadows withdrew. They returned to me, swirling over my skin and gathering at my back.

I stepped away, leaning against the opposite wall. I couldn't remove my eyes from where the shadows had just been.

"You didn't know you could do it?" Kalieth asked, reading it in my stare.

I shook my head.

"What made you think to try?"

"The shadows," I said. "They– like you."

His brows flew up. "Really?"

"Don't start."

He pressed a hand against his chest. He feigned a flattered gasp. "Does this mean we're meant for each other?"

I pushed off the wall, closing the distance between myself and the service door. "I will re-break your ribs."

"Promise?"

I threw the door open. Music flooded into the corridor, echoing into the rooms beyond. I was suddenly bathed in golden light and warmed by the many crackling fires.

I adjusted my dress and walked forward. I tried to keep my eyes to the floor so that no one would notice their silver color. I needed to keep the element of surprise for just a few more moments.

I turned to find Kalieth hanging back in the corridor. I arched a brow, and he responded by gesturing to his ripped shirt. It had no buttons left for him to use. He'd either have to stay behind or walk around the ballroom bare-chested.

With a plan forming in my head, I returned to the threshold for him. I wiped my thumb across my lip, coating it in lipstick, and smeared it across Kalieth's mouth and cheek. He grabbed my wrist quickly, glancing around at anyone who might be watching. "What are you doing?"

"Just follow my lead. Act like we've both had a little too much to drink, and we make for the main entrance. The others will be waiting outside the gates. We have to get them inside before Xaphan's speech."

Before he had a chance to question my plan, I narrowed my eyes to slits and stumbled backward into the ballroom. He jumped into character, stumbling after me and catching me just before I would've fallen to the floor. I giggled as he steadied me, wrapped my arms around his neck, and leaned into him heavily. He guided us toward the ballroom doors.

We walked relatively slow, stumbling every once in a while to sell our drunken façade. If people got too close, we would whisper and giggle sweet nothings to one another. Our public display of affection worked wonders in scaring the other guests away.

We were nearly at the doors when a group of young, low-level merchants recognized Kalieth. They called out to him, approaching quickly.

Kalieth pretended not to hear them. He kept his eyes on me, with a seductive smirk pulling at his lips. Once the merchants were in earshot, he leaned in close and said, "You made a grave mistake tonight. You let me have a taste of you. Your kiss was a dream wrapped in shadows and nightmares, and I'll do whatever it takes to feel it again."

I shivered at the utter sincerity in his words.

The group of merchants whistled and backed away from us, priding Kalieth for catching such a beauty. It took everything I had not to reach into my sleeves and throw one of my knives after hearing some of their comments. Kalieth, as if sensing my crumbling restraint, took my hands into his own. He interlaced our fingers and tightened his grip, knowing I might try to pull away.

"What's the harm if I kill them?" I muttered through the bared teeth of a fake smile.

"Has anyone ever told you that you're awfully violent?"

"Try telling me when my hands are free."

Kalieth chuckled. He let me go once we were only a few steps from the doors. They were closed now, likely in preparation for Xaphan's speech. I hoped that we could still slip through without drawing too much attention to ourselves.

Just as my hand found the doorknob, the sound of metal tapping against glass rang through the room. The chatter died out, replaced by an anxious silence. Xaphan's speech. It was time.

Kalieth and I exchanged a panicked glance. I returned my focus to the door, ready to slip away without anyone noticing, but the handle started to turn in my hand without my help. I withdrew my arm, watching as the door started to creak open.

Kalieth pulled me out of the way, jerking me back. We retreated into the crowd, unable to do anything but watch as the doors flew wide open, bouncing back off the walls. The sound they made echoed through the entire room, turning heads, and drawing surprised gasps from the crowd.

Standing in the doorway was none other than Alastor Vermillion. He wasn't in formal attire, instead he wore his armor. A cape hung from his shoulders, displaying the Vermillion family crest across his back. He raised his chin high, a cocky smile on his lips when all eyes turned to him. "Apologies, father," he said; his voice ringing through the room. "But I thought you'd like an early Dragon's Feast present."

He took a few steps into the room. Arrogance resided in his every stride. He looked around, reveling in the attention. He held out the silence, as if enjoying the suspense and tension he instilled.

Unable to hold out any longer, Alastor turned and gestured toward the doorway in a grand sweep of his arm. "We found them scouting the premises."

I heard the scuffling sounds of boots against the polished floor. I listened to the gasps and cries of those who stood in front of me. I felt the tension rise in the air, threatening to choke me as I struggled to see through the sea of people.

Four guards walked through the doors. Each one escorting someone. I could hear the struggle as the guards fought to keep their hold on the prisoners.

I pushed through two people, with Kalieth right behind me. There, on their knees before Alastor and Xaphan Vermillion, with their wrists bound and daggers pressed to their throats, was Bryce, Ryder, Quinn, and Ace.

CHAPTER 39

Bryce

The guard that held me did so leisurely. He knew I wouldn't fight him; knew I wouldn't call to the flames. Not while they had a dagger pressed against Ryder's throat. I wouldn't be able to protect us both.

I was forced to do absolutely nothing except weather Xaphan's piercing gaze as he surveyed us. I bit my tongue to keep from spitting at his feet or cursing him and bringing us all early deaths. I clenched my fists together so that no one could see my trembling hands.

"Well, well," Xaphan drawled. "Isn't this a delightful surprise?"

He stepped down from his dais. The bastard built himself a throne to sit upon while he watched the festivities. I suddenly found myself wondering how much influence the Vermillions had over the real royalty in the capital. Xaphan seemed to fancy himself the real king. That also made him the executioner, and we just might've walked straight into our sentencing.

"Where there's henchmen, there must be a Reaper lurking in the shadows," Xaphan said, glancing around the room. "Are you with us Reaper? I'd hate to kill your friends without you here to watch."

Murmurs and gasps spread through the crowd. Thank the gods, it was finally time for the city to get a look at Xaphan Vermillion's true colors. No matter how it ended tonight, they would know what he is. A god. A monster. The devil. Whatever they want to call him.

"Step away," I heard an all too familiar voice call from behind me. "That one's mine."

The guard keeping a dagger to my throat slipped away. The blade was replaced by a large, calloused hand wrapping around my neck, squeezing enough to labor my breath. He forced me to my feet, sliding an arm around my waist and tugging me flat against him.

The sounds of a struggle beside me told me that Ryder was fighting against his captor. It was a whole new kind of torture, I discovered, to be in Eligor's hold while Ryder watched. With no real way of knowing whether we would live long enough to be with one another again.

I felt tears gathering in my eyes, but I refused to let them fall. The Vermillions would relish seeing my distress, my pain. I wouldn't give them that satisfaction. Not when I was only minutes from joining my sister in the afterlife.

Xaphan was saying something. He was calling out to the crowd, searching the room again. I heard nothing he said. I couldn't because Eligor slid his fingers into my hair, gripping hard and yanking me back so that his lips were against my ear. "Listen to me and listen carefully," he hissed. "The Vermillion brothers will be bursting into the room any minute. We'll have seconds to use surprise to our advantage. I'll take care of the guards holding your friends. You hit Xaphan with all the power you've got."

Every thought I had seconds ago ebbed away. I relaxed in his hold, realizing that it didn't feel the same. It was gentle.

Utter confusion addled my brain. "Mara?" I whispered, the sound hardly audible. Had the Reaper discovered a new talent with the shadows?

"Is that her name? The one who's wearing my dress?"

My blood turned to ice in my veins. It was lucky she held me up, because my knees gave out with the last few words. Every muscle in my body started to tremble. The small question left me in a broken exhale that threatened to spill tears. "Alina?"

"Two years, it's been," she said. Her voice still disguised as Eligor's. "And you're still stealing my things."

I couldn't breathe. I couldn't remember how. I was reduced to the basic need to draw a breath in and blow it out. It was all I could do to keep myself from falling into a paralyzing shock that would only seal my fate tonight.

"You're lucky I felt merciful tonight," she added. "Because I planned to let you decide your own fate, even if it left you here in a cell. I planned to leave you to rot, just like you did to me."

Another wave of nauseating shock passed through me. It chilled me to the bone first, sending me into a fit of shivers. But the cool grip of panic soon brought heat to my face, my neck.

This was my worst fear. The nightmare that would chase sleep away. She lived through it all, and I left her here to face it alone. In the two years we'd been separated, she lived through the worst tortures the Vermillions could concoct while I pranced across rooftops with my new family. I failed her. I failed us both.

She was right to want to see me suffer. I would too if our roles were switched. This was my fault. All of it. I was the one stupid enough to get captured in the first place. I was the one who ran when she got shot down. I was the one to stay away instead of ripping this estate apart brick by brick until I'd found her again.

I was so lost in my own thoughts, reliving the past, that I didn't realize Xaphan's gaze had landed on me. He surveyed me, studying every detail of my face. His eyes then shifted to the fake Eligor behind me.

"You can't keep her this time, my son. We've lost her too many times. She goes to the Northern Kingdom with the others in the morning."

"As long as I get to have the night with her first," Alina replied, nailing Eligor's smug voice.

I heard Ryder grunt as he struggled against the guards once more. "I'll fucking kill you," he snapped at my sister. Of course, he had no way of knowing it wasn't the real Eligor that he spoke to. I wished I could tell him that it was okay, but frankly, even though I had my sister back, everything felt wrong.

Xaphan's eyes lit up at the sight of Ryder's anger. It was exactly what he thrived off of. What he lived for. He wanted Ryder angry. Wanted him ready to fight for me, just so that he could take all that hope, all that fight, and crush it. That was the Vermillion way, to torture us until we break.

Xaphan nodded to Ryder. "That one."

Two guards closed in on him from either side. They grabbed him by the arms, lifting him a few inches off the floor and dragged him forward.

"This one dies first, Reaper," Xaphan called, unsheathing his sword. He pressed the blade beneath Ryder's chin and forced him to look up. "Your sister, isn't it?"

My heart dropped to the floor.

"You gave yourself away by telling me this sword belonged to your father. So, if this is Ryder, who hides beneath the mask? I'm told there are two children. One boy. One girl. I'd simply love to meet you."

I tried to subtly search the crowd, but I saw no hint of black among the vibrant dresses. There were no silver or golden eyes staring back. I

464

wondered if she truly wasn't here. Maybe she would return to find us all dead on the ballroom floor. I had to admit, it wasn't exactly what I had in mind when I dreamed of attending a ball.

"Very well. The brother dies first, then the boy," Xaphan sighed. He looked to where Quinn knelt on the far right. Quinn gulped, shrinking away from Vermillion's stare. Ace moved almost imperceptibly closer, straightening to size-up the god. Xaphan didn't seem to notice. He raised his sword, his eyes fixed on the knot at the base of Ryder's throat.

I opened my mouth to release a scream of pure terror, but the sound never came. I only got as far as drawing in the breath before a door on the other side of the room was kicked open. From the small service door emerged Azazel, Tynan, Nox, Darcel, and finally, Eligor, with their weapons raised.

"Now!" Alina yelled, pushing me out toward Xaphan while she dove for the guards that restrained Ace and Quinn.

I watched in horror as Xaphan's sword came down for Ryder's throat. I could see the whole story play out. Ryder's death, and my unbound rage that would bathe the entire city in flame. Not tonight.

I threw my hands out, summoning all the fire I could muster, and hit Xaphan with a column of flames so powerful that it knocked him across the room just seconds before his blade would've touched Ryder's skin.

Alina managed to throw the guards off of Ace and Quinn, and with their help, they drove them off completely. Now we stood together, closing ranks into a small circle, as the Vermillion sons surrounded us. More and more guards flooded into the room. They shouted orders and formed their own lines until there were nearly two dozen of them between us and the nearest exit. The mystic mercenaries that Vermillion hired formed the front line, and I watched in horror as two mystics took their defensive positions on either side of me, one with lightning crackling between his fingers and another twirling small metal disks. We were outnumbered and outmatched.

Xaphan's shoes clicked against the floors as he approached calmly. He brushed out the few flames that burned at his blazer and smoothed out the scorched fabric. He sighed, as though he were disappointed in us, and clicked his tongue. "I expected more from this."

He waved a hand and turned away. "Kill them."

The crowd of guests shouted and gasped. To many of them, this would seem like a bizarre twist of events. But there was nothing they could do. The guards closed in on us. The Vermillion sons snickered and taunted us as they pressed their swords to our chests. We were backing into each other, pressing against one another. There was nowhere to go, no way to fight.

They continued to close in. I felt Eligor's blade dig into my skin. Felt the warmth of my own blood trail down my chest. Breathing became hard. There was nowhere left to go. Death was with us, waiting and ready. I could feel the cold chill of his fingers as they brushed over my arms, down my back, ready to lift my soul away.

No.

That wasn't it.

Not Death's grip. This was a welcomed chill that whispered to me. That assured me of safety and comfort.

I realized the shadows were with us in the same second that the glass dome above us shattered, and the darkness from the sky above poured into the ballroom.

Night itself came alive, and all hell broke loose.

CHAPTER 40

Mara

I knew that to have full, unbound control over the shadows, I was supposed to let all emotion flow through me like a peaceful river. I was meant to forgive and forget and use my power with no ill intent. Everything should be rainbows and butterflies.

I am anything but peaceful, and *fuck* forgiveness. Consequences be damned, the only thing I was using to call to my shadows now was rage. Pure and unrelenting. It built and festered for nearly four seasons now. It was time to let it all loose. It was time for Xaphan Vermillion to feel the full extent of my wrath.

The others were completely surrounded. They were being herded into one another like sheep to the slaughter while Kalieth and I hid in a corner. No more.

I made to step out, but Kalieth grabbed my arm. I turned to see his eyes through the shadows, which were growing and expanding outward, ready to summon Death himself. They curled over my arms and around his when he gripped me.

His eyes found mine, and for a long moment, we only stood there. There were unspoken words in our stares. We didn't have enough time to try to voice them. He cleared his throat and released my arm. "If we make it through this, we'll talk about that kiss."

I only nodded, words a delicacy I couldn't grasp. I turned back toward the chaos, leaving Kalieth behind to join the others. Time seemed to slow as I walked toward it all. This would be the end of suffering. The end of deceit. The end of the era of war.

I am the end.

I embraced the shadow. I saw all the darkness lurking inside of me, within my very soul, and I willed it to come out. I opened the box of world-ending anger that I'd locked away within myself for so long, and I commanded it to destroy.

Shadows erupted from me like an explosion of darkness. They seeped out of my back, my palms, my nose and mouth. They shot up to the ceiling, shattering the glass dome above and setting the night free. They spread through the room and snuffed out the light. I felt the primal magic in the dragon scales stirring with my show of power. They seemed to buzz with some sort of warmth and spark. I felt their power seeping into me, making my shadows more powerful. More deadly.

I sent a wave of my power toward my friends, knocking the Vermillion sons off their feet. The last thing I saw was Bryce burning the very ground beneath the guards' feet before the shadows filled the room, and there was nothing to be seen but complete and utter darkness. The kind of darkness that goes on for eternity, stretching on and on.

Over the screams of the crowd, and the pounding of their footsteps as they fled in all directions, Xaphan called to me. "Reaper, how nice of you to finally join us." His voice was a rolling purr.

I said nothing. I only walked toward the voice, stepping lightly, cursing the heels for the way they clicked against the floors.

"Tell me, did you learn how to kill a god? Or did you come to me prepared to die?"

The distant sounds of metal on metal told me that my friends were still fighting. There were far too many guards for them to take on their own, and more of them would be flooding in. Beyond that, the Vermillion brothers would be relentless in their pursuit. My friends needed backup, and I couldn't be there for them.

Then the shadows whispered to me again. *TheTaleTheTaleTheTale.* They said. *AzkrivaAzkrivaAzkriva.*

It was hard to clear my head long enough to understand what they meant. But it came to me, cracking through the murky waters of my mind like moonlight. They spoke of the old tales of the two kings. The better part of them may have been lies, but some things were based off Cheusi's truth.

Of course.

"...he could control any shadow he came across. Soon he commanded his own army of mindless beings that could not be killed..."

A hint. A truth buried in the deceit of a fake history. *Azkriva. Abominations.* They were described in records as beings who could control shadow, but that wasn't completely true. They were beings born from Cheusi's magic. They were her army of shadows.

I had no idea how to do it, but the shadows did. They were a celestial form of infinite wisdom. They'd lived a thousand lifetimes. They were there for the birth of the realms and they would continue to live on long after the death of the worlds. They were my teachers. It was my turn to listen.

I took a deep breath and closed my eyes. I opened my other senses to my surroundings, allowing them to expand through the room. The shadows became an extension of my touch, smell, and hearing. I felt the smooth, cool surface of the polished floors when the shadows brushed against them as if it were my own fingertips reaching out. The acrid smell of smoke filled my nose like I was right beside the doused flame. I listened to the frightened breathing of guests and felt their body heat against my own skin.

Once my senses were open to everything in the room, I turned my attention to the shadows. The darkened extensions of the people around me. The shadows of items bathed in moonlight from the windows. The shadows of guests who found a spare torch to light. The shadows of my friends,

471

illuminated by Bryce's flaming fingertips. Those were the ones I reached out to.

They were harder to control, the naturally occurring silhouettes. They wanted to stay with their counterparts. To continue living in a state of peace like they were designed to do. It was against their nature to follow me.

My influence was too great. The laws of nature bent to my will with little resistance. I ripped the shadows away from the living. I pulled them toward me, breathing life into them as they came. They rose from the floor, a swirling mass of black mist and nightmares. The sight of them enough to grip grown men with terror. They were my loyal servants. My harbingers of night. My *azkrivas*. The sight of them was a promise of decimation.

I sent them off to aid my friends in their battle against guards and cowards. They would protect all which I held dear while I cut the head off the snake.

I reached out with my senses once more. This time, I searched for another power signature. Aether. It was easy to detect. It gave off warmth and light like nothing else in this world. It also burned and blinded when in the wrong hands. That's what Xaphan planned to do, no doubt. Steal my aether and burn this world to ashes so he can create a new one. He and Morrighan.

He stood on his dais, unmoving. He was waiting for me there. He knew I would come. It was undoubtedly a trap, but I didn't care. I was blinded by rage, unable to think strategically. All I knew was the desire to kill. All I heard were the screams of innocents around me. All I felt was the tension in the room, so thick I could slice it with my sword. All I saw was one small light shining through my infinite night. A single star. I knew it was him.

"You know nothing of this world, Reaper," his voice cut through all other sounds. It drowned out the clashing swords. It rang over the chaos of fleeing guests.

I kept silent. He wanted to bait me into giving away my whereabouts. I would do no such thing.

"Do you even know what your father was the god of?"

I didn't. I never asked.

"Your father was becoming a pain in my side. *The God of Healing and Medicine.* The one all healers and sickly patients prayed to. Do you know what he did with his power? He went straight to the front lines to heal soldiers and try to persuade the commanders to end this war. He got too close, and I had to put an end to him."

A healer? *Of course.* Da only ever wanted to help people. He never got sick, not that I could remember. The only time I'd ever seen him injured was when I gazed upon his corpse.

"Unfortunately, his whole accelerated healing ability made killing him quite difficult. My power and aether alone couldn't do it. I needed help from a much more primal magic."

I was close now. I stayed out of his sight, lurking in the depths of the shadows. He stood tall. His eyes, glowing silver, searched his surroundings carefully, never leaving the shadows. In the palm of his hand, aether, tendrils of light swirling through his fingers, splayed the night. It illuminated his face in a white glow that made his pale skin look sickly.

"But once I absorbed his aether, I stole his healing power. So, Reaper, how exactly do you plan to kill me? What primal magic do you have?"

"I know exactly how I plan to kill you, Xaphan. Primal magic would be far too quick. Far too easy. I want to see you suffer first," I said.

Xaphan searched the shadows for me, finding nothing. I was already on the other side of him, walking in slow circles.

"For what? For killing your father? That can't be what all this fuss is about."

"For my father. For all the innocent lives lost in this war. For the people you've tortured and sold. If the authorities won't punish you, I'll find my own justice for the laws you've broken. The lives you've destroyed."

Xaphan scoffed, the sound set my blood to boil. "Laws? The voice of law speaks far too softly to be heard in the great noise of war."

I curled my fingers inward and clenched my fists so tight that my knuckles turned pale. The shadows closed in on Vermillion, clawing at his skin and seeping into his bones to send pain into his every nerve.

He hardly even flinched. I watched as the wounds my shadows inflicted healed within seconds. The two sides of the gashes sealed themselves together before blood could fall.

"You'll have to do better than that," he said, unimpressed.

I stepped out of the shadows then, into the small area of the room that was illuminated by the light of his aether. He stared at me. I stared at him. For the first time, he was seeing me for everything I truly am. A Reaper. A goddess. A woman.

He smiled then; the gesture predatory in nature. The aether in his palms flared and popped before it exploded into a blinding light that drove my shadows away. They screeched as they receded back into the night above.

I hid my face beneath my arm, and yet I could still see light burning through my closed eyes. An eerie silence settled over the room as the light faded. I made to lower my arm, but only got as far as opening my eyes before a hand slid into my hair, yanking my head back to make way for another hand to grip my throat.

Aether burned the skin of my neck as it poured from Xaphan's palms. I bit down on my tongue to keep from crying out. The motion was shortly followed with the metallic taste of my own blood.

"Is this your Reaper?" Xaphan called out, presenting me to the thinning crowd. "This farmgirl playing dress-up?"

The few people who were still there, who were unable to find a way out, looked upon us through wide eyes. I hated being on the receiving end of so many stares. Gazes filled with wonder and awe while others displayed hatred, fear, or disgust.

His hands tightened around my throat. I struggled to breathe. I clawed at his wrists, trying to relieve myself of the burning heat his hands provided. I tried to call to the shadows, but the blinding light seeping from Xaphan's palms burned them away.

I watched, horrified, as the Vermillion sons closed in on my friends. With my *azkriva* driven away by Xaphan's power, they had no help. There were far too many guards and mercenaries. One managed to strike a hard blow to Ryder's side. He fell to his knees, and another guard drew his sword back to plunge into my brother's chest. Ryder dropped to the ground, barely escaping the blade.

"You should be thanking me, Reaper. After all, what would you be without me? Not a goddess. Not a symbol of fear. You'd be another nobody. A mere blade of grass beneath the shade of a boot. I made you what you are." His grip tightened on my hair, answered by the searing pain in my scalp. He leaned in closer, his lips only a hair's breadth from my ear, and whispered, "*I made you.*"

His grip tightened on my throat. The aether flowing from his hands choked me. It travelled through my blood and cast away my shadows, leaving my skin vulnerable. The silver flames burned me horribly, and yet I couldn't scream. I couldn't do anything but watch as Alastor Vermillion dragged Quinn by his hair to the steps of the dais. He kicked in his knees and forced him to kneel.

The aether pouring from Xaphan's hands began to battle with the aether in my own blood. I felt him stealing it away from me, draining the life from my veins. My fingertips turned grey and lifeless. None of it mattered. All I could focus on was Quinn, and the terror in his wide eyes. The edge to his shrill voice as he begged me for help.

Bryce was screaming. She was burning the faces off the guards in front of her, fighting her way toward Quinn. Ryder was shouting something, reaching forward as if there was no distance between them. Kalieth was running, but Eligor and Azazel grabbed him, pinning him against one of the columns. None of them were close enough. None of them would make it.

But Ace could. He threw the guards off him as though they were light as feathers. He raised his bloodied fists, ready to show Alastor Vermillion how he earned his name, but Alastor sensed the presence behind him. He knew who was coming, and he knew he couldn't defeat him hand to hand. He spun around on his heel, and from his cloak he pulled a pistol. I heard the gunshot before I watched Ace fall, and within the same moment, Alastor withdrew his dagger and sliced Quinn's throat open, all with a smile on his face.

Quinn's eyes flew wide. His lips parted for a scream that never sounded. He clutched at his throat, his hands coming away slick with blood.

His gaze was still set upon me, a hand stretched out to me for help, when he collapsed to the ground.

CHAPTER 41

Quinn

The pain was secondary to the shock. In fact, the shock numbed me. It stretched out a few short seconds into a million so that I could enjoy my last breath of air in this world.

The warm, sticky feeling dripping down my chest was blood. I knew that without having to look. My sword fell from my hands, but I didn't hear it clatter against the floor. I couldn't hear anything over the ringing in my ears. I could only focus on my own heartbeat as it slowed.

I had no idea I was falling until my back hit the floor. The cold of the stone seeped into my skin, but I hardly noticed. The simple sensation of touch was fading now. The world was fading now.

Alastor was standing over me, saying something. Maybe a one-liner he practiced in the mirror beforehand. Maybe a spur of the moment snarky remark. I didn't care. I didn't listen.

The beat of my own heart was the only thing in the world. It was the beat of a war drum, echoing over the mountaintops of lands far away. It was ancient music, sung by many voices that I could barely hear, but they grew louder as the seconds ticked by. Would I be one of those singers? When the world turns black and I am nothing more than single flame burning in eternal night, will I remember all I've lived through here?

The steady beat began to slow. The war drums turned into a gentle tap, like individual drops of water falling into the sink.

I don't want to die. There is so much left in this world to discover. So many stories to write. So many adventures to take part in. I still have unread books on my shelves and unfinished letters I have to send. I'll never get to finish my training with Ryder or have my exclusive interviews with Mara. I won't see Bryce live through her royal fantasies. I'll never know if Kalieth will find peace after the end of his family. And Ace–

Ace.

I didn't want to leave him. I didn't get to say goodbye. What do you say to the man you could've loved if you had the time? What do you say to someone who was neither your friend nor your lover, but something beautiful in between? I wanted to say that I was leaving our story unfinished, but I don't think that's true. I always thought we were an epic romance, but maybe we were a tragedy all along. That's alright, I suppose. I would be the love snuffed out, if only to give him a love that burns for eternity.

It's closing in. The beyond. The after. The end and the beginning. The thing no one truly comprehends until it's too late.

The steady beat in my chest– my heart. My heart faltered. I felt it. It was the only thing left that I could feel. It missed a beat, then two.

It tried to keep up with my gasping breaths as my lungs struggled to take in air. It sluggishly dragged on, until it couldn't anymore.

It failed.

It failed– and everything in me seized. My muscles, my organs, my lungs and even my mind. It all came to a crashing halt. My body strained for relief from this agony. For air or blood or *something* to end this torment.

I reached out for someone. In the back of my mind, I knew that none of my friends were with me, but I reached out anyway, hoping against all odds. No one took my hand.

My eyes were wide, my gaze fixed on something far beyond the ceiling of this horrid estate. There was something there, in the silver starlight that reached for me. Something that called to me. Any part of me that fought to live had died with my heart, and all that was left wanted to be taken to the silver palace in the skies.

Death swept in far quicker than I ever could've imagined. It lifted me up into the night and enveloped me, almost like the warm embrace of a soul returned home. I left the physical world behind, and I found peace in the stars.

CHAPTER 42

Kaleith

Silence.

I heard only silence as blood spilled down the stairs of the dais and ran across the ballroom floor. There were the sounds of heels clicking against the floor as the guests fled. There were the shouts of the guards as they threw themselves on top of Ryder. The scream from Bryce as she fell to her knees, burning everything within a few feet of her. The angry roar from Ace as he tried and failed to get to his feet. Still, I heard none of it. I heard silence as I watched the blood finally stop spurting from Quinn's throat.

"*I made you,*" Xaphan hissed into Mara's ear yet again. "And you can never change that. You can't run from it." He smirked against the skin of her neck, their eyes glued to where Quinn's body still twitched. "You can't save them."

But he couldn't see what I saw. He couldn't see the absolute rage that twisted Mara's face, or the shadows that crawled across her skin, far too dark to be cast away by the light of his aether.

Wind picked up around them, stirring the dust and debris.

Xaphan's lips parted as he looked around in confusion. But Mara's stare was still set on Quinn's body. She hadn't looked away. She wouldn't. Her lower lip trembled, and her nostrils flared, but she would not look away.

It was fueling her. The rage she felt at the fact she failed to protect him. She needed to see it. She forced herself to look as punishment.

She always held rage in her heart. This, however, was different. This time, she wouldn't conceal it. She wouldn't stuff it into the darkest corners of herself and hold her head high to be the fearless leader of this group. That's not what we needed her to be anymore. We needed her angry. We needed her unleashed, and that's exactly what she planned to do– unleash her fury.

The wind picked up even more, and the shadows began to join it, circling around and around, pushing everyone back until we couldn't see Mara or Xaphan anymore. The last thing I saw was my father letting Mara go, backing away slowly, whether it was out of fear or shock, I couldn't tell.

Her hands found their way to the sides of her face. Her knees gave out. She fell to the floor. When she hit the ground, the earth shook beneath our feet.

The wind blew harder now. We were stuck in a column of air. It twisted around us, gaining strength. It whistled loud and whipped our hair.

She screamed.

A surge of power swept through the lands, knocking me off my feet. I had the column to support me, but my brothers were thrown across the room, into the walls behind us. Dust cascaded down as the ceiling itself began to crumble. The windows shattered and the curtains whipped around in the wake of the energy surge.

She was heard in the city. She was heard in the village of Nero. She was heard in the Northern Kingdom, and she was heard in lands still undiscovered, far beyond the end of the sea. The shrill call was a summons. An awakening.

When the wolf howls, the pack awakens.

The world answered her cry. All the glass in the entire city of Shadieh shattered. Water receded from distant shores only to race back in many monstrous waves. Snow plummeted from the summits of mountains far into the borders of the Northern Kingdom, and then her call razed those mountains completely. Trees in forests far away bent and ruptured into a thousand tiny splinters. Fruit fell from the trees in the farmlands in great troves. Birds scattered into the air. Soldiers on both sides of the war stopped firing for a moment, taking cover from what they thought was a mighty explosion. After centuries, silver eyes opened all across the lands.

Mara roared her fury to the oceans, mountains, and deserts. To the mortal realm, the stars, and to all the places in between. To the primal force that ruled over us all and the gods who may or may not be listening. She screamed and screamed with no end in sight.

The call of rage and sorrow will sweep across all lands.

The estate crumbled around us. I dodged falling chandeliers and pieces of the ceiling as her power grew in intensity. As I got closer to the swirling darkness, I saw a faint glow in the endless sea of shadow. I struggled to walk forward. Struggled to see what lied within.

The black dragon scales she wore glowed silver at the seams. Sparks flew from them as her shadows continued to flood from her back. The darkness grew and expanded until I saw it take shape. Two large, powerful, bat-like wings took root in the shadows. They had to measure twenty feet in length.

An earsplitting screech sounded, but this time I knew it wasn't Mara that caused the sound. The wings rose high above her and came down in one mighty beat. The shadows pulled from Mara's back, and she leaned forward, screaming again.

I fell back onto the ground as I watched the shadows swirl and grow until a dragon the size of a merchant's ship emerged from the darkness. It's sleek, black scales were the same size and shape of the ones Mara wore on her dress. Its eyes were the same silver color as hers. Each of its claws were as long as a sword, and both rows of its teeth looked as sharp as spears.

Every beat of its wings sent a surge of wind my way strong enough to throw a man off balance. It threw its head back and roared into the night, the sound echoing to the ends of the world. Silver flames spilled from its mouth, shooting up into the sky. I felt the heat. It was enough to melt the flesh off a man's bones within seconds.

When the fire finally stopped, the dragon dropped to the ground. The polished floors of the ballroom cracked beneath its giant claws.

The estate was a pile of debris. We were exposed to the night around us now, only a few columns still standing.

I felt hands snaking under my arms, helping me up, just as the wind and shadows finally died down. Ryder, Ace, Bryce, and I all watched, in awe and horror, as the dust settled. Mara stood, all her hair a glowing shade of white and shadows swirling around every inch of her, beneath her very skin.

The dragon stood tall beside her. A deep growling sound vibrated from its chest. It looked down on us, waiting for Mara's first command. I couldn't be sure, but I thought it just might be to burn this world to ashes.

The darkness that erupted from her was like nothing we'd seen before, as if she'd been holding back all this time. It was more than just tendrils of shadows now. The darkness was deeper, richer. Night itself spilled from her palms. Night Incarnate. That's what she was. The personification of darkness.

And when she opened her eyes...

I was used to Mara's cold stares, but this was different. There was nothing human behind that gaze. There was nothing at all within those irises of silver flames. A cold, dry light emanated from them. Her pupils were the dark pits in the voids beyond the worlds. She was not here with us. She looked at me, and she saw straight through me.

Then those empty eyes moved to my father. Any trace of smugness or humor was wiped clean. His own eyes widened in horror as he took a step back, shaking his head. "No, it's not possible," he whispered to himself. His hand shook as he raised it to her, as if splaying a hand in front of him would stop her wrath. He threw out a final blast of his power. All he could muster. She met it with her own. Light and dark collided in a blinding explosion. Glittering black dust from her and silver flames from him streaked through the room.

She advanced on him, slowly, so slowly. Her expression was hardened, unfeeling. She stared down her nose at him as he stepped back again, tripping down the dais stairs and falling onto his back. "I'm sorry," he said, the words breathy and shrill. "Please."

Mara's head tilted to the side, her eyes narrowing. Still, she walked toward him one step at a time. Each one calculated.

Then his back hit the wall and she stopped. She still stood a few feet away, but it made no difference. The darkness was curling around him, enveloping him.

And then his screams echoed into the night. The shadows *consumed* him. They lifted him high into the air, and all Mara had to do was *look* at him. His bones started to crack and shatter within his skin. Blood poured from his eyes, his nose, his ears. His spine curled until it caved. His jaw popped as his fingers broke. I watched the shadows dig into his flesh like claws and tear at him until he was an unrecognizable piece of shredded meat. But he was still alive. His chest rose and fell rapidly as he screamed and screamed. Then he dropped to the floor.

As Xaphan writhed in pain, screeching, the dragon finally left its mother's side. It chased after my brothers, who were fleeing into the gardens. It herded them back toward the house, snapping its teeth and growling.

Mara didn't even look in their direction. She leaned down to Xaphan, so close that her lips nearly touched his skin. Her unfeeling gaze swept over him, and she hardly blinked as she said, "You made me? How does it feel, then..." she asked slowly, each word deep and gravelly. "To have made your murderer?" She pulled away, a smirk on her lips. "The only thing that will be remembered about the great Xaphan Vermillion is that the night came for you, and it consumed you. *And you can never change that. You can't run from it.*" She put her hand against his chest, digging her nails into his torn skin until a pool of blood dripped onto the floor between them. Xaphan looked down at the hand she had against his chest. His silver eyes widened as realization hit him.

Beneath her curled fingers, aether stirred. She struggled to draw it out of him. Her hands shook with exertion, and she cried out as the power threatened to tear her apart.

The darkness that pooled from her palms entered his skin and returned carrying wisps of silver light. His aether. His soul. His essence.

With one last mighty pull, she ripped all the aether out of his body. He fell back onto the ground, his body greying and draining of all life. She held the aether between her palms, the cold light casting over her skin to make her look sickly. She turned away from him as the dragon closed in, purring deeply.

She walked toward me as the beast bathed my father in silver flames, just before it sank its teeth into his flesh and ripped him apart. She said nothing. She only stared with a blank expression on her face. There was no smile. No light in her eyes. No relief or satisfaction. She only walked slowly; her eyes trained on me.

The aether in her palm looked like one of the stars in the night sky if you could pluck them out.

I tensed as she neared. I looked to the others, wondering if Bryce, Ryder, or Ace knew what was happening. I was always being left out of things like this. The others were rigid too, glancing at one another out of utter shock. But they wouldn't dare say anything, not when they didn't recognize the person behind Mara's silver eyes.

Mara stopped mere inches away. Her eyes moved between the ball of light in her hand and me. She drew a long breath in and nodded to herself, as if she were encouraging herself to go through with it.

489

"This power was meant to be passed down to his strongest child..." She glanced up at me. "Do you swear to use this power to help me bring peace?"

CHAPTER 43

Ace

I leaned heavily against Ryder as we watched Mara offer Kalieth his father's power. I pressed a hand to my side, wincing when I saw the amount of blood that stained my hands. I ignored it, however, because now was no time to collapse. Now was the time for revenge. I wanted to watch Mara claw the Vermillion brothers from the inside out first. I wanted to see the smirk wiped from Alastor's face when she tears his soul out of his body. He deserved a slower death. He deserved all the tortures a mortal mind could think of. He deserved it because he killed *him.*

I couldn't say *his* name. I couldn't even think it. I refused to look toward the body only a few feet beside me. That would make it real. So, for now, I directed all my attention to the Reaper and Kalieth.

A sharp inhale forced Kalieth's chest to rise. He looked between the aether and Mara several times. It almost seemed like he was giving her time to reconsider this decision. But Mara didn't budge. She waited, fingers flexing, in the tense silence.

Kalieth nodded.

"Over my dead body," Azazel said. He raised his sword, lunging for Kalieth.

All Mara had to do was look his way, and the shadow from his own back wrapped around him, jerking him down onto the floor. Shadows curled down his arms, forcing him to drop his sword and put his hands behind his back. The shadows yanked him into a kneeling position where he would have to watch helplessly as his brother received their father's undeserved gifts. "All in good time," Mara muttered to him.

Alastor, Tynan, Nox, Darcel, and Eligor all tried to run, but they were knocked backward by a star-kissed wind. Their shadows turned against them too, dragging them to the ground and binding their limbs together.

When the brother's were bound, Mara returned her gaze to Kalieth. She lowered her hand onto his chest, letting the aether go. The light flooded Kalieth's veins. He gasped and fell to his knees, clutching at his chest as if there were a gaping wound there.

Mara bent to help him, but he pushed her away. "No," he gasped. "It's alright. I just need a second."

He spoke the truth, because after a long moment he was climbing back to his feet, taking deep breaths. The light dissipated beneath his skin, but his eyes still glowed silver.

Then there were only stares and glances. We all looked around at one another. It seemed that there were too many emotions, too many thoughts, to be able to comprehend it all so soon. It was over. We won. But... we lost. What were we meant to do now? Return to living normal lives? Mara and Kalieth were *gods* now. What would they do?

After a long, tense silence, Mara's eyes flicked over to where Quinn's body was splayed across the dais stairs. The veins in her neck popped as she drew in another breath. "Kalieth, Ryder, take Ace and Quinn to Artemis," she said, her voice dangerously low.

Ryder followed her gaze to meet Quinn's lifeless stare. "Mara... he's gone," he said, his voice barely above a whisper.

"His soul hasn't left yet. He has a chance. Take them to Artemis," she snapped.

Kalieth hesitantly walked toward Quinn, scooping him up into his arms.

Ryder straightened. He looked like he might say something more, but he bit his tongue and nodded. He tightened his grip on my waist to help me limp toward the door. I sneered, pushing away from him. "I'm not leaving. I want to see the Vermillions die."

"Then you will bleed out and join them," Mara replied, not missing a beat, as if she knew I'd say it and prepared a response.

I wanted to argue, but she was right. I felt lightheaded. It wouldn't be long until unconsciousness claimed me completely, and if I collapsed here and now, they wouldn't be able to drag me back to Artemis in time. I bit my tongue as I leaned into Ryder again. Together, we made our way toward the door.

"What about you?" Kalieth asked, nodding to Mara, Bryce, and Alina. "What about my brothers?"

Mara's head swiveled to the Vermillion brothers. "They had their chance. We'll have our revenge."

CHAPTER 44

Mara

We won.

There was no celebration. No laughs, cheers, or smiles. No crying or sobbing. There was only the rippling heat of rage to keep us warm in the chilled night air. All three of us stared at the Vermillion brothers we most wanted to kill. For Alina, it was Azazel. For Bryce, it was Eligor, and for me, it was Alastor. The other three would come later.

Bryce moved first.

She walked toward her abuser slowly. She flexed her fingers, and flames burst to life in her palms. Her chest rose and fell in calculated breaths. She stopped with her feet only inches away from his knees. She knelt to his level, holding her flaming hand between them.

Eligor tried to lean away, but she only made the flames burn higher. Eligor shook his head. He looked at her through eyes wide with terror.

"Please," he said. The word sounded like a broken plea.

A wicked smile came to Bryce's lips, something I'd never seen from her before. Something I'd never want to see again. The way her eyes lit up with excitement sent a chill down my spine.

"Please what?" she asked. Her voice sounded far too calm, too soft.

He was breathing heavily, trying his best to jerk away from the flames. "Please, mercy."

She cocked her head. Her brows lowered in concern. After a moment, she said, "Okay." She withdrew her hand, dousing the fire by a simple closing of her first. She offered her other hand to him, looking to me with a nod.

Unsure where she was going with this, I released one of Eligor's hands from his bonds of shadow. He looked around nervously, but Bryce only nodded to him, flexed her fingers, and waited.

He hesitantly put his hand in hers, and she responded with a soft smile. A smile that soon turned to hateful, bared teeth as she took one of his fingers and bent it back as far as she could, twisting it to an unnatural angle. She spat on his face and said, "Where was your mercy?"

Eligor cried out in pain. He tried to pull away, but Bryce's grip was firm. She moved onto the next finger, doing the same thing. Then the next, until all five of his fingers pointed in unnatural, painful angles.

When she was finished, she wrapped her other hand around his wrist. Her fingers curled and squeezed until I heard another bone pop. She still wasn't done, though. The fingers wrapped around his wrists started to glow red with the heat she summoned. The simmering sound of his burning skin could be heard between his violent screams. The acrid smell was inescapable.

Bryce only let go when she burned through skin and bone. Through all the nerves and muscle. She withdrew when his hand fell to the ground. Then, without wasting a second, she took his other hand and did it all again. Broke each of his fingers and then his wrist before she took off his whole hand, so that he would feel every bit of the pain.

Eligor's cries finally subsided. He slumped forward as the last of his energy left him. Bryce clicked her tongue and shook her head. She weaved her fingers into his hair and yanked him back, forcing him to look into her eyes.

"Oh no, don't go quiet on me now, love," she mocked. His shuddering breaths were the only response she got. She sighed and leaned in close. "If there is life after death, you should spend it running, because when I join you there, you will burn in my hellfire for an eternity."

She stood then, glaring down at him with almost as much disgust as her sister held in her eyes, and threw both hands out, columns of flames pouring from them.

Eligor had no chance. He had no second for words or thoughts. He was completely engulfed in flames. His body thrashed around as his screams echoed out into the night. Funny, how he looked almost exactly like his father did in his last few moments.

Bryce backed into one of the columns. She leaned her head against the marble, watching as Eligor burned alive. The flames reflected in her satisfied irises. She didn't look away for a single second. Neither did the other brothers. They watched in horror until Eligor's body was nothing but charred flesh and bone.

"Please," Tynan said, cowering in his shadow bonds. "I only ever did what he asked because I feared for my life. He killed our sister, Octavia, for not following his orders. I didn't want to meet the same fate."

Nox nodded, though the quick jerks of his head looked almost painful. "Me too. I never wanted any of this, I swear it!"

Darcel shook in his chains. "He would've done much worse to us if we turned against him."

Azazel stayed silent, keeping his eyes to the floor. Alastor glared at the two, betrayal blatant in his gaze.

Bryce looked to me to make the decision.

I considered it. Of all the Vermillion brothers, Tynan, Darcel, and Nox were the least problematic. As far as I knew, they had nothing to do with their father's secret business, and they lived in fear for years. I promised Kalieth I would give them a chance.

They trembled in my silence, and I enjoyed the sight of it so much that I stayed quiet for a moment longer than necessary. I gave each of them a long, stern look. "You will leave Shadieh. You will live in exile."

They were so relieved and pumped with adrenaline that they began to stumble over their words and talk over one another.

"Oh gods, we will!

"Yes, of course!"

"Thank you!"

I waved my hand, and the shadow bonds released them. They tripped over one another as they scrambled to their feet.

"*Fuck* that," someone scoffed. I blinked, and suddenly both Tynan and Nox were dead on the floor, twin blades embedded in their chests. Darcel was running for the doors, but he didn't make it far before a throwing knife found his back, and he collapsed to the floor. Alina stood over them. Their blood was splattered across her clothes, across her face, but she didn't seem to care.

Bryce rushed to her sister, yanking her away from the brothers, even though it was much too late to save them. "Alina!" Bryce cried. "What are you doing? They surrendered!"

Alina crossed her arms over her chest and gave Bryce a flat, narrow-eyed look. She stiffened at Bryce's angry tone, and her mouth twisted into a soured expression. "They're *Vermillions*," Alina replied, as if that answered every question we might have. Another second passed, and she looked at the bleeding corpses at her feet before she added, "They deserve nothing more than death." Her eyes snapped up to stare at me over Bryce's shoulder. A warning for me, because Kalieth would be next on her list after tonight. I raised my chin high, mirroring her cold stare for a long moment, sizing her up.

I was angered beyond words that she went against my orders and killed *my* prisoners. The only reason I didn't slay her where she stood was because she was Bryce's sister, and she'd been through hell over the past few months. I couldn't expect her to recognize my authority, but she would learn that my sympathy only stretched so far.

Bryce took a small step away from her sister. Alina noted the movement but said nothing. Bryce stared at her through lowered brows, sadness crossing over her face. "What happened to you?"

Alina cocked her head to the side. Her expression didn't change in the slightest.

It was Azazel's low chuckle that turned our heads. He stared at his brothers' bodies, but there was a smirk stretching across his face. "She's not the same person you left here to die," he said, looking to Bryce. "I made sure of that."

Alina turned to face him. The lack of emotion on her face when she faced her abuser, as opposed to Bryce, was disconcerting. There was no fear or hatred, but there was no excitement either. There was nothing in her eyes. Nothing.

"I'll be happy to face Death this night, knowing that I left my mark in this world through you, my dear. I will forever live on through you," Azazel said, a cocky grin on his face.

Alina crouched down until she was eye-level with him. "If your only mark left in this world is the stain you've left in my mind, then I would not rejoice. Just like your father, you made your own murderer. You toppled your own empire, and once you're gone, there will be nothing left of you. Your memory will fall into the shadow of a great name, and you will be forgotten by all those who come after you. Don't count on living through me, my dear Az, because when I burn this place to ash, and your corpse with it, I'll leave with a new face, and start a new life. Your name will never be uttered. Your story will never be told. Night came for your father, but you'll die knowing that it was Alina Reitenour who came for you."

The smirk died on Az's lips. He opened his mouth to say something, but the words never came. Alina slashed through his throat with clongated, inhuman claws that stretched from her hand. A talent unique to shapeshifters. His body leaned to the side before falling over completely. I had to step back to avoid the spray of blood.

Then, it was my turn. I looked to Alastor, the last of the brothers. I stalked over to him, a beast freed of my cage, and grabbed him by his throat. He struggled to free himself from my grasp, clawing at my hands, but it was no use. I slammed him hard against one of the columns, hoping to break something.

"What are you going to do? Break my fingers? Burn me alive? Slit my throat? I'm not afraid. Do

501

it," Alastor said, taking fast breaths in through his nose.

"No. There's a death far worse than that. A suffering I spared your brothers from, and even your father, in a way. If you could live through it, you'd have a new definition for pain. But you'll die, and I'll turn your soul to ash, and you'll be forgotten to this world, this realm, this universe. You won't even be able to join your family in the afterlife. There will be no afterlife for you. These words will be the last thing you hear before you're simply gone." As I spoke, my shadows curled down my arms in wisps, crawling toward Alastor's throat.

He would be feeling them against his skin like pins and needles piercing him as they went. He tried to hide his pain from me, but I could feel it in the way his muscles trembled beneath my hold.

The shadows entered through his nose and mouth, travelling down his throat. They spread through his veins, pulling all the little bits of his soul through his flesh and bone and up to my awaiting hand.

To rip a soul from a mortal body was a paralyzing pain. It was nearly impossible to live through, and even if a person could survive through all that unbridled torture, they would finally meet Death when the soul actually leaves the body. Their skin grey and lifeless. Their corpses instantly mummified, as if they'd been rotting away for centuries. That would be Alastor's fate.

The shadows dragged the aether out of his body through his face. I made sure it felt as painful

502

as possible, with the shadows ripping along his insides like claws and daggers as they stole his life's essence away.

Alastor screamed and thrashed against the wall. Nothing would loosen my hold on him. Not when I had the same vision of Quinn's lifeless eyes flashing through my head again and again.

The rot started in Alastor's fingers. The scrawny, grey skin spread up his arms and over his chest until he was nothing more than a living corpse in my grasp. Only then, with his soul gathered in my palm and the shadows returning to my skin, did I let him fall to the floor, utterly dead in every definition of the word.

All at once, silver orbs of light gathered at the chests of the remaining five Vermillions, including Xaphan. The orbs of light looked almost exactly like the aether, but different in that their movements weren't as serene. These lights blazed like silver fire. The souls of the others separated from the mortal bodies prematurely, triggered by the power I exerted when I stole Alastor's.

"Their souls," Bryce whispered. "I suppose that's your job now, with Cheusi gone."

I surveyed the room, looking to each individual soul. I held out my hands, calling to them all. They rose out of the bodies, hovering in the air for a moment before flying into my waiting palms at lightning speed. There, they combined in my hold, becoming one large ball of light that I could hardly contain with both hands. Disgust contorted my face as I looked down at it. It was all that was left of the Vermillion legacy. My fingers tensed and curled inward, and black

503

shadows swirled from my palms, creeping over the light and tainting it.

I didn't stop until the light was snuffed out completely. A ball of shadows sat in my hands now, and I started to compress it until it was no larger than a carriage wheel. That's when I fought against the opposing forces to clap my hands together, and the ball of swirling darkness exploded into a shimmering mess of black dust.

Bryce looked at me questioningly. Without turning to her, I said, "Their souls didn't deserve to join the others in the stars. This way, they're unmade. Never to be reborn."

Clap.

My head jerked back. I looked into the darkness surrounding us, but I saw nothing. My dragon, however, who'd been feasting happily on Xaphan's remains, raised its head. His lip curled over his blood-stained teeth, and he growled into the shadows.

Clap.

Bryce and Alina heard it this time. They joined me in looking around, turning aimlessly.

Clap.

A woman appeared from the shadows, her hands still raised to clap again. Her ruby red lips were stretched into a triumphant smirk. Her hair tumbled over her shoulders in waves of deep crimson. Even the dress she wore was a bright shade of red, spilling off her in large bunches of fabric and ruffles. Her heels clicked against the floor as she walked toward us, her chin held high.

When I saw her face, I realized I'd seen it before. Earlier in the night, during the ball, I'd seen her speaking to Vermillion. I saw her for no more than a few seconds, but I remembered, nonetheless. She was his guest. She stayed to watch his execution. She watched it all and still approached me with no fear.

I knew who she was, but I refused to admit it.

She stepped further into the light. Her pale skin rejected the moonlight. It made her look ill and decayed. But her eyes glowed blood red through the clouds of dust that still blew off the piles of debris around us.

Eichi's prophecy echoed in my mind. *The red eyes set upon the last dragon.*

She surveyed us, one by one, until her gaze dropped to the bodies of the Vermillion brothers. She rolled her lips between her teeth, raising a brow, before blowing out a sigh. "Well done. Mara, is it?"

My dragon was curling around me, ready to attack if I commanded. The newcomer noted the beast but didn't seem concerned for her life. Didn't seem surprised in the least to see an extinct species in front of her.

I narrowed my eyes. My chin jerked upward as I addressed her. "Who the hell are you?" Though, I was willing to wager that I knew the answer.

She didn't answer me, but she didn't have to. It was Bryce and Alina who caught my attention now. The former was frozen, lips parted on a gasp, and the latter was kneeling, her head bowed respectfully.

Bryce swallowed thickly. Her voice trembled as a single word croaked from her throat. "*Mom?*"

The woman smiled at Bryce before her gaze returned to me. It was a stare that tore daggers through my chest. A warning to stay away. "You may have won the battle, Reaper," she said, her voice cold. "But the war still rages." Then, she turned to her daughters, and the warmth returned to her face. "Come, my children. I'm taking you home."

I had no time to react, to do anything at all, before a wall of fire surrounded all three of them, and they disappeared into the flames.

CHAPTER 45

Kalieth

Artemis patched Ace back together with ease. I wanted to watch her work, but Ryder warned me repeatedly not to look into her eyes, which made me uneasy enough to avoid looking in her direction all together. I chose to stay silent too, since Ryder said to be careful what you say to her, right before telling me it was best for me to not speak at all.

Mara joined us a few minutes after we arrived. I had questions to ask her, about what she'd done to my brothers. But by the way her lips were set into a firm line, and she watched Artemis work on Ace through lowered brows, with her hands interlaced together against her mouth, I gathered that now was not a good time.

"The prisoners?" Ryder asked, stepping forward.

Mara nodded. "Released."

That seemed to be the end of it, but then a few minutes passed by, and no one followed the

Reaper into the cottage. She leaned against the threshold, alone.

Ryder tensed. "Bryce and Alina?"

Mara didn't even look his way. Her eyes were set on where Artemis finished up bandaging Ace's side. "Gone."

The breath in my lungs was stolen away with that one word. *Gone.* Gone where? Were they alive? We'd already lost one friend today, we couldn't lose another.

I knew Ace was healed when he struggled to get to his feet, earning a hiss from Artemis. "Stay still, you fool! Of course, a man stupid enough to step in front of a gun would try to stand the second I stitch him together." She muttered more curses under her breath. She pushed him back down onto the dining room table that she cleared for him to lay upon. The bed on the opposite wall was reserved for Quinn, though I wasn't sure he had much of a preference.

Mara stood and pinned Ace to the table with an arm against his shoulder. Ace's gaze slid to hers, and I saw something pass between them. An unspoken understanding. Ace stopped struggling. He relaxed against Mara's hold, though I could tell that he didn't like not being able to see what was happening with Quinn as Artemis made her way over to the bed.

All of that was lost on Ryder. He was tense as a bow string pulled back, ready to be released. Ready to lose all control. "*What do you mean 'gone'?*"

"We'll speak of it later," Mara muttered, still watching Artemis. Out of respect for Quinn, Ryder bit his tongue, but I knew his silence wouldn't last long. Not when Bryce was involved.

Artemis looked down upon Quinn. She shook her head to herself, as if she knew the answer to this question, but she humored us anyway. She reached out with one hand, hovering it just a hair's breadth over Quinn's face. She closed her eyes and tossed her head back, pointing her nose to the ceiling. Her hand moved up and down over Quinn's body as she searched for anything she could latch onto. Any part of him that still lived.

After a few seconds, her chest fell, and she lowered her head. She opened her reptile-like eyes and her lips fell into a frown. "He is gone."

"No." The word was a command. A threat to try harder or face Mara's wrath.

I didn't know much about the witch, but I knew disrespect was something she did not tolerate. I also knew that the power she had stemmed from a primal source, meaning that it could potentially rival Mara's. The two of them knew it, too. The tension between them choked everyone in the room.

Artemis cocked her head, her eyes narrowed. "He's dead." A forked tongue slipped out between her teeth as she spoke.

A sudden heaviness found my chest. I knew, long before the words passed her lips, but hearing them aloud was an entirely different sensation.

I wanted to say something. The thickness in my throat didn't allow me to. It was almost painful to try to speak. I was left to only the voice in my head. My own mind betrayed me by playing memories over and over. Memories of training in the snow, when I pelted Quinn with a snowball, and started a war that lasted all day. When I told him all the history I knew of my grandfather, and he listened intently, writing down every word he could remember.

I could hear his laugh. I could see his smile. There was no possible way for me to comprehend that I would never see him pacing around the safe houses, with a book in hand, oblivious to the world. I would never listen to him and Ace bicker over something so inconsequential that it was hilarious. There would never be another sarcastic comment for me to roll my eyes to.

He was gone. The nineteen-year-old genius, far too mature for his age. The kid who longed to explore this world and bring knowledge to everyone who came after him.

He was gone, forever.

"Bring him back," Mara snapped.

"Mara–" Ryder tried to stop it from happening, but it was too late.

"Careful, Reaper," Artemis hissed.

"His soul hasn't left his body yet. You can bring him back."

"You speak of necromancy. That's a dangerous game to play."

"Do it."

"Few times have those spells worked, and each time the dead did not return the same."

"I don't care. Do it."

"Mara, no," Ace said. I was surprised by the utter devastation in his voice. The absolute sorrow and despair that wrecked his face. The face I'd only ever seen depict boredom or annoyance. His eyes didn't even move from Quinn's body as he spoke. Not until everyone went silent and he looked to Mara for emphasis. "He wouldn't want that."

"Listen to the living, Reaper," Artemis said. "Dead men don't beg for life."

As she spoke, silver light pooled from Quinn's nose and mouth. It gathered there, just a few inches above his face, casting a pale glow over his pallid skin. It looked like a ball of dense fog bathed in the twilight hours of both moon and sun. It waited there, just above his body, for Mara to do something.

All eyes turned to the Reaper, but she made no move toward Quinn. She simply stared at the light with anger instilled in her gaze.

Artemis's hoarse voice sounded a bit softer as she said, "Give him peace."

Mara looked between Quinn and Artemis. There was no sadness in her stare. No remorse or guilt. There was only anger; deep rage that made the aether in her eyes blaze like an inferno. She looked to each of us individually with drawn brows. "You're giving up on him? All of you?"

511

Even though his thoughts weren't entirely with us, Ryder's mouth fell open. His head snapped toward his sister, and his entire body tensed. "Don't you *dare* accuse us of anything. Our friend is dead. There's nothing you can do to change that. You hear me? *Nothing.*"

The others didn't understand, but I did. I knew why she acted this way. I understood why she snapped and pushed them away instead of joining them in grief. Her worst fear came true tonight. She may not have failed to kill Vermillion, but she did fail at something much worse. She failed to protect the people she cared about. Failed to keep us together as a group.

She didn't snap at the others because she was angry at them. She was angry at herself and pushing everyone else away made it easier for her to contain that anger. Without the others to pester her, she could push the grief, desperation, and rage down into the void within herself.

Mara closed herself off from them in every way possible. She distanced herself from everyone by standing on the opposite side of the bed. She crossed her arms over her chest and dug her nails into her arms. Her unfeeling gaze swept over Quinn's body, and I watched her grind her teeth. As I watched her closely, I realized that she just might be the most grief-stricken one of us all. She was seconds from exploding, teetering on the edge.

Her fingers twitched– or, maybe they were shaking, as she reached for Quinn's soul. The shadows brought it to her, reaching out like extensions of her own fingers. Once she had it in her grasp, she turned, without saying anything, and walked straight out the front door, into the night.

The others didn't seem surprised. Ryder was the first to follow. His eyes were glazed over; his brows angled low as he retreated into his own mind.

I stayed behind to help Ace. I offered him my arm, but to my surprise, he pushed me away. He rolled off the table, onto his feet, and dropped to his knees in front of the bed. He lifted a trembling hand and found Quinn's arm.

I'd never seen Ace upset. Even when angry, there's a calm expression that hides his emotion. But this was so much different. He looked pained, in a way that had nothing to do with the patched-up wound on his side.

I watched as his chest caved in, and his spine curled as he collapsed in on himself. A choked sound left him as his brow found the floor. His arms flew up to hold either side of his head. "I'm sorry," he whispered into the floorboards. The words blended together as pure, raw emotion found its way into his voice. "*I'msorryI'msorryI'msorry.*"

His sobs rocked through him until he finally stilled. He didn't lift his head from the floor. He didn't even look my way as he muttered, "his pockets."

I looked around the room. I thought Artemis was still with us, but the creepy sorceress had disappeared. Ace and I were alone.

513

"What?" I asked, leaning forward.

"Check his pockets," Ace said. His voice was hoarse and almost unrecognizable.

I stepped over him to reach into Quinn's jacket. It felt wrong, in a way, to search a dead man's pockets, but I knew that if Ace was the one to ask, there was a reason behind it.

There was nothing in his exterior pockets. The interior one, however, held something bulky. I pulled out a few pencils, and then a large bundle of papers. They were coated in blood, but I could still see the ink enough for his words to be legible.

I turned to find Ace back on his feet. He leaned against the bedpost for support. He said nothing as he held out his hand. I placed the papers in his palm. He stared down at the blood and took a deep breath. He put them into his own pocket and made for the door. I knew better than to offer him help this time. Instead, I followed just a few paces behind.

Mara and Ryder waited for us outside. Artemis's house was on the very edge of the city. It faced open fields and the Eastern part of the Infernal River. A forest lied a few miles away. I could just make out the dark silhouettes of the trees through the night. To the north, far in the distance, I could see fire spilling from the sky as Mara's dragon burned the Vermillion Estate to the ground.

Mara still held Quinn's soul between her hands. Besides the moon above, it was the only source of light we had. They waited for us to join them before commencing with whatever it was Mara planned to do.

We stood in a wide circle. Each of us took a few feet to ourselves. There would come a time tonight when we would all lean into one another, but for now, we needed to process this on our own.

"Before you..." Ace trailed off. He had to clear his throat and try again. "He wrote this before tonight. Told me that if I read it before he left for the university, he'd write in one of his records that Kalieth beat me in a fight. I couldn't risk my reputation, so I agreed to keep my eyes off his letters until he told me it was time. I guess it's time now..."

He picked a single piece of paper out of the bundle. He was careful to unfold it. The blood made it especially fragile. He took a deep breath, glanced around the circle, and started to read.

To my friends,

If you're reading this, it means we magically survived this whole thing and I finally get to return to the University. I know you'll miss me dearly, but just know I am in a much, much better place. I will write our story, publish it, and make enough money to send you all to anger management. I'm sure one day we'll meet again. But just in case we don't, I wanted you to be the first to read one of the first records I ever wrote. I started it on the second week of being with this group, and I finished it the night we went out drinking together, before the ball.

Here it goes.

THE REAPER

Where I come from, the fate of a person relies solely on their shadow...

His record was a description of the Kings and the Shadow Realm, all the tales we once believed. It was a beautifully written dedication to the past, until he turned his sights to the present.

...Night is coming because the Reaper is bringing it with him.

I once believed the rumors. I once thought the Reaper came to the city to kill us all and bring a day of reckoning. I thought the Long Night was upon us and the sun would be doused like a candle.

I don't think I believe that anymore.

The Reaper is a mystery. People fear the unknown, but that doesn't exactly explain the horror he strikes into everyone's hearts. If all mysteries were terrifying, the world would be a horribly confusing place, because no one would have ever explored or experimented.

So, why do people fear him? I've come to realize, in my time with the group, that the only people who fear him are those that fear change. We've all grown up in war. Many of us would give anything to put a stop to it. But some, like the Vermillions, fear that change. It could hurt them and the empire they've built during the constant distraction of violence.

It's become obvious that the Seers of this generation are deceivers and con artists. No true Seer would spread the vicious rumors about the Reaper if they truly saw what I've seen in him. So, if the prophets won't tell you the truth about the masked assailant, I'll do it myself.

I hated the Reaper for making me a part of this group. I needed his protection, but I didn't want any part in his antics. I understand now that he was just trying to give me a higher purpose, and I never said thank you. I'd be six feet in the ground right now if it weren't for him.

"That's enough," Mara said firmly. Ace didn't listen. He continued without hesitation.

He gave me a family when I was most alone in this world. He gave me inspiration when I had nothing else. He made my dreams come true, because not only was I able to write history, but he made me a part of it.

Let it be known the Reaper and his henchmen are not demons or monsters or azkriva crawling out of shadows. We're a family. A bunch of misfits who couldn't make it alone in this world, so we grouped together and made our lives our own. We don't have sewn mouths or scarred faces. We bleed like you. We laugh, drink, fight, and love like you.

Let it be known that the Reaper, hated and loved, feared and worshipped, is a woman. Let the men in this country see what a true leader is. That it is not defined by a gender. That it is defined by love and loyalty. Inspiration and understanding.

Let it be known that...

Ace faltered. His eyes glanced over the words again.

Let it be known that Quinn Chinen was in love with Aerin Taziri. Let it be known that he was best friends with Bryce Reitenour and the man she has wrapped around her finger. Let it be known that he grew to respect Kalieth Vermillion and be the biggest pain in the ass the Reaper ever knew. Let it be known that Quinn Chinen found his home. His family. Let it be known that he will hold a place in his heart for each of them until the day he dies.

When he finished, Ace slipped the papers into his own pocket and crossed his arms over his chest. All eyes turned to Mara, who stared down at the aether in her hands. "You'll see to it that his records are published? All of them?" She glanced at Ace. He nodded.

She wasted no time. She threw Quinn's soul up to the night, and from her lifted palm, shadows erupted. They enveloped the ball of light, carrying it up into the night sky, and when Quinn finally found his place among the stars, great streaks of silver light danced through the sky, expanding out in all directions, as if announcing to the mortal world that one of the brightest souls had just joined their ancestors.

And so, it was done. All of it. Quinn Chinen faded into memory. Into legend.

Ryder slumped to his knees, rubbing a hand over his face. Ace stayed standing, his eyes glued on the new star that shined above our heads. The new star that shined brighter than any other.

There was no time for grief.

Mara's eyes left the stars to find Ryder. "Bryce was taken. She disappeared into a sea of flames and then they were gone."

518

Ryder tensed. "They?"

"She, Alina, and their mother."

All of us looked to Mara then, our attention solely hers. She nodded, sensing our gazes even though hers had dropped to the ground. "We were wrong. Bryce isn't *a* descendant of Morrighan. She's *the* descendant of Morrighan. Her daughter. The heir to the Northern Kingdom and the power of destruction."

"*Fuck,*" Ace said, the words being the tail end of a frustrated sigh.

"I should've known," Ryder said, shaking his head. "I *felt* her power changing, growing. I just didn't understand it. I should've asked. I should've–"

Mara was before him in an instant, kneeling down to his level and bringing him into an embrace. She held him there for a long time, until she felt the muscles in his back relax into her hold. Only then did she pull away and look straight into his eyes. "We'll get her back."

The knot in Ryder's throat bobbed as he met his sister's determined stare. "How?"

Her silver eyes returned to Ace and me, and I watched the aether swirl within her irises. "We ride North. I will slay the primal behind this war," she sneered. "Night is coming for the Northern Kingdom, and even the stars will flicker out in the wake of what I will unleash."

Acknowledgements

When I started writing this book, my goal was to write six very different personalities. It took weeks to carefully think of different backgrounds and inner conflicts for each character, and yet, they all still have one thing in common– me. I put my love for writing into Quinn. I put my sarcasm into Ace. I poured my love for my three beautiful sisters into Ryder. I shared my healing through Bryce. I wrote my humor and horrible flirting into Kalieth. And Mara– well, I gave her my fears and strengths alike. Mara and I never would've made it to the end without our friends and family supporting us every step of the way. For both our sakes, I'd like to offer thanks to everyone who helped me along this journey.

To my mother, there wasn't a single step along the way that you did not help me with. I have no idea what I would do without you. Thank you for being my mother, my best friend, my "momager," and my biggest fan all in one.

To my father, thank you for fostering my love for fantasy, from reading me the lord of the rings before bed to taking me to midnight showings of the hobbit on opening night. Without you, I never would've become a writer.

To my three sisters, Victoria, Whitney, and Rebecka, thank you for always being the people I can fall back on. Thank you for not only being my sisters, but also my best friends. Thank you for being the people I could rant to for hours on end and the people I could always count on to make me laugh. Rebecka, thank you for teaching me what found family is. We may not be blood, but you were there all throughout my life, doing my makeup for finding nemo, accidentally punching me in the head, encouraging my writing, and always, *always* eating zucchini. If we had a choice, I would choose you to be my sister in every lifetime.

To Talia Sigurdson, thank you for taking the time out of our busy freshman year to be one of my peer readers! Your encouraging comments kept me going when imposter syndrome snuck up on me.

To Zero and Amber Hutchins, who saw enough potential in my work to create the book cover and concept art. If I only knew when I first started this book centered around found family, that I was still finding my own. Thank you for being the first two people to bring my book alive in art. Thank you for being my best friends through a stressful first year of college. Thank you for being my emotional support humans. Thank you for being my chosen sisters.

To Marissa Tauber, Rayan Chatterjee, Aiden Gottschalk, Andrew Erbskorn, and Jalen Ready, who came into my life as fast and as chaotic as a hurricane, your constant support is more valuable than you will ever know.

To my forever friends, Marissa Saylor, Julia Saylor, Tori Stahl, Bella Potts, and Carly Hollenbach, who all don't read and probably won't get to this part of the book without skipping through, thank you. This book never would've been possible without you guys and the memories we've made together over the years.

About
the Author

Mya Richter is currently headed toward her sophomore year at the Savannah College of Art and Design, studying for a degree in Dramatic Writing. Lansdale, Pennsylvania is the place she calls home. When she is not writing, she may be critiquing movies with her sister, acting out her own book scenes in the mirror, cuddling with her Dobermans, or doing various normal things like hiking, cooking, and waiting tables. She is known to appear if you light some candles and play ominous Game of Thrones music.

CPSIA information can be obtained
at www.ICGtesting.com
Printed in the USA
BVHW030508060822
643861BV00001B/2